Joanne Rock credits her decision to write romance after a book she picked up during a flight delay engrossed her so thoroughly that she didn't mind at all when her flight was delayed two more times. Giving her readers the chance to escape into another world has motivated her to write over eighty books for a variety of Mills & Boon series.

Yahrah St. John is the proud author of forty-one books with Mills & Boon Desire and Kimani Romance as well as her own indie works. When she's not at home crafting one of her steamy romances with compelling heroes and feisty heroines with a dash of family drama, she is gourmet cooking or travelling the globe seeking out her next adventure. For more info, visit yahrahstjohn.com or find her on Facebook, Instagram, Twitter, BookBub or Goodreads.

Discover more at millsandboon.co.uk

ROCKY MOUNTAIN RIVALS

JOANNE ROCK

A GAME BETWEEN FRIENDS

YAHRAH ST. JOHN

MILLS & BOON

First Published in Great Britain 2022
by Mills & Boon, an imprint of HarperCollins*Publishers* Ltd
1 London Bridge Street, London, SE1 9GF

www.harpercollins.co.uk

HarperCollins*Publishers*
1st Floor, Watermarque Building,
Ringsend Road, Dublin 4, Ireland

Rocky Mountain Rivals © 2022 Joanne Rock
A Game Between Friends © 2022 Yahrah Yisrael

ISBN: 978-0-263-30380-3

ROCKY MOUNTAIN RIVALS

JOANNE ROCK

For my friends and readers
with complicated family dynamics.
Wishing you peace and patience to heal
where you can and wisdom to set
boundaries when you can't.

One

She hoped it was a good omen.

Lured by the Help Wanted sign in the window of the one and only restaurant in Catamount, Colorado, Fleur Barclay stepped out of her beat-up car to inquire inside. The heat of the summer sun warmed her face; the scent of barbecue carried on the breeze. The Cowboy Kitchen was a local institution that had been in business when Fleur and her family used to visit her grandmother in Catamount when she was a kid. The restaurant had remained a local staple through her teen years when Fleur had been the only Barclay still visiting Gran after her parents split and her sisters had chosen sides in the acrimonious divorce.

Now, five years removed from when Fleur fled this small town in the wake of an unhappy split of her own, she was heartened to see Cowboy Kitchen still in business. And in need of help.

Given that she was currently unemployed and needed to remain in town until she settled her grandmother's estate, Fleur chose to view the ad as a sign that her recent string of bad luck was changing.

The past few months had brought her beloved Gran's passing, and a spate of inappropriate advances by her boss that had made her work life impossible. She'd felt forced to leave her assistant chef position. The only tiny silver lining? At least she could live on her Gran's ranch while she readied the place for sale. She wouldn't have been able to pay her rent in Dallas for much longer anyhow, especially since finding a good gig in Texas would have been a challenge without her boss's recommendation.

Something she'd obviously never receive since she'd filed a discrimination complaint with the State.

Unwilling to think about that now, Fleur skirted through a handful of parked cars in front of the lodge-style building that housed a small hardware store and a post office service window in addition to the eatery. Well, *diner*, really. But she could hardly afford to be choosy when the place was just a few miles from Crooked Elm, Gran's ranch. She needed an income to pay her bills. She couldn't bear the thought of touching the savings earmarked for opening her own restaurant one day. And "one day" might come all the sooner if she could make enough from the sale of her grandmother's property.

A rusted bell chimed overhead as she stepped through the entrance. The scent of bacon hung heavy in the air even though it was long past noon. The decor remained the same as ever—white countertops, black-and-white laminate floors, chrome barstools with turquoise seats from a bygone era. The only thing remotely Western about the Cowboy Kitchen was the oversize painting of a faded brown Stetson on the wall above the counter. If there'd been a lunch crowd, it had since departed. A couple of old-timers dressed in faded coveralls sat at a table near the window, hunched over coffee cups. Another patron—younger but dressed like the others in boots and denim—scrolled through his phone at the counter.

"Be right with you!" A feminine voice called from somewhere in the back, probably in response to the doorbell.

Smoothing her blue cotton skirt wrinkled from travel, Fleur moved closer to the counter where a sleek computer monitor sat beside a simple credit card reader. The decor might be from another era, but someone had clearly upgraded the tech. Was that another good sign that a chef role would pay a reasonable wage? Fleur already knew there was no cash in Gran's estate, so until she could sell the Crooked Elm and split the proceeds evenly with her older sisters, she needed to be careful of her expenses.

And wasn't that the same as ever? Her property developer father had cut her off financially the day she'd turned eighteen, perceiving Fleur's efforts at smoothing the family rifts to be "taking her mother's side" in the never-ending divorce war. The feud was so over-the-top it would be laughable if it weren't heartbreaking at the same time. Another frustration she shoved to the back of her mind.

"And…how can I help you?" A smiling brunette pushed her way through the white swinging door from the kitchen to greet her. "Table for one?"

The woman had bright pink lipstick and an abundance of freckles, her dark hair in a long ponytail. She wore an all-white uniform with a silver name tag that read "Marta."

That's right. Marta Macon. Her family lived on the

outskirts of town. Fleur thought her dad might work at the hardware store.

"Actually, no. I was here about the sign in the window. Are you still hiring?" Fleur knew certain people in Catamount would view a diner job in her grandmother's rural hometown as a step down for her. Plenty of locals knew the great lengths she'd gone to in order to earn enough money for culinary school tuition.

Some of her peers had deemed entering regional pageants to earn scholarships as "giving herself airs." One man in particular had scoffed at her path, spouting tired opinions about rodeo pageants reinforcing gendered power dynamics and contributing to the objectification of women. Easy for wealthy Drake Alexander to judge her when he'd never had to worry about paying his own way for anything.

And just how had Drake crept into her thoughts after all this time? She chased him out of her head.

"We are most definitely hiring." Marta bent to retrieve a paper from beneath the counter while a Patsy Cline tune played on an overhead speaker. "You're one of the Barclay girls, aren't you?"

"That's right. I'm Fleur." She smiled politely, though she wasn't sure many people would recall her older sisters since neither Lark nor Jessamyn had spent time in Catamount for years. "We were in 4-H together."

Crooked Elm Ranch had been her summer home every year until she'd finished high school. Then she'd spent two straight years living in Colorado, working multiple jobs to save enough for culinary school.

Until she'd had no choice but to leave.

"I remember you. Have you waitressed before?"

"Yes." Was there any support role she hadn't taken

in the restaurant world? "But I hoped you might need help on the cook staff."

"Sorry." The other woman shook her head, dark ponytail shadowing her movements as she began straightening some napkins spilling out of a dispenser. "We're all set in the kitchen. Stella McRory never misses a shift, and she's been here longer than I have."

"Oh." She couldn't hide her disappointment. Not that she objected to food service. But the public-facing position would practically ensure she'd have to smile at too many people she hoped never to see again. Mostly Drake Alexander. "I'll have to think about it, in that case. Do you mind if I take the form?"

There would only be so much work available around town, after all. In another couple of weeks, she wouldn't have the option to be choosy when her savings dwindled.

"Sure thing." Marta moved on to the next napkin dispenser, straightening the paper products. "Just swing by with it if you decide to apply. It's a fun place to work. Everybody stops in sooner or later."

Just as she feared.

Fleur backed up a step, folding the application in half. Before she could reply, Marta continued.

"And the working environment has gotten nicer since the diner changed hands. The new owner is great. I even have a 401(k) now," Marta announced proudly, hands flying from one dispenser to the next, prepping for the dinner crowd with practiced ease.

The thought of a savings account had Fleur rethinking her need to work in a kitchen.

"Really? Who owns the place these days?" Unfolding the application again, she smoothed out the wrinkles as she studied the paper for a clue to the new management.

Behind her, the old-fashioned doorbell chimed. Marta's expression brightened.

"Here's the owner now," she offered in a cheery voice, gesturing toward the entrance.

Fleur turned expectantly.

And any hopes of her luck changing took a nosedive.

Seeing the imposing frame and chiseled features of the most unfeeling bastard she'd ever met, her chances for a job expired on the spot.

Marta, unaware, continued, "Do you remember Drake Alexander from your time in Catamount? He's our local rodeo star."

Fleur seemed to hear the words as if they were spoken from far away, her full attention locked on the man responsible for driving her from town five years ago. He'd always disliked her. Then, when she'd started dating Drake's younger brother, the enmity had redoubled.

Five years hadn't changed her nemesis.

Dark eyes and dark, waving hair that framed a face full of angles—sharp cheekbones, square chin, straight blade of a nose. He was slim hipped and broad shouldered, dressed all in black right down to the Stetson he clutched in one hand. No doubt, he was an excellent-looking man on the surface, except that all Fleur could see in front of her was a cold heart.

Even his smile looked more like a baring of white teeth as he spoke. "Miss Colorado Silver Spurs and I are well acquainted, Marta."

Fleur's grip on the work application tightened so hard the form crumpled in her fist. Which was just as well. Better to have her dreams go belly-up than subject herself to this man again. She jammed the ruined paper into the pocket of her jean jacket. Vaguely, she registered Marta saying something near them—but her focus remained on the man who'd broken up her engagement to his brother.

"How unfortunate to see you again, Drake," she said mildly, reminding herself she'd prepared for this moment. She'd understood that running into him again in this small town was inevitable. Thankfully, she didn't have to worry about seeing Colin in town since her former fiancé had relocated to Montana. "But at least now I know to avoid this place while I'm in Catamount for the summer."

"Hoping to recapture the old glory as rodeo royalty? Or are you leaving the field clear for newcomers?"

He wasted no time returning to their old antagonism. But then, that way it was easier for her to deal with the complicated feelings this man had always stirred inside her.

"I might ask you the same question. I hear your rodeo days are as far in the past as my pageants. But as much fun as it would be to chat about all the ways you torpedoed my life, I have places to be." She hitched the strap of her purse higher on one shoulder and turned toward Marta. "It was nice seeing you again, Marta."

Breezing past the tall, rangy form of Drake Alexander with a cool disdain at odds with the fiery anger inside her, Fleur shoved open the door of the Cowboy Kitchen and vowed never to enter the building again.

Inside the Cowboy Kitchen, Drake dropped into the booth closest to the door and told himself not to look out the front window to see where Fleur Barclay had gone.

Unfortunately, his eyes were already glued to her slender frame as she glided between the parked cars to wrench open the reluctant door of a compact rust bucket old enough to be a certifiable antique. Not exactly the ride he would have expected for the former rodeo queen, but then nothing about Fleur played to type.

Damn, but she looked more incredible than ever.

No amount of beauty, though, could cover a greedy heart. He resented her for trying to trap his younger brother into marriage, after dating only a couple of months. And even before then, he'd found plenty of reasons to avoid her.

But there was no denying that Fleur turned heads. His included. With endless legs and lips so full they launched torrid fantasies before she ever opened her mouth, Fleur appealed to him as much as she ticked him off. It was an awkward combination that meant he'd kept his distance from her. Especially when she was seven years younger and firmly off limits when they'd repeatedly run into one another on the rodeo circuit.

Until he'd found out about the sudden unwise engagement to his brother when she'd been just twenty years old. As de facto head of the Alexander family since his parents' deaths, Drake took his role in protecting his siblings seriously. So he'd told Fleur exactly what he thought of her marriage ploy. And within days, her engagement to his brother had ended, and Colin—blaming Drake for the split—had moved to Montana. Drake had hoped the anger his brother felt about his interference would fade, but in five years, Colin hadn't returned home once.

Now, watching Fleur step into her vehicle, Drake eyed the way her short blue skirt hugged her hips. A trio of silver necklaces caught the June sunlight where they dangled on the front of her plain white T, a fringed jean jacket the only nod to her old rodeo queen days.

A heavy mug clunked down onto the table in front of him, breaking his reverie. Marta stood beside his booth and filled the stoneware cup from a steaming glass pot, releasing the scent of coffee into the air.

"I would have given my right arm to be the national Miss Silver Spurs," she informed him with a sniff. "The horsemanship skills in that competition are very well respected."

"I'm sure they are," he acknowledged, guilt nipping his conscience. "I meant no offense to the rodeo pageants—"

"It sure sounded like you did," Marta shot back, her former sunny smile nowhere in sight. "Do you have any idea how many good works those women are involved in for their communities if they win?"

He did know, actually. And he needed to do better than to spout off like that just because Fleur had always gotten under his skin.

"I apologize. Fleur and I have a history and I shouldn't have spoken to her that way." He didn't want to rile his best waitress and manager. So he changed topics. "Did she say what she was here for, by the way?"

He guessed she'd come to town to settle her grandmother's estate. Hopefully, it would be the speediest process in the history of Catamount.

"She was looking for a job. But since she crumpled the application into pulp when she saw you, I doubt she'll be applying." Marta turned on a heel and stalked off to refill the cups of the only other diners in the establishment.

Fleur wanted a job?

Just how long was she planning on staying in Catamount?

He shouldn't have given in to the reflex to taunt her. Drake had been waiting for Crooked Elm to go up for sale for years. And now that it finally seemed like a viable possibility, his first move was to resort to sparring with Fleur a reflex from the old days when he'd worked hard to keep her at arm's length.

Why hadn't he offered her condolences about losing her grandmother? He'd always liked Antonia Barclay, even if she'd refused to sell him a key piece of her ranch property for years. She'd warned him that one day he would have to bargain with her granddaughters for the right to buy the land.

Now that day had come and he'd already started on the wrong foot. He'd just been caught off guard when he'd walked into the diner and saw a woman so gorgeous she'd sent a thrill through him. When she'd spun around enough that he'd recognized her…

All the old tangle of bitterness and hunger had him shoving his boot in his mouth.

He took a sip of the coffee and promptly scalded his tongue. Drake swore softly and glanced out the front windows again.

The rust-bucket car was still parked there—right beside his pickup truck. Through the windshield, he could see Fleur in the driver's seat, head bent over her phone.

Before he could think the better of it, he shot to his feet and pushed his way out of the exit. He clapped his Stetson on his head midstride, then squared his shoulders to face her.

He wanted to offer to buy Crooked Elm then and there. She'd been very willing to accept a payout from an Alexander man five years ago during the engagement to Colin. He'd overheard them discussing a prenup—with substantial provisions for Fleur—before the engagement was a week old. It had rubbed him raw to have his brother tied down when Fleur hadn't even had the chance to attend culinary school yet, prompting his visit to Fleur to tell her exactly what he thought of it. And while their argu-

m   d been effective in encouraging her to
ba   with his brother, it had also left a deep
so

th   nowledge now that he'd mishandled
h   ser now. So maybe he could convince
e   h without ever having to list the prop-

p   t she drove the beat-up car gave him
ti   n her off as a gold digger once upon a
i   l didn't fit with the car she was driv-
C   at she'd been looking for a job at the
e   of all places. It wasn't much as far as
a   it was the only food establishment in
J   nd Drake had been unwilling to let the
            en the former owner couldn't make the
            s anymore. He would never leave this
            it made sense to invest in the place.
            ll across the windshield, Fleur looked
            pping her phone before her gray eyes

            down her window, the hand crank
            ary to even turn on the engine.
            f a few more jabs?" she asked, blink-
            sunlight.

            to the bait. If there was any chance
            him, he couldn't fall into old habits.
            your grandmother. Everyone liked

            Whether from sadness at her loss or
            he hadn't stuck to their usual script,
he couldn't say.

"Thank you." The words were stiff. Forced. "I'll or-
ganize a memorial once I'm sure my sisters can be here."

He hadn't seen all three Barclay sisters in Catamount

at the same time since he'd been a teen. He'd never forget the day, either. There'd been a junior rodeo at the county fair shortly after the elder Barclays' breakup. Fleur's mother arrived with her oldest daughter, while Fleur's father had been in attendance with his mistress. Jessamyn, the middle daughter, had been in a barrel racing competition. Drake had been in the stands watching since the bull riding event started later in the day.

Security had to get involved after the mistress—the wife of a prominent divorce attorney, of all things—used her designer purse like a medieval mace, knocking Mrs. Barclay down a few stairs. Fleur had been in the early days of her rodeo career, so she'd been maybe nine years old at the time. She'd been dressed in red, white and blue satin, seated on horseback in the arena with a few other flag bearers, preparing for the opening laps. But she'd surprised the crowd by breaking into a spontaneous solo rendition of "America the Beautiful" after the fight broke out. The decision had seemed an odd choice to a lot of folks, since her mother could have very well been injured at the time, although Drake had suspected she'd been trying to deflect attention from the scene.

Later, he'd second-guessed the opinion, especially as he'd watched her grow into a dedicated pageant contestant, travelling all over the west for a shot at a title.

But for the rest of Catamount, Fleur's reputation for being self-centered had only grown from that day at the junior rodeo. He wasn't going to think about that now when he needed to convince her to sell him Crooked Elm. The ranch's rangelands had been overused by their current tenant and needed serious intervention to restore the soil quality. Conserving the land—using it in a way that gave back instead of stripping it—had been a goal of his parents. For that reason, it was an even more important goal for him.

"I'm sure you'll have a big turnout for her," he told Fleur belatedly, still deciding the best way to proceed. Should he make the offer now? Or backtrack and try to smooth over her impression of him to boost the chances she'd agree to it? Swallowing his pride in one hard lump, he tried to adopt a reasonably pleasant tone. "Marta mentioned you were in the market for a job?"

She laughed. A brisk, mirthless *ha!* "Only until I found out who owns the place."

He leaned against his pickup truck parked beside her car, then crossed one boot over the other as he picked his words carefully. Marta's admonishment about his judgmental words had reminded him he had no business needling Fleur anymore. She wasn't a kid any longer, and he couldn't still claim to be reeling from his parents' death. Time to rein in the sniping.

"We could keep clear of each other. I rarely set foot in there anyhow."

"This conversation just gets weirder and weirder." She shook her head, copper-colored curls jiggling with the motion. "Is this some kind of trick to humiliate me down the road? Do you want to invite your rich friends to heckle me while I wait on them?"

"Hardly." He'd do his damnedest to keep his friends away from a mercenary beauty queen. "I bought the diner because it was a good business move, not because I frequent the place. Don't let me keep you away if you want to work there."

"Now I know it's a trick," she said drily, bending forward to retrieve the phone she'd dropped on the car's floorboards. She sat up, eyes flaming. "There's no chance you would do anything to help me after the way you broke up my engagement and chased me out of Catamount last time. You're probably just angling to find the fastest method to send me running out of town again."

"That's not true—" he began, but she continued as if he'd never interrupted.

"No doubt you could make my life a living hell if you were my boss, so I'll pass. Thanks just the same." She jammed the phone into a cupholder and rolled up her window, effectively ending their conversation.

As efforts to smooth things over with her went, it wasn't half-bad.

It'd been almost civil. Or as civil as things had ever been between him and Fleur.

Still, as he watched the rusty car disappear up the road, Drake guessed he'd have to dig deeper on his campaign to win her over if he ever wanted her to sell him her grandmother's land.

Two

Standing in the bright yellow kitchen where she'd spent many happy hours cooking with her grandmother, Fleur leaned a hip against the Mexican tile countertop and adjusted her tablet on its stand. The oldest of the sisters, Lark, had FaceTimed her to finalize details for Antonia Barclay's memorial. Fleur was grateful for the virtual company when the house at Crooked Elm seemed to echo with loneliness now that Gran wasn't there. Not to mention, talking to Lark kept her mind off Drake and the frustration of their unexpected encounter.

Had it been her imagination or had he made an overture to friendliness after all this time? She knew she had to be misreading the situation. Better to focus on her plans for Antonia's memorial.

How many times had she and Gran sat at the table in the blue painted chairs, taste-testing one another's recipes? She glanced up at the decorative plates hung on the arch above the copper apron sink, remembering taking them down one day to clean them. Gran had narrated where and when she'd acquired each one, reminiscing about meeting Fleur's long-deceased grandfather when they were teens, then traveling the country with him before they settled on his family's ranch in Catamount. Fleur had treasured every story, her inner romantic thrilling to the idea that marriage didn't have to be the war zone that her parents had created.

Tugging her attention away from the plates, she refocused on Lark's face framed on the tablet screen. A practicing therapist, her older sister had glossy dark hair, arrow straight and reaching midway down her back. She wore it in a long braid today and her green eyes had shadows beneath them as she packed toys in her work satchel after counseling children in her home office in Los Angeles. Fleur guessed Lark must have some upcoming appointments on the road if she was loading her travel bag. Lark consulted with a couple of local schools in addition to her practice at home.

"Are you sure you can't spend the night after the memorial?" Fleur asked her for the second time.

She ached for family now, even more than usual. While her relationship with both Lark and Jessamyn was strained she was more likely to have sway with the eldest. Lark didn't hold as much of a grudge about Fleur's efforts as family peacekeeper as Jessamyn.

"I wish I could." Lark scooped up the last of the toys, a rag doll and a stuffed puppy with floppy ears, then pitched them in her duffel bag. "But I've had to draw big-time boundaries to protect myself from the drama with Dad. And I'm sad enough about Gran without adding his inevitable BS to the day."

Fleur clamped her teeth around her lower lip to prevent

herself from arguing. Her sister looked exhausted, and Fleur knew it would be tough for her to return to Catamount even without family dysfunction. Lark's hockey player ex-husband had purchased a ranch in Catamount where he'd planned to spend his retirement after his sports career ended—right next door to the Barclays. And although the marriage had fallen apart before that day had come, he still hadn't sold the place yet. Her very private sister hadn't shared the full scope of the breakup with Fleur, but she knew it had been bad.

And if there was one thing Fleur understood, it was a bad breakup. She bore the scars of hers to this day.

"I understand." She traced the pattern in one of the tiles on the countertop, her finger following the blue flower petals before outlining the green stems. "It's just so quiet here without Gran."

"I'm sorry." Setting down the bag of toys, Lark looked right at her, surely seeing the hurt Fleur couldn't begin to express. "It feels strange for me, too, seeing that bright, happy kitchen without her there. I can only imagine how hard it is for you."

Fleur nodded, not trusting her voice to speak with all the emotions welling up in her throat. Their grandmother had been more like a mom to her in the years when Fleur's mother had been recovering from the divorce and the depressive spiral that followed it. Jennifer Barclay had mustered energy to fight her husband in court at every juncture of their divorce proceedings, but once she'd won decisive judgments against him and the marriage was truly over, she seemed to lose all sense of purpose.

Lark had been a rock for their mom, ensuring she got the care she needed during those years. Jessamyn had moved in with their father, convinced their mom had persecuted Mateo Barclay unfairly. Their dad had cut off all contact and financial support to both Lark and Fleur as a result. That hadn't stopped Fleur from trying to mend things between them all over the years, but the more she tried to open a dialogue, the more she seemed to alienate everyone. After her breakup with Colin Alexander, she'd given up her peacekeeping efforts. But she still missed her family.

"I wish I'd been here more this past year," Fleur admitted, guilt piling on her shoulders. She'd been so focused on her job, saving up for her own establishment while trying to make a name for herself in the Dallas restaurant community.

She never wanted to be reliant on someone else's support again. She'd turned to Colin at a low point in her life, thinking he'd be a friend and partner. But their relationship hadn't been strong enough to withstand Drake's scorn. He was used to having women fall over him for his good looks and wealth, so maybe it was easy for him to think that's all she'd seen in Colin, too.

"So do I." Lark dropped to sit on a low leather hassock. A bright, inspirational painting of a rainbow over a green field spread out in the background behind her, at odds with her sister's sad expression. "I'll never forgive myself for avoiding Catamount these past few years because of Gibson. I missed out on that time with Gran."

Her sister drew in a slow, shaky breath while Fleur searched for the rights words to console her. Before she could come up with anything, Lark spoke again.

"I was surprised to hear from Drake Alexander this week," she blurted as she stood again, hitching her duffel over her shoulder as if ready to leave the office soon.

"Excuse me?" Straightening, Fleur dragged the tablet

closer to her so fast she knocked it sideways on the stand. "What did Drake want?"

"He was feeling me out about making an offer on Crooked Elm."

"What do you mean?" Fleur frowned, wondering why he had said nothing to her about it when he'd known she was the Barclay in residence.

Agitation quickened her pulse.

"He's interested in buying it. I think he hopes we'll sell directly to him without putting it on the market, but I think we should at least wait and see what kind of interest we get first." Lark dug in her bag and came up with a set of keys. "But I need to get to an appointment with a client's school counselor. Message me if you need help with Gran's service."

"I will. And thank you." Fleur nodded absently, still thinking about Drake approaching her sister. She disconnected the call, her tablet going dark before she left the kitchen to wander into the overgrown backyard.

Of course Drake would go behind her back to talk to Lark. But at least the anger chased away the melancholy she'd been feeling. Drake's underhanded tactics let her channel grief and mourning into frustrated outrage.

The rat bastard.

She kept to the flagstone path to avoid tall weeds around the small courtyard where Gran had surrounded a birdbath with perennials, thinking about the awkward conversation she'd had with Drake in the Cowboy Kitchen parking lot. It made a new kind of sense now. She'd been confused that he followed her outside and took the initiative to offer his condolences.

Hell, he'd offered her *a job.*

But all that time he'd simply been gauging her potential willingness to sell him her grandmother's land.

Bending to right the birdbath that had toppled sideways into the lavender and salvia, Fleur vowed not to accept any offer her nemesis made for Crooked Elm. He couldn't just avoid her because he'd made an enemy out of her.

He'd always thought the worst of her, even before the fiasco of her engagement to his brother. Those years when she'd been travelling to pageants in an effort to win the scholarship prizes, Drake had always been close by to chastise her about her outfits, about the company she kept, about the choices she'd made, nominating himself as a reluctant protector since they were both from the same town. But she hadn't asked for his help. And no matter how well-meaning it might have been at one time, it always came off as judgy. Superior.

But she never could have predicted the level of animosity he'd aimed her way once she got engaged to his brother. He'd been determined to convince her to end things with Colin, and she'd been so upset about how her motives had been misperceived that she'd done exactly that.

Of course, by that time, she'd miscarried, eliminating the secret reason for the engagement in the first place. Under the circumstances, she hadn't had the emotional resources to stand up to Drake and tell him exactly what she thought of his interference, so she'd simply given Colin back his ring.

Setting him free from a commitment he'd only made to her for the baby's sake. But she'd underestimated how devastated she would be—emotionally, physically and mentally—in the aftermath. She'd regretted sending Colin away when she'd needed someone to grieve with her.

But her anger had never been directed toward him,

even though he hadn't looked back once he'd left town. No. Her animosity had always been reserved for the man who'd told her she had no business marrying his brother in the first place.

Now, suddenly, Drake needed a favor from her. Well she wouldn't be swayed by his offering her a much-needed paycheck, or pretending to have cared about her grandmother.

Fleur brushed some dirt away from the design molded inside the bowl of the birdbath. Her fingers traced the lines of a sun with a smiling face. She needed to see the Crooked Elm house and grounds shine again even though she couldn't afford to keep the lands. She didn't have money to invest in the work, but she had time and sweat equity. Somehow, she'd find a job to pay her bills.

And just maybe, in the process, she'd figure out a way to heal her broken family, too.

But one thing was certain. She was done needing anything an Alexander man had to offer, ever again.

The scent of lilies and roses hanging thick in the air, Drake noted that the lack of receiving line following Antonia Barclay's memorial spoke volumes about the broken family dynamic.

His gaze swept over the crowd inside the rented hall behind the biggest church in Catamount, seeking the various Barclay sisters since they hadn't even sat together during the memorial. Now that the formal part of the service had finished, the women had dispersed to the opposite corners of the building as they prepared for a meal. And maybe, for his purposes, it was just as well that the siblings didn't have strong family bonds. He wasn't sure how Fleur would feel about him approaching Lark regarding the sale of Crooked Elm. But after the way she'd refused his job offer and reminded him she wouldn't ever trust him again, he'd figured he'd have a better chance of Lark hearing him out.

Too bad she'd seemed distracted when he'd phoned her the week before, telling him she had no plans to return to Catamount beyond the day of the memorial. Which meant this might be his only chance to reach out to the sisters in person.

He tugged his Stetson off his head before heading toward the buffet tables where he'd spied the glint of Fleur's distinctive copper-colored hair a moment before. It didn't make sense that his boots were walking in her direction when they didn't get along. Maybe his conscience hadn't rested easy after their last conversation. There was no love lost between them, but he knew the service had to have been difficult for her. She'd spoken only briefly, her words steady and well chosen, but the dark shadows under her eyes told the toll it had taken.

"Excuse me."

Her voice sounded suddenly behind him, and he turned to see Fleur. He hated the way his blood heated and pulse raced around her, but couldn't pull his gaze away. She wore a simple gray dress dotted with white flowers, understated but not somber. The hem fell just above her knees, and despite the occasion, he might have still been momentarily distracted by her legs if she hadn't been juggling two large trays. The salvers were heaped with a variety of the Spanish tapas that he recalled Antonia Barclay bringing to community potluck events—savory *croquetas*, some kind of fried potato dish, chorizo and cheeses.

"Whoa. Let me give you a hand." He reached for one of the trays to help, his fingers brushing hers briefly. The contact zinged through him while he turned back to make more room for the food on the closest buffet table. "Shouldn't the catering staff be giving you a hand with this?"

He settled the food between a chafing dish of skewers threaded with chicken and red peppers, and a warming tray full of something that looked like bruschetta, but he was guessing had a Spanish flair. Even the musician in the far corner of the hall played Spanish classical guitar, the whole event themed to showcase Antonia's heritage.

"I must have left my staff in Texas," Fleur snapped while she slid her platter into place near a carafe of red wine. "Along with my job. So I guess I'll just power through on my own."

Confused, Drake stared at all the dishes piled on the buffet tables. There was enough to feed the entire town, the scents of grilled meats and spices wafting through the building while more guests filled the room. The conversation level had increased in volume since the end of the memorial.

"Then who provided all the food?" He couldn't resist swiping one of the *croquetas* from the table, a dish he recalled with fondness.

"Surely not the shallow rodeo pageant queen who saved every cent to attend culinary school." She glared up at him, her eyebrows furrowed as she frowned. "How's the *croqueta*, by the way?"

Surprise made him gulp the food down too soon, but it didn't detract from the taste. Fleur Barclay might be an opportunist, but she was clearly an accomplished chef. And why was it bitter to learn that she had more determination and drive than he'd given her credit for?

"As good as Antonia's," he admitted.

Her expression softened, and the look in her eyes

stirred the old heat inside him. A heat he couldn't afford to feel around his brother's former fiancée. That had to be the reason he found himself saying, "And I'll bet attending culinary school turned out to be more rewarding than sacrificing your dreams for marriage, didn't it?"

Her lips flattened into a thin line. Her gray eyes narrowed.

"I don't know about that. I missed out on having you for a brother-in-law, Drake." She folded her arms, her gaze boring into his. "Think about all the fun we could have had silently seething at each other across your family living room every holiday."

The thought of being related to her sent a chill through him, actually. And it wasn't one bit like the charged sensation he'd experienced when their hands had touched. Whatever it was she made him feel, it wasn't an appropriate response to a woman Colin had loved.

"Or not so silently," he amended, hating the vision of Fleur in his brother's arms. "You always enjoyed getting a reaction by needling me."

He should have ignored her when their time on the rodeo circuit had overlapped—him as a bull rider in his twenties, and her showing up to pageants at fairs all over the West in her late teens. But she made it impossible when she constantly drew attention to herself, traipsing through the rodeo grounds in gowns and spangles, attracting all the wrong kinds of attention from guys who didn't know how young she was. Or did, but didn't care, which ticked him off even more. He'd come to her defense more times than she knew, but she'd never made it easy.

Drake might not have been born into the school of hard knocks like Fleur had been, but life had pulled the rug out from under him at eighteen when his parents had died in a freak accident on their property just at the time he was supposed to head to college. An old barn had collapsed, a structure they'd hoped to salvage as part of their life-long efforts to be good stewards of the land. They had been passionately devoted to conservancy, from local wetlands to limiting their carbon footprint, and they'd tried to save an old barn his mother had found "charming" even though it had an unstable stone foundation.

The day the building caved in devastated the family for years afterward. Drake had sacrificed his own rodeo dreams, keeping one foot on the circuit strictly for the extra earnings while he learned the ranching business for himself. Plus, the bull riding competitions had been flexible enough that he could be home with his younger brother and sister until they finished high school.

But no number of obstacles could have made him turn to using other people to get ahead, the way Fleur had with her engagement to Colin. They'd only dated a few weeks before Fleur had a ring on her finger and the promise of Colin's financial help even if things went south between them.

Why else would Fleur have suddenly decided to sacrifice culinary school to marry Colin instead?

"Good point." Fleur lowered her voice as a couple of older women moved past them to admire the buffet displays. Then, once they'd moved out of earshot, she leaned closer to him. "I could hardly stay silent when you're the type of man to go behind people's backs to get his own way."

The venom behind the words shouldn't surprise him when they'd never been friends. But then, maybe he'd fooled himself thinking she'd ultimately be glad to sell off Crooked Elm.

"I suppose you're referring to me contacting Lark?"

He peered around the rented hall again, looking for Fleur's sisters in the crowd.

He needed someone on his side for this conversation since the glint in Fleur's eyes concerned him. If she refused to sell him the ranch, would her siblings be able to override her? He couldn't see either Jessamyn or Lark in the sea of Catamount locals come to say goodbye to the well-liked Barclay widow.

"Of course I am." She tilted her chin at him. "You could have just told me what you wanted that day at the Cowboy Kitchen. Instead you tried to do me a great favor by giving me a job. Was that to make me so grateful I'd sign over Crooked Elm for a song?"

"I'm prepared to make a competitive offer, Fleur," he clarified, wondering if that fact had gotten lost somehow. "I thought it might save you time and trouble for me to take the ranch off your hands—"

"Off my hands?" Her voice rose, breasts rising and falling faster with every agitated breath. "As if it was a burden to spend time in the only place I've ever felt at home in the last sixteen years. Maybe I won't sell a single acre of it until I'm good and ready."

Her eyes shone with emotion as she spoke, and Drake had no doubt that she'd regretted letting him see those feelings by the way she bit down hard on her lower lip afterward.

She spun away from him before he could frame a response, and as much as he would have liked to have continued the conversation and clarify his intentions, he knew her grandmother's memorial was hardly the place. He barely had time to process the conversation when a heavy hand clapped him on the shoulder.

"What's this I hear about selling acres?" a too-jovial male voice asked.

Turning, Drake met the sharp, dark eyes of Mateo Barclay, Fleur's father. Antonia's only son wore a custom-tailored suit and Italian loafers in a crowd full of cowboy boots. His middle daughter, Jessamyn, stood beside him, dressed in a black jacket and matching pencil skirt, her dark wavy hair pinned high on her head. Drake had heard she'd spent the last six years working for her father's real estate development company in Manhattan.

"Hello, Mr. Barclay. I'm so sorry for your loss." Drake shook the other man's hand before offering condolences to Jessamyn.

"So did I hear correctly that you're interested in purchasing my mother's run-down ranch?" Mateo pressed, looking around the crowd as he spoke, as if already searching for someone more worthy of his conversation. He jingled his keys in his pocket and rocked on his heels while he spoke.

It irritated Drake that the guy would bad-mouth the property Fleur had just gotten done saying she loved. Not that he was suddenly on Fleur's side. But her father had struck him as a self-centered blowhard even before his behavior during the divorce.

"I'll be submitting an offer on it soon, yes." Drake wondered why Antonia hadn't given the property to her son but her granddaughters.

"More power to you," Mateo said conspiratorially. "I wouldn't touch the place. Property values out here haven't kept pace with land in vacation destination cities. I tried my best to convince Mom to come to New York, but she was set in her ways." He shook his head before turning to Jessamyn. "Well, I'd say we've put in enough time here. Are you ready to head out?"

"Dad, please," Jessamyn protested quietly. "We haven't even eaten."

"I'll leave you to your dinner, then," Drake said, excusing himself. He nodded to them both, very ready to part ways with Mateo. "Jessamyn, I'll cc you on the offer I make on Crooked Elm. Fleur told me the three of you need to agree when you're ready to sell."

He would have liked to explain his hopes for Crooked Elm, but this wasn't the time.

"Of course." She smiled warmly and passed him her card. "I'll look forward to hearing from you." And then she disappeared into the crowd with her father.

Stuffing the contact information in his jacket pocket, he headed toward the food tables, considering his next move with the Barclay family. He needed their property to continue his parents' legacy of conservation and land restoration efforts. Drake invested heavily in carrying out their work as a way to honor their memory, but he couldn't fulfill his goals in his own backyard while the Crooked Elm continued to be misused by the Barclay family's tenant. He'd tried more than once to convince Antonia Barclay to rent the rangelands to him instead, but she'd refused, insisting that her tenant was working on an irrigation system for the property as part of his reduced rent. Drake had seen little evidence of any such progress. As it stood, a creek that fed the White River wound through his property and the Barclays' ranch lands, and there was no way to restore the wetlands surrounding it without managing the nearby property.

All the ranch lands would be more valuable once he'd restored it. But better for him if Mateo Barclay—the real estate developer—kept thinking Crooked Elm was worthless. Drake didn't need him getting involved in the sale. He'd give Jessamyn a call during the week so they could speak privately.

For now, he'd wait until the meal was over to seek out

Fleur again. Not to talk about the deal. Just to smooth things over from earlier. If she was going to spend some time in Catamount enjoying her grandmother's ranch, at least that would mean Drake had more time to convince her to sell to him.

His first step? Making a few fresh memories with her so she could replace the old ones from the day when he'd decimated her hopes of marriage to his brother.

Three

Two hours after she'd served the food, Fleur eyed the buffet tables through the thinning crowd at her grandmother's memorial and decided she could begin cleaning up. Although the preparation for the meal had been a lot of work, she was grateful for the activity on a difficult day. Her grief was too deep to share with the others gathered for the celebration of Antonia's life, so it was better to stay busy now and process the loss later, when the hurt wasn't so fresh.

Excusing herself from a conversation with the local grocer, who'd been sharing a memory of Antonia's early attempts to order fresh octopus when she'd first moved to Colorado, Fleur wove through the people milling around the exit ready to leave. She'd almost reached the buffet when a tall, blonde beauty with hazel eyes approached her, a navy blue dress hugging her slim figure. It took her a moment to recognize Drake and Colin's younger sister, Emma Alexander.

Trepidation seized her even though they'd been friends once. She hadn't seen or spoken to Emma since Fleur had broken off her engagement to Colin.

"Fleur." Emma held her arms wide before wrapping her in a hug scented with the same perfume she'd always worn—something warm and spicy, with a hint of rose. Then, pulling back, she frowned. "I'm sorry about your grandmother. I was late to arrive since I was in Denver getting a last fitting on my wedding dress today, but I wanted you to know how much I loved Antonia. Colin's still living in Montana now, but I'm sure he'd also send his sympathies."

Her chest eased at the kind words and the woman's obvious sincerity. She was glad that Drake's disdain hadn't tainted Emma's view of her. Or if it had, the woman was too well-mannered to show it.

"Thank you so much. And congratulations on your wedding. I didn't know you were engaged." As soon as the words left her mouth, she worried they would call to mind her own failed relationship with Colin, but Emma only beamed.

Fleur could see a resemblance to her oldest brother around the eyes. But where Drake looked at her with dark cynicism, his sister seemed determined to see the good in people. For a moment, it occurred to her that Emma might have that ability because Drake had set aside his own dreams, sacrificing college and the rodeo to ensure his siblings could grow up in their childhood home. But she dismissed the idea again, not sure why her brain wanted to defend Drake Alexander.

"We've been engaged since last Christmas. Glen and I just moved up the wedding to the Fourth of July because we can't wait any longer to start our happily-ever-after." Her smile was infectious, her cheeks glowing pink.

"That's just a few weeks away. Will you have the ceremony locally?" Fleur thought to her own brief engagement. There'd been no thought of wedding dresses then.

There hadn't been time before things fell apart.

"Drake has said we can marry at the ranch, which will be perfect as it can be difficult to change the date with a big venue. But I've been in complete despair about finding anyone to cater it on short notice after the first company I contracted with went out of business suddenly." Emma gave her a sly smile. "Or at least, I despaired about it until today."

Emma pivoted on her nude pumps and gestured toward the buffet tables.

"What?" Confused, Fleur tried to follow her meaning. "I didn't have it catered, so I don't have a name to give you."

"Because you're a chef now!" the other woman said enthusiastically. "Just like you always wanted to be. And you fed half the town today on your own. Wouldn't you consider doing the same thing for my wedding? I have a very generous budget, too, but it's been impossible to find someone good to make the trip all the way out to Catamount, especially on short notice."

The request was so flattering, so exciting, she reeled. Still, even if she could pull off something like that, she wasn't sure it would be a good idea. She had no desire to see Colin again after the way they'd parted, and spending time around Drake—who'd never liked her—was surely an even worse idea.

"Oh no, Emma. I can't do a formal, sit-down meal or anything. I just thought this would be a nice way to remember Antonia—"

"Of course, this was perfect." Emma squeezed her arm gently. "You served all the things we remember her cooking. And that's why I'd love the same foods at my wedding. Antonia brought meals to my family for weeks after my parents died. She was so good to us. To me, in particular."

Emma was only ten at the time of her parents' deaths. Fleur remembered that awful summer when the barn had caved in with the Alexanders inside. She'd heard reports afterward that Mrs. Alexander had been pinned under debris and her husband had gone in to help, but then the rest of the structure fell, killing them both. She'd been one year older than Emma and had grown tongue-tied around the neighbor who'd been through something so traumatic.

"I hadn't realized," Fleur mused, touched anew by her grandmother's generous heart. She would have had her hands full keeping track of Fleur for months on end, yet she'd made time to extend herself to a motherless child, too. "Can I have a few days to think about it and get back to you next week?"

She hadn't secured a job yet, so the income would be welcome. But would the work put her too much in the path of Drake and Colin? She wasn't ready to face either of them anytime soon.

Then, as if called by her thoughts, she met Drake's dark-eyed stare from across the room. A buzz of awareness zipped through her, her nerve endings humming to life. No doubt that only happened because he made her wary. She needed to be on guard around this charismatic—ruthless—man. And yet, she couldn't deny the prickly sense of something...*more* between them.

"Certainly. And I'm sorry if this wasn't a good time to bring it up." The younger woman frowned.

She tore her attention from Drake, wondering if her attention had been obvious. Her cheeks warmed. "I'm glad we talked about the wedding. I'm thrilled for you, Emma."

"Can I help you with the cleanup?" she offered.

"No, thank you. I saw Lark head into the kitchen a few minutes ago. She'll help." Maybe. Her sisters had sat far from one another during the meal. *Would they avoid her in an effort to avoid each other?*

How would they ever agree on what to do with Crooked Elm and the rest of their grandmother's possessions if they never spoke to one another?

Once Emma left, Fleur busied herself with collecting empty trays and condensing leftovers onto a couple of plates. Then she backed through the swinging door into the kitchen, where Lark was already at the industrial-sized sink doing dishes, a borrowed canvas apron wrapped around her simple black sheath dress. But then Lark had never put much stock in appearances. Fleur's brainy sister believed in getting the job done, and had zero patience for fools. Hot water steamed around her while she scoured a chafing dish.

A rush of love for her sister soothed some of the hurts of the day.

"Thank you so much—" Fleur began.

"No need for thanks. If I didn't have a task to occupy my hands, I would have strangled our father. Jessamyn practically had to duct tape him into his chair to get him to stay at his own mother's memorial." Lark used her wrist to shove a hank of limp hair off her forehead.

Fleur scraped dishes and stacked them, choosing her words carefully since their father's favored daughter had frequently been a sore subject for Lark. For that matter, their father was an even sorer subject. "You know how differently people cope with grief. Dad's never done well with deep emotions."

Her sister made a derisive noise. "Right. Like love for his own daughters. Tough stuff."

Before Fleur could answer, the swinging door pushed open again, emitting a brief rush of conversation and Spanish guitar music. Jessamyn strode purposefully into the kitchen, balancing a tray stacked with glassware.

She looked so put together wearing her sleek designer watch, red-bottom heels and tailored suit. Jess's hair was the same shade as Lark's, but where Lark's had never known a curl, Jessamyn's waves were the stuff of shampoo commercials. Today she wore it tamed into an updo, where it was efficient and beautiful. Yet Fleur always liked seeing it twisted around her sister's shoulders like a living thing.

"The food was incredible, Fleur," Jessamyn announced as she settled the precarious load onto an empty spot. "I held it together through the whole service, but then one taste of the tortilla Española and I was overcome with nostalgia. It tasted exactly like Gran's."

Fleur's throat closed up at the compliment, especially from Jessamyn, who prided herself on not displaying messy emotions. Fleur had held it together all day, too, but the reminder of why she'd worked so hard to feed everyone threatened to unleash the grief she'd tucked away for later.

She glanced between Lark, the brainiac therapist, and Jessamyn, the corporate shark, and wished they could share their hurts more often.

"Thank you. It was weirdly comforting to cook in her kitchen. I thought it would be hard, and in some ways it was. But eventually, it felt peaceful, like I truly would always have a part of her with me." She blinked to keep the emotions at bay and noticed Lark had shut off the faucet to join them. "It almost seemed like she wanted me there."

"Oh, hon. Of course she did," Lark rushed to assure her, sliding an arm around her shoulders while Jessamyn reached to take her hand.

How sad that it took a loss in their family to bring them all together. Standing shoulder-to-shoulder with them reminded her of how many years they'd spent happily under one roof, doing all the things sisters take for granted when they're young. Braiding one another's hair. Sharing toys and books. Sleeping lumped in the same bed during thunderstorms.

Or later when their parents fought, and the sound of angry voices vibrated through the walls.

She could sense the instant her sisters began to retreat. Unwilling for the moment to end, she squeezed Jessamyn's hand tighter and clapped the other on top of Lark's so she couldn't let her go.

"Wait. I know you both have to leave tonight, but I want you to come back to the ranch this summer before we sell the place." She hadn't known she was going to ask it until the words left her mouth. Yes, she needed the money from the sale. But somehow she knew she couldn't allow her finances to dictate what happened next with Crooked Elm.

"Fleur, my work keeps me so busy," Jessamyn started while Lark protested, "I don't know how I can get the time off—"

"Please. Just think about trying to make it happen. If the ranch is our only shared legacy, then we should *share* it. However briefly." She eased her grip on her siblings' hands, understanding they needed to decide for themselves whether or not they would return.

But in the end, they both nodded.

"I'll try," Lark promised.

"Me, too," Jessamyn echoed, backing away. "But I should go. Dad and I are flying to New York tonight. We need to get on our way."

Fleur breathed easier, having secured that much from her sisters.

"Thank you for keeping him here this long," Fleur called after her while Lark remained silent beside her.

Jessamyn waved an acknowledgment as she sailed out the swinging door. Lark returned to the dishes, shoving up her sleeves and cranking on the faucet.

They were a long way from the sisters they'd been once. And maybe they'd never have that kind of love for one another again. But Fleur thought maybe one day, there was still a chance they could be a family.

Seated on his truck tailgate outside the town's rec center, Drake had started to wonder if Fleur had gone home with someone else. A thought that irritated him a lot more than it should.

The parking area was empty of every vehicle save hers. He'd moved his truck to the spot beside her and waited, needing to speak to her again. To clarify his intentions where Crooked Elm was concerned and make peace with her.

Especially now that Emma had approached Fleur about possibly catering her wedding. He'd been surprised by that news, considering how picky his sister had been about all the arrangements for her nuptials. Fleur might be an excellent cook, but she wasn't a caterer. He just hoped like hell she didn't refuse Emma because of her feelings about him. God knew, the woman could be prickly. He didn't want his sister hurt.

A moment later, a shaft of light spilled out onto the parking lot where the back door of the rec center opened. Fleur emerged, her hair now in a high ponytail as she balanced two large sacks on one arm and carried an open box in the other.

Drake shoved to his feet and jogged toward her. He'd gone home an hour ago to change into a pair of jeans and T-shirt, while Fleur was still in her gray wrap dress, the fabric hugging her curves in a way he sure as hell shouldn't be noticing.

"Let me help." He took the heavy box from her as soon as he reached her. "Is your car open?"

"No. My keys are in my bag. But what are you still doing here?" Her gaze drifted over him.

She was probably just noting the change of clothes. Still, he liked having her eyes on his body.

And damn it, but he needed to resolve the business between them so he could stay away from her. Bad enough to be attracted to his brother's former fiancée. But when it was also the woman he'd steered his sibling away from, the attraction felt all the more wrong.

"Once again, I find myself wanting to correct a bad impression I made on you when we spoke earlier." He set the box on the ground beside the trunk of her car before taking the sacks she carried out of her arms so she could find her keys.

Fleur nodded as she riffled through her bag. "Because you want to buy the land. Otherwise, you'd never dream of being nice to me."

She withdrew a small key ring with a silver medallion of a running horse from her purse. Inserting the key into the lock, her trunk lifted, albeit with a creaking protest.

"That's not entirely true." He settled the box inside the trunk next to a tire iron. "I've dreamed of being nice to you before." He hadn't meant to drop his tone an octave, but there was no help for it now. "What I mean is—it's not hard for me to be civil."

He busied himself with the other two bags, stowing them away.

"Fine. I'm all ears for this effort you're making to be...less wretched than I remember." She leaned a hip on the bumper of her car and tilted her head to one side to observe him.

Her ponytail slid off her shoulder, exposing an expanse of pale skin at her neck.

He battled the urge to shut his eyes and pinch the bridge of his nose to will away visions of tasting her there.

"Will you sit with me for a minute?" Shutting the trunk of her car, he gestured toward the open tailgate of his pickup, silver metallic paint gleaming in the moonlight. "It's a beautiful night."

Nodding, she straightened and walked closer. He fisted his hands to keep from offering her a boost, but he couldn't stop his gaze from going to the indent at her waist, where it would have been easy to lift her.

Once she'd hoisted herself up, he did the same. A barn owl screeched from somewhere nearby, filling the air with the unholy call.

"A beautiful night for alien invaders, maybe," Fleur muttered, wrapping her arms around herself. "What *is* that godawful sound?"

He laughed, grateful for a momentary reprieve from hammering out some kind of accord between them.

"That's a barn owl, city girl. You've been gone a long time."

She shivered. "Well, it's spooky enough to be a sound effect in a horror film."

"Have you been in Dallas this whole time?" He recalled that's where her family used to live when they first started coming to Catamount in the summers, before the divorce that catapulted the members to opposite coasts.

"Yes. I gravitated there after things went south with Colin. My mom is on the West Coast near Lark, and my father's business is based in New York, so that's where Jessamyn lives."

He wanted to ask why she hadn't gone to either of those places after her engagement ended, but he knew it was none of his business when he'd been the cause of the split. Or maybe he just didn't want to stir up bad memories.

"I noticed your father kept his distance today," he observed instead. "Lark still doesn't speak to him, either?"

She shook her head. "No. I, on the other hand, will always speak to him, but he makes sure we're never close enough for that to happen. Lark says he's prone to obsessive rumination, and he also has high anxiety levels, but I think he's just an excellent grudge holder."

The pale ribbon that tied her wrap dress fluttered in the breeze, and she captured it between her thumb and forefinger, smoothing them down the silky length.

"Tough to imagine anyone Antonia parented being so tightly wound." His gaze strayed to her calves where her legs swung off the tailgate. When he caught himself, he whipped his attention back to her face, cursing the wayward chemistry. "But I wanted to talk to you tonight so that you'd know my offer to buy Crooked Elm is both sincere and reflective of fair market value."

Her lips flattened into a frown. "It's not even on the market yet, and I haven't had time to research comparable properties."

"I assure you, I have researched it—"

She swung on him with a huff of indignation. "You can't believe I'd take your word for what's an appropriate figure given our relationship."

Something in her tone got under his skin.

"We don't have a relationship." He let the words linger a moment, giving them weight. "But I tried to be a good neighbor to Antonia, and I'd like to think she appreciated my efforts."

"Then why didn't you convince *her* to sell if you were on such great terms?" Her raised voice told Drake how far off track the conversation had gotten.

Hadn't he been trying to smooth things over with her? Wrestling down his annoyance, he explained, "I believe she would have sold to me if she hadn't been committed to giving her granddaughters the option of keeping the place if they chose. But from what I can see, it doesn't look like any of you want to make a life here."

"How would you know what I want?" She tipped her head up to look at the stars. "You don't understand the first thing about me."

"You haven't set foot in Catamount for five years. Not even for Antonia. Are you trying to tell me you suddenly want to be my neighbor?"

"I haven't been here because of *you*," she shot back, sliding off the truck bed and landing on her feet. "You did nothing to hide your distaste for me, and did everything you could to ruin my relationship with Colin. Especially when I needed his support. Do you have any idea how much I dreaded returning to this town with you in it?"

Seeing her this agitated—this hurt and furious—raked over his conscience for a moment. She hadn't let him glimpse those emotions five years ago. He'd been surprised, in fact, that she'd backed down about her engagement to his brother. He'd expected a battle from her, or at least some passionate defense of her love for his brother when Drake had lobbied for her to rethink marriage. Instead, she'd acquiesced.

Now, he latched on to her words. "What do you mean that you needed his support?" He'd thought she needed Colin's money. "Financially?"

An angry sound erupted from her throat before she pivoted on her heel and marched toward the driver's side of her car.

"Fleur?" He hopped off the tailgate to follow her, wondering what he'd missed. "Explain it to me. If you didn't mean money, what did you need from Colin?"

She spun around so fast the hem of her dress whipped at his legs and he had to stop short not to run into her.

"You know what, Drake? I don't owe you any explanations. I didn't then, and I don't now." She was so close he caught a hint of her perfume, vanilla and nutty. Her breath brushed his cheek. "For that matter, you're the last man on earth I'd take a cent from, so I won't be selling Crooked Elm to you."

Her warmth and scent so close to him distracted him from understanding her words for a fraction of a second. So by the time he'd processed the blow she'd just dealt, she was already sliding into the driver's seat.

"Fleur, wait." He'd screwed this up. Badly. And with the land at stake, he couldn't afford to make things personal with Fleur. "Don't make a decision now, while you're upset."

"Good night, Drake." She reached for the car door to pull it closed, then hesitated, glancing up at him. "And I'm not going to be the one to tell Emma you blew her chances of having me cater her wedding. That's on you for always assuming the worst of me. But then you don't have a great track record when it comes to talking to your siblings."

He would have argued, but since she shut the door, he thought it better to get his feet out of the way of her tires as she put the vehicle into reverse.

How could he lose the land he needed *and* mess up his sister's wedding plans at the same time? Yet he found it tough to ruminate on those things when Fleur's words still echoed in his mind about needing Colin's support. Had there been more to his brother's engagement than he'd known at the time?

Fleur's engine revved as she pulled onto the county road, and he realized he felt uneasy about how upset she'd been. Her anger had seemed genuine enough, making him question everything he'd thought he'd known about her in the past. All he'd known was that his brother went from an easygoing fellow when he started dating Fleur, to a tense, sadder man when they got engaged. He'd refused to talk about his relationship with Fleur, and once they'd broken up, Colin had hightailed it out of town. They'd barely spoken since.

He slammed the tailgate closed on his truck, listening to the barn owl still complaining overhead. Maybe Fleur was just a good actress, and her outrage had been for show. But if it wasn't—if Drake had missed something about his brother's rush to wed—then he needed to figure out what had happened. And since Fleur made it clear she wouldn't be giving him any explanations, that meant he'd need to give his brother a call.

Drumming his fingers on the cool metal of the truck fender, Drake suspected he should feel remorse at the possibility of screwing up Colin's love life five years ago. But with the memory of Fleur's fragrance stirring his senses, he couldn't help thinking it was still just as well that he'd come between them. Because what kind of special torment would it have been to feel like this about his brother's wife?

Four

"Volume up." Fleur gave the voice command to the Bluetooth speaker playing a traditional tango song, an almond scent filling the kitchen.

The lilt of guitars and bandonion had her swaying from the counter to the oven to check on the *polvorones*, almond cookies that her grandmother used to send to her every Christmas. Fleur had found four different recipes for the holiday treat in Antonia's notes, but none of them tasted quite like what she remembered. For the past two days, she'd been winging it, combining elements from the recipes to try to re-create the perfect texture.

After peering through the window into the turquoise oven dating from the seventies, Fleur pulled the door open and withdrew a cookie sheet, setting it on the stove top. A thumping noise made her think for a moment that the bass line in the tango song had sped up. But then she realized someone was knocking at the door.

The outline of a Stetson through the sidelights made her breath catch for a moment. She hadn't seen or heard from Drake since their encounter in the parking lot after her grandmother's memorial, and he'd been in her thoughts far more than he deserved ever since. She regretted losing her temper to the degree that she threatened not to cater Emma's wedding. Not only was it unnecessarily rude to Emma, whom she liked. But it was also cutting off her nose to spite her face since Fleur really needed the paycheck.

And the potential word-of-mouth clients that might come afterward.

An instant later, however, it became apparent from the size of the man's outline that it couldn't be Drake. The newcomer was both shorter and wider than the tall, muscular rancher next door.

Not that she'd given much thought to Drake's body, damn it. She called a voice command to the Bluetooth speaker to lower the volume on her tango music before opening the door.

"Hello. Can I help you?" she greeted the stranger.

A grizzled older man pushed his hat back on his head as he took her measure in the June sunlight. Dirt-smudged overalls suggested he'd been working with his hands.

"I'm not sure. I'm Josiah Cranston, your grandmother's tenant. I've been trying to reach you to find out your plans for Crooked Elm since I've been leasing most of the rangelands for the last five years."

"Fleur Barclay." She extended her hand, remembering the small cottage that had once served as the foreman's quarters for Crooked Elm. Her grandmother had rented out the house when she'd leased the acreage. "Thank you for stopping by. Would you like to come in?"

The man's lower lip curled, hesitating. "I'm not really fit for company since I've been in the fields. I just wanted to see if you're still planning to lease to me this year or if I'll need to make other arrangements?"

His voice was gruff, his tone impatient as he shuffled from foot to foot on the welcome mat.

"I apologize, Mr. Cranston. My sisters and I haven't had the chance to discuss our next move, but we are considering selling the ranch." There was no other way to afford her dream of owning a restaurant. And she understood the financial windfall would help Lark, who'd been struggling to make ends meet since her divorce after refusing her ex-husband's offer of alimony. Fleur understood all too well the need to be independent after the games their father had put them through with finances.

Jessamyn might not need the funds, but she certainly had no sentimental attachment to the Crooked Elm. A fact that struck Fleur as very sad when they'd all been happy here once.

The rancher on the porch narrowed pale blue eyes at her, then took a moment to spit over one side of the porch rail.

"Well, that's not going to make things easy for me. But that's no concern of yours, I suppose." Another spit. "The creek has been drying up, anyway. I don't think you're going to have much luck selling a property with no irrigation."

She wanted to ask him why he'd want to keep renting the land if it was no good, but his confrontational demeanor kept the thought on lockdown. "I'm surprised to hear about the creek. Maybe it's just a dry year?"

"Nope. Bad land management practices. But your grandma didn't have any money to put into the place." He rocked on his heels, old boots creaking under his weight.

She bristled at the slight.

"What do you mean 'bad land management'? Gran hadn't even ranched the land for over a decade." She should have made it a priority to walk more of the property. Or borrow a horse and ride it so she could see for herself what it looked like these days. Antonia had long ago sold off all but a few goats that she kept for making her own cheeses.

"Why don't you ask your neighbor about that?" he suggested, smiling in a way that looked more like a grimace, showing tobacco-stained teeth. "The Alexander boy is the local conservation hero. I'm sure he'll be too glad to tell you everything your grandmother was doing wrong here dating back to well before my time."

Drake? He was the last person she wanted to talk to these days, but before she could quiz Josiah any more, the man tipped his hat in a way that seemed more than a little patronizing as he wished her a "good day."

She fixed a polite expression on her face and said goodbye, but as soon as she closed the door she asked no one in particular, "How am I supposed to have a good day now?"

Worried, Fleur wandered over to the stove and lifted a spatula to move her *polvorones* to a cooling rack while she considered her next move. She didn't know anything about local conservation efforts or land management practices. Her ranching knowledge was limited to horseback riding, summer vacations at Gran's and whatever she'd learned in 4-H about animals. Oh, and she could make cheese from goat's milk, too. A good thing, since she'd inherited her grandmother's goats and had been caring for them daily.

Had Antonia known the creek was drying up? Or was Josiah just trying to worry Fleur about selling the land so she'd keep leasing it to him? Gran had kept her tenant on because the income paid the yearly land taxes and provided enough for Gran's living expenses. But would she have continued to lease to him if she'd known about the irrigation problems?

She had no way of knowing the answers to those questions, but she suspected Josiah was right that Drake would know. She'd overheard a conversation at the feed-store earlier in the week about how he'd expanded his father's operation and how successful he'd become with his yearling steers. Drake wasn't just playing at being a rancher. He was the real deal.

Maybe it was just as well that she had a reason to visit Alexander Ranch. She owed Emma an answer about her wedding, and if she had to eat humble pie in front of Drake for letting her temper get the better of her, she would do so. Emma had always been kind to her, even in the old pageant days when most of her peers had written her efforts off as attention-seeking.

Still, the thought of seeing Drake again stirred a hunger inside her...

With a curse, she swiped one of the warm cookies off the cooling rack and took a big bite. The rush of sugar and almond was perfect, as was the wave of nostalgia that followed. The crumbly, shortbread-like texture transported her to Christmases past when she would bite into the treats her grandmother shipped to their family. Excited, she knew she'd found the right combination for the recipe and made a note in her food binder.

Even better, she'd have a freshly baked confection to offer in a trade for information at the Alexander Ranch. *Polvorones* beat the taste of humble pie any day. Besides, she seemed to need a substitute snack lately whenever she thought of Drake after their last encounter. She'd never stood so close to him as she had in the parking lot under the stars.

And she recalled the precise moment during her tirade when her anger at him had suddenly felt like something entirely different. Something twitchy and hungry. Like maybe she wanted to throw herself into his arms instead of arguing with him.

Just remembering the moment inspired the need to fan herself. So, as she packed up the cookies in a container to walk over to the ranch next door, she reminded herself that Drake Alexander had assumed the worst about her five years ago, upsetting her so much that she'd done exactly what he'd suggested and broken things off with his brother.

Hurting herself in the process, since it meant losing Colin's support at the most difficult time of her life.

Come to think of it, had her behavior been all that different at the memorial when she'd allowed Drake to rile her so much she threatened not to cater Emma's wedding? Hadn't she learned anything in the last five years? Wasn't she a more responsible, level-headed woman than the one who'd left Catamount back then?

By the time she slipped on her boots and headed out the back door again, Fleur acknowledged that Drake had done her wrong, and she had every right to be angry about that. But she couldn't deny that when she thought about the past, the bigger anger she saved for herself.

With a shift of his knee, Drake nudged Pearl, his paint mare, closer to a feeder creek for the White River. Careful to avoid a patch of new wetland plants, he slowed Pearl's pace so he could withdraw his phone to take some photos of the area. The difference in the plant growth along the creek here, versus farther south after the waterway passed through the Crooked Elm rangelands, was dramatic.

He'd been working with the local conservancy group on better land management practices to bring the wetlands back these past three years. The efforts were time intensive, but the long-term benefits couldn't be overstated. If only Antonia Barclay had agreed.

Because it sure seemed like her stubborn granddaughter would never even hear him out. Too much bad blood for them to hold a civil conversation for more than five minutes. He huffed out a long exhale at the thought of Fleur, wondering if Colin would ever return his calls about her. Taking a gamble, he switched his phone out of camera mode and hit the button to dial his brother's number.

Again.

He'd already left messages. Texted. He hated that his relationship with his younger brother had disintegrated to this point, where they only spoke a couple of times a year. After their falling-out over Fleur, Colin had relocated to Montana, where he'd attended college.

"Drake?" Colin's voice in his ear surprised him after the radio silence this whole week. "Everything okay?"

"Yes, things are fine here." No surprise Colin would worry that something was wrong in the family since Drake hardly ever checked in. "Thanks for picking up. I've been trying to reach you all week."

He heard the judgment in his voice, but it was too late to scrub it out now. He tipped his head to view the cloudless blue sky, breathing in the cooler, pine-scented air blowing off the mountains to the east. This place had a way of calming him down and soothing the raw patches inside. He'd never leave this land that his parents had worked with their own hands, land they'd died trying to better.

"I figured I'd call you on the weekend," Colin muttered, a distant buzz sounding in the background of the call. A tractor, maybe. "We did a big gather this week and needed some outside hands, so I've been overseeing a lot."

Drake understood that moving a big herd over rough range could be time-consuming. He wished—not for the first time—that his brother had bought land closer to home. What was Drake pushing himself for to expand the Alexander Ranch operation if not for the benefit of Alexanders?

But he stuffed down those thoughts to focus on why he'd called. He urged Pearl away from the creek bed to head toward home. "Sorry to pester you. But a question has come up for me this week now that Fleur Barclay is back in Catamount."

The answering silence felt heavy. Hostile?

He hoped not. They hadn't spoken of her in five years. Unbidden, an image of Colin and Fleur laughing together over a basket of puppies flashed through his head. The foreman's Great Pyrenees, Myrtle, had birthed a litter and Colin had invited Fleur over to play with the pups. It had been the first—the only time—he'd seen the two of them together as a couple. The image had burned into him even then.

"Emma told me about Fleur's return," Colin said finally, voice even. If he still had feelings for Fleur, Drake couldn't have guessed it from his tone. "And I was sorry to hear about Antonia's passing." He paused a long moment before continuing. "You mentioned a question?"

"Fleur said something the other night, after her grandmother's memorial, that made me think there was more to your engagement than what you told me." He recalled her expression perfectly, pretty gray eyes full of distress and anger. Her expressive mouth pulled into an unhappy frown.

The split from Colin had upset her deeply. Was it just because they were so in love? The idea bothered him. Made him wonder if he'd read the situation all wrong back then. He'd been so sure they weren't right for each other, even if she *hadn't* been marrying Colin for the payout.

"First of all, my brother, that's not a question." Colin's voice had an edge. "Secondly you'll have to ask her if you want to know more about that subject. And if that's all you needed, I've got a pasture full of protective mama cows and calves that need moving."

"Wait—" Drake had a follow-up question, but his phone screen showed the call had already ended.

He shoved the device into the pocket of his jeans and was about to nudge Pearl faster when movement from a clearing caught his eye. Turning, he spied a distinctly feminine form in a bright red T-shirt and jean cutoffs heading toward him, a basket over one arm.

Fleur.

Her hair blew around her shoulders, the color more blond than red in the sunlight. And the T-shirt she wore didn't quite reach the waistband of her shorts, a sliver of skin visible as she moved toward him. What was it about that narrow strip of skin that mesmerized him? He wanted to slide his palms around her there, feel that smooth skin against his hands as he crushed her to him.

He could deny wanting her—and he'd tried that, damn it, he'd *tried*—but that had never eased his fascination with this woman. For a moment, he let the truth of that knowledge wash over him, wishing they could have met under different circumstances, without all the baggage of their shared past.

And his brother's old claim on her.

Standing still as she picked her way along the path between the ranches, Drake was grateful for how long it took her to close the distance between them. It took him every second of that time to get command of himself.

"I was on my way to Alexander Ranch to offer an olive branch," she announced once she neared him, her eyes fixed on Pearl and not him. "What a gorgeous horse you have. May I say hello to her?"

Wary of her motive behind a peace offering, Drake still needed to accept it when he had questions for her.

"Of course." He lifted his leg over the mare's back and slid to the ground. "This is Pearl, daughter to one of my mother's favorite mares, Black Pearl."

He didn't speak of his parents often, but he thought Fleur might recall the animal. And maybe the topic was his own attempt at a truce, reminding her of a time before the animosity between them.

"I remember Black Pearl," she whispered, stroking Pearl's all white nose. "I admired your mother's horsemanship. She always encouraged me in my riding." Her gaze darted toward him, perhaps checking for his reaction to a conversation about his mom.

He realized he wanted to hear what she had to say, however. His own store of memories about his parents was far too limited, and often overshadowed by the argument he'd had with them the last time they'd spoken.

Your siblings look up to you, Drake. You need to set a better example...

"Did she?" Drake prompted her, scratching behind Pearl's ear when Fleur's hand fell away.

She nodded. "I was never as good as Emma because we didn't have horses at our house in Dallas. But your mom always picked out a calm animal for me to ride and gave me new confidence."

Fleur's smile lit her entire face, the memory clearly a good one for her. He couldn't recall ever seeing that happy light in her eyes before. Not even when she'd been engaged to his brother.

The thought gave him pause, as he wondered if life had been tougher for her than he'd realized.

"I'm glad to know that about my mother, although it doesn't surprise me to hear." Clearing his throat, he put aside his own memories to focus on her. "Were you coming to the house? I'm not sure if Emma's around, but you're…welcome either way."

He couldn't help the halting words. He and Fleur had been opposing forces for too long. And Colin had insisted Fleur was the only one who could fill Drake in on the blanks in his mind about her broken engagement.

"I did plan to bring these to your sister." She lifted a yellow tea towel laid over the willow basket she carried to show him the sweets within. "I wanted to apologize for my hasty words and let her know I would cater her reception if she still has need of my services."

"If I promise I never told Emma otherwise, can I try one of these?" His hand hovered over the cookies as he inhaled the scent of almond and butter.

"They're *polvorones*, and thank you, Drake. Keeping quiet about my mean side in front of your sister deserves a reward. Please take one."

Her soft voice and conciliatory words stirred something inside him, and he shoved it ruthlessly aside to focus on the cookies.

Helping himself, he bit into one. They were delicious,

like everything else she made. "Oh wow. You didn't have these at the memorial or I would have remembered."

Another smile from her as she tucked the yellow linen around the baked goods again.

"I've been fine-tuning the recipe all week, and I'm really happy with this version."

"They're amazing. Better than anything we offer at the Cowboy Kitchen." He recalled that she needed a job, a job he hadn't been able to convince her to take at the restaurant he now owned. "You should consider selling them there."

"Really?" Her eyebrows lifted in surprise. "You don't think the cook would be opposed to having baked goods brought in from outside?"

Drake shrugged. "Can't hurt to ask." He polished off the rest before gesturing to Pearl. "And we can ride back to the house." He gestured to his horse.

"Oh, that's okay. I'm fine to walk." Her gaze darted between him and the animal.

Then high splotches of color appeared on her cheeks. That hint of awareness made him all the more determined to convince her.

"This is a day of olive branches, after all," he pressed.

Her gray eyes moved over the horse before darting back to him.

"You trust Pearl with two riders?"

"Yes, and she trusts me." Plus the house was less than a mile away. He wouldn't expect the animal to carry the extra weight for any real distance.

His words seemed to have the desired effect because she stepped closer, passing him the basket so she could mount.

He clipped the basket into a carabiner hook on the saddlebag, then held the reins while Fleur put a boot in the stirrup. She hoisted herself up, smooth and easy, like she belonged on horseback. Of course, despite the hard time he'd given Fleur about being a rodeo pageant queen, they didn't choose just anyone to represent the sport. The best were excellent horsewomen.

"Do you want to be in front?" She sat straight in the middle of the saddle, her legs bare and tanned to the tops of her cowboy boots.

"You take the reins." He already knew she rode well. Hell, his mother had given her a stamp of approval. "I'll ride behind."

Pearl would have headed home now even without a hand on the reins. Besides, Drake couldn't deny the desire to feel Fleur in his arms just this once. He knew her well enough to suspect the truce between them wouldn't last, so this could be the only chance he ever had.

Swinging up behind her, he wrapped an arm around her waist, remembering belatedly about the way her short T-shirt didn't quite meet the top of her cutoffs. His forearm pressed into smooth, bare skin, her belly sucking in on a gasp at the contact.

Same, sweetheart. Same.

He breathed in the vanilla scent of her as her back pressed his chest. Her curvy rump pressed...ah, damn. He had to grind his teeth together to keep from thinking about how *that* felt.

Instead, he nudged Pearl's side gently, glancing down to enjoy the way Fleur's legs looked riding along his jeans. Unable to stop himself, he cupped her hip in his palm, knowing full well this moment would be replayed in his head many, many times after today.

"So you decided you won't mind catering the wedding?" he asked to keep his brain rooted in reality and not the fantasy scenarios spinning through his brain.

Pearl took her time down the path toward the barn, slow and steady. She was a damned good horse to keep Fleur right where Drake wanted her. For now, at least.

"I've always liked your sister." She glanced up at him over her shoulder. "I wasn't sure how she felt about me after Colin and I—er, split up. She was away at college then, and I hesitated to reach out to her."

A bird startled out of the grass nearby with a squawk, and the mare did a double step, jarring the riders a bit. Drake's fingers flexed against Fleur's hip bone, his thumb resting in the curve of her waist.

Making it all the tougher to focus.

"Colin never talked about that to anyone that I know of." He forced his thoughts back to the conversation he'd had with his brother just before Fleur had arrived today. "In fact, I asked him again about the engagement after the conversation you and I had the other night. But he said if I wanted to know more, I'd have to ask you."

He waited, their hips rolling forward in synch as the mare went downhill. Fleur's shoulders tensed, but she never tightened her grip on the reins. A credit to her ability to put the horse first.

"It was kind of Colin to maintain my secret all this time, but maybe it would benefit us all to clear the air," she said finally.

"I don't understand." Frowning, he edged to one side to better gauge her expression.

Fleur turned to meet his gaze briefly, her eyes shining with emotion. "I never wanted anyone to know," she said quietly. "I was pregnant."

Five

The secret had spilled out of her more easily than she would have expected after all these years.

Fleur felt a burden slide from her shoulders. Not because she'd confided in Drake, necessarily. Just that she'd spoken the truth to *someone* at long last. But being on horseback with Drake, not fully facing him, had made it easier to divulge the old secret. Or, if she was totally honest with herself, maybe entrusting him with that closely guarded information had also been a way to distract herself from the hyperawareness she experienced being pressed against his hard, masculine body. Every breath she took was scented with pine and leather overlaid with musk and man.

She felt hot all over. On edge.

So perhaps sharing the angst of her past with Colin was an effort to douse the flames.

"My God, Fleur." Drake's voice sounded rough, as

if he had a weight on his chest. "I never guessed. And I can't believe Colin didn't say anything—"

"I swore him to secrecy. I wanted to figure out how to tell my parents and my grandmother first. But we planned on telling your family afterward." She peered up over one shoulder at him as the horse entered a tunnel of tall pine trees. The shade cast Drake's expression in shadow, but she could see the set of his jaw, the flat disapproval of his mouth.

"Still, he should have—" He shook his head, frustration clear as he stopped himself midsentence.

"What? He should have broken a promise to me to confide in you? I didn't want everyone to know we were marrying because of the baby, though they'd all figure it out soon enough." It had taken a while, but she'd forgiven Colin for his eagerness to flee town once she'd given him back his ring. Though she did have some resentment at how easy it had seemed for him to let go. Not just of her, but of the future they'd glimpsed together with their child—however briefly.

"That's not what I was going to say." Still holding her waist, Drake wrenched off his Stetson with his free hand, to rake his wrist along his forehead in an impatient gesture. "He had an obligation to you."

"You didn't think so at the time," she reminded him, taking a little too much pleasure in the outlet of bitterness.

"You're right. Of course." The words were softly spoken as he replaced his hat on his head. He exhaled a slow breath while his grip shifted on the waistband of her shorts, his thumb grazing the bare skin beneath her cropped top.

An accidental brush. No more.

Yet sensation sizzled through her despite everything.

Her pulse quickened and with it the need to lash out. To distance herself from what she felt around him.

"I'll mark it in my calendar as a first. Catamount's resident bull riding champion and ranching king agrees with me, the outcast rodeo queen." She kept her eye on the trail ahead, grateful to see the massive log-and-stone main house where she could dismount.

Had she really thought for a moment she could make peace with this man? His chest rubbed against her shoulder blades with the movement of the mount, his warmth and strength reminding her how long it had been since she'd been this close to any man. Surely that had to be why she couldn't stop picturing what it would be like to turn in his arms and plaster herself to him. Taste him. Touch him.

Why did she have to feel those things for a man who'd never understood her? A man who'd gone out of his way to make sure she knew he didn't approve of her.

"I'm man enough to admit when I'm wrong." His tone hadn't varied from the earlier gentleness.

Something about that—his kindness in the face of her attempts to restore some enmity—only messed with her head. She resisted the urge to look up and over her shoulder at him. They were so close she could have tipped her neck back and her head would have fit into the notch beneath his jaw.

Swallowing hard, she said nothing and silently willed Pearl to walk faster. The house was less than fifty yards away. Surrounded by aspen trees whispering in the light breeze, the sprawling home had to be well over ten thousand square feet. They approached from the back, where a feeder creek to the White River meandered into a wide bend, giving the wide stone patio an elegant water feature at its base. Adirondack chairs surrounded a stone firepit near the creek on one end of the patio, while a wooden dock thrust into the heart of the waterway at the other.

The creek didn't look dry here, the way Josiah Cranston had suggested. But she *had* noted that the waterway on the Barclay property didn't appear as robust. Still, she could hardly blurt out questions about land management no matter how much she didn't want to talk about the past.

"Fleur?" His voice sounded closer, the words warm against her hair even though he didn't touch her there.

The pine and musk scent of him made her want to breathe deeply. A shiver stole through her, and she closed her eyes briefly to ward away whatever illusion of attraction she was feeling.

"What?" She forced the word from her lips with more harshness than she'd intended.

"May I ask—" He swallowed, a movement she felt as he hesitated. "What became of the child?"

Old pain rose inside her, suddenly as jagged and deep as ever it had been. A sense of loss came with it, the rush of emptiness so poignant her hand went to the flat of her belly.

Right where Drake's forearm rested.

She didn't flinch away from him, though, her fingers landing lightly on his skin as she remembered the baby that wasn't meant to be.

"I miscarried early," she admitted, her eyes hot with unshed tears. "Right after Colin drew up the prenup with generous terms for me in case things didn't work out between us. He'd done it to make me feel more secure about giving marriage a try." She needed to press that point, knowing Drake had been convinced she was only marrying Colin for a payday. "When you asked me to break things off, I was no longer pregnant. That's why I agreed."

Behind her, Drake was utterly still. The horse had halted on the grass close to the patio. Pearl gave a shake of her head as if to ward off an itch, but otherwise, stood patiently as the creek babbled past.

"I'm so damned sorry, Fleur." At some point, Drake had tucked her even closer to him, his brawny arm holding her tighter. His cheek rested against her hair. She could feel his heartbeat against her spine. While she knew she should probably pull away, she couldn't find the will to ignore this comfort that she'd never received for her lost child.

And it did feel like comfort. For a moment, she breathed it in, allowing herself a moment of healing peace that came from his apology.

From his touch.

A tear plopped from her eye onto his forearm. She stared at the wet drop as it melted into the space between her hand and Drake's skin.

"Thank you. It was a long time ago." It had been a confusing time since she'd been scared about the pregnancy and the ways it would change her life, but she'd never *not* wanted the baby.

At the time, it had felt like one more way she'd been denied a family, something she'd been lacking ever since her parents' marriage had imploded. Until she'd miscarried, she hadn't realized how many hopes she'd already built around the life inside her.

"It was a long time ago, which makes my apology not only inadequate, but also overdue." Drake gave her a slight squeeze before releasing her again.

He swung a leg over Pearl's back to dismount, then held up his hands to help her down. A courtesy she hardly required. But considering she felt a bit unsteady, she didn't protest. And somehow, looking into his brown eyes as he eased her to her feet added to the sparks lighting up her insides.

Unwelcome sparks, damn it.

Just because she'd welcomed his comfort didn't mean she would cave to the new awareness of him that grew every time she saw him.

Stepping out of his arms, she reached to unfasten the carabiner that held the basket of freshly baked cookies she'd brought. Belatedly, she remembered her mission today had nothing to do with anything they'd talked about. How could she speak to Drake about wetlands and land management when her pulse was thrumming and her skin felt too tight because of his touch?

"I can get it," he offered, his fingers brushing against hers as he pinched the heavy clip open.

She opened her mouth to argue—she really needed the barrier of a disagreement right now—but her gaze collided with his again. And it amazed her how much different it felt for him to peer at her with warmth and curiosity instead of cold scorn.

Her throat dried up. She sucked in a fast breath, struggling for equilibrium as they stood side by side, their hands on either end of the basket as he freed it.

His attention lowered to her mouth, as if he'd heard that intake of air and understood what it meant. Her heart rattled her ribs so loudly she wondered if he heard that, too.

Mesmerized, she might have turned toward him a fraction.

Until a feminine voice shouted from the house.

"Fleur, it's you!" Emma called to them, making Fleur

leap back a step, her basket in her hands. "Drake Alexander, you'd better be inviting her to dinner."

A sigh of relief—it must be relief and not a twinge of disappointment that the moment had been broken—dispelled the turmoil that had been whipping through her a moment ago. Fleur told herself she'd speak to Drake another time, when she wasn't all twisted around and confused about him. She stretched her lips into a welcoming smile for her friend.

"Emma, I'm so glad to see you."

Agitated, Drake spoke softly to Pearl to lead her to the barn. The mare nickered and followed him, her soft nose pressing into his shoulder every now and again, as if to pick up his pace so she could get to her oats faster.

Fleur had been pregnant with Colin's child.

The news floored him. Maybe he should have guessed as much, considering how fast they'd gotten engaged and how uneasy Colin had seemed. Even Fleur hadn't seemed like an eager bride. Which had made Drake wary of their motivations and love. But a pregnancy had never crossed his mind.

And shouldn't that tell him something about how quick he'd been to draw assumptions about Fleur? He regretted that, if only because his interference could have had devastating consequences for the Alexander family line. Yes, she'd said she'd already miscarried by the time Drake convinced her to break the engagement. But what if she hadn't? Would she have still caved to Drake's insistence they were all wrong for one another?

He would have been responsible for separating Colin from the mother of his child. No wonder his brother didn't speak to him.

Reaching the barn, he clipped Pearl into the cross-ties

to groom her before her meal. There were ranch hands nearby if he'd wanted to hand off the task, but the simple ritual of brushing down his horse would be a welcome distraction when his mind was working double time.

Because even if he could set aside the fact that Fleur and Colin had shared a deeper connection than Drake had understood, he couldn't escape the other thing circling around and around his brain. There'd been a breathless, heated moment with her just now when he'd nearly kissed her. He would have sworn—in that instant, at least—that she'd wanted him, too.

He removed the saddle and bridle, returning the pieces to the tack room before he retrieved the brush. The stables were empty with the other horses out to pasture, but an older gelding stood near the open doors to the barn in a shady spot he favored.

"Hello, Pharoah." Drake paused to greet the tall palomino with a scratch along the flank.

While he stood there, one foot in the barn and one foot out, he could look at the main house and see the stone patio where his sister and Fleur now sat in the Adirondack chairs by the creek bend. The willow basket of almond cookies sat on a low wooden table between them along with a clear glass pitcher of lemonade Emma must have brought from the house. From almost two hundred yards away, he couldn't hear them, but he could see Fleur's face in profile well enough, her smile and relaxed posture telling him that Emma had put her at ease.

He felt relieved to know Fleur could put aside their conversation enough to enjoy her time with his sister. Fleur had been visibly upset talking about the miscarriage. It had surprised him when she'd attempted to downplay his role in breaking up her engagement to Colin by assuring him she'd already miscarried by then. He'd been reeling so much from the news of the pregnancy, she could have delivered a knockout blow if she'd allowed him to think he'd robbed her of the father's support at a critical juncture.

Yet she hadn't. Even though he'd most certainly done so.

On the patio, she turned toward him suddenly, as if she'd felt his regard. Awareness crackled to life, like a flame called from red-hot embers beneath the thinnest veneer of ash.

He nodded to Fleur along with a final pat to Pharoah before returning to the cool shadows inside the barn. Finding a currycomb and brushes for Pearl, he returned to the task of grooming the black-and-white dappled paint.

As he worked over the animal, he contemplated his next move, knowing he needed to be warier around the woman. The old enmity between them was fading. How could it stand based on what he knew now?

He'd done Fleur Barclay wrong.

As he'd told her, he could admit a failure. That wasn't the problem wedged between his shoulder blades. Right now, all he could think of was how she'd fit against him when they rode together. How her breath had quickened when his thumb skimmed the band of bare flesh at her waist. How her gray eyes had turned a molten silver in the protracted moment when he'd thought about kissing her.

That was a far bigger problem than the mistake he made five years ago. Because it meant he wanted the woman his brother had loved.

And if he hoped to repair the damage he'd already done to the relationship with his sibling, he could never, ever act on that.

"Would you like any more chicken?" Emma asked Fleur as they finished their dinner that evening. Her hostess had somehow managed to barbecue in a white denim skirt and blousy orange top without getting a drop of sauce on her outfit. Her pear-shaped solitaire engagement ring glinted as she brandished the platter of poultry. "Or should I bring out the *polvorones* for our dessert?"

The two of them sat on the patio as the sun sank lower on the horizon. Emma had produced salads and fresh bread to go with the chicken for an impromptu meal that had been delicious. It had taken a while for Fleur to relax enough to enjoy herself since she kept thinking Drake would join them.

Indeed, Emma remarked on it more than once that he usually joined her for supper. So perhaps he was staying away from the table because of Fleur. Which was just as well, of course. She preferred it, even. The old way of relating to Drake—ignoring him, hating him—was simpler than whatever had happened between them earlier that afternoon when things had turned unexpectedly heated.

"I couldn't eat another bite of anything, Emma. But thank you. All the food was delicious, and I really enjoyed the meal." Fleur shook out her napkin over the grass closest to the picnic table on the patio, then folded the red-and-white gingham linen to lay beside her empty plate.

She had almost convinced herself that she'd imagined those breathless moments with Drake when the air between them crackled with electricity and she swore he would have kissed her.

They'd never even liked each other.

So clearly, her thinking that she'd almost kissed Drake Alexander was just a fanciful imagining.

Reaching across the wrought-iron table, Emma gave Fleur's forearm a squeeze. "It was my pleasure to cook for you and have some time together. I'm just so thrilled you decided to cater the wedding."

Fleur smiled, gladness stealing through her. After navigating the difficult relationships with her sisters, she often felt gun-shy about female friendships. As a result, she hadn't made those deep bonds that some women form with their friends, and her life was the poorer for it. She hadn't expected Emma to extend her the warmth of friendship so readily after the broken engagement.

The thought brought her former fiancé's face to mind. She really needed to ask Emma an awkward question.

"Erm. One thing about the wedding." She shifted position on the bench, forcing herself to meet Emma's wide hazel eyes. As much as she wanted this job—and she really, really needed the income at this point—she didn't want to create unease in the Alexander family. "You know things ended unhappily between Colin and me. You're not concerned it might be awkward for him? Having me so involved in your big day?"

Emma's head tilted to one side, her lips drawing into a small frown. "I hope it won't be hard for him, but given how little effort he's made to patch things up with Drake since their falling-out over you, I won't let his feelings dictate my choices."

Fleur reared back a bit, trying to get a handle on what she'd just heard. Her bare thighs beneath her cutoffs raked along the wrought-iron seat at the movement.

"They quarreled?" She hadn't known there was tension between them—then or now. "And you think it was over me?"

"You didn't know?" Emma's eyes went round as she shoved aside her plate and leaned her elbows on the table. "When Colin moved to Montana, he intended it as a way to put distance between him and Drake. He hasn't been home since…you know." She looked abashed, her voice dropping. "Things ended with you."

Fleur shook her head, unable to believe that she'd been the cause of that sort of standoff.

"There had to be more to it than me. Colin and I— we weren't meant to be. He knew that as well as I did." She just hadn't always liked to admit that to herself since hanging on to her anger with Drake had been easier than blaming Colin, who'd been her friend before he'd been her lover, however briefly.

She thought back to his brief visit to her at her grand-mother's house when she'd told him there was no point in remaining together since she'd miscarried their baby. He'd been kind. Tender, even. And he'd wished her well when she'd given him back his ring.

It would have all been a distant memory for her ex-cept that she'd been deep in her own grief. His depar-ture from her life, when she needed someone to grieve with her, or to at least hold her while she cried, had been devastating. Only after he walked out her door for good did she give in to the emotions overwhelming her. She'd cried for days. Weeks, maybe. Time had been a slippery concept in those days of despair and, she realized later, a huge shift in hormones that made it even tougher to get her emotions under control.

Yet she hadn't blamed Colin, choosing to see his brother as the one responsible for pressing her to end the engagement. Now, she had to wonder why she'd been content to paint Drake as the villain in their drama. Why did she reserve all her animosity for him? But then, Drake had always inspired strong emotions in her.

Even now, her thoughts went to him and not to his brother far away in Montana.

"Do you really think so?" Emma mused, toying with the blond ends of her ponytail. Around them, the gas-fueled tiki torches around the patio flamed to life, giving a golden cast to the evening as the sun disappeared behind tall pines. "I'll be honest that I never saw the two of you as the right fit for one another." Her hazel gaze was shrewd for a moment before she smiled. "Either way, if he wanted a say in my wedding planning, he could have come home to congratulate me or visit me anytime in the past five years."

A new uneasiness returned as Fleur considered what she'd learned. There were dynamics at work in the Alexander family she'd been unaware of and felt unprepared to deal with during the catering job. She empathized, having dysfunction galore in her own family, though it made her uncomfortable that she could be the source of Drake and Colin's conflict. But since she wouldn't be able to afford to keep the electric on at the ranch next month if she didn't have some kind of work, she planned to forge ahead anyhow.

She stood to help Emma clear the table, changing the subject to other wedding details in an effort to lighten the mood. But even as Emma described her dress in detail, and explained her plans for exchanging vows beside the creek in her own backyard, Fleur's thoughts kept returning to Drake.

Not just the way he held her on horseback. Or the charged moment when she thought he might have kissed her. She also wondered what had happened between the Drake brothers to make Colin leave Catamount for good.

What if the misunderstanding concerned her, or was in her power to fix? Fleur knew how much it hurt to have warring siblings.

Making up her mind to talk to Drake about it when she approached him about the land management issue, she said good-night to Emma, knowing she should start the walk home before it got any darker.

The women exchanged a hug.

"Let me give you a ride home," Emma offered.

Fleur shook her head. "That's okay. The fresh air will do me good."

She had too much on her mind, especially that exchange with Drake.

"Then you can take one of the horses," Emma insisted as they stood on the flagstones, the creek rippling at their feet. "It's too far to walk, especially at this hour. And Drake is probably still in the barn. He can saddle one for you."

"I'll be fine," Fleur vowed as she edged onto the damp grass. Because even though she'd decided to speak to Drake, she hadn't quite recovered enough from their last conversation to spend more time with him tonight. "I'll take the path that follows the creek."

"And what if you step into a bog?" Emma argued, distracted by her vibrating phone. She checked it briefly before stuffing the device into her skirt pocket. "A horse will keep you safe and give you some company."

Fleur retreated another step, knowing she'd taken too much of the woman's time already. "Don't think twice about it. Thanks again for a really nice evening—*Oof!*" she exclaimed as she backed into a warm, muscular wall.

Drake's hands were on her arms, steadying her from behind. At the same time, he called to his sister over Fleur's head.

"I've got her, Emma. I can drive her home."

Fleur's heart pounded too hard from the contact to gainsay him. And the last thing she wanted was to argue with her friend's brother in front of Emma, who was giving her a juicy contract for a catering job.

So she tamped down the surge of awareness and channeled it all into agitation, glaring at Drake as she stomped across a gravel road to where his pickup was parked near an equipment barn. She waited until he'd helped her up into his truck.

Once he'd closed the door behind her and climbed into the driver's seat, she whirled on him. "What do you think you're doing?"

Six

Excellent question.

Drake had asked himself the same thing only about twenty times since the offer to drive Fleur home had leaped from his mouth. What the hell had he been thinking when he'd skipped dinner to avoid her, spending the time berating himself for coveting the woman he'd warned his brother against? He was supposed to be finding a way to befriend her enough to convince her to sell Crooked Elm to him, a goal directly in opposition to avoiding the attraction he felt for her.

Grinding his teeth as he put the pickup in Reverse, he kept his focus on the rearview mirror instead of the woman beside him.

"I'm taking you home," he managed once he'd unlocked his jaw enough to speak. "That's what I'm doing."

The sound of her windy sigh expressed the same exasperation he felt. He put the truck in gear and headed for the main road. Walking the back way between their ranches was only about three miles. The county route took longer, remaining on the outskirts of both properties.

"What I mean is, why would you volunteer for the job now, after how awkward the ride over here was?" Her voice filled the truck cabin, feminine and sweet somehow, even through her frustration. It made him think about the confidences shared earlier when he'd pressed her close. "And don't say it wasn't, since you went out of your way to disappoint Emma by not showing up for the meal she made. I know it was because you didn't want to see me."

He considered the question carefully while the headlights shone a path through the darkness. He'd always liked the lack of ambient light out here, the way the stars seemed closer. But right now, driving Fleur home, he focused on the woods close to the road, alert for critters that could jump out in front of the vehicle.

"I didn't skip dinner just to avoid you," he said quietly. "I needed the time to think about what you told me. It changes…things. Between my brother and me."

When she didn't answer right away, he stole a glance over at her. She stared out the passenger window, while one finger traced a slow pattern on the pane.

"I hadn't realized until tonight that your relationship with Colin was strained," she said at last. "I assumed that once Colin and I broke our engagement, things went back to normal between the two of you."

How much to say about the heated argument he'd had with Colin that day five years ago? Drake's first instinct was to keep Alexander family matters private. But given how integral a role Fleur had played—and that she'd be there when Colin returned for Emma's wedding—he thought it best to share something of what happened.

Besides, he had to start somewhere with building some trust between them.

"Everything came to a head for us the day I heard you two talking about the pre-nup. I told him about my concerns the day before I confronted you." He didn't like to recall the argument, but he dredged up some sound bites now in order to paint a picture for her. "My insistence that he was too young to marry and you hadn't been dating long enough turned into him rebelling against everything I'd tried to do since becoming head of the family. He accused me of planning his life for him. From the college he'd attended to the way he spent his weekends, since I'd expected him to continue pitching in on the ranch."

Drake had been angry, wondering how his younger brother could have the audacity to suggest *his* life had been plotted out for him. Did he honestly think Drake had been able to make his own choices? Everything he'd done had been to protect his brother and sister, to ensure their future. He'd forsaken a college scholarship and all but quit rodeo, giving up any serious pursuit of a sport he'd once been poised to dominate. Staying on the fringes, entering weekend competitions for prize money, had only rubbed salt in the wound of all he hadn't been able to accomplish.

"But Colin was twenty-three years old at the time, not a kid in school." She sounded puzzled, but she was facing him again, giving the conversation her full attention. "He was done with college. I thought he really enjoyed working here. We even talked about settling in Catamount for good."

Did she know how wistful she sounded? he wondered. The idea reminded him of his responsibility in breaking them up, and the new sense of guilt mingled with resentment that she should want Colin while Drake couldn't help thinking about *her*.

Turning onto the main road, his grip on the wheel tightened.

"Perhaps he only said that to be agreeable." He couldn't help the harshness in his tone. "He'd told me more than once he wanted out of the family business. I assumed it was because he disliked cattle ranching, so it came as a surprise when he bought his own spread two states away. Turns out it wasn't the work he objected to. Just me."

Despite everything he'd done to ensure his siblings were secure after their parents died. Colin had been fourteen at the time. He would have gone into foster care if Drake hadn't given up his own college scholarship to stay at home to oversee things. Not just his siblings, but the ranch, too. Thank God he'd been eighteen then. He shuddered to think what would have happened to all of them if he'd been even one year younger.

He hadn't expected thanks. He would have never made a different decision. But he would have never guessed that Colin would resent him.

In the silence afterward, Fleur's hand dropped lightly on his thigh.

"It might not have anything to do with you," she suggested softly. "My siblings ran to opposite coasts as soon as they could after my parents' divorce. I don't think they wanted to escape me so much as the site of their unhappiness."

He appreciated the idea. Would have found comfort in the words even, except that her hand on his thigh made it tough to think about anything but touching more of her.

His muscle tensed under her palm. Everything tensed,

for that matter. His blood ran hotter around this woman, and there was no help for it.

So he was glad to spot the turnoff for her grandmother's house just ahead. The sooner he dropped her off safely, the faster he could stop thinking about exploring the sparks that flared brighter every time they were together. Another day, he'd figure out how to win her over enough to sell Crooked Elm to him. For tonight, he needed to retreat until he figured out how to deal with the unexpected revelation that a red-hot fire burned beneath their old animosity.

"All those months where you and I were on the road at rodeos all over the West—the bull rider and the rodeo queen—" he glanced over at her, a cool smile in place "—who would have thought we'd be the ones to keep the home fires burning?"

Her hand evaporated from his leg like it had never been there—as he'd known it would. Their enmity had begun on the road, from the early days when he'd teased her about how seriously she took her pageant roles, to later years when she'd pranked him by making a fake dating profile for him. She'd only been a kid—eighteen when he'd quit the rodeo circuit, and she hadn't been well supervised, with her mother or sisters showing up only sporadically.

He should have cut her more slack.

Now he missed her touch immediately. Yet he was also grateful for the reprieve, however brief, from this growing hunger to kiss her until they were both breathless.

"You didn't know I had a sentimental streak, did you?" she shot back, sticking close to the passenger side door as he slowed to a stop in front of her grandmother's house. "It was always tough for you to see underneath the spangled dresses and leather fringe, but it's there."

The last thing he needed was to start imagining the body under her clothes. Especially when those cutoff shorts had him fantasizing about her thighs all day long.

But her wry tone and tight smile made him feel like a first-class ass for not simply accepting the comfort she'd offered. But discovering he was more attracted to Fleur than ever was still screwing with his head, and he couldn't afford another breathless moment of staring at her lips, like he'd experienced earlier today. Better to send her on her way mad at him.

"If you say so." Braking to a stop, he glanced over at her before parking the truck. "Good night, Miss Silver Spurs."

He wasn't surprised when she slammed the door in his face.

Arriving at the Cowboy Kitchen just as they flipped over the sign to Open, her car full of freshly baked treats for the diner to sell, Fleur hoped she could maintain her running streak of avoiding Drake. Surely that would be a benefit of rising long before dawn to start baking—getting in and out of the Cowboy Kitchen without running into the owner. It had been ten days since Drake had driven her home after her dinner with Emma, and she guessed he was taking the same pains to stay away from her as she was from him.

She recognized his tactics that night when he'd dropped her off. Right at the moment when he'd showed her something deeper, something real, he'd shifted the heartfelt conversation into verbal combat.

Truly, she'd never seen him so clearly as she had at that moment. He hid behind the old quarrels as surely as she did—shoving aside any hint of tenderness behind the safety of contentious words.

The realization, and the empathy that came with it, had rattled her. His truck wasn't in the parking lot of the local eatery, however, and that had to be a good sign. She'd followed his suggestion and checked with the manager—who turned out to be Marta, her old friend from 4-H who also waitressed there—about stocking cookies, tarts and cakes in the display case a couple of times each week. Marta had been enthusiastic, and they'd test run some things last week.

Two days ago, Marta had informed Fleur everything sold out, and they were ready to order more. The order had come in the nick of time to pay some of Fleur's most pressing bills since she wouldn't receive the bulk of the payment for catering Emma's wedding until after the event. Even now, the first payment was contingent on a tasting that she'd set up with Emma for tonight. They'd finalize the menu afterward so Fleur could order everything she needed. The wedding was less than two weeks away.

And although both of her newfound income sources were connected to Drake Alexander, at least she wasn't working directly for him, the way she would have been if she'd taken a job at Cowboy Kitchen. This way, she was an independent contractor, doing business with one of his businesses, right? She didn't have to feel dependent on Drake, even though the rich rancher seemed to support the entire town of Catamount in one way or another. Even the local nature conservancy had sung his praises when they stopped by yesterday to make an appointment with her to discuss the diminished condition of wetlands on Crooked Elm property. She'd put them off for a couple of more days, certain whatever they wanted would be expensive when she couldn't afford to invest any more in the property.

But every day she spent working in her grand-mother's kitchen made her wish she didn't have to sell Crooked Elm.

Now, stepping out of her rattletrap vehicle, Fleur turned to open the creaking back door to unload her carefully packed baked goods when her cell chimed. At six in the morning? Surprised, she tugged the phone from the pocket of her denim skirt to check the screen.

Jessamyn.

Her sister never contacted her just to chat. Knowing it was either business or an emergency, Fleur accepted the call.

"Hello?" She shifted to lean against the trunk of her car, careful to avoid a spot on the fender where silver paint and rust were both flaking away.

"Sorry to call so early, Fleur, but I wanted to touch base before Dad gets in the office." Her sister's voice sounded weary, which might not have been unusual for some women at that hour, but Jessamyn had long been a disciple of the school of hustle and grind. She thrived on long hours and doing anything to get ahead.

"It's fine. Everything okay there?" She tipped her head back to feel the sun's early rays on her face, the cooler air welcome after a couple of hot days.

She'd always loved the weather in Colorado. Even the hottest days were tempered by lower humidity than Dallas. She swore her recipes were better here, too, but that might have more to do with her mood than the weather. Not even Drake's presence in her life could diminish the joy she took in being at her Gran's house. She just wished she hadn't waited so long to return.

"Yes, but I wanted to alert you that Dad's been receiving mail from local conservation groups near Catamount concerned about land management practices at Crooked

Elm. Were you aware of this?" Jessamyn's blunt way of speaking always felt vaguely accusatory, and Fleur had to remind herself not to take offense where none was meant.

Being raised in a household of warring factions definitely made Fleur even more prickly. It had occurred to her after her last exchange with Drake that her tendency to snipe and be defensive had shaped her relationship with him early on. But those rodeo years that he liked to tease her about had been hell for her. Did he think she enjoyed all the times she'd dressed up in gowns she found at consignment shops to compete for prizes to afford her education? Even before her dad had cut off support to her, he'd warned her he wouldn't be helping with college. She'd hit the pageant circuit hard at sixteen.

In theory, Fleur had loved a lot of things about rodeo life. Behind the scenes had a culture of its own, however, and in her experience, it hadn't always been warmhearted and supportive. She shook off the mental wandering and focused on Jessamyn's question.

"Gran's tenant for the rangelands mentioned it to me." She didn't say anything about the visit from the local conservation group yet, keying in on the other piece of information that troubled her. "Why is mail going to Dad about Crooked Elm?"

The last thing they needed was for their father to be involved in how the property was managed until they sold it. Antonia had been very deliberate about willing the place to her three granddaughters, not her son who had turned his back on the old ranch long ago.

"I don't know." Jessamyn sounded puzzled. "I've been meaning to look into that. Maybe he's paid tax bills for Gran before."

Worry tickled along her senses since her sister didn't sound confident of the answer.

"Dad won't contest the will or anything, right? Isn't it too late for that?" She did not know how the legalities worked, assuming her grandmother's will would be enough for them to move forward.

"Technically, no. It's not too late since the court still has to have a hearing to confirm the will, but I'm sure everything is in order." Jessamyn huffed out a windy sigh. "Anyway, I'm trying to clear my schedule for next month, so I can work on the house before we put it up for sale once the estate is settled. In the meantime, I'm sending a picture of this letter so you can look into it. We don't want any legalities to tie up the property."

She plucked at her blouse with nervous fingers, hoping Jessamyn was just being overly cautious. A big green tractor rumbled past on the main road, making it hard to hear anything else for a moment.

"I'll figure it out," she said once the farm vehicle had moved away, the words more to reassure herself than as an actual statement of fact. "Thanks for letting me know."

On the other end of the call, her sister seemed to hesitate before answering.

"If it's too much for us, Fleur, we can ask Dad for help. He hires companies all the time to fix up houses—"

"Never." She bit the word out with more vehemence than she'd intended considering Jessamyn had long supported their father's stance on most everything. "He would do it to help you, Jess, but he would resent every cent that might benefit Lark or me."

Her sister's tone softened. "I don't think that's true anymore."

Biting her lip against the urge to argue, Fleur straightened away from her car and turned back to the stacks of plastic containers buckled into the safety harness.

"Either way, I would never accept his help now." He'd

abandoned her when she'd needed a father's love, never showing up for any of her pageants or putting in time to chaperone her when she'd been tying herself in knots to earn college scholarships. Was it any wonder she'd developed a reputation as a haughty ice queen on the rodeo circuit? She'd had her reasons for seeming untouchable, a kid's coping mechanism for unwanted attention. Then again, maybe if she'd kept up the old hauteur to avoid attention, she wouldn't have had to quit her last job, where the kitchen manager had no concept of personal space. Or keeping his hands to himself. "Unlike Dad, I don't believe the almighty dollar solves every problem."

He'd been more concerned with guarding his fortune against his ex-wife and anyone who sympathized with her. And while Fleur tried not to be the kind of cringeworthy adult who blamed her problems on her parents, Fleur had found herself frequently unpacking baggage from that time in her life, from her father's decision that she wasn't worthy of recognition as his daughter. At least now, she was more aware of her own behavior because of it.

Recognizing it didn't always make her change, however.

"Heard and understood," Jessamyn retorted, the biting tone sounding more like her old self. "Far be it for anyone in this family to do things the easy way."

After saying goodbye, Fleur tucked her phone in her pocket and withdrew the first stack of boxes filled with cookies and tarts to bring inside the restaurant. While she'd been standing in the parking lot, two other cars had pulled in with patrons for the diner, and the scent of ham and bacon wafted on the breeze every time the door opened.

Unwilling to miss out on potential sales because she'd

been gabbing with her sister, Fleur hurried inside with the containers, thanking Marta as the other woman appeared in time to open the front door for her, her dark ponytail bouncing on one shoulder in time with her energetic walk.

"Good morning," Fleur greeted her, taking care not to jostle her cargo as she wound her way through the tables toward the counter, where an old-fashioned bakery case had been scrubbed clean. "I still have more outside."

A handful of patrons glanced her way while a George Jones tune played softly over hidden speakers. The scent of coffee hung in the air while pans and utensils banged in the back. Fleur missed working in a restaurant, the rhythms of a shared kitchen workspace calling to her.

One day, if she could sell Crooked Elm, she really had a shot at opening her own place.

"Do you need help? I can dart out for a minute—"

She shook her head once she'd settled the boxes near the case. "That's okay, but thank you. It's a huge help to have you get the door."

"I'll follow you out, then." Marta paused to pick up a coffeepot behind the counter so she could refill a patron's cup. "I'm right behind you."

Fleur nodded, respecting the other woman's ease with doing multiple things at once, a coveted skill in any busy eating establishment. "Sounds perfect."

"And be thinking about what you want for breakfast. Drake said to give you a meal on the house whenever you brought us items to sell." As she spoke, Marta had already moved to start filling the bakery case with fresh pastries.

Fleur noticed an older couple getting up from their seats to check out the wares, but her pleasure in their obvious interest was diminished by Marta's words.

Had Drake told Marta to buy from Fleur in the first

place? She'd been okay with him recommending that she try Cowboy Kitchen as an outlet, but she was less comfortable with him paving the way for her if she hadn't earned it. And she definitely wasn't accepting meals from another man who thought he could buy his way through life.

Especially one who also assumed that Fleur could be bought. Just as he'd thought when he found out about her engagement to Colin. Drake had been so sure she only wanted to marry him for financial security.

Pushing her way out the front door, bells chiming, Fleur retrieved the rest of her wares. Yet her joy in the act was diminished with the possibility of Drake's interference weighing on her.

As much as she didn't want to see him again—attraction be damned—she really should clear the air with the man who seemed to have all of Catamount under his thumb. She would explain that she didn't need his help securing work, or feeding herself, for crying out loud. Besides, she still wanted to ask him more about the local conservation efforts since Josiah Cranston had implied Drake was something of an expert.

So, after unloading the last stack of baked goods and politely declining Marta's efforts to feed her, Fleur stepped out into the sunshine and got out her phone again.

Without giving herself time to overthink it, she found Drake's contact information. He'd insisted she take it almost a decade ago when he'd appointed himself her disapproving guardian on those times they'd ended up at the same rodeos.

Even then, he'd been judgmental and condescending toward her, convinced everything she did was to make a spectacle of herself. Why would she have thought he'd changed just because he made her heart race faster now?

Thumbs flying over the screen, she typed:

Emma's tasting for the reception is tonight at Crooked Elm. I hope you'll join us.

And sent it before she could have time to regret it.

Seven

Standing outside the goat pen at Crooked Elm Ranch, Drake scratched the head of a floppy-eared Nubian in the hope of quieting her. The mottled brown-and-white animal had been bleating with urgency during the last half hour of the tasting Fleur had arranged for Emma. Drake had used the distracting calls as an excuse to let his sister make her selections for the reception menu.

Or maybe he'd just latched on to the first excuse he could think of to step away from the draw of their hostess.

While two other goats ambled over to greet him—both black and white—Drake felt his attention yanked back to the picnic table draped in a sunny yellow tablecloth, where Fleur reviewed wedding cake ideas on a tablet. She wore a white tank top and a pale green skirt printed with flowers that ended just above her knees. Her copper-colored hair was tied into a low ponytail with a sheer pink scarf. He'd spent half the tasting thinking about untying the fabric and teasing the ends over her skin.

But the other half of the time, he'd spent forcing himself to admit that not only had he misjudged her in the past, he'd also failed to recognize that she'd become a force to be reckoned with in her own right.

He'd been so sure she'd only rolled into town to serve her own ends by selling off the ranch to the highest bidder so she could count up her profit. Yet she'd surprised him by moving into the place for the summer and connecting with the residents of Catamount again. After seeing the effort she'd put into baking, he'd insisted Marta give her an outlet for her goods at Cowboy Kitchen. And he wasn't the only one who'd noticed her talents. He'd heard from Emma that she'd booked small catering jobs with two of her friends—someone's baby shower and a retirement party for a local farmer.

Yet until this evening, when he'd watched Fleur in sales mode going over the possibilities for Emma's wedding foods, he hadn't really acknowledged that she possessed far more drive and determination than he'd ever given her credit for. She'd achieved a lot in five years, and her skill for cooking came through in her discussion of preparation and presentation. She wasn't catering just to make a buck. She was clearly passionate about it.

"They like you!" Fleur called over to him. She and Emma had both lifted their eyes from the tablet to watch him pet the three jostling goats. "This is the most content they've been since I got here."

The remark brought to mind how long she'd been in town. What kind of job had she left behind in Dallas that she didn't need to return yet?

"I'm not bad with animals," he observed lightly, wishing for a moment that he possessed some of the same ease with people.

His brother, namely. But now he also wished he had a way to prove to Fleur that his sole purpose in life wasn't just to give her a tough time. He didn't want to be continually at odds with her. He simply found it convenient at the times when the thought of tasting her proved so all-consuming he didn't know how else to handle it.

Before she could reply, Emma's fiancé, Glen, arrived, jogging across the backyard in his cargoes and a polo with his ranch's brand printed on the pocket, as if he'd only just finished up his work.

Leaving the goats to their own devices and giving time for Glen to be caught up on the wedding menu, Drake strolled the perimeter of the yard, where Fleur's handiwork was evident. The last time he'd visited Antonia at Crooked Elm, the birdbath fountain had been caked in moss and the perennials surrounding it were a wild thicket. But the stonework had been cleaned, and the water feature restored so that it babbled softly. New plants mingled with old ones that had been thinned out and separated, a fresh layer of mulch protecting the soil.

Beyond the birdbath, a firepit had been raked clean and the rocks reset. The heavy wooden furniture surrounding it had been recently painted.

All of it made the setting for Fleur's sales pitch that much more appealing. She'd set out tall candles surrounded by glass globes to protect them from the breeze, and as the daylight faded into early evening, the candlelight gave the yard a romantic vibe.

"Are you done working your Doctor Doolittle magic on the goats?" Fleur's voice sounded just behind him, alerting him that she must have stepped away from the engaged couple for the moment. Perhaps she noticed him swiveling his attention back to his sister, because Fleur explained quickly, "I thought I'd give them some privacy to talk over my menu ideas. I don't want your sister to feel obligated to accept my suggestions just because we're friends or—for any reason."

His gaze stuck on her silvery-gray eyes as she turned to him, and he wondered if she'd always been thoughtful, and he'd just been too stubborn to recognize it. He scraped a hand over his jaw, seized with the need to touch her again. He hadn't forgotten how she'd felt tucked up against him in the saddle that day. How soft her skin had been when his thumb had brushed a bare patch at her waist.

"I was surprised you invited me tonight." His voice had dipped an octave, his thoughts getting the better of him. "Especially after how we parted last time."

He'd sniped at her to put distance between them, recognizing he was in danger of kissing her otherwise.

"I have a couple of things I hoped to discuss with you." She peered over her shoulder to where Emma and Glen studied the tablet together, their heads close as they sat side by side at the picnic table. Then Fleur looked up at him again. "Privately. Would you be able to stay after Emma finishes up? I'm guessing Glen is already signing off on the food items she selected."

His blood heated at the thought of being alone with Fleur, even though he knew she wouldn't have anything remotely intimate in mind. Still, just being around her amped him up.

"That's a safe bet." Drake had noticed the two of them seemed like-minded in many ways. It was one of the reasons he'd given the guy his approval to ask for Emma's hand. He took his role as head of the family seriously, and that meant ensuring his sister's happiness. "And as long as Glen can drop Emma back at home, I'll stay."

Even though it was surely unwise. Even though he'd told himself it would only worsen his relationship with his brother to spend time with Colin's former fiancée.

Fleur's shoulders relaxed a fraction.

"Thank you." Nodding, she seemed relieved at his quick agreement. As if she'd been worried he wouldn't give her an audience. The idea made him feel like a heel. "I'll just go see if they're ready to wrap things up."

Drake watched her walk away from him, his eyes drifting to the sway of her hips despite his best intentions.

He was going to need all his restraint to keep his hands off her. And he refused to fall back on the old knee-jerk method of bickering like a couple of kids. She deserved better than that.

But considering how long the attraction had been simmering inside him, he feared the slightest wrong move could start an inferno they wouldn't be able to ignore.

Fifteen minutes later, the tasting appointment had concluded and Fleur had a signed contract in her possession for Emma Alexander's wedding reception. Thankfully, the income would allow her to pay the bills this month and give her more time to work out her next steps. After thanking the future bride and groom, she stood in her driveway beside Drake to wave goodbye to them.

Glen would accompany Emma home, so that Drake could remain behind to speak to her, just as she'd requested. That should be a good thing. Except, as Glen's black extended-cab pickup vanished in a cloud of dust and country rock music, Fleur became more aware of Drake's muscular frame just behind her. His shoulders cast a shadow on her back, preventing the last rays of the sun from reaching her skin as it slipped lower in the sky. A shiver tripped over her, and she couldn't even pretend it was because of a chill in the air.

Her senses attuned to his presence. His deep, even breathing. A hint of his pine and musk scent. A thrill shot through her at the way her pulse zipped faster, even when she knew she had to ignore the signs of her body's obvious attraction to the man.

She hadn't called him here tonight for that.

"Thank you for staying," she said crisply as she turned to face him.

And promptly confronted a whole new set of compelling Drake attributes. His dark eyes locked on hers, searching. Was it her imagination, or did they lack some of the judgment they normally contained anytime he looked at her?

A frivolous thought. Wishful thinking that only distracted her from her purpose.

"Would you like to take a seat?" she blurted, needing to break the connection. Desperate to have the conversation ended so she could send him on his way before she allowed herself to be hypnotized by that magnetic gaze of his.

"Sure. Thank you for agreeing to cater the reception," he returned, shoving his hands in the pockets of his dark jeans. He still wore a black Stetson tonight, but he'd traded his boots for loafers. A white T-shirt and a subtly patterned gray-and-black sport coat, custom-tailored to his athletic form, reminded her that there was more to him than a bull rider. "It makes me happy to see Emma so pleased with the wedding arrangements."

He walked with her toward the picnic table, the candles inside the hurricane lamp flickering golden as the sky began its evening shift from pink to violet. There was rain in the forecast tonight, but so far the cloudy sky only made the sunset prettier.

The sincerity in his tone shouldn't have surprised her. She knew that Drake took his brother's and sister's happiness seriously, since she'd once been a casualty of that protectiveness once herself.

Still, she couldn't help the warmth that stole through her at having won this demanding man's approval in at least one area. She hadn't sought it. But considering how often she'd fallen short of earning praise from anyone in her own family, having Drake notice her efforts felt… nice.

"It's my pleasure." She stopped near the picnic table and turned her back to it so she could use the bench while facing away from the work surface. "I'll do everything in my power to ensure my responsibilities for that day exceed her expectations."

Drake took a seat on the same side, but he straddled the bench to face her directly, laying one arm along the table.

"But I'm guessing you didn't ask me to stay behind so we could discuss the wedding plans," he observed drily, and she welcomed the challenge in his voice.

Why was it so much easier to talk to Drake as her adversary?

"And you would be correct." Crossing her legs, she shifted toward him. "There are two reasons I needed to see you. First, to ask if you directed Marta to purchase food items from me in the hope of securing my good will in potentially selling Crooked Elm to you."

He reared back at the words. "Excuse me?"

"You didn't do that?" She thought his surprise seemed genuine.

Was it possible he hadn't been using their financial

disparity to his advantage? She knew it was a hot button for her after her father's games with money.

"Of course not." He took off his Stetson and set it on the far side of the picnic table before tunneling impatient fingers through his hair. "Marta and the cook, Stella McRory, have autonomy over there. I wouldn't know the first thing about running a diner."

"Because Marta told me you said she should feed me when I bring baked goods," she added, distracted by the flexing of his square jaw. The hint of bristle made her wonder what his face would feel like against her palm.

Not that she would ever find out.

"I also set the employees up with better health insurance and comped one meal a day for everyone who works there. I won't apologize for good employee retention tactics, or for making sure local suppliers like working with us."

"Marta seemed really pleased to have a 401(k)," she remarked, recalling the other woman's pride when she'd said as much.

"There you go." He nodded, seeming satisfied. Vindicated. Then his expression softened. "I had no ulterior motive when I told Marta to extend you a courtesy meal. Though I guess I can't be surprised you would assume the worst of me, given our history."

"It's not just our history that made me uncomfortable with the idea." She flexed her toes inside her metallic silver sandals, noticing that her pink nail polish had faded. She'd been so busy for the past week and a half, she went to bed exhausted every night, with little time for anything but work. "My father enjoys flexing the power of his financial might in front of people. Especially Lark and me."

"I'm not sure the cost of a couple of fried eggs and toast at the diner would be an impressive display of my net worth if I were that kind of guy." The teasing note in his voice made her smile despite herself. "It's just a gesture, plain and simple."

"Right. Sorry to misread that." She didn't mention the other incident in her life that made her wary of men with power over her financial future. Her creep of a former boss wasn't worth bringing up.

The silence stretched for a moment while the katydids clicked and called in the nearby bushes. The sound was peaceful, making her realize the goats must be content now, too. All was quiet in their pen.

"You said there were two things?" Drake prompted a moment later. He slid the hurricane lamp closer to them on the picnic table, casting his features in a sudden golden glow.

All at once, a vivid memory slammed into her brain from the days when they'd attended some of the same rodeos. They'd been in Evergreen, Colorado, and Fleur had been excited about her chances in the princess pageant for the younger age group, plus both her mother and Lark had been able to attend with her. Having her oldest sister nearby had made the whole event less stressful, since Fleur could focus on her performance, her riding and her presentation instead of the inevitable logistics of food, lodging and transportation to the various events. She'd been particularly happy after doing well in the horsemanship competition, and Lark had taken her to sit in the stands near some people she knew from Catamount—including Drake.

Lark was Drake's age, seven years older than Fleur. That had seemed a lifetime apart when she'd been fifteen. But Drake had praised Fleur's riding that night, and for one evening at least, hadn't seemed judgmental.

She'd even been a little starry-eyed that he'd paid attention to her at all.

Until one of Lark's friends breezed into the group, draping herself across Drake's lap like she owned real estate there. The raven-haired woman had kissed him full on the mouth before stage-whispering to Lark that she was ready to take Drake back to her hotel so she could get the *real* rodeo started. Drake had chastised the bold brunette, his eyes flicking to Fleur, making her aware it was *her* fault that he had to rein in his girlfriend.

A shiver pulsed up her spine now at the memory that had no business flashing across her thoughts now.

"Fleur?" Drake's straight, dark eyebrows scrunched in confusion. "Are you okay?"

"Yes." She nodded jerkily, wishing she could shove aside the vision of Drake giving some random woman the ride of her life. "Um. I've heard you're a bit of an expert on the local conservation efforts."

Her voice sounded funny. Too high and thin.

As if she'd been having inappropriate thoughts of the man she would prefer to hate.

"It would be a stretch to say I'm an expert, but I've certainly invested in measures to preserve the natural ecosystem wherever possible. Good land management benefits the cattle, the land, native species—the list goes on. Why do you ask?"

"Well, I have reason to believe that—"

His shin grazed her calf as he stretched his legs.

"Sorry," he said automatically, gaze snapping to hers.

The momentary touch was like connecting an electrical circuit, the heat of his body apparent right through the fabric of his pants.

Her breathing quickened, the rapid intake of breath

sounding loud in her ears when the only other sound was the katydid concert.

"I'm worried Crooked Elm is in violation of some environmental initiatives." She grabbed on to the conversation like a lifeline, confident there was nothing remotely sexy in the topic. "Jessamyn told me my father has been receiving mail from an agency that threatened citations on a few counts, but from what I could gather, they're most concerned about the creek."

She'd reviewed the letter Jessamyn had forwarded, but there were references to other regulatory documents she hadn't unearthed yet.

Drake nodded. "Antonia's tenant lets his cattle range too close to the water. The damage he's doing is going to take years to fix."

"You think that's it?" The problem seemed simple to fix if she spoke to Josiah Cranston. Then again, the surly rancher might not be amenable to changing his practices now.

What she needed to do was give him notice of the lease termination.

A cold breeze kicked up from the east, blowing her hair along her shoulders. She tucked a strand behind one ear to keep it out of her line of vision.

"There could be other problems, but I'm guessing that's the biggest area of concern. You should follow the creek next time you visit Emma and see how different the vegetation along it looks on your land compared to mine."

Frowning, she realized she would have bristled at words like that a few days ago. But she'd reached a new accord with Drake.

Even, she realized, a new trust. Because no matter their differences in the past, she believed in his passionate commitment to the land. He wouldn't steer her wrong about that.

When another breeze stirred even stronger this time, the ends of her hair floated dangerously close to the open top of the hurricane lamp. Drake darted forward, capturing the strands with one hand and pushing away the lamp with the other.

"Storm's coming," he announced, his voice gravelly as he kept her hair in his fist for a moment longer than necessary.

Then two.

Heat thrummed through her, pulsing in time with her heartbeat. She couldn't feel his touch, yet the thought of him tugging her head back with that hold on her hair turned her knees to liquid. Did something flicker in his dark gaze, or was that just the reflected candlelight?

A low rumble of thunder in the distance was probably a warning they should both be heeding. Instead, it felt like a drumroll overture for whatever madness was about to take place between them next.

She licked her dry lips as he resettled her hair behind her back. And then his hand was there, on her shoulder.

A warm, anchoring weight.

"Drake." His name left her lips in wonder. A plea.

And when another roll of thunder sounded, she felt the static in the air, the charged pull of the night and the man.

Except the thunder sounded different. Nearer. Like charging hooves galloping closer.

At the same moment the thought formed, Drake sprang from the bench. Breaking into a run, he called over his shoulder, "The goats are loose."

Eight

"Nimue, don't you want your dinner?" Fleur coaxed the small black-and-white goat, the only one they hadn't been able to capture.

Drake watched Fleur swing a bright blue pail to tempt the escapee, while the other two does inside the pen bleated and called, the yard partially lit by a couple of outdoor fixtures mounted to the barn. The brown-and-white Nubian—Morgan le Fay, he'd been informed—had returned to the enclosure as soon as Drake had herded her toward it. The larger of the black-and-white animals—Guinevere—had romped around the yard with more enthusiasm until she'd gotten distracted by a tasty patch of grass, and Fleur had been able to slip a lead around its neck.

Now only one holdout remained. He worked on securing the pen where a board along the top of the woven mesh fencing had given way, while Fleur pleaded with the last jail breaker. Considering how his evening had progressed with Fleur before the animals escaped, Drake was ready to tie up the goat adventure. He could have sworn they'd been moments away from locking lips when a blur of horns and fur had streaked past them.

"I'm surprised it never came to my attention that Antonia named her goats after Arthurian legends," he observed as he hammered in a nail to fasten a replacement board into place. He'd been fortunate to find a stack of precut lumber inside the big barn and had made quick work of the job.

Another flash of lightning split the sky, illuminating Fleur's face as she cooed at the unrepentant animal. Drake set aside the hammer and turned his attention to helping her since a storm was imminent. He knew he should leave considering how badly he wanted to stay and find out if that kiss would still happen. Yet how could he have left her to deal with the broken fence alone when she already thought poorly of him? With good reason.

He'd misjudged this woman more than once, and now he wanted to offer an olive branch of his own. He would help her tonight, and offer whatever advice she needed to help her settle the land management citations.

Now Nimue looked ready to play, her floppy ears swinging as she trotted around the birdbath in the center of the lawn. He retrieved the lead rope Fleur had used with Guinevere and moved closer to the goat as the thunder sounded more and more ominous.

The air smelled like rain.

"Gran didn't have them for long. She rescued them two years ago from a shelter near Grand Junction." Fleur took a handful of grain and extended it, her hair whipping around her head as the wind picked up force. "She texted me a photo of them later that week, telling me she liked the idea of names that were regal and magical for the spindly little trio, convinced it would give them something to aspire to."

When the lightning lit up the sky again, Drake could see her smiling to herself at the memory. He only had a moment to enjoy the vision she made, wind wreaking havoc with her skirt, her natural beauty drawing his eye more than the days of spangles and big hair.

He was almost close enough to drop the lead rope over Nimue's head when the downpour started.

Fleur squealed at the same time the goat bleated, a chorus of feminine surprise. He was drenched instantly, the rainfall hard and cold. Time was running out, and he didn't want to chase the beast in the rain. Drake dropped the rope over the little runaway's head.

Thank God.

He raised his voice to be heard over the racket of the deluge sluicing over them. "I've got her. Go inside, and I'll make sure she's secure."

Fleur must have understood, because she bolted toward the abandoned picnic table, wet skirt clinging to her legs as she ran. Before he could lose himself in staring at her, he turned the opposite way, leading a humbled doe back to the pen, where she would have access to a warm barn and dry hay. Inside the enclosure, Drake tugged off the rope so the animal could take refuge with her friends. He closed and locked the gate before doing a visual sweep of the yard.

No sign of Fleur.

He hesitated for a fraction of a second, not sure if he should head straight for his truck or go inside to say good-night, but Fleur solved that dilemma by calling to him from a back door.

"Come in!" she called.

He only had an instant to note the white tank top hugging her body before he wrenched his gaze up to her eyes.

An instant that sent his pulse pounding.

Jogging toward the door, he paused under the narrow overhang outside the threshold.

"Are you sure—?" The unfinished question lingered for a split second, a world of meanings filling in the blank as they stared at one another, clothes dripping.

Any hesitation seemed overridden by her sense of hospitality because she gripped his wrist and drew him indoors.

"I insist." She let go of him once he was safely inside. After closing the door behind him, she passed him a white towel from a fluffy stack on a nearby deacon's bench with a tall mirror behind it. "At least dry off and wait for the worst of it to pass over. I appreciate you helping me with the goats."

She sounded breathless from running around in the rain. She'd discarded her shoes and now stood in bare feet on the gray ceramic tile floor. Water pooled at her feet, but she grabbed a towel off the tall pile and dropped it onto the floor. Her slender curves were outlined thanks to the soaked skirt and tank top; the picture she made burning itself onto the backs of his eyelids forever. She grabbed yet another towel, wrapping it around herself, but it wasn't fast enough for his liking. He forced his gaze away.

They stood in a dimly lit mudroom that he hadn't been in for many years. His younger brother and sister had spent more time than him playing with the neighbor's granddaughters in the summers that Lark, Jessamyn and Fleur had been in residence. As the oldest of his siblings, he'd been expected to learn the ranch business at an early age. Since his father was a self-made man, he'd wanted

Drake to understand what it was like to work all the jobs on the ranch, from stable hand to foreman and—eventually—ranch manager—before taking over one day. Drake had chafed at pouring every available moment into the ranch during his senior year of high school, resenting that he never had a free weekend to do anything besides work. Now he would give anything for the chance to spend another day with his father.

But Drake shook off the unhappy thoughts as he mopped off the worst of the water on his face and arms. Beyond the darkened mudroom, Drake saw the bright yellow kitchen with mosaic tile countertops and an old fireplace built into the far wall.

"Is the fireplace safe to use?" he asked, seeing the log holder full of split wood. "I could start us a fire while you…dry off."

He needed her to change clothes. If not for her sake, for his.

She bit her lip, her face washed clean of any makeup, if she'd even been wearing any in the first place. Her eyelashes were spiky with water. The natural pink tint of her mouth turned a deeper shade of rose where her teeth stabbed the plump lower lip.

His focus lasered in on that spot, and he could almost imagine what she tasted like there.

"It's no trouble," he urged her, voice raking over his throat that seemed the only dry place on his body right now. "And we never finished talking about the land management issues you asked about. I've got a change of clothes in the truck, too. I'll just—"

His words dried up when Fleur bent forward to wring out the worst of the water from her skirt. Between the quick flash of thigh she bared and the soft bounce of her breasts while she worked, he wasn't sure how he'd make it through the evening. Not waiting for her to reply either way, he grabbed one of the overcoats he'd spotted on the rack full of pegs by the back door, and threw it over himself.

"Be right back," he barked over his shoulder, lurching toward the door.

But he already knew the cold rain wouldn't put a dent in the heat building inside him, all of it for Fleur.

An hour later, seated beside Drake on the long, traditional sofa upholstered in the same dark blue wool-blend fabric of her childhood, Fleur congratulated herself on successfully navigating the land mines of the evening with him.

He sat forward on the couch, explaining the cheapest ways to remedy the local waterway, his finger tracing an old map of the property. Once they'd both changed—her into a simple cotton knit dress that fell to her knees and him into dry, faded blue jeans and a black T-shirt that he'd had stashed in his truck—they'd moved to the living area to enjoy the fire more comfortably. The hearth was open on both sides so the kitchen and living room both received the heat.

Fleur had made hot cocoa and brought out almond croissants to nosh on, determined to keep her hands busy and her brain off the tempting man in her house. She'd spent the last hour peppering him with questions about potential issues with the rangelands that could impede the sale of Crooked Elm. Drake had been knowledgeable and helpful, explaining the problems with degraded water quality due to heavy grazing and concentration of livestock.

The map of the property had come in handy as he showed her the borders of where Josiah Cranston was supposed to graze his cattle versus the land he actually used.

Shoving aside her empty stoneware plate dotted with a few leftover almond slivers, Fleur edged closer to Drake to see where he pointed.

"You mean to tell me that Cranston is using more of the land than he's renting?" Indignation swelled inside her as she recalled the man's face as he'd scowled and spit that day he came to the ranch house. "Effectively violating the lease?"

The fire snapped and popped in the hearth, spitting a red spark against the screen.

Drake nodded. "He convinced Antonia to lease it for a reduced price with the understanding that he'd install an irrigation system to fill that dry pond basin up here." He tapped his finger against the spot, and Fleur's cheek grazed his shoulder as she tracked the place.

Lightning crackled through her, making the storm outside feel like an afterthought. The scent of him—pine and leather, a hint of musk—made her want to bury her face in his shirt and inhale deeply. The low rumble of his voice in the quiet room vibrated along her senses, making her shiver. She repressed the need to scramble away from him, trying to downplay the jolt she felt from the contact. Instead, she tilted her head, keeping focused on the dried pond.

The broken lease agreement.

Right.

"He told me there was no irrigation on the land." She latched on to the memory of that conversation, knowing it was important. Critical to readying the Crooked Elm for sale. She should be thinking about that instead of all the ways she found Drake appealing now. "Do you think that means he never installed the system he promised?"

Indignation on her grandmother's behalf speared through her, along with a wave of guilt that she hadn't been around more to help. To see if Gran needed her. Instead, her grandmother had been trying to manage on her own with a swindler whose word she trusted.

Fleur cursed her pride for not returning sooner. She'd allowed her hurt and anger about the past to keep her far from Catamount, where she was needed.

"He definitely didn't install a system. And I've seen his cattle at the creek illegally. There is access to another reservoir up here." Drake wrapped a knuckle on another spot, far from the main ranch house. "But I've seen that system recently, and I know it's dangerously low."

"Did Gran know about all of this?" And if so, why hadn't she confided in Fleur? If she'd known, she would have returned to Catamount no matter how things stood with the Alexander men.

"I know she did. I spoke to her about it last fall to make sure she knew Cranston wasn't keeping his end of the bargain." Sliding the map onto the heavy oak coffee table, Drake picked up his gray stoneware mug and drained the remains of his hot cocoa.

"What did she say?"

He shook his head. "She said she wasn't worried about it. That she knew Cranston would 'come around.'" With a shrug, he met her eyes in the firelight. "She made it clear she didn't want me to confront him about it."

"I wish you'd contacted me." She held his dark gaze, wanting him to know she spoke truthfully. Notching her chin higher, she continued, "No matter our differences, I would have thought you'd know I'd be here if she needed help." She hesitated, knowing he'd viewed her as shallow. Superficial. "Or if you couldn't abide the thought of talking to me, you could have messaged one of my sisters."

A log shifted in the fireplace, dimming the light in the room from bright golden to a dull orange.

"You're right." His response surprised her. "I should have gotten in touch with one of you." His lips flattened into a thoughtful line before he spoke again, with slow deliberation. "With you."

She hid the shiver that coursed through her at his words. Forcing a smile, she had to ask, "You really think I would have been the one you would have messaged?"

"Maybe not. But it should have been. You spent the most time here. It was obvious—even to me—you cared deeply about your grandmother."

The recognition of that simple truth by someone who would never give her credit she didn't deserve soothed a little of her unease about what she'd just learned. As much as it hurt that her grandmother hadn't reached out to her, it also felt vindicating to have Drake recognize her commitment to the one person in her life whose love had been unconditional.

"Yes, I did." She tucked a strand of her still damp hair behind her ear. The locks had curled, making it harder to smooth back. "But even so, I failed her. I should have done more for her, been here more."

"Don't say that." A reassuring hand fell on her knee, giving her a gentle squeeze. "Take it from someone who has chased himself through all seven levels of hell since losing loved ones. You can't spend your life regretting things you did or didn't do while they were here."

The grit in his tone told her that wisdom had been hard won. Painful. And, knowing the loss of his parents had to have been extremely traumatic, she slipped her hand over his where it rested on her knee.

"I'm sorry you've done that." She would have never guessed he'd have regrets about anything. He'd been all of eighteen when they died, and he'd always seemed like a model son, working the family ranch from childhood. "I'm sure your parents would be incredibly proud of you to see all you've accomplished here. Making the ranch a model of good environmental initiatives. Swooping in to save the local diner. Trying to keep your neighbors safe from unscrupulous tenants."

It meant a lot to her that he'd kept an eye on Gran, even if he hadn't contacted Fleur when he'd worried about Antonia. That he'd looked in on her touched Fleur. And suggested there was more to this man than she'd ever allowed herself to believe.

"I'd like to think they'd be proud of the choices I've made since…since then." His attention dipped to their joined hands, and she wondered if he took comfort from her touch, or if the contact stirred the same things in him that it did for her. "But at the time, I wasn't always the best son."

She guessed the quiet admission was one he hadn't made often. Maybe ever.

The room seemed unnaturally still, the only sound their breathing now that the fire had settled into a dull glow. Outside, the rain had eased into a steady, softer rhythm.

Something about the regret in his words plucked at so many of her own sore places. She understood how it felt to disappoint people you cared about. She was surprised that he did, too.

"Drake—"

He wrenched his head back up to meet her eyes again. "It's okay, Fleur. I've made peace with the past. Mostly. I just mean to say that there's no need to blame yourself."

She understood what he hadn't said. That he didn't want her comfort. He only wanted to give some. Which seemed in keeping with what she knew about this strong man, who'd not only ruled over a financial empire since he was eighteen but grown it.

Still, she hadn't expected this kindness from him after their acrimonious past. And she sure hadn't expected to be, for all intents and purposes, holding his hand right now while they sat side by side on her grandmother's couch.

Telling herself she needed to pull back now, before his dark eyes mesmerized her any more, she flexed her fingers to free them from his.

Just as his thumb circled a spot on the inside of her knee.

Slowly. Deliberately.

And if that didn't have her melting inside, then the twin flames in his eyes would have done the job. The electric connection that had been leaping between them all day—or, who was she kidding, ever since she'd returned to Catamount—returned with a vengeance.

She'd run fast and hard from it before tonight, telling herself that she didn't like Drake Alexander. That she didn't want to get involved with her ex-fiancé's brother. The one responsible for splitting up a relationship at a critical time in her life.

But right now, in the quiet living room with her guard down, her fears exposed and Drake looking at her like she was the answer to all his questions, she couldn't run anymore.

She didn't want to. This man had bulldozed right through her defenses, destroying the aloofness that had been her salvation in the past.

Part of her wanted to tell him as much. To rail at him for the confusion he made her feel. To blame him for showing her this side of him she hadn't known existed.

But when she opened her mouth to say so, she found herself asking, "What are we doing?"

The words curled like paper in a fire, thin and disintegrating under the heat of need that had been building for weeks.

Drake shifted beside her, facing her fully, his hand never leaving her knee just below the hem of her dress. Still, his thumb grazed her sensitive skin, sending ribbons of longing up her thigh.

Higher.

"For years, I thought I would regret it if I ever let myself get close to you." The words were unexpectedly harsh. But then, he'd never sugarcoated anything with her, had he? She felt a momentary flash of hurt, until she locked into the first part of what he'd said.

"For years?" Had he known this was underneath the animosity?

Closing the gap between them, he shook his head impatiently. As if he didn't want to answer the question? Or as if the answer were obvious?

Her heart sped at his nearness. At what she craved.

"But now," he continued, his voice dropping deeper. His forehead touching hers. "I know I'll regret it more if I don't."

Nine

Just one taste.

Drake told himself that was all he needed. Okay, he ached for more than that. But a single taste was all he'd allow himself of this woman who tempted him more than any other.

One kiss, and he'd have the answer to questions that had haunted the corners of his mind for longer than he cared to think about. What if he hadn't brought Colin with him to that final rodeo? What if Colin hadn't driven Fleur back to Catamount after she'd failed to capture the Miss Colorado Rodeo title that would have given her the rest of the scholarship money she'd needed for college?

Drake had seen Fleur with different eyes that summer. She'd been twenty years old. No longer a kid he needed to protect. Some of her defensive armor had worn off by then, perhaps because she'd been developing a new confidence in herself and her ability to attend culinary school without her family's help. He'd recognized then that he wanted her, but he hadn't acted on it, knowing she had big dreams that didn't include Catamount or him.

His brother had acted, though. And the next time he'd seen Fleur had been weeks later when he'd discovered them engaged. His reaction had been out of bounds. Not just because he knew it was a bad idea for both of them.

But because he'd wanted her, too.

He'd ignored that hunger for so long, reminding himself of every fault he'd ever scavenged to find with her, that his appetite had only grown more urgent. Unavoidable. Undeniable.

Just one taste.

Fleur's eyelashes fluttered, her breath huffing damp and warm along his mouth as she considered his words. Her cheeks were flush with desire, with promise.

"I think I'd regret it, too," she said finally, dragging her gray eyes up to his. "If we didn't find out—"

Her tongue darted out to swipe along the upper lip. The glistening moisture proved to be his kryptonite.

His restraint shredded until he held on by a thread. Hunger to taste her had him salivating. His grip tightened on her knee by a fraction, squeezing gently. The red knit dress she wore skimmed her luscious curves the way he wanted to.

"Find out what, Fleur?" he prompted, body throbbing with need. "Tell me."

The corner of her lips curled up on one side. "What it would be like if we kissed instead of argued."

Yes. Relief that she wanted him twined with a new imperative to kiss her in a way she'd never forget. Fleur's hands moved to his shoulders, nails digging into the fabric of his T-shirt to grasp the muscle.

Testosterone gripped Drake below the belt.

Still, he stroked one hand up her neck, feeling the delicate warmth of her pulse beat beneath his fingertips. He would not rush this. He wanted to savor the moment, savor her. Then he cradled her jaw, angling her the way he wanted before his mouth descended on hers.

His groan chorused with her sigh as she sank into him, her back arching, so her breasts tilted up, pressing into his chest.

Just one taste.

He ignored the cautionary reminder in his head, fading by the moment, and hauled her slender form into his lap. Her hip grazed the erection imprinted on his zipper and the sound she made—half sob, half whimper—vibrated up her throat to rattle through the kiss.

Her fingers tunneled through his hair, pulling him closer, tugging on the strands. He calculated how fast he could have her dress off, as if he had any intention of taking this further. But he couldn't. Wouldn't.

But that didn't stop the thoughts blasting through his head as his hand slid up her thigh, careful to keep the fabric of her dress between his palm and her leg. Because the connection was setting off fireworks, and he knew he needed to get the moment back under control somehow.

Hadn't he promised himself he wouldn't take this any further than a kiss?

He cupped her hip, imagining her straddling him instead of sitting crossways on his thighs. A dangerous, delectable image. One that would be so easy to re-create in reality now.

Fleur swayed against him, soft breasts molding to his chest, the tight points calling to his mouth. He could do that much, couldn't he, without crossing the line? A taste there, too.

Palming one high, curved mound, he slipped his

thumb inside the splice neck of the dress and dragged away the fabric to expose the red lace and silk of the bra, the rose-colored peak straining the sheer material. He fastened his lips around her there, drawing her in his mouth, sampling her flavor through fragile lace. He caught the vanilla and nutty scent of her perfume, a fragrance he always associated with her, and inhaled deeply while she rocked closer.

Closer.

"Drake." His name on her lips set him afire.

Her fingers scrabbled along his shoulders, looking for purchase or…pushing him away?

Releasing her, he edged back enough to look into her eyes. Assess what she wanted. Had he misread?

"Too much?" His whole body reverberated with need while he focused on her.

"No. Not enough." She spoke with quiet certainty even though her gray eyes remained passion-dazed. Lips still damp from his mouth.

Relieved he hadn't pushed an advantage, he savored the hungry look in her eyes that reflected everything he was feeling. Even so, the moment reminded him how close they were to taking this into a direction from which there was no coming back.

If they let this heat carry them away, would she resent him later?

"It wasn't enough for me, either," he admitted, trying to drag in a cooling breath. He scrubbed his hand over his face. "But I know this isn't why you asked me here tonight. I shouldn't—"

His gaze snagged on the swell of her breast above red lace. Whatever he'd been trying to say vaporized out of his head again, his pulse strumming an urgent rhythm in his blood.

Fleur's hand smoothed over his shoulder, and he forced himself to pull the fabric of her dress back into place to cover her up.

She closed her eyes for a moment. Swallowed hard. "Shouldn't? Or won't?"

"It's not about what I want." He thought of the devastation one wrong move could cause for her. For his brother, who would be in town for Emma's wedding soon. "I've already hurt Colin enough."

Fleur scrambled back, off his lap. "*Colin?* You think it was Colin who took the worst of it when you convinced me to call things off between us?"

Ah, damn. He regretted the words he hadn't thought through. Already he missed the warmth of her in his arms, and hated that he'd taken her right back to resenting him.

"No. I know I hurt you, too. It wasn't fair of me to make assumptions, to act out of—"

What? Anger? Jealousy?

He recalled the fire in his blood the day he'd come home to find Fleur and Colin in the dining room at the Alexander Ranch, his brother's arm around her while he kissed Fleur's forehead. A big diamond on Fleur's ring finger and plans for a new home in San Antonio spread before them.

"Go ahead, you can say it." Fleur shrugged a shoulder and tugged at the front of her dress, as if she could tuck herself deeper into the fabric. "You assumed I wanted to cash in on Colin's trust, and you treated me accordingly. Like a gold-digging opportunist."

Heat sprang up the back of his neck at an accusation that was all wrong because he'd willingly allowed her to think as much all these years.

"That's not true." He pressed the heels of his hands

into his eye sockets and rubbed ruthless circles before letting go again. Met her flashing gray gaze. "I reacted badly that day because I envied him, Fleur. Even then, I wanted you, and I was furious with Colin—with myself—that I'd never taken a chance with you. And by then, it was far too late."

In the stunned silence of his declaration, Fleur's jaw dropped open before snapping shut again. She blinked fast, uncomprehending. Then, finally, her vision cleared as she seemed to understand all too well.

"You can't be serious," she half whispered. "You've never liked me—"

"I fought against liking you too much." He had been honorable. He'd set the right example for his siblings every damned day since his parents had died because his father had warned him in that last argument that he wasn't being a good role model.

"Why would you do that? Was I so horrible that you couldn't stand the idea of being attracted to me?"

"Hell no. You were too young for me." He'd been her defender. Her protector. He'd made sure someone was looking out for her when her family couldn't be bothered to watch over her, because even when they'd attended her shows, they'd been wrapped up in their own dramas. "By the time I could acknowledge that maybe you weren't too young anymore, you were with my brother."

Her nose wrinkled in confusion. "All the scowls. The put-downs. Why would you do that?"

"I was scowling at everyone who looked at you too long." Exasperated, he lifted his arms with a shoulder shrug. "And if I sniped at you, it was a misguided effort to keep reprobate cowboys from trying to get you alone."

For long moments, the crackling fire was the only

sound in the room while Fleur seemed to play this over in her mind.

"You told me to end things with Colin because of that?" The questioning look on her face said how she still didn't buy into what he'd shared. "Because of some unrequited feeling—"

"Absolutely not." He let her hear the unequivocal truth in the words, allowed them to sink in before he continued. "I didn't handle the situation as diplomatically as I should have because of my feelings for you. But either way, I would have still counseled Colin to think twice about marriage when you hadn't even gone to culinary school yet. You hadn't had a chance to live your dreams. It wouldn't have been fair of him then—of anyone—to tie you down."

Shocked at Drake's revelation, Fleur didn't know how much time had passed afterward when he rose from the seat beside her.

"The rain has let up. I should get going." He paced away from her and the couch where they'd kissed, his sock feet silent on the hardwood floor. "I'm sorry if I've overstepped tonight."

He was leaving?

Her whole body still hummed from the heat he'd aroused with his touch. His mouth.

And she didn't want to regret leaving things unsaid. She needed them to talk this through.

"You didn't overstep." She sprang to her feet, too, not sure what she wanted to say or what should happen next. But she knew that him leaving wasn't the best option. Not when she was in a muddle with her feelings and desire for him still weighed heavy in her limbs. "I'm just trying to make sense of what you said and…what it means."

She found it difficult to believe that this man who'd always pushed her away had—at times—wanted to pull her closer. And she couldn't deny that what he'd said about not wanting anyone to tie her down before she'd had a chance to pursue her dream had made her feel...seen.

Drake Alexander, her longtime nemesis, had understood things about her that no one else had taken the time to discover.

He paused near the fireplace mantel, his gaze going to a framed photo of her on graduation day from her culinary school. It wasn't a professional shot, just an image a friend had taken of her jumping for joy—tennis shoes visible under her graduation gown—near a downtown bridge close to the campus in San Antonio.

"It means that I've tried hard to do the right thing where you are concerned, but that I have a special knack for falling short." A self-deprecating smile curved his lips. "If you need help with the land improvements, you know where to find me."

He moved closer to the front door as if to leave, but she darted to stand in his path, her heart hammering against the wall of her chest.

"What if I need something else?" She didn't know what she was doing. Her brain hadn't mapped out a plan; she was just moving on instinct.

Because she recognized deep in her gut that she didn't want Drake to leave. Not with her lips trembling from the pressure of his mouth on hers. Her breasts aching from the exquisite pleasure of the kiss he'd given her there, too.

Desire flared hot in his dark eyes. It wasn't just the reflection of the flames from the hearth in his gaze. She could clearly read the same hunger she felt.

"That would be madness." His harsh words didn't deter her.

Especially when his nostrils flared, his breathing deepening the closer she came.

This man had been trying to send her running for as long as she'd known him. Yet tonight, he'd given her an insight into his behavior that she wouldn't soon forget. The heat behind all those old feelings was rooted in something more complex than simple enmity.

Something she wanted desperately to explore.

"You can't scare me off that easily anymore." She laid her palm on the warm wall of his chest. She felt the racket of his heart beneath her hand, the beating as strong and erratic as her own. "Especially not now, when I know what it's like to be the center of your attention."

Where she got her boldness right now, she had no idea. She only knew that if he left here tonight, she might never have the opportunity to delve into the attraction beneath his cool exterior again. And she craved that chance. Too many people in her life had overlooked her. Written her off.

Having Drake look at her this way now, like he wanted to devour her more than he wanted another breath, stirred a need in her that she couldn't ignore.

He dragged in a deep breath, and something in his expression told her he was going to push her away. Make some excuse about not touching her because of her brief, ill-fated engagement to his brother before he bolted for the door. But Colin had never looked at her like this. Colin never tied her in knots the way Drake did with just one heated look.

So she didn't wait for another argument. Even as a cool draft from the rainy evening filtered through the drafty door at her back, she wound her arms around his neck, pressing herself to the warmth of Drake's strong, hard body.

"Just one more kiss," she urged, speaking the words over his mouth before she let her lips graze his.

The growl of agreement he made rumbled through his chest and into hers, vibrating along her spine. A thrill shot through her, pleasure like a drug in her veins.

His arms banded around her waist, lifting her against him, sealing their bodies together. His mouth moved over hers hungrily, tasting, teasing, exploring every inch. She raised her palms to his shoulders, digging into the muscle there, holding herself steady for the sensual onslaught.

The kiss transported her, teasing a response from her that she hadn't known she was capable of feeling from a talented, generous mouth working over hers. But Drake kissed her like he had all night, like there was nothing more important in the world to him than finding out what made her sigh and wriggle, what made her go boneless in his arms.

His hold on her shifted as he backed her against the front door, his hands trailing down her thighs to lift them. Wrap them around his hips.

The position lined up her mound with the bulge in his jeans. Even with her dress and a layer of denim still between them it gave her a sweet spasm.

He captured her cry of pleasure in his mouth before he broke the kiss. She gulped in air, realizing she'd forgotten to breathe for who knew how long.

"You have no idea how long I've wanted to kiss you like this." His fingers tunneled beneath her skirt to stroke his way up her thighs. At the same time, his hips tilted forward, applying pressure right where she needed it most.

Fireworks danced behind her eyelids.

"Please, more," she murmured against his mouth, wondering if it was possible to wriggle out of the dress without ever leaving his arms.

She hadn't been touched this way since…ever. Because the encounters she'd had with other men were nothing—anemic simulations of sex—compared to this. And they hadn't even taken off their clothes yet.

"After I've dreamed about you for years, Fleur, I'm not taking you against a door the first time." The rough edge to his voice made her nipples tighten almost painfully.

And then, she realized what he'd said.

Would he really take her?

Would it really be the first of more than one time?

"My room is that way." She pointed toward the back of the house, to her old bedroom near the kitchen. "But I'd like to go on record as being fine with a first time against the door."

She flexed the muscles of her thighs, squeezing his hips and also rubbing their bodies together in a way that made her toes curl.

Instead of answering her, he cradled her chin in one hand, tilting her face up as if to study her.

"Are you certain?" His voice sounded ragged, raked over a dry throat.

As if the hungry ache was eating him from the inside out.

Or maybe she was projecting since that's exactly how she felt.

"Positive. I need you." Her words sounded every bit as desperate as she felt, but they must have satisfied him, because a moment later, he curved his forearm beneath her ass and carried her toward her bedroom.

His long strides rocked their bodies together, and her hold tightened on his neck. She tucked her forehead against his chest, rubbing her cheek over the warmth of his skin through his cotton T-shirt.

But he stopped at the threshold, not taking that last step.

"I don't have protection. Not even in the truck. I don't—"

"I have some," she admitted, splaying her hand along the bristles of his jaw. "I've replenished a stash faithfully every year since—"

She'd gotten pregnant. Miscarried his brother's baby.

Was it her imagination or did a chill descend between them? It felt as if the molecules in the air around her all moved and shifted to accommodate this new information. But just when she thought he would set her on her feet and walk away from her again, he exhaled a long breath.

His grip on her thighs tightened.

"Good. We're going to need as many as you have."

Ten

Her wordless hum of pleasure was the sweetest sound he'd ever heard.

He would have battled his own need for her for Fleur's sake. He'd have forced it down if she didn't want him. Ruthlessly ignored it, no matter how much it cost him.

But he didn't have a prayer of refusing her.

I need you.

Her soft words still circled around his brain, a command he wouldn't walk away from. Not after the way he'd hurt her five years ago. Not after how long he'd spent denying his feelings for her.

So Drake crossed the threshold of her darkened bedroom, still carrying her in his arms. She remained wrapped around him, ankles locked around his back. Every step he took across the cool plank floor created friction between their bodies, the warmth of her sex riding him.

"Where are the condoms?" He tightened his grip on her, needing to minimize the bump and grind motion until he was planted inside her. Deep inside her. He was beyond revved up from knowing that she wanted him, hearing the desire in her voice and seeing the way her eyelashes fluttered at each brush of his body against hers.

"I'll get them," she murmured, unwinding her legs from his waist so she could jump to the floor.

As she disappeared into a bathroom off to one side, Drake tugged off his T-shirt and strode deeper into her bedroom. It was a small space in a home that had been built in a different era, when a sleeping chamber was meant solely for that. But ivory walls and minimal furnishings—a full-size bed draped in a simple white duvet, a faded steamer trunk for a nightstand, a single chest of drawers—provided the necessary comforts. He tilted the dark plantation shutters that covered the lone window, allowing slivers of moonlight to fall on the bed.

He'd reached for the button on his jeans, flicking the first open, when Fleur returned. Her bare feet padded silently across the hardwood floor, her red knit dress swishing around her thighs even as it clung to her breasts where he'd eased open the bodice earlier.

Did she have any idea how sexy she was?

"I found them," she announced breathlessly.

He slipped his arms around her waist, hauling her against his chest. Then he let his hands roam all over her, savoring the feel of her perfect-size breasts, the stiff points of her nipples.

"Do you remember the shared horseback ride?" he spoke the words into her ear, giving himself a view down the front of her dress where her chest rose and fell in quick, hard pants. "When I held you in front of me, just like this?"

Her hair caught on his whiskers as she nodded, her head lolling to one side in a way that left her neck exposed. Greedily, he bent to taste her there, kissing and licking his way up her throat. The warm vanilla scent of her intensified as he reached behind her ear.

"This is how I wanted to touch you that day." He dragged one shoulder of her dress down her arm, baring the red lace cup of her bra and the creamy swell of breast above it.

With one hand, he palmed the soft weight, squeezing and molding, teasing the tight peak with his thumb. With his other hand, he dragged up the hem of her dress until a red scrap of satin between her thighs was visible. He must have stared a second too long, mesmerized by the body he'd fantasized about so many times, because Fleur arched her back in a way that tilted her hips against his lap.

"You did?" She reached up to encircle his neck with her arms, the action lifting her breasts in a way that nearly brought them right out of the bra.

"Damned right, I did," he growled low, knowing he needed her naked soon. "And I've been imagining it ever since."

He cupped the V between her thighs, her damp panties clinging to her. He nearly lost it then and there, knowing she wanted him almost as much as he craved her.

"Show me," she urged him on, her eyes closed, dark lashes fanning over her cheeks. "You don't have to imagine anymore."

Something about the way she said it—her tone, maybe, or the languid movements of her hips as she rocked against him—told him how much she liked what he was doing to her. So he took his time making her feel good, drawing out the pleasure. Narrating it for her.

"I wanted to see these first." He hauled down the lacy cup of her bra, peeling it away from her breast. Then, trapping the nipple between his fingers, he squeezed lightly. "Find out what touches you liked best here."

He couldn't wait to lick her there, too, but he wasn't finished reminding her of that ride when he'd been pressed up against her, his hand brushing her bare waist from that too-short top that didn't cover her.

"What else did you think about?" she demanded, her legs shifting restlessly now. Her thighs twitched around his hand, where he clamped an uncompromising hold between her legs. "I find it hard to believe my breasts would have captured *all* your attention."

"You will not disparage these on my watch," he warned her, tugging the other shoulder of her dress off so he could fondle the warm weight. "They're perfect."

"Drake." She made the word a plea, swaying and undulating against him. "Hurry, please. More."

He'd never had a lap dance until today and now, he'd never want another after the way Fleur moved with a hypnotic roll of her hips.

"I want this, too. Have wanted it for so long," he admitted, slipping two fingers beneath the damp satin panties.

Discovering something infinitely softer. Sweeter. Hotter.

He captured the tight bundle of nerves at her apex and rolled it between his fingers, mimicking what he'd done to her nipple. She gasped. Tensed. Her whole body coiled and went still, waiting.

And then it released. Waves went through her body, and she relaxed.

He'd never seen anything more beautiful. Never felt

more privileged. It humbled him. And only made him more urgent to be inside her.

"Fleur." He breathed her name on a hard exhale, his pulse gone wild. "Come with me."

She went boneless against him, and he scooped her off her feet easily, stripping her clothes off as he laid her in the center of that pristine white duvet. When she was naked, her copper-colored hair spilling over the pillow and her gray eyes following his every movement, he finished unfastening his pants.

Shed them and the rest of his clothes as quickly as possible. Every heartbeat seemed to echo with her name.

Fleur. Fleur. Fleur.

A rapid tattoo of urgency.

He ripped open the box of condoms and sheathed himself. On the bed, Fleur roused from her release, propping herself on her elbow to watch him. And having her hungry eyes on him only made him burn hotter to bury himself in her.

She reached for him as he climbed on top of her. Covering her. Her arms pulled him down, surrounding him in her softness and her scent.

He spread her thighs wider as he positioned himself, his gaze locked on hers when he nudged his way inside. Inch by inch he spread her, going slow and giving her time to adjust, but the fit was tight. Her breathing was fast, her arms clinging to him, and he would have sold his soul before he rushed her.

Still, his arms shook from the need to have more of her. Sweat beaded along his back. His forehead.

"It's okay. I'm okay," she chanted softly to herself as much as to him.

"Are you?" He tilted her chin to look in her eyes, wondering if he'd missed something. "Is it really okay?"

She nodded fast. "Yes. It's just—" She hesitated, sipping on her lower lip for a moment before she went on. "My second time ever. And it's been so long."

The revelation had contradictory effects. He wanted to redo the night and take even more time. Cherish her. But the caveman part of him that wanted to claim her— to imprint himself on her so that she'd never want anyone else—was a primal instinct that was impossible to ignore.

So of course, he *would* ignore it. Because he knew better than to act on the caveman side.

"Fleur." He held himself very, very still while he got command of himself. He should withdraw perhaps. Give her another orgasm.

But while he weighed the options, she arched her back and rolled her hips again. Her breathy sighs coming faster.

"There," she exclaimed, her gray eyes alight with new fire. New purpose. "I just needed a minute."

She thrust her hips forward in a move so unexpected he was pretty sure he saw the promised land for a moment.

"Fleur." Her name was a strangled sound in his throat, his body demanding more. Demanding that he move. Take her.

Never let her go.

"I'm good now," she vowed, her voice turning sultry as she worked her hips in another thrust intended to erase all his thinking faculties. "I'm ready."

And he hoped like hell she meant it, because nothing could have prevented him from surging deeper. Again. And again.

But with her slender legs wrapping around him, holding him there, he knew she needed the same thing he did. He cradled her hip with one hand, rocking her closer, finding the rhythm that sent them both catapulting over the edge. The squeeze of her feminine muscles began a moment before his control snapped.

The release rocketed from the base of his spine, steam-rolling through him for so long he wasn't sure his legs could hold him up afterward. He sank to the bed beside her, unwilling to collapse on her but not sure he could bear his own weight for a minute.

In the aftermath, as the world righted itself again and his breathing slowed, he wondered what should happen next. He drew her closer, unable to resist the need to kiss her shoulder. Stroke her tangled hair off her face. She tasted sweet and salty at the same time, her clean skin now dotted with sweat. His and hers.

"You're thinking so hard, I hear the wheels turning," she mused from beside him, burrowing closer to lay her cheek on his arm. "Would you mind if we waited to talk about…what just happened? Table it until daybreak maybe?"

His stomach clenched at the words, even as he recognized she was giving him a grace period. A chance to get his head together before they had to face what they'd done tonight. Or—if nothing else—to at least enjoy this cease-fire between them and all the sensual rewards that could come with it.

Still, he couldn't help suspecting that she was already working out a way to pull away from him. And how messed up was it that he dreaded that thought, even as he, too, weighed how to extricate himself with the least possible damage? He might have screwed up the sale of the ranch. Probably damaged his relationship with his brother irreparably. And as for Fleur herself?

His stomach knotted tighter.

But he brushed aside all of that as he combed his fingers through tousled auburn strands. Right now, he just wanted to lie by her side. Hold her.

"I never thought I would say these words to you, Fleur Barclay, but I agree with you one hundred percent."

Tomorrow would be soon enough to deal with the fallout that was inevitable from their night together.

Fleur wasn't certain how long she slept.

Her bedroom remained dark save for moonlight, and the rain outside had slowed to a gentle patter on the roof. The sound normally soothed her, but with Drake stretched beside her, his hand still cupping her hip even as he dozed, she felt a spike of nerves.

What had she done?

Shifting on her pillow so she could watch the man beside her, Fleur's gaze swept over his strong, square shoulder where he lay on his side. His body tapered toward his waist and hips, an impressive V. She wanted to reach out and trace that slope along his lateral muscles, but she didn't wish to wake him.

Not when she needed to think.

Because sleeping with Drake hadn't been any part of her plan. Ever.

She lifted her gaze to his face, where she could see the shadow of dark bristles along his jaw. The moonlight filtering through the shutters turned everything a shade of gray in the room, giving the moment an otherworldly feel. As if Drake were a night phantom who might disappear into thin air.

But that wouldn't happen. His presence was solid. Real. He'd made her feel things she'd only dreamed of before given the way she'd put off sleeping with anyone else after the disaster of her relationship with Colin.

Who got pregnant after having sex exactly once?

Fleur, that's who. The only guy she'd ever been with intimately—before Drake—had left her pregnant. Then he'd walked away without so much as a goodbye, heeding his brother's advice to abandon her. No doubt the relationship with Colin had been a mistake. An unwise decision by her twenty-year-old self longing for someone permanent, a family. She'd been shaking when she told Colin about the baby. But after the first shock he'd been honorable, proposing marriage and letting her take the lead in announcing the pregnancy. He'd been scared, but would do the right thing. Even though he hadn't been in love with her—nor she with him. Not in any real way.

But knowing that now didn't fix the damage. Damage that Drake had played a large role in. Because after being disinherited and ignored by her father, Fleur hadn't possessed the best coping mechanisms for dealing with Drake's interference in her life and Colin's departure.

Hurt and grieving, she'd been a loner through culinary school, only to end up working for a kitchen manager who couldn't keep his hands to himself. Where was her strength? Her willingness to be a badass and fight for herself when the situation called for it? Filing a sexual harassment claim seemed like too tame a response to something that infuriated her.

Coming home to Catamount had awoken something inside her. Her grandmother's spirit, maybe. Or just a connection to the person she used to be before her family had fractured. Baking in the kitchen at Crooked Elm had reminded her it wasn't up to her to repair her family.

She could only repair herself.

Beside her, Drake stirred, jolting her from her thoughts. His fingers flexed on her hip where his hand lay, the warm pressure of his palm enough to remind her of what they'd shared earlier. A blazing hot connection. Possibly the kind that would burn her if she wasn't careful.

"Hmm, why are you awake?" he said in a raspy, groggy voice. "I thought we weren't supposed to be thinking deep thoughts until the morning." He dragged her closer, an effortless move with just one hand.

And what made that easy strength so arousing? Her heart skipped faster.

"Maybe I was just contemplating all the wicked ways I could wake you up." She walked her fingers up his chest, reveling in the way his muscles jumped under her touch.

"Why do I have the feeling you're trying to distract me with sex?" His hand skimmed higher, settling in the curve of her waist as his gaze searched hers.

"Is it working?" She dipped her finger into the notch at the base of his throat before tracing his collarbone.

"I'm definitely distracted," he admitted, wrapping his arm around her waist as one strong thigh slid between her legs. "But I won't let that keep me from talking to you if you're concerned about something." He stroked her hair from her face. "You looked worried when I opened my eyes."

She could feel his concern. It was clear in the way he looked at her. In the way he didn't seize on the sensual out she'd offered him from this conversation. Her heart turned over at the sensation of feeling…cared for.

Swallowing past the emotions that swelled inside her, she thought about how to express all the things the night had awakened in her.

"Do you remember that rodeo in town, right after my parents split, where I sang 'America the Beautiful'?" She felt sure he'd been there. He must have teased her about it before, but she couldn't recall for certain.

"All of Catamount remembers that day." His fingers traced idle circles on her lower back.

"I didn't know until afterward that everyone had the impression that I did it to call attention to myself. Some sort of ploy for the spotlight." She had been hurt by that. But then again, she'd never explained herself to anyone, either. Never fought for herself.

"It might have been the timing of the song more than anything." He ventured the opinion slowly, perhaps checking her reaction. "Your mother might have been injured."

Had she been?

It wouldn't have been serious or Fleur would have remembered, although a pang hit that the thought hadn't occurred to her at the time.

"I couldn't see well from where I was in the arena." The lights had been bright. The tension so thick it felt like it was crushing her when she'd heard her father and mother shouting at one another. There'd been no other sound in the whole arena except for their raised, furious voices. "I just knew they were fighting for the whole town to hear. It was so painful. So needless and wrong. I did the only thing I could think of to cover it up."

"You sang."

"I burst into song." Shrugging, she wasn't sure she could relate a nine-year-old girl's decisions in a way that would make sense to a grown man. "Not just so *I* didn't have to hear them, but so the rest of Catamount wouldn't be talking about my cheating father and my out-of-control mother all day. Or maybe I did it so my parents would be forced to listen to me for those two minutes where I was center stage."

Once the words tumbled from her lips—the last part a surprise even to her—Fleur wished she could call them back. Hadn't she wanted to find some personal strength? Admitting something that sounded so self-pitying hardly seemed like a good start. But before she could backpedal, Drake's voice rumbled between them, his chest vibrating against hers where they touched.

"You and your sisters navigated some rough waters when your folks split." He watched her with curious eyes, no doubt wondering why she'd brought up the story.

"We definitely spent too much time focused on their misery instead of looking forward." She should own that much without being self-pitying, after all. If she wanted to grow, to change, she needed to look back at all of her journey and not just the better parts. "But I always felt happiest when I was here. In Catamount."

"Because of your grandmother." He nodded, his expression clearing as if he understood now. "You must be missing her so much this summer."

"I am. But at the same time, I feel close to her here. I have good memories in this house, and I feel like being at Crooked Elm is helping me find myself after being a little lost these last five years." She'd run from her broken engagement, and from memories of the pregnancy she'd lost.

But staying away for so long had been a mistake she could never fix. And nothing would give her back that lost time with Gran, the person who'd loved her most.

"I'm glad to hear it." He trailed a knuckle down her arm, a lingering caress that sent a shiver through her. "It's been good seeing you again."

His gaze dipped to her lips, his hand lifting to cradle her face. He tilted her chin toward him.

But she couldn't kiss him without telling him her point. A decision that she'd only just come to tonight as she lay here tangled in the sheets with him.

"I'm not sure you'll still think that when I tell you I'm considering staying in Catamount." She steeled herself, ready to be strong again. To fight for what she wanted. "I don't want to sell Crooked Elm."

Eleven

"Staying. In Catamount." Drake repeated the words, giving himself more time to absorb the bombshell she'd just dropped on him.

Hadn't she wanted to delay a conversation about what had happened between them tonight? And yet she'd waded into a conversation about something with far more potential to splinter the fragile bond they'd forged together.

His pulse jumped in a more merciless rhythm than any bull he'd ever ridden, his brain searching for a response. Because while he wanted to be supportive of her, he could also see the potential for disaster. Between them. Between him and his brother if Drake continued to see Fleur. And as for his quest to purchase the land for himself to restore the waterway, a task he felt honor bound to complete in his parents' memory?

That had just gone up in flames.

"Yes, that's what I said." Fleur had gone still in his arms. "My catering business is doing better than I expected. There could be a viable opportunity for me here. Not just in catering, but maybe one day expanding into a restaurant."

He couldn't help a shocked laugh as he levered up on one elbow. "The profit and loss statements from Cowboy Kitchen would make you think twice about that. I only bought it as a kindness to the community—a way to keep a local business open."

She propped herself up on a pillow, her bared shoulders tense.

"Perhaps that's why you're not making a profit," she said carefully, seeming to take his measure as she spoke. "You're not passionate about the restaurant business the way I am. I can see real potential for the right establishment."

Her prickly body language told him he'd offended her, so he shifted away from that topic. There were a hundred other problems with her plan he could tackle, after all.

Swiping a hand over his face, he shoved himself into a sitting position, sheet pooling around his waist. "What about the land management issues? How can you address the impending conservation citations when you won't have capital to invest?"

The problems with the waterway on Crooked Elm property already had a tremendous ripple effect on the water and land quality at Alexander Ranch, to say nothing of the properties downstream from his. He had a responsibility to his cattle to take care of it.

"I haven't worked out all the answers yet." She gripped the edge of the duvet tightly in her fist, drawing it closer to her body. "I'm just exploring the possibility."

The wounded note in her voice came through clearly,

and he regretted his approach. He reached for her, wanting to recapture the closeness they'd shared earlier, the scent of her still filling his every breath.

"You're right. There's time to figure out how to make it work." From where he touched her arm, he felt the tension still thrumming through her, and knew he needed to dig deeper. Try harder. "I can help you. There are some measures you can take with the land that require more sweat equity than cash—"

"You know what?" Avoiding his gaze, she slid off the bed, plucking her simple cotton dress off the floor before dropping it over her head. "I probably shouldn't have said anything yet. My plans are still half-formed at best, and I'm not ready to think through things like that at this hour."

"Fleur, I didn't mean to discourage you—" he began, hurrying to get to his feet and drag on his boxers.

Already, he missed the warmth of her nakedness beside him.

"Are you sure about that?" she asked softly, busying her fingers with the dress's sash at her waist.

"That definitely was not my intention." He settled his palms on her shoulders, wishing he could draw her back to bed but understanding from her body language that their time together was done.

For tonight, he reminded himself fiercely, determined not to let this one time with her be his only taste of Fleur. They'd shared something deeper than a physical hunger for one another, and he fully intended to explore it.

When she remained quiet, he took her hands in his, trying to reclaim her attention. He needed her eyes on him.

"I'm sorry. I was only concerned for you and the obstacles you might encounter." He lifted both her hands to his mouth and kissed her knuckles. "If I had to do it all over again, I would simply say that Crooked Elm suits you."

Finally, her lips quirked. A hint of a smile.

Or maybe just a reprieve for the night.

"Thank you." Her eyes searched his for a moment before she took a step away. "But since I'm wide-awake now, I think I'll start the baking for the diner. I've sold out every time so far, so I'd like to make more than usual."

He didn't need to see the clock to know that dawn was still hours away. But he clamped his teeth around his tongue to keep from arguing with her. To prevent himself from running his hands over her curves and tucking her against him so he could kiss her thoroughly.

He wouldn't give her cause to regret anything that happened between them. He nodded as he reached for his shirt, then pulled it over his head.

"It sounds like the rain has stopped." He continued to dress, keeping his tone light. Easy. Maybe a retreat now was wisest. It would give him time to consider his next course of action with the sale of Crooked Elm. And with Fleur herself. "I'll get going. But how about dinner at my place tonight? We should talk."

About her plans. About the wedding and Colin's impending arrival in Catamount. About what had happened between them tonight.

She nodded, but she was already heading toward the door.

"I'll let you know." Turning the handle, she stepped into the corridor before he'd even finished the last button on his jeans.

Drake had an uneasy feeling. He felt her pulling away, and they'd shared too much tonight to just turn their backs on each other now.

Facing her in the hallway, he didn't know how to express himself in words. So he gave her the kiss he'd been longing to have since he'd awoken next to her in her bed.

"I'll call you." He headed toward the back door, where he'd left his shoes, telling himself there was still a chance they could figure this out without either one of them getting hurt.

Without hurting his brother any more than he already had.

He had no idea how to carry out his parents' legacy with the land if she remained at Crooked Elm, let alone what kind of relationship they might have as…neighbors? More? The idea tantalized and tormented him at the same time since, no matter what tonight meant for their future, they needed a plan before Colin returned.

"Are you sure you want to handle this on your own?" Jessamyn asked Fleur from the tablet screen propped on Gran's kitchen table. "We can hire a third party to legally serve Cranston the lease termination papers."

Fleur paused in rolling out biscuit dough so she could look at her perfectly coiffed sister. Fleur had been working for days on the prep for Emma Alexander's wedding, baking and freezing anything that could be made ahead of time, shopping and organizing foods that would be assembled later. She'd needed to fill her time ever since the awkward aftermath of her night with Drake.

Why had she been foolish enough to confide her plans to him? And how much more obvious could he have made it that he wasn't thrilled with the idea of her staying in Catamount? Memories of his deer-in-the-headlights eyes after her confession had taunted her hourly since then.

"If I can cater a wedding for two hundred on my own," Fleur replied, swiping a thumb across the tablet to remove a flour smudge that didn't belong on Jessamyn's face, "I think I can manage giving Josiah Cranston a few lease termination papers."

She might have ended her night with Drake on an uncomfortable note, but she had every faith in his advice about what was going wrong on the Crooked Elm Ranch acreage. If she wanted to address the land management issues, she needed to begin by canceling the lease agreement with her grandmother's uncooperative tenant. Her sister had provided her with appropriate forms for Fleur to initiate the process.

"How's the wedding planning going?" Jessamyn asked, surprising Fleur with a question that wasn't business-related. "You look exhausted."

"I am a little tired," she confessed, thinking about her lack of sleep in the hours before she awoke early to bake for the Cowboy Kitchen. "But aside from that," and the recurring sadness over misreading Drake, she silently added, "I feel good about things. The wedding. Crooked Elm. Being here is filling a place inside me I hadn't realized was empty."

Funny how she'd pinned all her hopes and dreams on opening a restaurant, yet she loved baking and cooking right here more than she had anywhere else. And it wasn't just nostalgia for Gran. Fleur felt productive here. Sure of herself. Like she needed to come home to recover all the pieces of who she'd been and glue them into one whole.

She'd even had some good news from the Texas Workforce Commission. They'd taken her claims of sexual harassment seriously. Her old boss would never be able to pull those tricks on anyone else.

Seated in front of her office window with the expansive view of Central Park, Jessamyn looked thoughtful, her expression softening. "I've been thinking about what you said—that we should spend some time at the ranch this summer so we could share the legacy Gran left us."

"You have?" Fleur set aside the rolling pin, giving her sister her full attention. She hadn't really expected Lark or Jessamyn—especially Jessamyn—to give the idea another thought.

Her heartbeat quickened even as she told herself not to get her hopes up. Her sister probably just wanted to explain why it couldn't possibly work out with her schedule.

"I've thought about it a lot, actually. There have been some things here—small issues I'm having with Patrick…" She cleared her throat at the mention of their father's protégé and the man Jessamyn and been dating for months. "Nothing major. But I've booked a flight for the week after Emma's wedding. I didn't want to descend on you until you finished your catering job."

Warmth and gratitude filled Fleur's chest, but she tried to modify her reaction to fit her all-business sibling. If she squealed in joy or got teary-eyed about a possible reunion, she could probably scare Jessamyn into canceling.

After their mother's over-the-top emotional displays, Jessamyn had gone the other direction. Nothing messy for her.

"I'm so happy you're going to be here," Fleur settled on saying, meaning it with every fiber of her being. How many times had she despaired of having any semblance of her family together again? "Thank you, Jess."

On the screen, Jessamyn was already bending over her desk phone, asking an assistant to send in her three o'clock before she nodded at Fleur. "I need to get going. But good luck with Josiah Cranston, and the wedding."

"Thank you." Fleur gave a little wave to her sister before disconnecting the video call.

She would have returned to her biscuits—part of the

Southern-inspired portion of the menu since she had suggested Emma serve a mix of appetizers at her evening wedding—except her phone rang.

Knowing the biscuits wouldn't bake themselves, she thought about ignoring it, but Drake's name was on the caller ID screen.

Again.

She'd dodged him since their night together, unwilling to hear him make any more excuses for why he didn't want her to stay in Catamount. But with the wedding a week away, she knew she couldn't continue avoiding him.

And maybe a part of her still longed to hear his voice.

"Hello?" Switching her phone to hands-free mode, she settled it beside the tablet and then lifted the round biscuit cutter.

"Fleur." He heaved out a long exhale that sounded… relieved? "I was beginning to think you were blocking my calls."

Her cheeks warmed, and she attempted to deflect that subject. "Just busy with wedding preparations. How are things going over there? Emma must be working on the barn by now."

"She's in full-scale General Emma mode, issuing orders faster than I can carry them out." His tone, confiding and fondly teasing, reminded her of their time together chasing the goats.

He'd been kind to her, refusing to leave her on her own to round up the escapees and mend the fence, even though she'd told him she could manage. So much had happened between them. So much more than just the sex, although her thoughts had probably strayed to that most often over the past few days. Well, that, and how it ended.

"I admire a woman who knows what she wants." Fleur pressed the cutter into the dough over and over again until she'd used every possible square inch. "Now that I've had a few more clients for catered events, I can appreciate your sister's decisiveness all the more."

"Your business is doing well?" he asked, seeming in no hurry to get to his point for calling.

Her nerves twisted at the thought as she used a metal spatula to lift the biscuits onto a baking sheet. Because she didn't know what she wanted where Drake was concerned. She only knew that she couldn't risk hurt from him when she was only just beginning to find her footing again.

"Business is better than I would have ever expected." She'd gotten two more jobs after agreeing to cater the wedding. "Thanks in part to your sister. She's been great about spreading the word."

"I'm glad to hear it. Marta says the things you bring into the diner are always gone by noon."

She couldn't help the swell of pride about that as she slid the last baking sheet into the oven.

"The foreman over on Ryder Wakefield's ranch has started sending someone into the Cowboy Kitchen first thing every morning to bring breakfast to all the hands." Cleaning up the kitchen counter, she checked the time, hoping to intercept Josiah Cranston before he returned home for the evening. "Is there anything else? I'm planning to take a ride around the range roads to see if I can find Gran's tenant so I can formally let him know that we're terminating the lease."

"There's most definitely something else." His voice pitched lower, and the effect on her was immediate.

Her breath caught. Her skin tightened. Memories of how he'd looked at her, undressed her, played through her mind in a tantalizing show.

"Oh. Um. What is it?" She cursed herself for sounding like an overexcited teenager. Especially when he'd seemed so taken aback by the thought of her staying in Catamount.

She set the dishrag aside and lifted the phone to her ear, focusing solely on the conversation.

"I'd really like to make you dinner. Are you free this evening?"

"I don't know, Drake." She closed her eyes, trying to shut out the way the sound of his voice made her feel. The way it made her remember so many moments from their night together—from corralling goats to tearing each other's clothes off. "Is it really wise for us to get involved when…"

Trailing off, she guessed he could fill in the blanks for all the reasons it wasn't a good idea for them to see each other. She didn't want to make things any more uncomfortable for him or Colin at the wedding.

"It's a little late for second-guessing that. After our last evening together, I would say involvement has already happened."

She bit her lip, knowing he was right.

"We never got to talk about it afterward," he reminded her, his tone softening. "Dinner would give us a chance to do that."

"To talk?" she clarified, uncertain if she could sign on for anything more than that.

Even though just hearing him made her insides heat and her body ache for him all the way to the roots of her hair.

"Don't you think we should at least come to terms with it? Maybe make a plan for the wedding, so it's not hopelessly awkward." As he spoke she heard a soft noise in the background.

An animal snort, she guessed. But then, he probably spent a lot of his time around his cattle.

"That makes sense," she agreed, wanting Emma's day to be flawless. Not just because Fleur was doing the catering, but also because she really liked Drake's sister. "I can do dinner tonight, but first I need to visit Josiah Cranston. I want to put those lease termination papers into his hands so the clock starts ticking on his thirty days to vacate the property."

She needed to keep her distance over dinner. Just a meal to work out logistics for how to be around each other at the wedding, and then she'd return home. No dwelling on what had happened between them last time.

No kisses that set her on fire or orgasms that catapulted her into the stratosphere. She couldn't deny the disappointment never to feel those things again, but she also felt a deep resolve at what had to be done.

"That works out perfectly," Drake agreed, sounding satisfied. Also, in the background, a bleating noise.

A calf, maybe, since there were no sheep on Alexander Ranch. She shook off the musing that didn't matter and tried to get her head on straight for the evening. Keep her distance. Settle what happened between them, make a plan for the wedding. Move on.

"Okay. I'll message you after I find Cranston and let you know when I can be there." Even as she told herself she wasn't going to swoon at Drake Alexander's feet again, she couldn't help but warm to his offer.

She had to be careful around this man or she could wind up with feelings she wasn't ready to have for him.

"I've got a better plan. Why don't I drive you around the rangelands and help you find Cranston? Then I can bring you home with me." Another bleating in the background, and the sound of Drake shifting around the phone.

She didn't see the need to spend extra time with him when it would be difficult enough to resist him over dinner.

"That's okay. I'm ready to leave now and—"

"Excellent. Because I'm right outside playing with Guinevere." The deep timbre of his voice teased over her senses. "I'm ready to go when you are."

Twelve

Watching Fleur exit the house and walk toward him in her simple white T-shirt and cutoff shorts, a pair of scuffed brown boots on her feet, Drake couldn't help but think how at home she looked here. Her copper-colored braid lay on one shoulder, a wilted yellow ribbon tied around the end, as she paused to scratch the brown-and-white ears of Morgan le Fay.

When Fleur had first told him she was thinking about staying in Catamount, he had assumed it would be a mistake. That an ambitious chef from Dallas wouldn't be happy in this remote Colorado small town. But how many of his assumptions about her were based on their rodeo days when she'd held herself apart from everyone else? He'd thought she was too proud, too full of herself. But he recognized now how insecure she might have felt after her parents' split. He understood better than most people how much influence a parent's judgment could have over a person.

How many of his own decisions had been reactionary measures to his parents' request that he set a better example for his siblings? That one argument had so much weight because it had been the last time he'd spoken to them.

Whatever the reason for his old notions about Fleur, the truth was that she thrived in Catamount now. She'd started a business here. Connected with locals like Marta and his sister. And, maybe most importantly, her good memories with her grandmother were here. Who was he to chase her out of town because he wanted to buy her land? The idea stirred unease.

Fleur stopped a few inches from him, her lips curving in a smile he hadn't expected but was so damned glad to see. How many times had he thought about her since their night together, reliving every moment of having her all to himself?

"You might have told me earlier in the phone conversation that you were standing outside my house the whole time," she chastised, her gray eyes meeting his for a moment before sliding lower.

Heat surged through him before she snapped her gaze back up to his, her cheeks flushing just a little.

That one moment made the days apart hurt a lot less. She hadn't forgotten their connection.

"I didn't want to spoil the surprise." His hands ached to wrap around her waist and pull her to him, but he needed to proceed with caution. "Should we go track down your tenant?"

He tipped his head in the direction of his truck in her driveway, the insects singing in the trees as the sun sank lower on the horizon.

"That would be great." She shadowed him as he led the way to the vehicle, holding the door for her to step up the running board. "If you want to make a loop around the property, I'll give him the papers when we find him."

"Sure thing. I saw his truck on the far western edge when I drove over here." He closed her door behind her and then rounded the front to climb in the driver's seat.

After starting the engine and pulling out onto the dirt access road around the rangelands, Drake's thoughts returned to his concern about buying Crooked Elm out from under her. He really didn't want to displace her or upset her.

And, what's more, a part of him liked the idea of her staying in town. Would they see each other more if she remained right next door?

She nodded. "I'm just eager to deliver the news and start the process of him leaving so we can figure out what's next for Crooked Elm."

He remained in low gear, mindful of his vehicle on a road traversed more frequently by tractors. He wished he could throttle his thoughts the same way he kept a rein on the engine, but he found himself asking more about the Barclay sisters' inherited spread.

"Would you consider keeping your grandmother's house and selling off just the lands?" The idea seemed perfect for both of them. So perfect that he couldn't stop himself from pressing the point a bit more. "That way, you could maintain your connection to the part of the property that means the most to you, but you'd still have some income from selling the lands you don't use."

When she remained quiet for a moment, he glanced her way to see her lips pursed as she seemed to mull it over.

"I hadn't thought of something like that. The house

seems such a part of the land, it never occurred to me to split them up." Her attention moved to the green grazing pasture off to their left, empty of cattle.

"So you like the idea?" Hope sparked. If she agreed to the plan, he could improve the lands without running her off. She could stay here and grow her business.

They would have the time to explore their attraction.

"I can't say for certain," she admitted, trailing a finger along the leather of the interior door. "And I would need both Lark and Jessamyn to agree, no matter what we do."

"Of course." He recalled as much, but for the first time, he saw a viable solution. A way for them both to be happy.

His conversations with his sisters had suggested they'd be open to a sale, so he couldn't imagine them objecting now.

"There's Josiah Cranston," she announced suddenly, shaking him from his musing. "You can pull over up there."

She pointed to a wide spot in the access road, close to a pasture gate.

Drake spotted the old-timer's vehicle in the distance, prepared for resistance from the unethical rancher who hadn't honored his agreement with Antonia Barclay.

"I'll drive you closer," he pressed, seeing an overgrown road alongside the field. His tires crunched through the undergrowth, the tall weeds brushing the undercarriage.

Beside him, Fleur reached in the back pocket of her cutoffs to withdraw a packet of folded papers.

The lease termination.

She already had her fingers in the door handle when he braked to a halt. "I'll just be a minute."

"I'm going with you." He shut off the engine and reached for the door.

"No, thank you." Her voice was sharp despite the polite words. "I'd like to handle my own business."

"And what if he's upset?" He shook his head, his gaze going to Cranston, where the guy seemed to be finishing up a phone call and tucking the device in his shirt pocket. "He already cheated Antonia with the irrigation—"

Fleur's hand landed on his arm. Firm. Certain.

"I'll handle him. It's my family's land, and it's my responsibility now." Her eyes locked on him. Determined.

Drake didn't like letting her confront the guy by herself, knowing that Josiah Cranston wasn't a particularly honorable person. But he could see this meant something to Fleur.

Reluctantly, he nodded. "I'll be right here if you need me."

Still, tension knotted in his shoulders as he watched her walk away to speak to him. Did she have any idea how tough it was for him to let her go alone? Not that he expected the surly rancher would lash out physically or anything. But Drake recognized that his protective streak had strengthened since his parents' deaths. It wasn't easy for him to watch people that he cared face anything he perceived as a potential danger.

That's why it had been impossible for him to let Colin marry Fleur without saying something. Even Emma had needed to tell him to back off sometimes. Now, with Fleur, the need to be by her side was even stronger. And what did that say about his feelings for her?

He ground his teeth together, reminding himself he had a clear view of them, at least. As a distraction, he picked up his phone and opened up a message to Jessamyn Barclay.

The idea of buying the Crooked Elm Ranch lands, but not the house, had seemed so promising he thought he'd run it by her, especially since Fleur already seemed open to the idea.

Tapping out a text, he reminded Jessamyn that his offer to buy the acreage would mean he'd take care of any citations from the local land management agencies. Surely that would make the proposal all the more appealing if they were anxious to resolve the issues. He hit Send, hoping the Barclay sisters would agree to his plan.

That way, his pledge to his parents' memory would be fulfilled, and the only thing keeping him from exploring the attraction with Fleur was an obligation to disclose a relationship to his brother.

Drake still didn't know how to do that. But Colin wouldn't be in town for the wedding for a few more days, so he still had time to figure it out. And as Fleur walked toward the truck, her meeting with Cranston apparently finished, Drake was very ready to focus on convincing her that their one night together wasn't nearly enough.

Back at Alexander Ranch an hour later, Fleur stole a sidelong glance at Drake as she walked toward a recently restored barn with him. She was still surprised to acknowledge this rugged rancher was no longer her adversary.

"Are you sure you're not hungry yet?" he asked, pausing outside the old barn.

The clean scents of pine and straw were strong here, the minimalist gray barn pretty enough to be on a magazine cover. Tall purple flowers she didn't recognize were planted on either side of the huge sliding door.

"I'd like to see the wedding venue first," she insisted, and while the answer was honest, she also knew she felt a little nervous about the evening meal she'd agreed to with Drake.

Something had shifted in his demeanor toward her since their night together. Which shouldn't surprise her, since she considered sleeping together a big step, too. And yet, she still hadn't figured out what it meant for them. What she wanted it to mean.

"Fair enough." He pivoted so that he faced her, meeting her gaze head-on. He spread his arms wide, his smile a hundred-watt level. "Prepare yourself for the site of the catering event that's going to launch your cooking career into the stratosphere."

She laughed, grateful for the moment of levity. Between the confrontation with Josiah Cranston—which had gone as well as could be expected, even if he hadn't been pleased—and the tension mounting about her evening with Drake, she appreciated the distraction.

All the more so when his nearness stirred a hunger to touch and taste him. To indulge all the pent-up longings that were part of her complicated feelings for this man.

"Let's hope you're right." Her voice sounded a little too breathless, but she tried to hide it by continuing, "The barn restoration is beautiful. I'm not surprised Emma wanted to have her wedding here."

She felt Drake's gaze linger on her a moment longer before he moved away, pushing open the huge door.

"Thank you. My father had notes for restoring everything on the ranch, from the buildings to the land. His plans emphasized sustainability and efficiency, from energy and materials to structure and design." There was a serious note in his voice that she hadn't heard before. Or maybe it was the expression on his face as he peered up at the gray timber exterior capped by a dark roof covered with solar panels on one side.

"You continued to follow your father's plans with the barn?" She found herself looking at the space with new eyes. Because she could see now that it was more than a wedding venue for Drake.

This building had been a tribute.

"Yes, I did." He stepped forward into the barn, stretching out an arm to flip on overhead lights. "His outlines were meticulous about everything from the kinds of recycled materials he wanted to use to the rainwater collection systems he envisioned for the house and barns."

Her step stuttered. "You restored other buildings, too?"

"Everything." His clipped answer somehow spoke volumes about how important that had been to him. "The house interior will be completely different from any memory you might have from when you were younger."

She hadn't been inside the Alexander home when she'd had dinner with Emma on the patio, she realized, other than to carry a few things outside from an enclosed porch.

Still, she didn't step inside the restored barn, her attention too fixated on this discovery about Drake's remodeling activity. Had his siblings minded? she wondered. How might they have felt about changes to the places in their home where they might have had special family memories? She recalled how much it meant to her to step into Gran's kitchen and have it look exactly the way she remembered.

"That must have been a tremendous undertaking." She found herself wanting to explore the whole ranch more carefully, now that she knew as much.

"And I'm not done yet." The determination in his eyes was unmistakable. "Reviving the waterway was supposed to be his crowning achievement."

Understanding dawned. His drive to buy Crooked Elm

was rooted in something so much deeper than she'd imagined. Pushing her to sell hadn't simply been a way to chase her out of town or throw around his net worth. He'd wanted to fulfill his father's vision.

But before she could respond, Drake extended his hand to her. "Come on in. You should see what Emma's done in here."

When her fingers settled in the warmth of his palm, a shiver ran up her spine. She couldn't deny her connection to this man, and all at once she knew that tonight, she wasn't going to try.

She wanted to lose herself in him again, to chase the feelings that only he had ever inspired. But for now, she drew in a deep breath and entered the barn, every step, every moment of waiting ramping the desire coursing through her veins.

"Oh, how beautiful," she murmured, her gaze going upward where yards and yards of pale pink tulle wove through the rafters, creating a soft canopy dotted with white lights woven through the fabric.

Below, the reclaimed wood support beams were wound with tulle and white ribbons, like giant Maypoles. Candelabra stands were already in place around the room, the white candles protected inside tiny glass globes. On the wooden floor, rectangular tables were laid out at angles. The focus on the head table adorned with white linen and skirted with more tulle.

"There will be greenery and pink peonies on almost every surface." Drake gestured around the room with his free hand. "My job was the tulle, and Emma assured me any spots that I missed would be covered with flowers."

"You did an incredible job." She wondered what it would be like to have a brother—or even a sister—make that kind of loving effort. To have a sibling who cared so deeply about her happiness. "Emma must be thrilled."

Fleur could feel her heart beat in the palm of her hand where it rested against Drake's, her emotions swelling too big to contain. She wanted to wrap herself in the hidden kindness of this man, the generosity of spirit in someone who would make a life's work of his parents' dreams, or set everything else aside to decorate a barn for a beloved sister.

"I think so. Now you just need to come through with the food—"

Fleur touched his jaw, turning his face toward her so she could look him in the eye. Then, stretching up on her toes, she brushed a kiss over his lips. Once. Twice.

When she settled on her feet, she noticed with pleasure that his eyes remained closed for a moment afterward. He blinked them open again, heated appreciation in their depths.

"What was that for?" he asked softly, letting go of her hand to wrap his arms around her waist.

"That was my way of apologizing for ever thinking you were a bad sibling." She'd believed the worst of him for years and he hadn't deserved it.

"You can think whatever you like about me if you apologize that way," he murmured, his arms flexing in a way that brought her closer still.

"I just remembered I've actually had a lot of wicked thoughts about you over the years." She kissed his cheek and down to his jaw. Taking her time, breathing in the pine and musk scent of his skin. "Atoning thoroughly could take a while."

With a hungry groan of appreciation he backed her deeper into the building. Gently, but so very deliberately.

"In that case, I need to show you my favorite part of

the restoration." He gripped one of her thighs on either side of his waist while she kept her arms around his neck. He lifted her into position.

She rocked against him, reveling in the hard length of him all too apparent through the denim of his jeans as he walked.

"What might that be?" She paused in her kisses long enough to peer over her shoulder so she could see where he was taking her.

"We converted the old hayloft to private guest quarters since the restored barn is going to be used strictly as a place for entertaining." His long strides brought them to an open staircase at the back of the building. He began to climb the wide wooden steps, still holding her, and she could see a small landing with open doors on either side.

"Are we really going to fool around in the hayloft?" A smile pulled at her lips at the thought.

A moment later, his mouth claimed hers for a slow, thorough tasting. When he finished, she was breathing hard, growing taut with desire.

"With any luck we're going to do a whole lot more than that." Entering one of the open rooms with her still in his arms, Drake kicked the heavy door closed behind them.

Fleur's heart sped, her limbs growing heavy as she pressed herself to him. She worked her fingers under the sleeves of his T-shirt, gripping the muscles there.

"If you get these clothes off, you'd find out for yourself." She kissed along the neckline of his shirt, then licked a path underneath it to his collarbone. "But until then, my mouth can only make amends for so much."

Thirteen

Fleur saw the way her words affected him.

Drake's fingers flexed into her thighs, a raw squeeze before he lifted her off him to settle her on the white duvet in the guest bedroom. She tried to catch her breath, as she sat on the edge of the mattress, her palms smoothing over the cotton fabric encasing thick eiderdown. But it wasn't easy to steady herself while she watched Drake peel his dark T-shirt up and over his head.

Baring the hard, carved muscles of a man in his prime, his body a map she couldn't wait to explore. Behind him, the white walls and gray reclaimed wood floor faded, the man dominating everything else. Besides, she couldn't think about how much work he'd put into this place. Her heart might dissolve in a puddle of tenderness she wasn't ready to feel.

Instead, she tried to focus on the practicalities.

"Are there condoms here?" She needed to ask before she lost all focus.

A moment fast approaching when he moved his hand to the button on his jeans. She registered the ache deep inside her, a need only he could fill. Her thighs pressed together, her hands reaching for him before he'd even kicked free of the denim and boxers.

"In the bathroom. The housekeeper stocks guest amenities in here." He took her hands in his, tugging her forward as he bent closer to kiss her lips. "I'll be right back."

She hadn't even registered the words when he pulled away. It took her a moment as her eyes blinked open to understand what he'd said and where he'd gone, his broad shoulders disappearing through an open door off to one side of the room.

How was it possible she could lose herself in him—in this feeling he sparked—so thoroughly? She hadn't missed sex in the years between her first, unwise introduction to coupling and the second, toe-curling experience Drake had given her when they were together before. She'd been focused on culinary school and work.

But right now, with her fingers shaking a little as she drew off her T-shirt and reached for the snap on her jean shorts, she wondered how she could go for a week without this feeling, let alone months. Years.

She'd never known it could be this way.

And that was her last rational thought before Drake reappeared in the bedroom, his dark brown eyes lasering in on her near nakedness, his steps charging toward her like a man on a mission.

Her breath caught on a gasp, and then his arms were around her, his mouth on hers, capturing the air. She melted into him as he laid her on the bed, her limbs turning to liquid when he stretched out over her. Covering her.

His skin felt hot against hers, and she craved his warmth. His strength. The scents she associated with him filled her nostrils as his tongue stroked possessively over hers. Her hips tilted toward him, seeking more. Craving connection.

"Drake, please," she urged him faster, her hands roaming over his body to catalog the ripples of muscles and the stretch of ligaments, her fingers fascinated with every sinew and plane. "I need you."

Was it too revealing that she hungered for him this badly? No, she told herself. It was physical. A sensual appetite that could surely be appeased.

If her own passion intimidated her, at least his seemed to match it. Hooking a finger in the lace of her white thong, he dragged the insubstantial fabric down her thighs and off, leaving her in just the matching lace bra.

His hands moved to that next, though, slipping the straps down her shoulders as he kissed each nipple through the decorative cups, turning the peaks into tight points.

Then he licked a path through the valley between her breasts, flicking open the fastening there with one finger so he could feast on her hungrily.

All the while she arched and writhed against him, wanting to feel him inside her.

When she reached between them to stroke over his erection from base to tip, the ragged growl he made sent thrills through her.

"You don't make it easy for me to take my time with you, do you?" He asked the question as he kissed his way back up her chest to her throat and along her jaw to her ear, where he nipped the lobe gently.

A shiver tripped down her spine.

"I've thought about this too many times since we were

together last," she admitted, the words tumbling out with zero filters. It couldn't be helped, though.

Something inside her had been unleashed, and she couldn't seem to call it back now.

"You're all I've thought about, Fleur," he rasped out between kisses, and she took his face in her hand to steer his mouth to hers, wanting to drink in what he'd said. To taste the need on her tongue and savor it.

The greedy way he kissed her, the press of his hips against hers underscored his words. She reached blindly around the bed for the condom and unwrapped the package, her fingers fumbling but fueled by desire.

"Let me." He took the condom from her, sheathing himself in one easy move before he levered up to sit on the edge of the bed, taking her with him.

For a moment, she wasn't sure where he wanted her, but then he lifted her onto his lap to straddle him. Their eyes met. Held.

When he lifted her again, he positioned her right where she needed to be so that she sank down, down and deeper down onto him. The feeling was perfect, filling her completely, so that she wanted to stay there forever.

Except then Drake moved, and she realized that was exactly what she needed. Her legs locked around him while his hips withdrew and then pistoned forward. Again and again.

Each thrust took her higher. Every moment of sharing her body with him seemed to tangle him in her heart. Deeper and deeper.

The thought was a dangerous one, but it was as inescapable as the release shimmering just out of reach. So close.

"Fleur." His breath stirred her hair, the word soft and passionate as any prayer. "Let go with me. Feel me."

For a moment, she met his intense gaze and everything inside her stopped. Held. Even time seemed to slow.

Then her orgasm crashed over her, her feminine muscles contracting and releasing in lush spasms that seemed to shake her whole body. As if from far away, she felt Drake tensing, every part of him going taut while she convulsed through the sweetness of her release. And then he was right there with her, his shout of satisfaction making her thighs clamp him tighter.

Bliss.

There was no other word for the sensual perfection of the moment, and Fleur let it fill her up as she slumped against him, his shoulder anchoring her where she rested her forehead for long minutes afterward.

Slowly, reason returned. It was almost disorienting to come back to the guest bedroom in the restored barn, to recognize how completely she'd lost her senses to this man and what they'd shared. She remembered how it had been the same way with him the first time, and she'd had to ask for a reprieve in discussing what their relationship meant.

And here she was again, still not ready to talk to him about that. Even though now, she feared she understood all too well what she was feeling.

Somehow, despite all her best intentions, she'd fallen in love with Drake Alexander.

Tensing at the realization, she wondered if she'd be able to hide it from him. She had to, of course. Drake hadn't even wanted her to stay in Catamount when she'd first told him about her wish to remain here.

His new idea of trying to buy the lands while she and her sisters kept the house hadn't been formed with any hope of having a relationship with her, either. He'd just wanted to fulfill his father's wishes.

"Hey." Drake shifted beneath her, his shoulder moving in a way that made her straighten to face him. "Everything okay?"

No. She was in complete and utter crisis.

She was in love.

But she swallowed down the unwise thoughts and forced a smile.

"That was amazing." She settled on a true statement that would have to do for now. "I was just trying to recover my senses."

For a moment, his dark eyes searched hers, as if he could tell there was more at work than what she'd confessed. But in the end, he nodded.

"Me, too. But I'm still going to make you dinner." He stroked one hand through her hair, her braid having fallen out at some point without her even realizing. He sifted through the waves now, gently untangling the strands. "You'll feel good as new after that."

Fleur wasn't so sure about that, but until she could contemplate her next move, she just reached for her clothes. She needed some kind of barrier between them before her feelings became all too apparent.

Something had shifted between them.

Drake could feel their equilibrium was all off-balance even though they shared a nice meal. His steaks had turned out perfectly, the side dishes simple but well cooked. And while he knew that Fleur was a professional chef, he didn't think the food had been that much of a disappointment.

If anything, she'd seemed genuinely pleased that he'd gone to the effort of cooking for her.

No, there was something else brewing between them. As he finished putting away the leftovers in the double-sized refrigerator, he stole a glance at Fleur where she wiped down the white quartz countertop where they'd eaten.

"I appreciate you letting me use this kitchen as a home base for catering the wedding," she remarked as she walked toward him. She rinsed out the dishcloth before squeezing out the excess water and draping it over the divider between the stainless steel sinks. "It's so roomy, and the appliances are a caterer's dream."

She ran a finger over the knobs at the industrial-sized gas stove when her cell phone chimed. Hesitating, she glanced his way.

"Feel free to take that," he encouraged her as he closed the refrigerator door. "I can step into the next room if you need privacy."

Withdrawing her phone from her pocket, she checked the screen. "No need. It's Jessamyn."

Fleur lowered herself into one of the counter stools at the island, where they'd eaten.

"Hello?" she answered the call, her gray eyes flicking to his while Jessamyn spoke for a minute.

For a moment, he wondered if her sister was calling with good news for them both—that she liked the idea of selling Drake the Crooked Elm Ranch acreage while the Barclay sisters kept the house.

But as he moved closer to the island to take a seat beside Fleur, he could tell that it wasn't good news. At first, a line appeared between her eyebrows, a confused furrow. But then, as her sister continued to speak, her jaw went slack with surprise.

"Are you serious?" Her breathing quickened as she shot up out of her seat. She appeared agitated as she paced around the island. "Can Dad even do that?"

Drake tensed, not liking to see her unhappy. His protective instincts fired, and he stood, too. Not that he could take action until he knew what was wrong, but he hated for her to be upset.

What had her father done?

He moved to close the distance between them, instinctively wanting to offer comfort. But just before he reached her, Fleur's shoulders tightened, and her mouth compressed into a thin, flat line.

Worse? Her gray eyes lifted to meet his. And he could have sworn all that anger was directed at…him?

"What is it?" he asked, feeling involved somehow in her conversation, even though she still held the phone to her ear.

But Fleur didn't answer him. Still locking gazes with him, she spoke again into the phone.

"Jess, I have Drake with me right now. If I put you on speaker, would you please repeat that so he knows?"

Worry speared through him as Fleur stabbed a button on her screen.

"Of course." Jessamyn's brusque tone came through the speaker as Fleur held the device between them. "I was just telling Fleur that our father intercepted Drake's message to me about wanting to buy the Crooked Elm rangelands. He's noticed Drake's interest in the property, apparently, both at Gran's memorial and then with the follow-up call and text about buying the parcel even with the citations pending. Now Dad thinks maybe those acres are worth more than he realized."

Drake shook his head, not understanding what was wrong.

"Does he think I should offer more for them?" he asked, unsure what he was missing. "I can increase my offer."

Why was Fleur so angry?

"Tell him," Fleur said, her words as sharp as any she'd

shot at him when they'd been enemies. "Explain what his need to force his own agenda has led to."

On the other end of the call, Jessamyn continued in that clipped business tone. Yet there was no mistaking the steely anger beneath it.

"Money isn't the issue. Now our father is contesting Antonia's will, Drake. It could be tied up in probate court for months. Or more. Bottom line, you won't be able to buy the land anyway until the case is settled."

The news devastated him. So he understood it had to devastate Fleur one hundred times as much. His gut sank.

"Fleur, I'm so sorry." He wanted to comfort her. To find a way to bear the news that must be crushing to her. "There must be some way—"

"There isn't." She snapped, her eyes flinty with anger before they moved away from him and back to her phone. "Jessamyn, I appreciate the update. Do you think I'm even legally allowed to live there?"

Drake speared his fingers through his hair, unable to believe what he was hearing. How could Mateo do this to his daughters?

"You should be fine since you were already there before Dad contested the will. But in yet more bad news, Josiah Cranston legally doesn't have to vacate the property now until probate is cleared."

Hell. Anger coursed through his veins even as Drake knew he had no right to it. Fleur and her sisters were the ones who deserved to be furious about this.

"It's a lot to absorb at once," Fleur said finally, her voice shaking slightly. "I'll call you later once I get my head around this, okay?"

"Sure thing, Fleur," Jessamyn returned, sounding exhausted as she heaved out a small sigh. "I'll get in touch with Lark."

Fleur disconnected and tucked the phone into her pocket, her movements deliberate. Slow.

Still, he recalled how her voice had a tremor in it a moment ago.

"I'm so sorry," he repeated, his hands landing on her shoulders. "We can hire an attorney who specializes in probate—"

"We?" Her voice rose an octave as she glared at him before spinning away from his touch. "*We* aren't doing anything together, Drake." She removed the place mats from the counter and replaced them in a buffet drawer, her movements abrupt. Jerky. "This is a problem for my sisters and me to deal with. It's not one you can manage with money and influence. In fact, it doesn't have anything to do with you."

His brain worked fast to try to follow what she was angry at him for, but the pieces didn't add up.

"Fleur, it's not my fault your father contested the will."

"Oh no?" She fisted her hands and settled them on her hips, the emotion practically steaming off her as she faced him. "Did you miss the part where my sister said your interest in the land made our money-hungry dad want to get involved? You're so gung ho to buy it that of course my big shot real estate developer father wants to know if he can make a buck on it."

He knew she was upset, and she had every reason to be. So he told himself not to argue with her. But damn it, how could he allow her to think the worst of him when he hadn't done anything but try to help?

"I couldn't have possibly known that he would view my interest that way. I only spoke to Jessamyn about it, not him."

Hadn't they been in bed together just a few hours ago? He'd shared more with her than any other woman. So it shredded him to see her look at him now as if he'd hurt her on purpose.

"Right. You spoke to my sister because you couldn't wait for me to do that, even though I'm back in Catamount to find some kind of peace among my siblings again. Why couldn't you just allow me to work at my own pace to settle things? I invited them here this summer so that we could talk face–to-face, but that wasn't good enough for you. Why did your wants have to come first?" She spoke faster with each sentence, her hurt more and more evident.

Her eyes shone with unshed tears, and he sensed the need to do something, say something, to fix things. Fast.

"They didn't. I hoped that I was helping you at the same time I was helping myself." He wasn't the bad guy here, but damned if he could make her see that.

"Did you really?" She folded her arms, her shoulders practically vibrating with her anger. "Or did you tell yourself that to justify throwing your money around to get what you wanted?"

Was that true?

The idea sat uncomfortably on him for a moment.

"If that's what I did, I promise you it was never my intention to hurt you." His heart pounded as if he needed any reminders that he was screwing this up. Saying all the wrong things.

She shook her head, taking a step back and grabbing her purse. "Too late. And your big offer isn't going to get you what you wanted this time anyway, so all your efforts to speed things up were for nothing."

"Fleur, wait." He followed her toward the door, unwilling to see her walk away upset. "Let's talk about this—"

"No." She held her ground in the hall entrance, pausing long enough to make sure he understood that much.

"We won't be talking about this, or anything else, either. I'll be here for Emma's wedding, but I have no interest in seeing you then or at any other time."

The words pummeled him harder than any thrashing he'd ever taken in the bull riding arena. And they sure as hell made him feel worse than any fall.

But as if that weren't bad enough, she punctuated them by turning on her heel and walking out the door.

Fourteen

Every day that passed without Fleur in his life hurt more than the one before.

Standing outside Emma's wedding reception as the sun dropped out of sight beyond the trees, Drake regarded the festivities in the hope of catching sight of Fleur as she catered the reception. A local band played upbeat country music inside the barn, the main doors both swung open so that guests could enjoy cocktails outside, too. White lights canopied the outdoor bar and a few tables were set up for guests who wished to take a breather from the dancing indoors. A bonfire burned in a firepit nearby, the flames ready for later in the evening when there would be s'more roasting for the kids.

Everything looked perfect. His parents' dreams for this day were fulfilled to the letter, and he felt good about that. But inside, everything seemed wrong. He hadn't spoken to his brother beyond the most superficial of greetings.

And worse, he hadn't seen Fleur.

He'd seen signs of her presence everywhere today. From the thoughtful favors she'd created for Emma with bags of spiced nuts for all the guests, to the abundant buffet table stacked with the Spanish tapas she specialized in making, Fleur's influence was all around him. And yet, she'd remained so thoroughly in the background that he'd never caught a single glimpse of her. Was she avoiding him? Did she even care enough to feel that strong of an emotion for him? Or was she just…indifferent? That possibility stung the most.

Even now his gaze went down to the main house where the kitchen lights were visible from the barn. She'd hired helpers who carried fresh trays up from the kitchen and took away the empties. Allowing her to stay firmly in the background.

An unexpected voice rumbled low behind him. "Dad and Mom would be proud to see this day."

Shaking off his thoughts, Drake turned to find Colin approach from the shadows. Clad in a tux and black Stetson just like his own, the two men looked similar enough on the outside. Yet how different were they inside when they'd barely spoken in years beyond the occasional necessary exchange about family business.

And that *was* his fault. Drake might not agree with Fleur's assessment of his mistakes where she was concerned. But he couldn't deny that he'd done his brother a grave disservice five years ago when he'd insisted Fleur break things off with him. It pained him to admit that now. Especially when acknowledging as much to Colin could drive his brother to seek Fleur again.

The possibility sent a crushing weight down onto his solar plexus.

"Glen is a good man," Drake acknowledged, trying to get a read on Colin. "I think Mom and Dad would approve."

"I don't mean Glen." Colin shook his head as he leaned against the trunk of a small cherry tree. "I mean the ranch. The barns. The land. It all looks just like what Dad wanted to accomplish."

A couple of older kids ran past them in their wedding finery carrying sparklers, an early nod to the fireworks planned for later when the sky fully darkened.

"You think so?" Drake wasn't fishing for compliments from his brother. He knew Colin wouldn't BS him about that of all things. "There were times I questioned the plans, wishing I could just ask him what he wanted—"

The emotion that rose in his throat made it necessary to cut himself off. Normally, he was good about tucking those old hurts away, but on Emma's wedding day, standing beside his long-estranged brother, he felt the full weight of the mistakes he'd made as head of the family.

"I wish I could ask him things, too. Both of them." Colin scuffed his dress boots through the grass. "Being home makes me wish that all the more."

Drake looked up fast at that. "Is this still home for you? I haven't spoiled that?"

"In spite of everything, yes, I guess it is." Colin tipped his hat back farther on his head as he rocked on his heels. "Montana is nice, and I'm not returning here anytime soon. But I'll always think of this place as home."

Drake's throat closed at the thought of his brother never around for more than the occasional wedding. The country music and the laugher from inside the barn seemed miles away as he dug deep to make a long-over-due apology.

"I'm sorry to hear that you're not coming back. All the more so because it's my fault you left. I had no right to interfere with you when you wanted to marry." He couldn't bring himself to say *when you wanted to marry Fleur.* Because he couldn't even put their names together in his head without pain spiking throughout him.

"Your fault?" Colin shook his head, seeming genuinely surprised. "For what, saying the obvious that Fleur Barclay and I would never work in a million years? Don't think I didn't know that, brother."

Reeling, Drake swept off his hat and scratched a hand through hair, sifting through his brother's words. He wanted to make sure he wasn't just hearing what he wished to hear.

"I thought you were furious with me for asking her to end the engagement." He knew Fleur had blamed him. Deservedly so.

"Hell no. I was furious with myself for hurting her in the first place when she and I—we were never going to be more than friends." Colin turned a tortured expression his way, his eyes pained. "All this time, I thought you knew. I was ashamed I went after her when I knew you liked her."

What? Had he been that obvious?

"Me?" He felt like someone had pulled the rug out from under him. He was left standing upright, but he wasn't quite sure how. "Why would you think that when we couldn't even stand to be around one another?"

Even as he spoke the words, Colin's eyes shot heavenward. "It's one thing to kid yourself, Drake, but you're not fooling me. Then, or now. You've always liked Fleur. From the time you assigned yourself as her personal protector at every rodeo, chasing guys away with bared teeth, to when you nearly took my head off for sleeping with her."

Drake bristled, his fingers fisting. And if just *hearing* those words did that to him—maybe his brother had a point.

He swore softly under his breath.

"I hated myself even before you came home and found out about us." Colin tipped his head to look at the sky where an early firework from a far-off neighbor sparkled red through the night.

"Let's say for argument's sake that I did have feelings for Fleur." Did? The reality of his feelings was staring him in the face every time he stared at the kitchen windows down the hill and willed himself to catch a glimpse of her.

He loved Fleur.

Deeply. Passionately. And his brother had known it long before he had.

"All right," his brother agreed. "We'll say that."

"Why would you be with her? I know we didn't always see eye to eye, but I thought we got along well enough."

Colin's dark eyebrows shot together as he frowned. "It had more to do with me than you. I resented you too much for having your life together while I was always struggling in your shadow. I missed having a brother once you decided to step into Dad's shoes and you called all the shots around here. You name it, I pinned it on you."

A burst of laughter from inside the barn reminded Drake he should return to the reception soon. Share this day with Emma. And yet, he'd waited half a lifetime for this conversation with his brother. He couldn't walk away from it now.

"I've only just started to realize that I may be more controlling than I should be."

"May be?" his brother said with the quirk of an eyebrow.

Drake shrugged sheepishly. He recalled Fleur's words too well about pushing his own agenda. And for what? He'd only hurt her by not giving her space to work through the legalities of the ranch inheritance in her own way. "And for that matter, I've also only started to understand that I have feelings for Fleur." His heart felt full. Heavy with the knowledge he needed to share.

"I love her," Drake admitted. "And I've been as hardheaded and blind with her as I have been with you."

Another firework exploded silently from some distant point, the shimmer of yellow and green lights flashing across the sky.

Colin straightened from where he'd leaned against the cherry tree and clapped a heavy hand on Drake's shoulder.

"If I've learned one thing in the past five years, it's that it's never too late to make better choices. Starting my own spread forced me to be my own man." Colin nodded toward the building that housed the kitchen where Fleur worked. "I apologized to Fleur tonight for the mistakes I made in the past, and it felt good to know there were no hard feelings."

Colin had already spoken to Fleur? Drake turned his gaze to the kitchen window once more, understanding that his whole life—his future—was inside that room right now. He needed to go down there and tell her as much, whether or not she forgave him.

He wouldn't allow this argument to fester for five years the way he'd done with Colin.

"Thank you." Not sure what else to say, he wrapped his brother in a hug. "And this is always your home."

Colin squeezed his shoulder before letting go. "Good. Then I will be the representative Alexander male of the hour, while you go patch things up with Fleur."

"Deal." Feeling lighter than he had in years, Drake smiled. He knew he had a long way to go to heal things with his sibling, but tonight was a start. And it felt damned good to have Colin here again.

He just hoped he could express himself to Fleur more effectively than he had in the past. He couldn't control whether or not she wanted him in her life. But he could make certain she understood how much he loved her, and he wasn't leaving that kitchen until he'd made his point.

Staring through the window at the silver lights exploding in a starfish pattern over the creek, Fleur chastised herself for being too chicken to leave the kitchen to go outside and enjoy the Fourth of July display.

Plus, she was still feeling emotional from her earlier encounter with Colin. They'd managed to talk, express their sorrow over the loss of their child, and come to terms with their relationship. She felt a pang as she realized her feelings for Colin had never been deep or strong or complicated. He'd been a safety net for her, and she a rebellion against his brother's rules for him. They'd parted on a good note.

So far, only the lights from neighboring ranches had arced across the sky. But Emma and Glen had a show planned for dusk, a newlywed celebration to cap off their wedding day. There'd been a time when Fleur might have imagined her enjoying that moment with Drake beside her.

But after their fight last week—after the way he'd

flexed his financial might hoping to make the sale of Crooked Elm happen faster—she had told him she didn't want to see him anymore. As much as it hurt to think of not being with him again, she also knew herself well enough to understand she couldn't spend her life feeling like her wishes were secondary to a man with money. Her father had made her feel less than enough for one lifetime.

Now she made her own decisions. Called her own shots.

And it was a lonely battle to have won.

The one bright moment was the talk she'd had with Colin. They were better as friends, they'd agreed. And she felt a weight off her mind thinking about that. Her conscience was eased regarding her past with Colin. They'd forgiven each other.

Returning to the counter, she stacked up the cleaned serving trays and slid them into their canvas carrying case. The evening had seemed like a success even though she hadn't visited the reception herself yet. And she needed to, soon. Emma deserved her personal congratulations.

When a side door opened, she expected to see Marta walk into the room with another empty tray. But when she looked up, Drake stood before her.

Dressed in a tuxedo and black Stetson, he had a pink rose boutonniere. She'd never seen him so devastatingly handsome, although she suspected it had more to do with how long it had been since she'd seen him than with what he wore.

"Fleur." He spoke her name like an answer to all his questions.

And it hurt her because she knew that wasn't the case.

"Does the bride need something?" she asked, channeling Jessamyn and turning on her business mode. "I can send Marta up with more *croquetas*."

She bustled toward the refrigerator, willing herself not to think about how handsome Drake looked. Or about what he might want.

Or how much she wanted him.

"Emma doesn't need anything," Drake asserted, stepping deeper into the room while still maintaining some distance. "The food was incredible and all the guests are singing your praises while they dance."

She really would have liked to have overseen things personally, so she appreciated hearing that. She'd stayed away to safeguard her heart. And keep from causing a scene.

"I'm glad to hear it." She thought of the heavy apron she wore. That her hair was in a net in deference to the food prep. Swiftly, she withdrew the net and untied the apron.

Because the cooking was finished, of course. Not because Drake stood there looking so good it made her hurt.

She tucked the items into her duffel bag and ran a self-conscious hand over her matted hair.

"You look beautiful." His low voice curled through her like smoke wisps as his gaze roamed over her yellow tea-length dress, the tulle skirt embroidered with daisies.

Swallowing her nerves, she tucked her hands under her elbows, folding her arms tightly.

"I know you're not here to talk about that. What can I do for you?"

"Emma wanted me to make sure you didn't miss the fireworks." He tugged off his Stetson and set it on a counter stool. "But that's only half the truth. I realized that I need to make better choices with you if I want any chance of convincing you not to walk away from what's happening between us."

Irritation flared.

"Isn't that how we got here in the first place? You making all the choices?" She'd had days to think about what had happened between them and she still felt frustrated. Resentful. "I understand you didn't mean to undermine me by going directly to my sister, Drake. But that's how it felt to me. And I'm extremely sensitive to that after the way my father played god with his financial power."

"I overstepped," he acknowledged, his expression disconsolate. "I took it for granted that you would want help, and I thought I was helping. In hindsight, I can see that I had no business assuming that. But I've accomplished a lot charging ahead without asking anyone's permission, and I failed to notice that it hurts people I care about."

"People?" Curiosity prompted her to ask.

Especially now that she noticed the violet shadows under his eyes. Almost as if he'd lost as much sleep this week as she had.

"You. And Colin, too." He flicked open the button on his tuxedo jacket before dipping a finger into his bow tie and loosening that as well. "We spoke just now, and I realized that what I perceived as being protective has been viewed as domineering to those around me."

Her heart softened a fraction at the despairing note in his voice.

"Colin said that?" She found her thoughts returning to the time she'd spent with him. They'd always been friends, their interactions easy and fun, unlike the way she and Drake had sparked friction.

Those weeks she and Colin had dated, she remembered him complaining that Drake was hard to live with, his expectations too high for anyone to meet. At the time, she'd thought she'd understood since she had her own strained relationships with Lark and Jessamyn. But maybe the fractures had gone deeper between the brothers.

"Apparently, he left for Montana because of it." His dark eyes met hers. "Or at least, that was one of his reasons. But it made me realize that I don't want to be that man who thinks he knows best. I didn't see the damage I was doing by getting involved in your business, Fleur, but I can change."

There was an earnestness in his voice, a depth of concern that she hadn't heard before.

It awakened her empathy. Her hope.

"Anyone can *change*," she agreed, her heart hammering so loudly it was all she heard. "If they want to. If it really means something to them."

How many times had she thought that about her family? All the Barclays had laughed at her attempts at peacekeeping in their dysfunctional clan, but she was still idealistic enough to believe people could change if they cared enough to try. Her failures hadn't taken that away from her.

And this was the first time anyone she'd loved had suggested they wanted to change.

"Fleur." Drake moved closer to her now, his dark cowboy boots covering the steps between them so that he stood before her. He lifted one of her hands and held it between both of his. "I love you. And I can't think of any more compelling reason in the world to change than for love."

The warmth of his touch anchored her as her heart soared on those words. Because coming from Drake Alexander, she knew it wasn't merely a phrase to toss out lightly. She'd seen firsthand how he kept his pledges to his parents.

Her chest expanded, a joy exploding inside it like the fireworks she'd seen through the kitchen window. Yet before she could speak, he continued.

"I know that I don't deserve you. Not yet." His dark eyes were serious. Somber. He squeezed her hands lightly, his voice lowering. "But if you'll give me a chance, I am confident that I can show you that you mean everything in the world to me."

Something shifted inside her, a new tenderness opening wide that gave her a different perspective of him. No doubt he was a man of strong principle and fierce loyalty. And now, he wanted to envelop her in all of those deep feelings.

A relationship with Drake promised her a depth of love—and passion—unlike anything she'd ever experienced before.

"I love you, too, Drake. So much." She spoke the words aloud that had been circling around her thoughts every hour since they'd been together last, and it felt beautiful to share.

He crushed her to him, holding her tightly. And she knew without question that he'd been as frantically worried about losing her as she'd been about him. She understand that desperate hug because it echoed everything inside her. She sighed into him.

And it felt like coming home.

"I will always want to fix everything I can for you," he spoke the words through her hair, kissing her in between words. "But you can tell me when I can't, and I promise that I will listen."

The last of her worries fell away, her heart full and so

very happy. A smile curved her lips, the rightness of the moment filling her whole being.

"I will hold you to that," she told him simply, leaning back to look him in the eyes, this proud, hardworking rancher that she loved.

And he stared at her like she'd solved all his problems. His eyes held a wealth of tenderness, and she wanted to melt right into it.

"I'm going to do everything I can to make you happy, you know." He stroked his hand over her cheek, slowing the touch so he could trace her lips with his thumb.

Her knees went weak from just that caress.

Although knowing he loved her might have had a little to do with the way she felt weightless and buoyantly joyful.

"I like the sound of that. I hope it involves you cooking for me again."

"It means standing behind you with whatever you decide to do. Offering advice when you need it. Letting you fight your battles with your father but being a sounding board when you want it. Whatever you and your sisters decide to do, you'll have my full support."

His eyes lit with promise as the sound of fireworks exploded outside over the creek. Up at the barn, the wedding guests cheered.

She knew they needed to join Emma and celebrate her wedding, but Drake held her there a moment longer.

"I'm going to do so much more than that," he vowed. "And when you want to start a restaurant, I hope you'll keep in mind that I just happen to have one."

She laughed, dizzy with the promise of the life they could share together. There were still problems ahead. Things that needed to be resolved with her sisters and their legacy from their grandmother. But knowing that this man was in her corner was a dream come true.

"I'll keep it in mind. For now, we'd better go watch the fireworks." Taking his hand, she tugged him toward the side door. "This is the perfect time to celebrate a happily-ever-after."

"I like the sound of that," he said in her ear, right before he swept her off her feet and into his arms. "Almost as much as I'm going to like calling you *Mrs.* Silver Spurs."

* * * * *

A GAME
BETWEEN FRIENDS

YAHRAH ST. JOHN

To my mom, Asilee Mitchell,
for showing me what true courage looks like.

Prologue

"Darling, I'm thrilled you could join us this evening," Angelique Lockett gushed when her son Xavier arrived at the skybox lounge at the Atlanta Cougars stadium.

His older brothers, Roman and Julian, and sister, Giana, had already arrived to watch the game. His new sister-in-law, Shantel, was also there.

"Hey, Ma." Xavier approached his mother and kissed her cheek. She eyed his ensemble. He'd come casually dressed in dark jeans, Jordan sneakers and, in a nod to his mother, a button-down blue shirt.

His work schedule as a sportscaster usually didn't allow him to attend Sunday games during the football season, but the network wanted to test out a new weekend commentator, so Xavier was sitting this one out. And before taking this job, Xavier had never had much opportunity to enjoy the family's private skybox, with its plush beige carpet, upholstered chairs, mahogany-paneled walls holding large television screens, and the huge marble-encased bar. *That was* because he'd been on the football field. But that was another lifetime.

The knee injury he'd sustained three years ago when he'd been the Cougars quarterback ended any chance he'd ever have of playing ball again. Xavier felt like a failure. He'd let down his old man. Let the team down. Before he was injured, the Atlanta Cougars were on a winning streak and poised to win their first championship, but then Xavier had made a wrong move that landed him under a mountain of men. He'd been carried off the field on a stretcher. It had been demoralizing.

"Should I be concerned you're not on-air?" his father inquired. Josiah had used his connections to help Xavier get the job, but that wasn't why he'd kept it. Xavier excelled at everything he did and once he found his groove, sportscasting had been no different. "You know there's always a place in the coaching department of the Atlanta Cougars."

"Everything's fine," Xavier replied and came toward the bar where Julian was stationed, drinking a tumbler of dark liquid. It wasn't the first time his father had brought up the possibility of him coaching the team, and Xavier suspected it wouldn't be the last.

"You avoided the hot seat," Julian said with a grin. "Must be one of our turns."

Xavier grinned back. There was no love lost between Julian and their father. They were incompatible. "Sorry, bro."

Julian was a smooth talker, and the ladies loved his toffee coloring, curly fade, light brown eyes and perpetual five-o'clock shadow. He was fashionably dressed in navy trousers and a silk shirt. He made Xavier his usual, a Scotch on the rocks, which he accepted. Xavier took a generous swallow to take the edge off—being here at the stadium was never easy. Brought back too many memories.

"The game should be starting soon," his mother announced. "I'll have the staff bring around the canapés."

Xavier and Julian both chuckled. Usually, they ate football fare when watching a game, like wings, nachos, bratwurst or chips and dip, but if their mother was in attendance? Only elevated appetizers would do.

"What are you two whispering about?" Giana asked, coming toward them. His beautiful, chocolate-hued sister wore a jean jumpsuit with a large belt wrapped around her slender waist. She wasn't quite as tall as Xavier, but she was statuesque and reached his shoulders. Her ebony hair was the same as their mother's, except Giana wore hers with wispy bangs.

"Staying off Dad's radar," Julian responded.

"Good luck with that." Giana chuckled.

"You better hope he doesn't ask you about Wynn Starks and why you haven't secured a sports drink endorsement contract with him yet," Julian quipped.

Giana rolled her eyes. "Don't you worry about a thing. I always get my man." She gave him a wink.

Their attention turned to the ninety-two-inch television screen. The game hadn't started, but the commentators were talking about the odds of the Atlanta Cougars winning, now that they had a new quarterback in Wayne Brown.

"Darn straight," Josiah shouted from across the room. "He's a terrific addition to the team and will get us a championship."

Is that a dig at me? Xavier wondered.

A light had gone out in Josiah's eyes when the doctors told Xavier he would never play football again. Xavier didn't know who was more upset, he or his father. So he'd allowed Josiah to bring in doctor after doctor, specialist after specialist until eventually Xavier had told him to stop. He was never going to be fixed.

Did that also mean he wasn't good enough to be Josiah's son?

It had taken Xavier months in therapy to realize he couldn't let football define him. The counselor had helped him see his life was his own and he could and *should* make choices that made *him* happy. Instead, as soon as he returned to Atlanta from the clinic, his father had pushed his agenda. Become a sports commentator, he'd said. And being the dutiful son, Xavier had complied.

"You're awfully quiet," Giana said from his side. "Are you okay?"

Xavier sipped his drink. "Sure."

She eyed him suspiciously. "I don't believe that for a second."

Xavier shrugged and focused his attention on the television screen because he couldn't believe his eyes. Standing in the middle of the field was Porscha Childs. Xavier blinked several times to be sure he wasn't hallucinating.

He wasn't.

Damn, she still looked good.

No, correct that. She looked *better.*

The years had been kind to her. The singer's tawny-brown skin gleamed. Her deep-set light brown eyes sparkled while her long jet-black hair hung in tussled waves down her slender back. She was smoking hot in a royal blue tuxedo dress with a deep V neckline. Her lush lips were bright red and totally kissable.

It made Xavier recall another time when he'd gotten to taste Porscha's lips.

Xavier had been at a wellness facility in Colorado that

specialized in care for the mind and body. The facility was frequented by athletes and celebrities, so Xavier had signed up to attend and rehabilitate his knee but also work on his mental health. Losing his lifelong dream had resulted in a deep depression.

Before arriving at the clinic, he'd wallowed for months until his father gave him a kick in the butt and told him to work out his issues. It was exactly what Xavier needed to jump-start him on the road to recovery. And so he'd flown to the facility in Colorado, and every day he dutifully worked the program, physical therapy in the mornings and group therapy in the afternoons.

It was there that he met the most stunning creature he'd ever seen. The first time he saw her, she was trying her best to be unassuming in a large kimono sweater wrapped around her frame. Her long black hair hung in a ponytail down her back, but it was her light brown eyes that spoke to him. Maybe because it was clear she didn't want to be there. She looked terrified of being called on by the group leader, who was known for putting newbies on the spot to get them to talk. It hadn't been easy for Xavier, either, to explain to the group why he was in therapy, but he'd done it, and she would, too.

He'd moved toward her and as he approached, her eyes landed on him. Xavier took a seat beside her. "Hey, name's Xavier."

Her eyes had drifted downward, and he'd wondered if she was going to speak, but then she'd said, "Hi."

"Is that all I get? I told you my name." He'd offered her a smile.

When she glanced up at him, he'd groaned and squeezed his eyes shut for a split second before opening them again. Heavens! Up close, her eyes were designed to make a man melt. She'd given him a half smile and his eyes zoomed to her delicious mouth, which had a tint of pink lipstick. "I'm Porscha." She'd held out her small hand.

Xavier took it in his and shook it. He'd been ready to say they could be friends during their stay, but something told him he and Porscha were going to be more than friends. *Much more.*

"She's amazing, isn't she?" Giana said from Xavier's side, bringing him back to the present as Porscha belted out the national anthem. "I love all her music."

"Yeah, she's all right," Julian commented from behind them. "I don't know if I could handle all the attention that comes with being with someone as famous as her."

"You get plenty of press," Xavier responded, defending Porscha.

Julian shrugged. "Local stuff. But her—" he pointed to the television "—the national press dogs her. That's a lot of pressure to live up to."

They had no idea, Xavier thought.

He recalled his and Porscha's discussion in the clinic about how she was always trying to keep up with her public persona and how when she failed, the public were quick to criticize. It was hard living up to the idealized version they had in their mind of who and what she should be.

He missed Porscha.

They'd been good together *in* and *out* of bed.

Maybe he could do something about that.

Xavier placed his drink on the bar. "I'll be right back." He knew his family would probably think he needed a break because of the game. He tended to avoid the stadium, but that wasn't it. He had to see Porscha.

"Where are you going?" his father asked. "The game is about to start."

"I'll be back," Xavier murmured and quickly left the

skybox. Once in the corridor, he raced toward the elevator that would take him to the lower level. He was betting Porscha wouldn't immediately leave the stadium but would instead go back to the dressing room and grab her things before escaping.

Xavier hoped he wasn't wrong.

Porscha was exhausted. She'd taken a red-eye from Germany, where she'd held a concert the night before at a military base. All she wanted was to go home, curl up in her own bed and go to sleep. Instead, her mother and manager, Diane Childs, had insisted she take this last-minute request to sing the national anthem for the Atlanta Cougars after another songstress bowed out due to a bout of laryngitis.

"The next six months are crucial," Diane had said once they were in the dressing room after last night's performance. "It's the final stretch before the Grammys. We want to keep your name on everyone's lips. The more exposure for you, the better."

And Porscha had relented.

She had worked too hard to get to this point. She had come from nothing. Her mother had gotten pregnant at eighteen and married her father, who'd eventually left them in relative poverty for another woman, whom he married and started another family with. Her mother had been devastated and consequently put all her focus on Porscha. When she had discovered Porscha could sing, she put her in singing competitions. Eventually, Porscha was picked up by a small record label.

Her first album had been a multiplatinum success, garnering her three Grammys and countless awards from Billboard to American Music. But success had brought its own scrutiny. The press were tough because she wasn't the average model size. Porscha thought the world was her oyster and then the second album came, bringing with it the sophomore jinx. *It bombed.* The press had been critical, and she'd fallen off the pedestal.

Afterward, she'd tumbled into a vicious depression, which only became worse when her father died a short while later. Although he'd contributed financially, she hadn't had a relationship with him prior to his passing, so his death, and the fact she would never get a resolution to the anger and disappoint she felt, hit her hard. That's when Diane had suggested she check into a wellness clinic in Denver that celebrities went to. Therapy had been a wake-up call, and Porscha fought her way back tooth and nail, although she hadn't done it by herself. She'd had help.

Xavier Lockett.

Sometimes just saying his name made her breath catch.

During her time at the clinic, they'd had a passionate affair, but Porscha had made the mistake of thinking it meant more. She'd thought they shared a connection. Then she'd overheard him discussing their relationship with another group member. He told the man that they were friends and nothing more. That was when she'd realized it had all been an illusion, but she'd been too caught up in the amazing sex to see the difference. Their breakup had been less than amicable.

It was why she limited her visits to Atlanta, because Xavier lived here. And for three years, she'd done good with only one visit to the stadium for a stop on her third album tour. But this? Singing the national anthem for the Atlanta Cougars was a recipe for disaster. There was a real possibility they could run into each other.

Although she'd done her best to steer clear of him, once in a while she looked Xavier up online to see what he was up to. He was a sports commentator for ASN and appeared to be doing well. She noticed that in the years since their breakup, he'd begun collecting women like trophies, showing them off at sports industry parties or high-profile events in Atlanta. Yet he never stayed with any of them for long. As soon as they lost their shiny newness, he discarded them, and it was on to the next best thing.

Porscha didn't have time for romance. Her career was her focus. She'd learned the hard way that she was a sucker when it came to men, so she'd been celibate. No man had ever aroused her passion like Xavier had.

She pushed Xavier out of her mind, determined to focus on the movie she was filming and its upcoming soundtrack. All she needed to do was change and get out of Lockett territory as fast as she could.

Xavier rushed past the locker rooms, physical therapy and recovery areas and arrived at the dressing rooms. Several bodyguards greeted him.

"Excuse me, sir. You're going to have to go back where you came from," one of the tall, beefy guards said, looking him up and down.

Luckily, Xavier still had his credentials on his lanyard and quickly showed them.

"I'm sorry, sir, I didn't realize you were one of the Locketts," the guard apologized. "Please…" He motioned Xavier forward.

"No worries. Where's Ms. Childs's room?" Xavier inquired. "I wanted to thank her for her rendition of the national anthem."

The guard led him down the hall to a door with a banner stating *Talent*.

"Thank you. I've got it from here." Xavier sucked in a breath and prepared himself for the less than enthusiastic greeting he was sure to receive. He and Porscha had broken up on bad terms. She thought he was a player using her for sex, but that had been far from true. They shared a bond and had gotten each other through the worst time in their lives.

Xavier knocked on the door. "Come in," a soft female voice said. He stepped inside the room and heard, "What the hell are *you* doing here?"

Porscha supposed she shouldn't be surprised. She'd known she could run into Xavier, but she didn't think he would seek her out because he hadn't in three years. And despite the surge of anger that sprang up from his sudden appearance, she had butterflies fluttering around in her tummy.

How was it possible he could *still* affect her like this?

In defiance of that revelation, she went with contempt. "I'll ask you again, what are you doing here?"

"I would think that's obvious," Xavier responded. "I came to see you."

"Ha!" Porscha laughed without humor.

Her mother rose from the couch she'd been sitting on. Diane Childs. She was tall with a slim build. She preferred trousers to dresses because they suited her more. She wore her hair in a sophisticated bob and preferred a swipe of lipstick and mascara to wearing any real makeup over her smooth fawn complexion. "Xavier Lockett, I presume?" she asked sizing him up.

"One and the same, ma'am."

"Then you know you shouldn't be here. Porscha is on a tight schedule."

"Perhaps, Porscha—" Xavier leaned sideways to glance behind Diane "—can speak for herself."

"I'm her manager."

"Mom, it's okay, I've got this." Porscha had a lot to say. Words she should have said three years ago.

Her mother turned to peer at her. "If you're sure?"

Porscha nodded. Diane stared at her for several seconds before she exited the room, leaving her and Xavier alone.

"It's good to see you. You look amazing," Xavier said.

"Of course, you'd say that." Porscha folded her arms across her bosom. "Because you were only interested in me for one thing."

"C'mon, Porscha. You know that's not true."

"Do I, Xavier?" she asked from a safe distance on the other side of the room because she knew she couldn't get any closer. Xavier had a way of pulling her in and she couldn't let that happen. She wasn't that easy. Or at least that was what she told herself.

"Yes, you do," he responded hotly. His eyes zeroed in on hers and Porscha found she couldn't look away. "It wasn't just physical. We helped get each other through a rough patch."

"That's not what you said back then."

"Because I wasn't about to put our business on blast to everyone in the clinic. It was private. Just between us."

"And you really expect me to believe that?" Porscha asked. "It's been three years, Xavier, and you've never tried to clear the air. So why now?"

"When I saw you upstairs on that television screen, I knew it wasn't over between us, Porscha." Xavier moved from the spot he'd been rooted to and strolled toward her. Porscha stepped backward until her hip hit the mirrored cabinet behind her. There was no place for her to run. "And seeing you up close and in person, I'm certain of it."

"You don't know what you're talking about."

"Maybe, but I don't think so," Xavier responded. "I haven't seen you date often over the last three years."

Porscha snorted. "Unlike you, who's been seen with lots of women."

Xavier smiled. "So you've been following me, huh?"

Porscha tossed her mane of jet-black curls over her shoulder. "Not really."

"Liar." He took a step toward her.

Porscha wanted to push him backward away from her, to batter his shoulders, but deep down she didn't want to.

So when he reached out and tunneled his hand through her hair, bringing her closer, she let him. He lowered his head and when she was inches away from his face, he said, "Tell me you don't want this." His tone was deep, smoky and sexy, causing a shiver to course down her spine.

Within seconds, she reached up and pulled him down toward her. Their mouths came together in an explosive kiss that sent a shock wave of lust through her body.

They kissed and kissed and kissed. Porscha tried to stay in the present, but the past merged with the present, flooding her with memories of how insatiable she'd once been for this man.

She refused to moan at the bliss of his kiss, but he tasted divine. When he used his tongue to lick across the seam of her lips, she opened to the demanding thrust of his tongue, relishing the erotic play. Xavier's lips were firm yet gentle, teasing hers until she gasped and whimpered, clinging to him. How was it that just one kiss from this man could make her frenzied with need? She could feel the place between her legs swell to life and moisten with excitement.

When Xavier pulled away, a craving for more built inside her. "Are we over, Porscha?" He looked down into her passion-glazed eyes and there was only one answer she could give.

No.

One

Six months later

"So nice of you to join us, Xavier," Vincent Chandler, the producer of Atlanta Sports Night, said when Xavier strolled into the rundown meeting on Monday, wearing a royal blue T-shirt and dark-washed jeans.

Xavier glanced down at his Rolex. "I'm sorry, am I late? The meeting is always at ten."

"I pushed it forward to nine thirty," Vincent responded. "And you'd know that if you looked at your texts."

Xavier rolled his eyes. He didn't need Vincent busting his chops. He'd come a long way the last few years from the rookie he'd been when he first joined the show. It had taken him some time to find his footing. He was used to playing football, not commenting on it.

"Sorry," he shrugged and sat beside Marcus Elliot, his partner in crime on their show.

"Long night?" Marcus asked.

"You could say that," Xavier replied. He'd stayed up with a certain graceful R and B singer.

"In addition to your commentating," Vincent was saying, "we'd like you to do an in-depth interview with De'Sean Jones."

"Why me?" Xavier inquired. He wasn't the most seasoned sportscaster on the network. In fact, he was considered by most to be wet behind the ears. Why would they give him an interview with De'Sean, the biggest draft pick of the year, instead of Marcus?

"Because you know what it's like to be in his shoes," Vincent replied. "You won a Heisman."

Don't remind me, Xavier thought.

He'd tried his best to put those glory days behind him, but Vincent wasn't making this easy. "I really think Marcus would be better suited." Xavier understood interviews like this would advance his career, but he didn't want to be reminded of the life he'd once had but never would again. Plus, Xavier still struggled with whether sportscasting was the right place for him. Had he merely done his father's bidding?

"The network would like to switch things up a bit," Vincent explained. "They'd like to see a fresh perspective, and since you've lived a day in the life, we think you're the perfect candidate."

"I doubt that." Xavier laughed dryly.

"It wasn't a request," Vincent replied.

Xavier turned and glowered at him. Vincent had had it out for him since the moment he arrived at ASN. He'd heard rumors it had something to do with the fact Vincent had a commentator already picked but had been pushed to give Xavier the position because Xavier's father had an existing relationship with the head of ASN.

"Fine. Where and when?" Xavier asked.

Later, once Xavier made it back to his cubicle, Marcus stopped by. "Don't worry about anything, X. I've got you covered. I've done plenty of interviews."

"I know, but it should have been you," Xavier said, leaning back in his chair to regard him.

Marcus shrugged and leaned against the cubicle wall. "These things happen."

"It's not fair. You've done a lot to build this network." Xavier believed in paying your dues before you got your big break, like he'd done on the football field. But this world was much different than being on the field.

"That may be true. But if you want staying power in this business, you don't want to ruffle any feathers and you've got to know how to play the game. The network likes you. Leverage it to work in your favor."

After Marcus left, Xavier thought about his advice. Perhaps he was going about this all wrong. He'd always been bitter about his father helping him get the job. He didn't need anyone to fight his battles, but now that Xavier was in the driver's seat with the network, he could use them to raise his profile and garner support for his charity work. ASN had better get ready because things were about to change.

"Yes, like that, Porscha." The photographer gave her direction, and she dutifully angled her face into the flow of the air gushing from the wind machine, so her mane of sable hair wafted in a cloud around her. "Okay, give me sexy. A little more pout."

Porscha leaned in and tried to ignore her irritation

and discomfort at how many times she had her makeup retouched and hair teased. She moved as she was told to move. She was a canvas for others to paint their vision of how they saw her. It was all part of the process. The photo shoot was for the soundtrack album cover for her new film with Ryan Mills. No doubt her face would be splashed across every magazine cover in the United States and beyond once the movie was released, because Ryan was extremely popular.

To get in the mood, Porscha daydreamed about Xavier and how he'd taken her up against the wall the night before. She'd been helpless to resist the raw, animal magnetism oozing from his every pore. She'd reveled in his powerfully naked body and the way he could extract every bit of pleasure from hers.

"Oh, yes, you've got it, Porscha. Just like that!"

After a half hour, the photo shoot ended and her personal assistant, Erin Connell, came by with a robe and wrapped it around Porscha's shoulders. "Thank you," Porscha said.

Erin was an affable young woman of average height, with fiery red hair and a sprinkling of freckles over her pale skin. She'd applied for the job as Porscha's assistant after graduating from UCLA with a degree in marketing. Her hope was to make it in the entertainment business someday, but initially she'd found it hard to get a job. Porscha had liked her immediately and hired her after the background check.

"You did great out there," her mother said from the sidelines.

"Thanks," Porscha replied as she walked toward the dressing room.

Ever since she and Xavier had picked up their affair again, she had been doing double duty flying between Atlanta and Los Angeles. She told her mother it was because of the soundtrack. That was partly true. At her request, the label had found a great producer in Atlanta to work on the soundtrack album, but that had ended a couple of months ago. She was doing the photo shoot here because of Xavier—because she couldn't get enough of him.

"What's next?" Porscha asked, glancing in her assistant's direction.

"You have an appearance at a radio station and that's it," Erin replied, leading Porscha to her dressing room.

Once there, Porscha stripped off her robe, even though her mother, Erin, Rachel Simone, her wardrobe stylist, and Kristen Love, her hair and makeup artist, were all in the room. She'd long ago given up any pretense of privacy in her world. These people were her glam squad, the team who ensured she always looked good. After her sophomore slump, Porscha refused to have any more unflattering photos of her published. It was why she never went in public without looking her best.

"Have you found a dress for the BET Awards?" Porscha asked, looking over at Rachel. She would be making an appearance on the awards show, the first of many appearances on the awards show circuit before the Grammys.

"No, but I will have a rack of options for you in a few days," Rachel replied. The blue-eyed blonde had a killer taste in fashion. Rachel usually dressed in designer clothes that would have seemed dowdy on Porscha, but on Rachel looked like she'd just come off the runway.

"Let's not leave it too late," Diane said, typing on her phone. "We want Porscha's ensemble to be talked about."

"Absolutely, Ms. Childs." Rachel knew her mother's lofty standards.

"But it's not the be-all and end-all," Porscha stated as Rachel helped her change into her street clothes.

Porscha was more concerned about her performance in her first film. She knew a lot of famous actresses had wanted the role, but in the end the director had chosen Porscha, an unproven talent, as the leading lady. As a result, she'd taken acting lessons because she was desperate to nail the story.

"Are you worried about the movie?" her mother inquired.

"Of course, Mama. It's my first. What if the critics think I'm terrible?"

Porscha had a love-hate relationship with the press. She considered the negativity part of the reason why she'd gone into a depression.

"I think you're doing fabulous."

Porscha laughed. "You have to say that. You're my mother."

"I agree with Diane," Erin interjected. "Your acting shows just the right amount of vulnerability."

"But we have to keep you in the spotlight," her mother continued. "This film could do for you what *The Bodyguard* did for Whitney Houston."

"Those are mighty big shoes to fill. I doubt anyone could," Porscha responded.

"Don't be defeatist. I didn't raise you to give up. You have to continue to elevate your game."

"How many more levels are in this game?" Porscha sighed. "I'm exhausted. I feel like I'm in a never-ending game of Super Mario Brothers. When does it end?"

"When you stop being relevant," her mother replied. "When people stop buying your music. Baby girl, your third album, *Metamorphosis*, revitalized your career. And now you have the soundtrack. You must ride the wave.

It's why Maybelline and L'Oréal came running and we have your new fragrance coming out next year. We need your brand diversified so if one part of your career slows, you have another to keep you afloat."

Porscha wondered if she meant keep *Diane Childs* afloat. Ever since her mother had discovered she could sing, it had been Porscha who kept the lights on and the rent paid once her father's financial support began to wane after he had other children. When she won prize money, it went to the coffers to take care of her, Diane said. But Porscha rarely saw any until she'd turned eighteen. That was when, with the help of the record label, she'd gotten an attorney and hashed out a manager contract with her mother.

Diane hadn't been happy about it, but Porscha was tired of working her butt off and seeing very little reward. Now she knew where her money went without having to ask for a handout whenever she wanted to buy something.

"Can you have the car brought around?" Porscha asked Erin.

"Already done. I anticipated you wanted to get out of Dodge."

She most certainly did. She was in the mood to burn off some steam with her secret lover. She hoped he was up for it, because she had a lot of tension to get rid of.

"So how is the wedding planning coming?" Xavier asked Giana when he stopped by her and Wynn's home later that evening.

Eventually, his sister had gotten her man. She not only convinced Wynn Starks to sign a contract with the Cougars allowing the team to represent his sports drinks company, but while they were sparring over business, the two had fallen madly in love. After they'd gotten engaged on New Year's Eve, Giana had moved straight out of the Lockett family guesthouse and into Wynn's place. Luckily, he lived in Tuxedo Park, keeping Giana as the only girl child nearby their mother, who was practically giddy with excitement at finally having a wedding to plan. Both Xavier's brothers had put the cart before the horse. Their brides had been expecting when they put a ring on it and they'd both held small weddings.

"Xavier, Mama is driving me crazy," Giana said. "She wants it to be the wedding of the year." She used her hands to make air quotes. "You would think she would never get another opportunity. There's still you."

Xavier snorted. "Don't go talking blasphemy, Gigi. I'm content with my life."

Giana cocked her head to stare at him. "Are you really, Xavier? You've been seeing someone secretly for months. You don't want more?" His sister had discovered their affair when he'd come back to the family mansion late one night a few months ago.

"No," he lied. Although he wasn't looking for commitment, he wouldn't mind taking Porscha out on an official date—to a nice dinner or maybe even a movie—but she wasn't the average woman he dated. Porscha was a celebrity and with that came another set of rules. He understood why she wanted to keep their relationship a secret and avoid speculation. The last six months, he'd done things her way, and he'd enjoyed their trysts. The passion between them was off the charts.

"I don't believe you, Xavier," Giana said. "But I'm not going to push. I wasn't looking for love when Wynn came around. I just wanted the Atlanta Cougars to represent his sports drink LEAN."

"Well, you got your man," Xavier stated. "Just like you said you would."

A large grin spread across his sister's lips. "Yes, I did, and I couldn't be happier, but Wynn didn't make it easy."

"No, he didn't."

Xavier recalled how Wynn had flipped when he saw Giana meeting with his competitor Blaine Smith last December. He'd accused Giana of using their relationship as a way to get closer to him and instantly regretted his lack of trust in her. Eventually, he'd recruited Xavier's help to win his sister back.

It had worked.

"Are you happy, Xavier?" Giana inquired, regarding him. "And I don't mean with your secret lover because I can read between the lines."

Xavier shrugged. "What do you want me to say, Gigi? Nothing is ever going to replace football."

"Maybe instead of pushing it away, you should embrace it."

"C'mon, don't tell me you're on Dad's side and think I should coach the team?"

"That's not what I'm suggesting."

"Then what?" His family knew his feelings on the subject. He was never going to be the Xavier they remembered. Playing football had given him a purpose, and although he'd found an alternate life as a sportscaster, it wasn't the same. He'd *lived* to play the game.

"Don't get defensive, Xavier," Giana responded. "I was merely going to suggest you consider coming back to the Atlanta Cougars as a mentor to some of the younger players."

"A mentor?" The thought had never crossed his mind.

"Yes. You know what it's like to be in their shoes and the struggles they face in this business. You could give them advice on the pitfalls. And who knows, it could help you and them. What do you say?"

Xavier was about to say no, but Giana interrupted him. "And before you nix the idea, mull it over."

"I'll think about it."

"Why am I not convinced? I thought being at the clinic had brought you some peace."

"I wouldn't say that, but it helped me accept the things I couldn't change. Accept my limitations."

"You're only limited here—" Giana pointed to her temple "—if you let yourself be."

After he left Giana's, Xavier wondered if she was right, and he wasn't giving himself enough credit. Being a sports commentator left him a lot of free time, which he usually spent in the gym or helping the many charities at the Lockett Foundation.

He especially enjoyed the foundation's work with local and African orphanages to help ensure kids got the absolute best out of life, from the basics like food, clothing and shelter to an education. Xavier recognized how fortunate he was to come from privilege and never wanted to take it for granted. It was why he sat on the board of the foundation: he wanted to make a difference.

His mother had been proud when one of her children took up her charitable efforts, because his siblings had other focuses.

Roman and Giana were all about Atlanta Cougars business while Julian, as a sports doctor, took care of the players. But Xavier wanted to do more. During his brief time as the star quarterback, he'd donated half his earnings to charity. That hadn't changed once he became a sports commentator. His agent had helped secure a salary in the millions, which allowed him to continue his efforts.

Xavier was on his way home when his phone buzzed. Glancing down, he saw it was Porscha. "Hello?"

"Hi, it's me. Are you busy?" Porscha's silky voice asked from the other end of the line.

"No, I just left Giana's and was on my way home."

"I was hoping we could meet at our spot," she said. "It's been a tough day and I need a release."

Xavier laughed. "I can be there in twenty."

"Great, I'll see you soon." She was off the phone before he could say goodbye.

Twenty minutes later, he was pulling his Porsche convertible up to the gate. He'd recruited his good friend John Summers, who'd sold Roman his house last year, to find them a secret hideaway. And John had come through. The location was in an upper-class neighborhood with complete privacy and security. Xavier walked up the paved driveway and punched in the code and the door opened.

Flicking on the light, he quickly used the alarm code she'd given him to turn off the security system. He glanced around the house, which was tastefully decorated in beige and earth tones. He walked inside and made himself comfortable in the nicely appointed kitchen, complete with a small bar in a nook near the living room. He found his favorite Scotch and prepared a drink while he waited for Porscha.

In most of his relationships, Xavier set the pace. This time, however, Porscha wanted to be in charge, and he'd accepted it because she awakened a ferocious lust he hadn't felt with other women.

He didn't have to wait long for her arrival. Within a half hour, he saw lights in the driveway, and seconds later, Porscha walked through the front door.

"Can you wait out here, Jose?"

"Absolutely, ma'am," he heard a male voice say.

Porscha came toward him dressed in a sexy gold mesh

top that showed off her round breasts, a fringed miniskirt that barely covered her bottom, and some high-heeled booties showing off her shapely legs. She looked hot.

"Wow!" Xavier couldn't stop ogling.

She grinned, spinning around. "I'm glad you approve, but this getup was entirely for my mother's benefit, to make her believe I was going out with friends instead of my real agenda, which was coming here."

"I take it she wouldn't approve?"

"I don't care if she approves or not. I'm here because I want to be." She reached behind her, and to his surprise the mesh top she'd been wearing fell to the floor, revealing her bare bosom underneath.

Xavier swore.

He closed the gap between them with slow but sure steps, fixing her with a heated stare. Her nipples beaded as he approached. He cupped the small weight of her swelling breasts, thumbed the cresting peaks, and then lowered his head to feast on one stiff nipple. Porscha threw her head back and let him take his fill. He tugged and suckled her steadily until her back arched.

He finally lifted his head and said, "Do you know how beautiful you are?"

She smiled at his praise. "You don't have to say that."

His finger traced her lower lip. "Don't doubt it. Because you are." Her eyelids lowered. Xavier remembered Porscha's insecurities about her body, but she was perfect in every way to him, and he would remind her tonight and any other night she let him.

He dropped to his knees and pulled down the miniskirt and the scarlet thong in one fell swoop. He looked up at her as he cupped her bare bottom. "Missed me?"

"Yes," she croaked. Her eyes were glazed with passion because she matched his ardor.

"Let's see how much," Xavier replied and put one of her legs over his shoulders. "I can't wait to taste you." Then he lowered his head so he could reacquaint himself with the place between her thighs.

"Ohmigod!" Porscha let out a loud sigh and clung to Xavier's shoulders for support. Her daydreams about how good the sex with Xavier was didn't do the man justice. There was no thought of shyness or self-consciousness. Instead, she abandoned herself completely to every stroke of Xavier's tongue and fingers inside her wet heat. Teasing, licking, flicking and swirling, Xavier brought her to the edge using all the skills she'd never been able to forget.

He made her cross boundaries she never would have before—like coming to this house so scantily clad. If she had her way, she'd dress in sweats, but the music business required she show off more skin than she was comfortable with. But Xavier always exulted in her body and made her want to show off the progress she'd made. Since leaving Colorado, she'd gotten to her target weight that was managed by a personal chef who ensured she ate a balanced diet and a trainer who had her on a rigorous exercise regime.

And now she could feel comfortable with the man who gave her powerful orgasms.

"Xavier!" She cried his name when her climax struck, trembling and quaking as she came face-to-face with the oblivion she craved. Gazing down at him, she saw a smoky, sensual pride gleaming in his brown eyes.

"Are you ready for round two?" Xavier inquired.

Before she could answer, he rose and swept her lethargic body into his arms and headed to the bedroom.

He strode down the hall with her in his arms as if

she weighed nothing. Then he was pressing her down onto the coverlet of the master bed, drawing it back so he could lay her on the cool sheets. Porscha watched with amazement as Xavier stripped off his clothes and sheathed himself. His desire for her was blatant and she welcomed it; she couldn't wait to run her palms across his smooth and muscled torso. And when he joined her on the bed, she did exactly that.

When he flattened her breasts against his hard chest, she ran her hands over his back, glorying in its muscled strength. She loved his full build, broad shoulders and ample behind. She reached behind him to grip his butt, bringing them skin to skin. "I need you inside me, *now*," she moaned and opened her thighs wider. "Please, give me what I want."

"I'm happy to oblige." He leaned over her and pushed his body into hers in one sure, swift stroke. Porscha undulated beneath him, and Xavier's hips rocked as he settled into a fast, hard rhythm that she eagerly matched.

He pressed a kiss to the side of her neck and began taking nips of her earlobe. Porscha shuddered as passion and pleasure rushed through her. "Oh, yes, like that!"

Xavier fought to regain control as Porscha took him deeper inside her. He was large, but her muscles clamped around him, milking him and drawing him in fully.

His release was so close, but it was too soon. He wanted to draw out the moment, but his skin was rippling with goose bumps. He slipped his hand down between them to delve inside her wet heat and Porscha gave a high-pitched cry of pleasure. Xavier closed his eyes as shock waves coursed through her and detonated inside of him, sucking his last vestige of control. He gripped her tightly and began pumping hard.

Porscha's body welcomed his and when she squeezed his butt and locked her legs around his hips, it was over. He took her mouth in a hard, deep kiss, swallowing her cries as another round of tremors erupted through her. Only then did he surrender and tumble over the edge of the world, with Porscha around him cushioning him as he fell.

They stayed together like that in each other's arms until eventually she drifted off to sleep. That was when Xavier rose from the bed and headed to the shower. He and Porscha never spent the night together.

Her rules.

Not his.

They'd fallen fast and quick their first time around and neither of them was eager for a repeat performance. Porscha didn't trust him, had believed the worst of him, and that hurt more than he'd ever let on. Xavier was willing to continue their physical relationship because they were compatible in bed, but he refused to go deeper for fear that if he wasn't careful, he would fall headlong into disaster again with this woman, and his heart couldn't take another beating. He kept Porscha at arm's length just like she wanted, and in so doing, he protected his heart.

Two

"Good morning, Ma," Xavier said when he came to the breakfast table the next morning, wearing a T-shirt and sweatpants. She was in the morning room alone drinking a cup of coffee while perusing the news on her tablet.

He lived at home with his parents in the separate wing of the house. When he'd been the Cougars quarterback and always on the road, Xavier hadn't seen the need for his own place. And after the injury, he'd been depressed, and having family nearby helped. He didn't have to cook or clean for himself and generally his parents left him to his own devices. Plus with his siblings hitched, his mother loved having one of her children nearby so she could be a mother hen.

"Good morning. Did you sleep well?" Angelique Lockett was an ageless beauty with a peanut butter complexion and light brown eyes. She looked flawless in slender slacks and a flowery tunic. Her normally shoulder-length jet-black hair was in a carefully blown, sleek chignon.

"Yes, I did." Xavier had been exhausted by last night's extracurricular activities. When he finally came home, he'd passed out.

"What do you have planned for today?" his mother asked. Since it was off-season now for football, his agent wanted him to meet with several networks about coming on board as a game analyst for other sports. And Xavier intended to, but he was more interested in his charitable projects.

"I hope it's coming to the stadium to talk to the head coach, John Russell," his father said, walking into the room before Xavier could get a word in edgewise. "It's not too late to get you in for next season."

"C'mon, Dad. I told you I don't want a coaching position."

"It's only because you're afraid to get back in the saddle. You need to get over your fear."

"Stop it!" Xavier shouted, slamming his palm against the table and causing the dishes on top to rattle. "Can't I enjoy my breakfast in peace? If that's not possible, I'll happily move out. I've stayed here much too long anyway. With Giana gone, it's not the same." He hadn't felt the need to leave before, but the longer he and Porscha continued their fling, the more he realized he needed his own space.

"Darling, no!" His mother leaned over and touched his hand. "Please don't go." She scowled at his father. "We don't want you to. Do we, Josiah?"

His father rolled his eyes and reached for the coffee carafe to pour himself a cup of joe. "The boy is a grown man, Angie. If he wants to move out, let him. He's not your baby boy anymore."

"He'll always be my baby." His mother smiled in Xavier's direction. "Even when you're old and gray."

Xavier appreciated his mother trying to lighten the mood, but it was time for him to move on. "How about this? I'll move into the guesthouse. In the meantime, I'm heading to the Lockett Foundation. I'm meeting with the director of the youth complex we're building for after-school athletic programs and summer camps."

The foundation helped support several youth organizations within the Atlanta community by providing new uniforms and athletic equipment to underprivileged kids, but the complex they'd just built was a huge win for the community.

"I'm so proud of you, Xavier. You're the only one of my children who's taken up the baton with the foundation," his mother replied.

"Thanks, Ma." Xavier kissed her cheek and made a swift exit. He needed to leave before his father continued to press him about coming on as an assistant coach with the Atlanta Cougars. Once again, Josiah was trying to tell him what to do. He probably felt entitled because all his life Xavier had followed the path his father laid out. Football. Football. And more football.

Those days, however, were over. Xavier was his own man now, with his own thoughts and ideas about the direction of his life. And when he was ready to make his next move, he would. But it wouldn't be because the great Josiah Lockett ordained it.

"Right this way," the announcer said as Porscha, her mom, Erin and the rest of her team walked down the hall toward the stage for the Lois Howard talk show several days later in New York.

In between filming her new movie, Porscha had several appearances lined up to sing a popular hit off her third album. She was sitting down with Lois on her popular syndicated talk show for a Q and A. Since Lois was known for asking guests to dance, Porscha had made sure her ensemble—of an oversize, abstract-print blazer with a deep V cut and skinny capris with high-heeled booties—was not only chic and flattering to her figure, but nimble enough for her to do a few dance moves.

Once they arrived backstage, Kristen powdered her nose to take off any shine, but it was her mother who fiddled with her outfit, brushing off invisible lint and making sure not a hair was out of place. When her name was announced and the soft strands of one of her most popular ballads, "The One Who Loves You," came on, Porscha sashayed onstage.

Bright lights and a lone spotlight greeted Porscha along with an in-person studio audience, but she blocked it out of her mind. Instead, she focused on the beautiful lyrics, letting the music take her along the journey. The song started off slow and quiet, allowing her to look at the audience and connect with them. But as the melody grew stronger and the song came to its crescendo, so did Porscha's voice. She opened her arms, sweeping them wide as the note climbed with the music.

Her eyes closed as she sang the last refrains of the song. When she opened them and looked out over the audience, she saw tears in the eyes of several people right before she bowed.

Applause erupted.

The cameras cut to a commercial break.

Lois, holding several index cards in her hand, came out to greet Porscha. "That was amazing!" Her platinum blonde hair was neatly pulled back into a ponytail, and she wore a simple white silk blouse, black slacks and low heels.

Porscha beamed with pride. "Thank you."

"No, seriously, your voice is like warm syrup over pancakes," Lois responded.

Porscha laughed. "I don't think I've ever been described that way. Do you mind if I powder my nose?"

"No, of course not. We'll be back in five minutes."

Porscha rushed off the stage and found her mother and Kristen waiting to touch up her makeup and fix her hair.

"That was great, Porscha, really," her mother said. "Though next time, I would like to see you hold that last note just a bit longer, you know, milk the crowd for all their worth."

Porscha narrowed her eyes. Her mother wasn't a singer, but she certainly could be critical of a skill she'd never acquired. "Thanks, I'll remember that."

After a quick brush of powder, she was back on set with the talk show host. Lois was funny and charming, and Porscha could see why her show was popular around the globe. "How's the filming of your new movie with Ryan Mills going?" Lois inquired.

"It's fantastic," Porscha gushed. "To work with someone of his caliber is wonderful, especially for my first film."

"Were you nervous when you first met him?"

Porscha knew exactly what to do. She had to stroke her costar's ego. He'd been voted Sexiest Man Alive by People *twice* in the last decade. "Oh, absolutely! I'm his biggest fan!"

When the time came, Lois didn't hesitate to ask Porscha to show one of her best dance moves and she was ready. Porscha knew her limitations. She was no dancer, but she executed a few shakes and wiggles of her hips that she'd practiced with her choreographer. It appeased Lois and before she knew it, the interview was over.

"Everyone, let's give Porscha Childs a big thank-you for coming on the show," Lois said, clapping her hands.

The audience not only gave her a roaring applause, but a standing ovation as well. Porscha was humbled. It felt great to be on top again. She'd taken it for granted with her first album, thinking the public's goodwill would last forever. It had been humiliating when her sophomore album bombed. The press hadn't been kind. In fact, they'd been downright brutal about the weight she had gained with her depression and grief over losing her father.

Once offstage, Porscha didn't go back to the green room but followed her mother and Erin toward the rear exit, where a car was waiting outside. She saw a crowd of fans had gathered to see her. Many of them were holding up posters with her picture and the magazine she'd recently been featured on.

"Porscha, you don't have time for this," her mother whispered in her ear.

"Yes, I do," Porscha hissed, pulling away. "They're my fans." With a smile on her face, she walked over to the group, and her bodyguard Jose joined her.

"Ohmigod, I love you, Porscha!" a young man gushed when she approached. "Can I have a picture?"

"Sure." Porscha leaned in for a quick selfie. Then she autographed several more photos and a magazine before waving and heading back to the car.

Jose held open the door and Porscha slid inside. Her mother was waiting for her but didn't harangue. She pivoted to a new topic. "Great interview, Porscha. The media ate up how you gushed over Ryan."

Porscha frowned. "I didn't gush."

Her mother shrugged as she looked down at her phone. "Doesn't matter. An audience member already tweeted about it and there's speculation that the two of you are an item."

"They got all of that from me saying I'm a huge fan of Ryan's?" Porscha rolled her eyes upward. "That's crazy."

They arrived at the popular NYC hotel where they were staying, and once again, she was greeted by a flock of paparazzi and fans. Reaching inside her bag for her compact, Porscha checked her face and hair one more time before exiting the vehicle.

She smiled in front of the cameras, but Porscha wondered if anyone ever really saw her. The *real* her. Certainly not her mother, who was only interested in the image Porscha presented to the world and how it affected their pocketbook. Once her mother realized she had talent at an early age, she'd pushed Porscha to ensure her daughter would live up to *her* wildest dreams. The only one who had ever seemed to really want to get to know Porscha was Xavier.

Porscha walked into the hotel in a daze and thought back to when they had been at the clinic. She'd let Xavier in, allowed him to see the real her without all the trappings. And she didn't mean just hair or makeup, though back then she had taken out her weave and worn her hair in its natural state. But more than that, she'd shared her fears and dreams and he'd listened. For the first time in a long time, she thought someone cared about her.

That was why it hurt when he'd indicated that they were friends and nothing more. He devalued their relationship and it had wounded not only her heart, but her pride. She'd vowed never to give a man that kind of power over her again, especially after what happened with her ex-boyfriend Gil Harris. Six years ago, she'd foolishly believed Gil cared for her, too, but he'd only been using her for fame and fortune. As soon as a big payday came, he'd dropped Porscha like a hot potato. She'd been heartbroken and looked like a fool to the world after talking about how madly in love with him she was.

Xavier's reemergence in her life threw her. She'd wanted to act as if she didn't care, but the passion she felt for him was still there. And when he kissed her, she'd been as lost as she had been three years ago. She'd fallen in love with him then, but her feelings were not returned. This time, she'd told herself that if they had a fling, she could rid herself of the long-buried feelings she had for him.

That had been six months ago.

She was no closer to figuring out where her emotions stood. Instead, whenever she felt herself spinning out of control and needing an anchor, she called Xavier. She could talk to him about anything, and he listened. *Had she gotten it wrong all those years ago?*

No, no, this was a fool's mission. She was going down the same road and expecting a different result. Sure, he talked to her on the phone, but in all the times they'd been intimate, not once had Xavier mentioned wanting more than sex. He played up his single lifestyle in his social media. What was she supposed to think? She had to stop yearning for something she would never have and focus on her career, because it was all she had.

"You really have a knack for this, Xavier," Andrew Chapman, director of the Lockett Foundation, stated once the room cleared out of their weekly meeting that afternoon.

"I'm really passionate about what we do here."

Ever since Xavier was a high school senior and had gone to an away game and seen the conditions other teams played in, he'd wanted to make a difference. Once he'd been drafted, Xavier realized his platform could help further causes he was interested in. He used part of his earnings to support those charities. And after he discussed it with his mother, she'd agreed the foundation would help with his efforts.

"We are certainly lucky to have you," Andrew said. "I have to head into another meeting, but I'll talk to you later."

Xavier nodded. He was on his way to his office when he decided to make a U-turn and head to the medical clinic on the lower level of the foundation's offices. Usually, Julian volunteered there during the off-season.

Opening the clinic door, he found his brother in the reception area, chatting with one of the staff members. "Xavier!" Julian smiled when he entered and came from around the counter to greet him. "What brings you to this neck of the woods?"

"Can't I come see my brother?"

"Of course, but you don't usually come down to interact with the lower rung of the family."

Xavier laughed, ignoring Julian's dig, and gave him a hug. "How's it going?"

"I saw a few patients earlier, but it's been a slow day."

"Care to take a walk?"

"Of course." Julian turned and glanced back at the receptionist. "Call me if you need me."

"Sure thing, boss," she replied, giving him a salute.

Julian followed Xavier down the hall. They were both silent until they were out of earshot of others and outside walking the grounds.

"What's on your mind?" Julian asked.

"Dad. He keeps pushing me to join the coaching staff."

"I thought that was a moot point. You said no."

"I did. I refuse to let Dad run roughshod over me. He's always pushed me, you know?"

"He did that to all of us, Xavier," Julian responded, sitting on a nearby bench. "When he wasn't putting a football in your hand, he was placing Roman as an intern with the Cougars and making sure he learned the business from the ground up. After Rome, I was next, but I didn't fit the mold of the son he envisioned. I was always more Mama's child, into arts and culture."

"How did you handle that?" Xavier joined him on the bench.

"I rebelled. I did things just to spite Josiah. But did that stop him? No, if I wasn't going to play ball, I was going into sports medicine. He was determined I have a role with the organization. And surprisingly, I found I enjoyed it. I could help the players and still not feel like an outsider in my own family."

"You felt like an outcast?"

Julian laughed. "Now, there's the understatement of the year, but this isn't about me. I made my peace with Josiah, and we live in a comfortable truce. Now that I have Elyse, I don't sweat the small stuff anymore. But you, you've always been the apple of his eye."

"That's the problem, Julian. It's hard to live up to this idealized version Dad has in his mind of me. I'm never going to be a quarterback again."

"True, but you are gifted, Xavier. You always have been. Whenever they put that football in your hand, you knew exactly what to do with it. You shouldn't sell yourself short."

"I don't do that."

"Yes, you do. Look at what you've done with the Lockett Foundation."

"I couldn't mope forever," Xavier responded. Giving back to those less fortunate helped put his position in perspective. He was young, in relatively good health, and had a lifetime ahead of him. So what if he walked with a slight limp? "I've learned not to let football define me, and

I'm afraid if I go back, it will suck me into this vortex of negativity because I can't get out there and play myself."

Julian nodded. "I can see where that would give you pause. But sometimes helping others is its own reward."

"Agreed. I've decided to step my foot back into the organization and take Giana up on her offer to mentor some of the younger players."

"That's fantastic! I'm sure she'll be pleased."

"I'm not doing it for her."

Xavier was doing it for himself, because he suspected it would help him move forward to recapturing the man he used to be.

"How did it go today?" Xavier asked Porscha later that night as she lay in her New York hotel room. Somehow this had become their routine when they were apart, or she was on the road. They would call each other and talk for hours about everything and nothing. Sometimes the calls were naughty, which was why Porscha was in a baby doll nightie right now.

"The song went fantastic, and Lois was wonderful. She made me feel at ease, so I was able to talk about my music."

"I know how much that means to you."

"Sometimes I think my mom forgets that at the end of the day all I have ever wanted to do is sing. All she talks about is my brand and expanding my reach. I mean this acting thing, it wasn't my idea, you know?"

"Then why don't you speak up? Tell her how you feel?"

Because Porscha was afraid. She knew how much her success meant to her mother. She'd sacrificed a lot to ensure Porscha had everything she needed to achieve her dream. But how long did Porscha have to pay the debt?

"I don't know," Porscha said. "She's done so much for me."

"Yeah, but you don't owe her your entire life. It's up to you to choose what's best for you."

"I don't see you putting your foot down and telling Josiah in no uncertain terms that you don't want to coach," Porscha countered defensively.

"Are you trying to start a fight, Porscha?" His curt voice lashed at her. "Because this wasn't about me."

"No, I'm not spoiling for an argument," she sighed. "But I'm also pointing out what we share in common. Two domineering parents who think they know what's best for us."

"*We* have to put them in their place."

"And how's that working for you?" Porscha inquired.

"No better than you," Xavier admitted honestly, and she appreciated he wasn't afraid of speaking his truth. "But at least I have my work at the foundation. I love what I do there. If I were to go to back to football, it would take away from my charity work."

"*You* have to decide what's more important to you, Xavier. Don't try to fit yourself into the image others have of you and deny who or what you've become. Our therapy taught us to face our fears and that's what you have to do."

They ended the call soon after, with Xavier still being miffed by her words, but Porscha refused to take them back. She knew it was unfair. She talked a good game, but could she heed her own advice? Could she stand up to her mother and tell her what *she* wanted and how *she* wanted to run her career? The task seemed daunting, so the little girl within pulled the covers over her head and fell asleep.

Three

"I have to say I'm not surprised," Giana said when Xavier strolled into the Atlanta Cougars managers meeting in the corporate headquarters conference room on Monday morning in a shirt and tie. He was fifteen minutes early.

He needed the extra time to deal with coming to the corporate headquarters. Xavier hadn't been back here since the injury that ended his career, but he had to face his own demons. And when he'd walked the halls just now, it felt like coming home, but it was also bittersweet because he was a visitor instead of a player.

This place had felt more like home than the family mansion in Tuxedo Park. He'd grown up here. From practicing as a teen in the youth camps to eventually running plays as a quarterback, it was part of his DNA. But he'd turned his back on it the last few years. He had to for his own self-preservation—until he could come to terms with the fact he'd never play ball again.

"Don't be smug," Xavier finally said, sitting by her side at the table.

"Why not?" Giana quirked a brow and glanced sideways at him. "I can't bask in the win? I told you mentoring was a promising idea and now everyone else will know it, too."

"Know what?" Roman asked, coming into the room. "What'd I miss?" He looked every bit the role of general manager in a bespoke navy suit with a blue-and-silver-striped tie. His smooth chocolate skin was similar to Giana's, but he had an expertly shorn beard.

"That Xavier is coming back to the team," Giana replied.

"In a limited capacity," Xavier added. He didn't want his family to put the cart before the horse. He'd thought long and hard about the advice Julian and Porscha gave him. And at the end of the day, he realized that helping others was something he did well. If he could offer new Cougars players some sound wisdom, he would.

"Nonetheless, we're happy to see you here, little brother," Roman said with a grin.

And looking into his brother's ebony eyes, Xavier believed him. Rome had been raised to be heir apparent and the role suited him, but he'd never hung it over any of their heads or made his siblings feel less than. He always played fair, which made him a great leader.

The rest of the department heads eventually trickled in, but their father wasn't one of them. Xavier was surprised the old man was actually letting go of the reins as he'd promised. It had been a source of friction between him and Roman last year, but their father had stepped down as general manager. Now Roman was running the show and Giana was his number two.

His brother got the meeting underway, and he and Giana spoke about what was coming next in the off-season. They'd had a successful scouting combine a few weeks ago and had their eyes on a few players who performed at top physical and mental condition. There was a lot of talk of the draft this month and what it would take to secure the players they needed.

Xavier was amazed. He'd never been privy to the behind-the-scenes of how football teams recruited players because he'd been on the field. There was a lot of wheeling and dealing, and Roman and Giana were more than up to the task. Eventually the meeting agenda ventured to new business. Giana brought up the mentorship program. When she made the announcement that Xavier would lead the effort, there were loud whispers among the department heads. Xavier had steered clear of any role in the Cougars since he'd retired from being a quarterback. Eventually, it was the head coach, John Russell, who spoke up.

"Do you really think that's a good idea?" John asked.

"I think it's a mighty fine proposal, John," Roman said, and he would have gone further, but Xavier stood and faced all the naysayers in the room. Some of them knew how tough it had been for Xavier to walk away from the game. There had been rumors he'd gone to a rehab facility that specialized in more than just ensuring he could walk again. They probably wondered if he was the right person to mentor other players.

"All of you know me," Xavier started, glancing around the table. "You watched me grow up on the field. You saw my successes and my failures. And yes, when I failed, it was spectacular. But that's also why I'm uniquely qualified to talk to new players about the pitfalls of success and how to keep themselves healthy. If you're looking for a poster child of the perfect football player, you won't find it in me." He looked around the room. "But I can tell them how to get back up when they fall."

John stared at him for a long time. Xavier knew he understood because John had played football, too, and Xavier had been a huge fan. He'd watched John's reels on many occasions, hoping that one day he could live up to his legacy. And for a brief time, he had.

"Then I'm on board," John replied. "Welcome back, Xavier."

John had no idea how much his words of encouragement meant to Xavier. And he told him so later after the meeting wrapped.

"I think it's great," John added. "You have a lot of advice you can offer some of these players. But I'm curious what made you decide to come back now."

Xavier thought about a petite singer on the other side of the country. She'd given him the final push he needed when she'd asked how long he was going to continue to deny his passion.

"I got a little push."

Later that morning, Porscha sat obediently in her trailer on the film set and watched as her mother took the hash browns off her breakfast plate of egg whites, grilled tomato and grapefruit. She rolled her eyes. She hated when Diane clocked what she ate, but Porscha knew she had to stay off carbs. They were not her friend and went straight to her hips.

"'Forever Love' is getting great coverage," her mother said. "It's in heavy rotation on all the major radio stations. It's going to be as big a hit as 'My Heart Will Go On' was for Celine Dion."

Porscha grinned. "That's wonderful news."

"We have to continue to capitalize on the moment," her mother stated. "Between the soundtrack and this film, who knows? You could be up for an Oscar and a Grammy next year."

"You really think so?"

"Absolutely."

As a young girl, she'd wanted to win a Grammy, and later she had, with her first album, more than one, but her second album hadn't produced a Billboard hit. Luckily, she'd rebounded, and the record label's hope that lightning would strike twice had been fulfilled. Her third album was a critical success and garnered several top singles along with another two Grammys. Her single "Forever Love" for the film's soundtrack was poised to do even better. Porscha knew it the moment she'd heard the song, but an Oscar? She hadn't wanted to dream too big, but perhaps it was possible to have it all?

A knock sounded on her trailer door and the production assistant poked his head in. "Porscha, we're ready for you."

"Be right there." She smoothed down the dress she'd be wearing in the scene.

"Knock their socks off, Porscha," Erin said. Her assistant was always there to give Porscha a boost when she needed it.

"Thanks, Erin."

Her mother stayed behind because Porscha told her having her on set made Porscha nervous and she didn't want to flub her lines. Diane hadn't liked it—she always wanted to be in the thick of the action where her daughter was concerned, but Porscha had been adamant.

When she left the trailer, Porscha followed the production assistant over to the set. Ryan was already there and smiled as she approached. With his light brown skin, curly hair and neat goatee, Ryan was easy on the eyes. Porscha could see why he was considered a heartthrob. Although slightly under six feet, he boasted an athletic build.

"You ready for this?" Ryan asked, ignoring the person dabbing makeup on his face.

"Yes." Porscha put on a good front to belie the inner turmoil roiling her tummy. Although they'd been on set for several weeks, Porscha still got nervous when it was time to film. It might come easy for Ryan but acting was new to her.

"I want to thank you for the positive press," Ryan said with a grin. "I never knew you had such a crush on me."

Porscha laughed at his cockiness. "Don't go getting a big head. That was purely for show."

"Ouch. You mean to tell me you don't want to marry me and have my babies like the tabloids say?" he teased.

Porscha shook her head. "Afraid not."

He clutched his heart. "You've wounded me."

"Positions, everyone!" the director yelled.

Ryan rose from his chair and they both got on their markers, and soon the cameras were rolling. Porscha forgot about where she was and transported herself into the role of an aspiring singer who meets Ryan, a talent manager at a local nightclub. They fall in love as he helps her with her career, but he's killed tragically in a robbery. Her character finds a way to go on without him and make a success of herself because that was what he would have wanted.

"Cut!" the director yelled. "That was wonderful, Porscha. Really fantastic job. We'll take a fifteen-minute break and come back."

Porscha exited the soundstage and walked to Erin, who waited with her phone. "Thanks." She took the device and noticed she'd missed a text from Xavier.

Break a leg.

Xavier knew how hard acting was for her. Porscha searched for an empty room and stepped inside, closing the door. She leaned against it and took a deep, cleansing breath. She'd done it. It wasn't easy pretending that she knew what she was doing. She dialed Xavier.

"How was the scene?" he asked without preamble.

"Good. I was nervous, but it's getting easier."

"Told ya. You have nothing to worry about. You're a natural."

"You're biased," she responded. One evening, when she'd been in Atlanta, she'd been nervous about an upcoming scene and Xavier had offered to run lines with her. He'd been complimentary, but Porscha wasn't sure she could believe him. He was sleeping with her after all.

"Yeah, well, I know talent when I see it," Xavier shot back hotly.

"And you? Did you decide about the mentorship?" She was curious if Xavier had gone along with his sister's suggestion that he mentor the younger members of the Atlanta Cougars.

"I did."

"And? Don't make keep me in suspense."

"I said yes." She heard the smile in Xavier's voice, and it made her happy. She wanted that for him—wanted him to do what he was passionate about.

"I'm glad."

"Then perhaps you'll agree to help with a special project of mine?" Xavier asked. "I wasn't going to ask, but I need a favor. We had a local artist drop out of singing at the opening of the Lockett Foundation's new youth center and I need a replacement."

Porscha frowned. Why hadn't he asked *her* to perform first? She would have attended if her schedule permitted. That was what she didn't understand. Sometimes they acted like a couple, calling and texting each other, but other times, Xavier acted as if she didn't exist, like going elsewhere for talent when he could come to her.

"If it's too much trouble, I can ask someone else," Xavier said when she remained silent on the other end of the line.

"I can do it."

"You're upset with me?" Xavier asked, intuitively understanding her reluctance. "Because I didn't ask you first. I'm sorry, Porsch. I didn't want you to think you owed me anything because…because we're sleeping together."

"I would never think that. So next time, ask me. What's the date?"

"Friday. Are you free?"

"I have to be back on set Monday, but I'll make it work."

"Thanks, Porscha. The kids are going to be so excited."

"You know I would do anything for children," Porscha responded and ended the call. What she really wanted to say was that she'd do anything for Xavier, but they weren't in a place where they could say that to each other.

Never had been.

She'd defined the parameters of their affair and she

had to stick to the terms. Otherwise it would only confuse them both.

There was a knock. "Porscha, they are ready for you back on set," the production assistant said from the other side of the door.

Porscha opened the door. "Let's do it."

Xavier put the phone down on his desk. He got the distinct impression Porscha was miffed because he hadn't asked her first, to do the appearance. They didn't have that kind of relationship. He'd agreed to be Porscha's plaything on the side and because he wanted her, he'd accepted the terms.

He'd thought the chemistry between them would burn itself out like most of his relationships. Before Porscha, Xavier kept women at a distance because nothing could come between him and football, his first real love. So his dealings with the opposite sex were of the physical variety, and after a release, it was on to the next one. But then he met Porscha, and he lost his head. He could remember the first time they'd been together.

After taking a long walk together at the facility in Colorado, he'd taken a blanket from his room and spread it on the grass in a secluded spot. Then they'd undressed and he'd found everything he didn't know he'd been looking for. It made Xavier wonder if they could give this long-distance relationship a try even though he lived in Atlanta and she lived in Los Angeles.

However, when she overheard him at the clinic talking to another group member, she'd gotten it all wrong. He hadn't been about to share his confidence with the man or confirm or deny his assumptions. At the time, Porscha had been under a heavy amount of scrutiny. He would never kiss and tell, so he said they were friends and there was nothing between them.

Then he'd turned around and seen Porscha standing in his doorway. The hurt expression in her eyes told him she'd heard every word. Xavier tried to apologize, but all she could hear was that she didn't mean anything to him. She accused him of using her to get through his time at the clinic. Her words had been like acid because they hadn't been true. He'd retaliated by stating she used him for the orgasms he gave her. The moment he said the words Xavier had regretted them because Porscha stepped backward as if he'd struck her. It was a low blow and not in his nature, but once they were out there, he couldn't take them back.

Porscha told him they were over. She never wanted to see him and then she'd walked out of his life. Porscha Childs was one of Xavier's biggest regrets. *She* was the one who got away. Was that why, since his stint in the clinic, he'd become even more guarded? Every time a woman tried to get close, his walls came up. The closest Xavier had ever gotten to feeling he could love someone was with Porscha.

Which was why there was going to come a point when the two of them would have *the talk* and find out where they wanted this affair to go. But for now he would leave things as they were.

Four

"Porscha, the press is eating up this bit about you and Ryan," her mother said. "It hasn't died down. We really should be playing this up."

"But it's not true," Porscha returned. "We're not dating."

"Does it matter? Why are you fighting me on this?" her mother asked in the limo on the way to Xavier's grand opening event for his youth complex on Friday afternoon. "It would be great press for you."

The media were claiming she and Ryan were an item. For the last half hour since they landed at the airport, her mother had been suggesting Porscha go along with the story to boost her career. After her interview with Lois, the rumor had gained traction and was picked up by several national entertainment outlets.

"Is it because of your relationship with Xavier?"

Porscha had had to confide in her mother about her relationship with Xavier because she'd been relentless in wanting to know why they kept coming back to Atlanta and why Porscha was singing at some "random" youth complex. She wished she hadn't told her mother, because she harped on the fact Xavier wasn't as famous as Ryan.

She'd defended Xavier when her mother called him washed-up. Porscha explained his family were Atlanta royalty and owned the Atlanta Cougars, but Diane countered that he was a small fish. They'd gone round and round until her mother realized Porscha wasn't changing her mind and she'd better get used to Xavier being a fixture in her life.

But today, Diane Childs was in rare form. She wanted Porscha to go out on a date with Ryan to fuel the gossip flames and hopefully boost sales of the soundtrack single. It wasn't a bad idea, but Porscha didn't like her mother thinking she had the final say.

"This has nothing to do with my relationship with Xavier," Porscha said, returning to her earlier comment. "We're not together like that." She was still hurt that he'd only asked her to sing at the event because another artist had dropped out. That stung. She thought they were friends as well as lovers.

"What are you saying?"

Porscha was tired of her mother constantly pushing her own agenda. Maybe if she agreed to the one date, she could get Diane off her back. "I'm saying… I'm willing to go on a publicized date to take advantage of the extra publicity."

Her mother clapped her hands. "Excellent. I'll get the ball rolling with Ryan's people. You won't regret this."

Porscha didn't think so. Going on this date was a stopgap measure to distance herself from Xavier and prevent herself from falling in love with a man who wasn't the commitment type. She'd learned that about him the hard way three years ago when she thought they were on the relationship track and Xavier said they were friends and nothing more. She wouldn't make that mistake again.

The car stopped in front of the youth complex and a massive crowd was waiting *for her*. It was heady, because she had always dreamed of being here one day but had never thought about what came with the fame.

Stepping out of the vehicle, Porscha waved at fans. When a young girl called out for her autograph and handed her a marker, Porscha scribbled her name on the girl's T-shirt and walked quickly toward the front door.

Standing in the doorway was none other than Xavier Lockett.

And her heart stopped.

He looked magnificent in a blue denim shirt, dark denim jeans and white sneakers. His curls were neatly faded, and she loved how his groomed beard felt against her thighs when his face was buried between her legs.

Oh, yes, she was in deep with this man and that frightened her most of all.

Xavier sucked in a breath when Porscha's town car pulled up outside the complex. He tried not to stare when she strutted toward him in a chic white pantsuit and pointy, nude Christian Louboutin stilettos. Her lustrous hair was piled high in an intricate arrangement of curls, but it was her smile and the dimple in her right cheek that were her best features.

As Porscha moved toward him, Xavier found himself unable to look away. His pulse pounded as she came forward.

"Xavier."

"Ms. Childs, so great of you to be able to join us today."

Her eyebrow rose when he didn't use her first name, but she affected a smile. "I'm happy to be here."

"Thanks for coming. The children are so excited. Please follow me to the side entrance," Xavier led her to the gymnasium when he would have preferred to catch her hips and bring her closer so he could sweep his lips over hers. But it wasn't going to happen.

Her entourage was in pursuit behind them. He wasn't going to get any alone time with Porscha, but he had a special surprise for her later up his sleeve. He'd been in cahoots with Erin, and she'd helped clear Porscha's schedule so she would be his tonight and all day tomorrow until she had to head back to Los Angeles for filming on Sunday.

"Here we are," Xavier said, opening the side door and leading them to a green room. "If you can wait here, I'll come back for you. There's refreshment and light snacks."

Diane glanced down at the food he had laid out. "Porscha can't eat any of that. It's all carbs except maybe the fresh fruit."

Xavier nodded. "Noted. I'll see what else we have." He knew Diane wasn't his biggest fan and he wasn't hers, either. He'd heard about women like her who used their children to get ahead, but he would never say that to Porscha. Diane was her mother after all. He was about to leave, when Porscha grabbed his arm. He found her looking up at him expectantly and he realized he hadn't said thank-you. "If I forget to say it, thank you for coming. You're doing me a huge favor."

She smiled. "You're welcome. I'll have to think of a way you can repay me."

"Oh, I have plenty of ways of showing my appreciation," Xavier whispered in her ear. Then he stroked her cheek with his palm and left the room.

It was hard to have a clear mind when Porscha was in the room. Xavier tended to lead with his libido instead of his head around her. He was thankful when he saw his mother gliding across the hall toward him with his father in tow. She looked regal in an all-white suit while his father wore his trademark pin-striped blue suit.

"Great work, my darling," his mother kissed Xavier's cheek. "What you've done here is nothing short of amazing."

"I have to agree with your mother on this one," Josiah said. "You knocked it out of the ballpark."

Earning his father's respect was a rare occurrence, so Xavier appreciated the attaboy. "Thanks, Dad."

"You ready to go out there and give your speech?" his father asked.

Xavier was more than ready and walked with his parents to the gymnasium, where the entire crowd was gathered—the youth who would use the sports complex, along with their families, the press and leaders in the community. Xavier noticed that Roman and Shantel, Julian and Elyse as well as Giana and Wynn were in the audience rooting him on.

Xavier headed to the podium. "I want to thank everyone for coming today. This project has been a labor of love not only for me, but for the Lockett Foundation. We want to be part of the fabric of our community and supporting the next generation of young talent, who need our help. They need uniforms and equipment, summer training camps and more, to reach their full potential. And this sports complex is my family's and the Atlanta Cougars' way of giving back."

"Why is this so important to you, Xavier?" one of the reporters shouted from the crowd.

"As many of you know, I had a short-lived career with

the league, but before, I played in many high school and football arenas and stadiums around the state. I saw how desperate many of these teams were for basic necessities. I wanted other players to have the same resources I had. And now, with this complex, they'll have the facilities they need. But we won't stop there. Through the Lockett Foundation they'll get everything they need."

Xavier finished his speech. "We are excited to have a special guest here today to help kick off the grand opening of the complex. Please give a warm welcome to the one, the only, Porscha Childs!"

The crowd erupted in applause and Xavier turned and watched as Porscha came through the side entrance to the front of the room with a microphone in her hand.

"Hi, everyone." She waved. "I want to thank the Lockett Foundation for inviting me to today's opening. Supporting our youth is near and dear to my heart. So would you like a song?"

"Yes!" The crowd cheered.

The melody from one of her most popular songs began playing and Xavier became enraptured as he listened to Porscha sing. He doubted he'd ever tire of hearing her voice.

After the song ended and the many congratulations from the kids, staff and his family, Xavier wanted to see only one person, but Porscha was nowhere to be found.

"Looking for someone in particular?" Giana inquired when Xavier peered beyond her through the dwindling crowd in the gymnasium.

Xavier returned his gaze to his sister. "Hmm…?" He just hoped Erin would live up to her end of the bargain and ensure Porscha arrived at their hideaway as planned.

"Well, you've answered my question as to who your secret lover is," Giana replied.

"Listen, Gigi." Xavier grabbed her arm and pulled her aside, away from the crowd.

"Don't backpedal now," Giana said, laughing. "Having her sing at my engagement party was one thing, but at the opening of our youth complex? C'mon, Xavier. You must think I don't have two eyes. I see the way you look at her."

"Is it that obvious?"

"Only to those who know you. Anyway, I was hoping to get to know Porscha, but she left in a flash."

"Don't get ahead of yourself, sis, we're just kicking it."

Giana raised a brow. "Ha, you can fool yourself if you want to, but no woman flies all the way across the country to sing a song for just a booty call. You mean something to her."

Hours later, when he arrived at their secret spot, Xavier wondered if Giana was right. Did Porscha care for him? He could admit Porscha was special to him. She didn't belong in his usual "love 'em and leave 'em" category. That was why he was unloading bags of groceries to make her dinner tonight. They were having their first official date.

When they'd been at the clinic, it was about leaning on each other for support both emotionally and physically. The last seven months were about sex, lots of it, and although he wouldn't trade a single second, tonight was about the two of them. And if Giana was right, Porscha would welcome seeing more from him. Xavier took the bags to the kitchen and immediately began laying out his game plan for dinner. He donned his apron and set to work.

An hour later, the candlelit table was set, and the meal was in the oven. Xavier didn't often cook, but there were a few dishes he'd mastered from his mother. One of which was shrimp and andouille sausage grits; he hoped Porscha liked it. He was putting the finishing touches on his butter-and-rum sauce for the bananas Foster when the alarm panel alerted him to the door opening.

She'd come.

Seconds later, Porscha walked into the kitchen in a crystal-encrusted corset top with black V-straps and a fringed miniskirt with Chanel ankle boots. "Wow!" She glanced around at the dining room, from the muted candlelight to the elaborate dinner settings to the bucket of champagne chilling. "You did all this?"

Xavier shrugged. "Do you like it?"

"I *love* it!" Porscha rushed toward him and to his delight jumped into his arms, her svelte legs wrapped around his waist forcing Xavier to hold her pert bottom. She rewarded him with a long, luxurious kiss.

When they parted, they were both breathless. Xavier eased Porscha down to her feet, because as much as he'd have loved nothing better than to take her upstairs to the bedroom, tonight was about showing Porscha there was more to them than just sex. Though he intended to have a lot of *that* before the night was over.

"I can't believe you went to all this trouble," Porscha said. "No one has ever cooked for me."

"What about your mom?"

"Diane is terrible in the kitchen. She can't even cook eggs. It's how I got into bad eating habits, because we were always eating out."

"My mom comes from New Orleans, and cooking is in her blood. She made sure each of us had a few signature dishes in our repertoire. Shrimp and grits is my specialty."

"I can't wait to try it."

"Would you like some wine? I opened a bottle to breathe."

"Yes, please."

Xavier busied himself getting wineglasses from the sparsely furnished cupboard. Since it was a rental, only the basics were included, but it was enough for him to make Porscha a delicious meal. It was the first time they would focus on conversation rather than ripping each other's clothes off.

He poured them each a glass and led her over to the low sofas in the living room so they could talk.

"What was it like growing up in the Lockett household?" Porscha inquired, sipping her wine.

"Intense," Xavier responded, swirling the claret-colored liquid around in his glass so it left trickles running down the sides. "Roman was an athlete, much like myself, but it wasn't his passion. Instead, he followed our father around everywhere, learning everything he could so he could lead the Cougars someday. Then there was Julian. He always had his head in a book or was writing poetry, and my father hated it. He wanted him to be more like Roman, so they butted heads constantly."

"And Giana? How did she fit into all this machismo?"

"She was a tomboy, constantly trying to show our father she could do anything Roman could. She was desperate to be seen as something other than a weak female."

"Well, she's done that. Isn't she CEO of the Cougars?"

Xavier nodded. "That's right. And I'm darn proud of her. She proved everyone wrong, including our father, who thought all women should be barefoot, pregnant and in the kitchen."

Porscha cocked her head to one side. "And you?"

"I was born several years after the initial trio. At that point, my father had given up ever hoping for a son who would follow in his footsteps. You see, my dad played football in his youth, but was never quite good enough to make it in the big leagues. So he and his former business partner, Frank Robinson, purchased the Atlanta Cougars."

"I had no idea."

"Imagine his joy when I came along and loved football," Xavier replied. "He was at every youth football league game, but once he realized how good I was, it took a turn from doting father to drill sergeant. He constantly pushed me to practice. And losing, well, that wasn't allowed. *'There are only winners and losers in life, son,—'* Xavier imitated his father's deep baritone voice "*—and you are a winner,'* he'd always say."

"That was a lot of pressure to put on you at such a young age."

Xavier shrugged and took a slow mouthful of the dark red wine and swished it around before swallowing. "It was either excel or deal with the wrath of Josiah Lockett. I chose excellence."

"But then you were injured."

He nodded. "Suddenly, I wasn't the golden child anymore. I was a disappointment. A stain on the Lockett legacy."

Porscha reached for his hand. "You're not a stain, Xavier. You're an incredible man."

"Oh, don't go giving me praise. I'm no Boy Scout." When he'd been a quarterback, he'd been a notorious ladies' man with women lined up at his door, but the injury had brought him back to reality real quick. "The Xavier of three years ago had a big chip on his shoulder and thought he was God's gift to women."

"You've changed, right?" Porscha asked. "I think we all have the capacity for growth."

Xavier was glad she felt that way, because by the end of the night he was hoping she would see a way forward to them being more than bed buddies.

Porscha found herself relaxing as the evening progressed. They dined by candlelight and enjoyed the delicious meal Xavier had prepared. The shrimp, andouille sausage and grits were divine. She wished they could share more chill nights like this when she could let her hair down literally and figuratively. She rarely got the opportunity to do so. She was always *on* in case someone was photographing or filming her. She appreciated this respite.

"So," Porscha said, staring at Xavier intently from across the table while they enjoyed their dessert of bananas Foster. "Why dinner? Why all the romance?" She inclined her head to the candlelit table.

"Truth?"

She nodded. "That would be appreciated."

His gaze held hers. Porscha doubted she would tire of looking into his dark eyes rimmed with thick curling black lashes and well-defined brows. But it was his words that caught her by surprise. "We have no problem in the bedroom department, Porscha. We never have. We have a communication and trust issue. And tonight was about seeing if there's more to us than just sex."

Porscha was shocked by his words. She did want more than a sexual relationship with Xavier. She wanted the friendship and companionship they'd found those weeks at the clinic. She wanted to believe him, but she'd been burned before. Her experience with Gil and then her earlier disappointment over Xavier had scarred her. She wasn't sure if she could trust her own judgment again.

At the clinic, when she heard Xavier mention they

were just friends and nothing more, it triggered flash-backs of Gil and her father. It made her feel worthless and unlovable. "I want to believe you, Xavier."

"Haven't I proven I can be trusted?" he asked. "All these months we've played completely by your rules, and I've gone along."

"Yes, you have." Xavier was as hungry for her as she was for him. She certainly hadn't experienced this strong an attraction with any other man. It was as if the memory of Xavier's lovemaking had haunted her the years they'd been apart.

"Maybe we could try dating and see where that leads. That's if you're willing to take a risk on me."

She wanted to, but she was afraid. She didn't want to get her heart broken again. It had taken too long to recover from their last affair. Xavier's reputation couldn't be forgotten, either. She had to stay in control of this situation. It had to be on her terms. Her rules.

"Let's take baby steps, okay?"

"If that's the way you want it."

"I do. And we can start with tonight."

Five

Xavier understood Porscha's reluctance. He'd made a mess of things between them before, and he knew his reputation as a playboy gave her pause. He would have to take it as a win that she wasn't saying no to dating altogether. It wasn't like he was ready to put a ring on it, but he wanted something more than a casual affair.

After clearing the table, they found themselves doing the mundane task of washing the dishes. He washed while she rinsed and put them in the drying rack.

"I can't remember the last time I did dishes," Porscha said. "I feel like I've been living out of a suitcase. The only time I haven't been was after the second album and my father's death."

Porscha rarely talked about that time in her life. Xavier knew it was a painful topic because she'd spiraled into a depression afterward. And it was exacerbated by the press because her sophomore effort hadn't lived up to the acclaim of her first one.

"You can talk to me about it," Xavier said as he finished up the last of the pots and pans and placed them on a drying mat on the counter.

Porscha paused, put down the drying towel and leaned against the counter to regard him. "My dad was my universe. Much like your father treats Giana, he treated me like a princess. But then he and my mom divorced when I was eight and suddenly my whole world was turned on its axis. He remarried. Started a new family, and I was persona non grata with the new wife."

"That had to be difficult." Xavier was fortunate his parents were still happily married and as much in love as they'd been the day they wed.

"It was. After the divorce, Mama became fixated on my talent. Before it had been sort of a hobby. I did a few singing competitions here and there. But then it all changed—instead of focusing on the heartbreak of losing my father, my mother poured all her time and energy into me and making sure I was a success. Voice and dance lessons. Rehearsals. Recitals. It was all an endless merry-go-round. Soon, I didn't even have time to see my father because we were always on the go chasing the dream."

"Do you think she was trying to keep you away from him?"

"Consciously? No. But it certainly felt that way at the time. It didn't help that I wasn't a fan of my stepmother's. I mean, she's the one who stole my father away. Needless to say, it caused a strain on our relationship, and he chose not to visit me and vice versa. I think my mother tried to overcompensate, so consequently I felt smothered. Over-mothered. Still do sometimes."

"Have you told her how you feel?"

"She gets defensive. Acts as if I don't love her or appreciate all she's done for me. But she doesn't get it, Xavier. I've sacrificed a lot, too. My entire childhood, *my life*, trying to fit the image of what *she* and the public want from me. It only became worse when Dad passed away. I went into a downward spiral of depression brought on by my guilt because I hadn't spent enough time with him, and the constant media scrutiny."

Xavier recalled seeing her picture splashed across the magazines and on social media. He hadn't known her then, but the press had been relentless.

"I stopped caring what I looked like. I ate one too many pints of Ben & Jerry's and gained a few pounds, but the press made it seem as if I was out of control. I helped them sell magazines, but it was hurtful. Here I am trying to deal with my own grief and being made a mockery of in the media. All the time, effort and hard work I put into my career was suddenly going down the drain. I had to get away. Get my head on straight. The clinic did that for me and it brought you to me."

"Come here." Xavier pulled her into his arms and hugged her tightly. He kissed the top of her head. "I'm glad you felt comfortable enough to share all of that with me."

"You bring me peace in the storm." She glanced up at him and Xavier got lost in her light brown gaze as she wrapped her arms around his waist. She felt warm and so damn good. Desire warred with an irritating wash of chivalry.

He'd brought Porscha here tonight to show her they could be more than bedmates. And he'd done that. She'd opened up to him and he wanted to protect her, but he couldn't deny his heart was pounding hard in his chest at having her so snug against him. She fit so perfectly. He wanted her.

Which was why he should pull away. She must have sensed his hesitance because she snaked her hand behind his neck and pulled him down to her. Her kiss was soft and gentle, yet unyielding. A thousand fireworks exploded inside his head as her lips opened beneath his.

"Porscha." He groaned her name as he reacquainted himself with her taste. She swayed in his arms, responding to his fervor. He couldn't help but touch her. His fingertips moved over her body, lingering at her waist. Skating upward to her hips. Cupping her buttocks and pulling her more firmly to him.

She gasped and it broke the spell. Xavier eased back and looked down at her. "I'm sorry. I didn't bring you here to seduce you, Porscha."

"I know." She smiled. "Now take me to bed."

"With pleasure." He picked her up in his arms and carried her to the bedroom.

Xavier kicked open the door and carefully laid Porscha down on the bed as if she were fragile. Then he gave her a long, leisurely kiss, which soon turned into something more, something deeper and more intense. They kissed until they were both gasping for air. Eventually, Xavier dragged his mouth from her lips to her throat. He could feel her pulse beating against his lips and felt himself growing hard.

He had to slow things down. He crouched down so he could unbuckle her impossibly high-heeled shoes and ease them off one at a time. When he began massaging her ankles and then her feet, Porscha moaned in ecstasy as if he was giving her the best orgasm she'd ever had.

He looked up at her. "Do you have any idea what

you're doing to me when you make sounds like that?" He couldn't wait for her to make more when he made love to her. With an impatient tug, he pulled the straps of the corset free so he could lift it up and over her head. Then he was palming her breasts.

Porscha made a mewing sound like a cat, inciting him to kiss her again. He moved his lips over hers, teasing and coaxing a response from her until she parted her lips. Then his tongue slipped between them to dance with hers, but Porscha wasn't going to be an inactive participant.

"You have too many clothes on." She reached for the silk shirt he wore and pulled it out of his jeans. Then she began attacking each one of the buttons until one flew off. He gave a low laugh of pleasure at her impatience.

"Easy, love!" he teased.

"Don't easy me," she retorted. "I want you naked." She reached for the zipper of his jeans and before Xavier knew it, she was tugging them along with his briefs down his legs, allowing his erection to spring forward. When she took his length in her hand and began to stroke him with her palm, it was too much for him to handle.

He took back the power by kissing her and exploring her body, especially her tightly budded nipples. He anointed them with his tongue and grazed them with his teeth. Pleasure pulsed through every cell of his being. He couldn't wait to make her his, but he wanted to be sure she was ready. So he moved lower, blazing a trail to her stomach with his lips while simultaneously stroking his fingers up her legs.

She gasped when he peeled off her miniskirt and panties, especially when his fingers slicked into her honeyed heat. He moved them against her sensitive female flesh. She cried, she shook, and she shuddered. And when he couldn't take it any longer, Xavier moved away long enough to get a condom and tear the wrapper between his teeth. Her eyes widened as he smoothed it on. Then he positioned himself over her, lifted her bottom and entered her with one powerful movement. Pleasure exploded through him when her body gripped him, welcoming him in. He found himself retreating, then plunging again deep inside her tight, slick body.

Tingles shot up his spine as Porscha clutched his back, all the while entwining her smooth legs with his hair-roughened ones. She angled up to meet his feverish thrusts and Xavier's pulse raced with excitement. *This* was what he needed. He leaned forward to give her a soft kiss and she answered the call by teasing and cajoling his tongue with her own.

Porscha captivated his senses and Xavier wanted more. There was nothing cool or controlled about his movements. He began rhythmically thrusting harder and faster inside her. Desire ruled his brain, wiping out everything else. His hands cupped Porscha's bottom and moved her to accept him exactly the way he needed.

Their breaths began coming in short, sharp gasps. Porscha broke first and her body convulsed powerfully around his. Xavier heard her soft cries as he released a low, guttural groan, and his mind went blank as ecstasy in the purest form surged through him.

Porscha was barely aware of Xavier extricating himself to deal with the contraception. She felt turned inside out. Her hair was like rumpled silk across the pillows, but inside she was suffused with a sense of satisfaction that made her want to sleep for a thousand years.

Eventually, Xavier rejoined her in bed with a satisfied smile. "That was epic," he said, sliding between the covers.

She wished she understood what it was about him that she couldn't say no to. He seemed to know how to light up every single one of her nerve endings and make her body tremble at his touch. Even now, in the aftermath of their lovemaking, when her body should have been spent, she wanted him again. But she wasn't sure she could trust her feelings.

Had Xavier ever been in love? Because love was what she sought if their relationship was going to go any further. But they'd never discussed their past loves. She had no idea if there had ever been a woman who meant something to him, and she sure hadn't shared the terrible lapse in judgment she'd made with Gil. It was embarrassing to talk about what a fool she'd been. Porscha was determined not to repeat her past mistakes. Time would tell if Xavier's intentions were real.

Six

As he drove to the Atlanta Cougars corporate headquarters the following Monday, Xavier felt good about how the weekend had gone. Although he and Porscha had the best sex of his life Friday night, they didn't stay in bed on Saturday like they usually did most weekends. Instead, they'd gone for a long run on one of the running trails, with the paparazzi being none the wiser.

The press had no idea to look for Porscha in an upper-middle-class neighborhood in Atlanta. When they returned, they showered and spent the remainder of the day ordering pizza, eating popcorn and binge-watching Netflix. Eventually, they climbed into bed for another explosive lovemaking session that lasted well into the wee hours of the morning when Porscha finally sneaked away to head back to her place. Xavier felt like he'd proved to Porscha they had the makings of a relationship.

It was surprising to Xavier to want more than just a

physical release: with other women he didn't *feel* anything other than pleasure. He didn't have to go deep because most of them only cared about his looks, his body or what being with him represented. Even though he wasn't a quarterback anymore, he was still part of the illustrious Lockett dynasty, and the ladies were eager to share in the glory.

But with Porscha he could be vulnerable. He'd shared with her what it was like growing up in the Lockett household. It wasn't easy when you fell from the top of the mountain in your father's eyes.

He was going to change the narrative. It was why he'd agreed to the mentorship program Giana suggested.

She'd emailed him info on a few players last week that she wanted him to meet with. There was last year's recruit, popular wide receiver Curtis Jackson. His father, Tim Jackson, was strict about the image his son presented. When Curtis got caught in a scandal last fall after trying to play hero, Julian's wife, Elyse, in her role as a publicist, had helped with the fallout. Consequently, Curtis was their most popular player. Then there was Wayne Brown, their new quarterback. Wayne was twenty-two and feeling himself. He was into the partying lifestyle and could soon find himself in a world of trouble if he wasn't careful. Xavier intended to have a serious chat with the young man.

Xavier pulled his Porsche convertible into one of the spots reserved for the Lockett family. Turning off the ignition, he hopped out and strode toward the door. Since he wanted to present a relaxed but professional image, he'd dressed in trousers and a navy button-down shirt. Instead of going toward the locker rooms or fitness center, he took the elevator to the executive suites and ran into Giana on the way.

"Xavier! I'm so happy to see you." Giana put her arm through his. "I have an office set up for you."

Xavier shook his head. "That's too much, Giana. I don't need one."

"Of course, you do." She walked him down the hall until they reached a door with his name on it. "I want you to feel part of the team. You're a Lockett after all. So let me do this for you, okay?"

"Fine." Xavier sighed and allowed her to walk him inside the office, which was decorated in cool blues and grays. He turned around. "It looks great. Now I want to meet the new players."

Xavier wasn't one for sitting on his butt. He was a man of action. Although he'd only played professionally for a few years, he'd parlayed that into sneaker and travel endorsements. Though some of those faded away after his injury, he'd invested well, and with his sportscaster salary, he wasn't hurting for cash.

"Okay, I can come with you." Giana started to follow him, but Xavier put a hand up.

"I don't need a babysitter." Xavier knew she meant well, but he didn't need his sister smothering him to death.

"Of course," Giana replied smoothly. "I'm here if you need me."

"Thanks." Xavier strode down the hall to the elevator bank. Within seconds, he was walking down corridors toward the weight room. He was sure to find the young men pumping iron because that was exactly where he would be—staying in tip-top shape for the new season. He ignored the ghosts of years past, but it was hard remembering how it felt to be running to the field in his uniform, helmet in hand.

Xavier blinked and reminded himself to focus on the future, because there was no turning back. But that didn't mean he wasn't affected. Football had meant *everything* to him. Had taken up his entire world until it was so nar-

row there was no room for anything else. He hadn't realized that until he'd come to care for Porscha. If he'd been
a quarterback, he wouldn't have even considered wanting
more from their relationship than sex.

The weight room wasn't crowded when he arrived.
Wayne and Curtis along with a few other players were
working out. Curtis was using the chest press while Wayne
bench-lifted. They both glanced up when Xavier entered
the room.

"Well, if isn't the legend." Wayne came toward him with
his hand outstretched. Wayne was a charismatic young
man with midnight-dark hair, blue eyes and an athletic
physique made for being a quarterback.

"Xavier Lockett."

"Oh, I know who you are," Wayne responded with a
large grin on his smooth brown face. "I've watched a lot
of your film and I know I have big shoes to fill."

"You need only be your authentic self," Xavier replied.
"The team hired you for a reason."

Wayne nodded. "I appreciate that. Thanks, man."

"You're welcome." Xavier glanced behind him toward
the huskier young man behind him. "Curtis, good to see
you." They'd met last year when his father brought Curtis to
meet the Locketts prior to signing with the Atlanta Cougars.

"You, too, Mr. Lockett," Curtis replied.

Xavier laughed. "Just call me Xavier."

"Are you sure?"

"Absolutely," Xavier said. "I was hoping I could buy
you both a smoothie and talk to you about the new mentorship program we're rolling out at the Atlanta Cougars.
What do you say?"

"I presume you were off with the cad this weekend?"
her mother asked when Porscha came down the stairs of

her Pacific Palisades home on Monday morning in search of breakfast. She'd arrived late last night from Atlanta, while her mother and her team had come back here on Friday night.

Porscha rolled her eyes and went to the warmer on the counter near the stove and pulled out the spinach and mushroom omelet her personal chef had left for her. She wasn't about to get into an argument with her mother again about her and Xavier. She'd made her choice and Diane was going to have to live with it. After grabbing a fork from the drawer, she took her plate to the limestone countertop and began to enjoy her meal.

"You're not going to answer me?" Her mother huffed, putting her coffee mug on the counter. "Fine. Then I'll just tell you we leaked a photo of you from filming. You were looking adoringly at Ryan and now the entire world thinks you're an item."

"Is that really necessary?"

"Of course. It will heighten the public's interest."

Porscha sighed. "Well, that's what you wanted."

"It's what you wanted, too," her mother chided. "Ryan is one of the most popular actors in the world. Having your name linked with his would be a great boost to your career. Ryan's team were more than agreeable to the date."

Porscha wasn't excited by the idea of fake-dating Ryan. This weekend, her affair with Xavier had taken a turn. Xavier wanted more than just sex. He wanted them to date. But he hadn't indicated if they were going to be monogamous.

Did she even want that?

Maybe.

But she feared getting hurt again. Gil had a done a number on her head and her self-confidence. Porscha wasn't sure she could trust her feelings when it came to men.

What was the harm in going out on a fake date with Ryan Mills? The exposure would help her career, but it would also allow her to keep some perspective where Xavier was concerned and see if she could trust him. Only time would tell.

"Xavier, thanks so much, dude," Curtis said, shaking his hand after their mentorship session ended in one of the many conference rooms at the Cougars' corporate head-quarters. Xavier had already spoken with Wayne, and he'd left a short while ago. "I appreciate all your advice. It hasn't been easy navigating this new world of fame and fortune."

"From what I've seen so far," Xavier began, "you have a rather good head on your shoulders. Your behavior last year, stepping in before that woman was assaulted at that hotel party, shows your character."

"I couldn't let that happen. Not on my watch."

"You did a good thing and I'm sure she appreciated it. Plus, it showed the media and any naysayers that you're exactly *who* you've represented yourself to be."

"I have my pops to thank for that," Curtis replied. "My father says selflessness, humility and truthfulness are the marks of an honorable man."

"Very well said. How would you feel about joining me in one of my charitable projects at the Lockett Founda-tion?"

"I'd like that." Curtis beamed. "I've been looking for the right vehicle to lend my name and support. Helping underprivileged youth means a lot to me."

They decided to meet up the following week. Xavier felt good about his first mentorship meetings. Giving ad-vice about what he'd learned and the struggles he'd faced while playing professionally had been cathartic.

"So how did it go?" a deep tenor voice asked from behind him.

Xavier turned around and saw Roman standing in the doorway of the conference room. He smiled. "It went well. Actually, correct that, it went superbly."

"I'm glad." Roman came inside and closed the door. "I have to admit I was a bit worried when Giana made the suggestion. You haven't deigned to walk these hallowed halls since your injury."

"I needed to come back in my own time."

A wide grin spread across Roman's face. "Well, we are happy to have you back in the fold. Care for some lunch? I had a cancellation."

"Sure, I'd like that." It had been too long since the two of them broke bread. During the season, Xavier was always on the air and sometimes traveling for work. And over the past year, Roman's entire life had changed. He'd gotten a wife and a baby all for the price of one.

They headed to the high-end restaurant on the top floor that was strictly for executives. Once they were seated, Xavier couldn't help but ask, "How's married life? Fatherhood?"

Roman had been a popular bachelor before he settled down. Xavier wondered how the transition was going, because Roman's wife, Shantel, had given birth to their son, Ethan Julian Lockett, late last fall.

"It's a lot," Roman grinned. "But I wouldn't change it for anything. Shantel is the love of my life and I'm lucky to have married her. Otherwise, who knows? She might have ended up with Julian."

"Good afternoon," the waiter interrupted them. Once he'd taken their order, they returned to their previous conversation.

Xavier laughed. "Really? How's that?"

"Oh, our brother had Shantel as his backup plan. Julian assumed Shantel would always be waiting in the wings if he ever tired of his playboy ways, but I beat him to the punch, and we fell head over heels in love, which is just as well because he wouldn't have met Elyse or be expecting his first child."

"Things happen the way they were meant to."

"True. And with Giana next in line for matrimony, that leaves you, baby brother, in Mama's crosshairs."

"I enjoy my life as it is," Xavier responded.

"And the woman you've been seeing on the side?" Roman inquired. "Don't think I've forgotten how Father mentioned her during our Christmas trip. Someone you don't want anyone to know about."

Xavier snorted. He was hoping Roman didn't recall the family holiday trip in which Josiah dropped the bomb that he knew Xavier's secrets. Their father hadn't named names, but he knew there was a woman in his life. "I was hoping you'd forgotten about that."

"Nah." Roman shook his head. "So, what gives? What's going on with you two?"

"It's nothing serious." Though this weekend had been different. They'd done a lot more talking than having sex. And after hitting the sheets, they'd cuddled and fell asleep.

"That's all?"

"Does there have to be more?" Xavier asked.

The waiter returned with Roman's Perrier and Xavier's Coke Zero.

"I don't know. That depends. How long have you been seeing each other?" Roman responded.

"Seven months, give or take."

"Sounds like a relationship to me."

Xavier denied it. "Porscha didn't want one. At least not

at first. She was insistent we stay bed buddies, but nothing more. But she's willing to consider more now."

"Wait a minute." Roman glanced around to be sure no one was around and then looked back at Xavier. "Porscha? As in Porscha Childs who sang at Giana's engagement party last month? And sang at the youth complex?"

Oh, Lord. Xavier rolled his eyes upward. He had just put his foot in his mouth. He'd promised Porscha he'd keep their relationship private, but the cat was out of the bag now. "How else do you think someone as famous as Porscha would come to a private party?"

Roman shrugged. "I don't know. I assumed Giana with her connections arranged it. I had no idea you and Porscha were hooking up. How did that happen?"

"Denver."

"But that was nearly four years ago," Roman stated.

"We became friends while in therapy," Xavier replied. "And friends turned to lovers, but then I messed up. She heard me tell another patient we were friends and nothing else. She felt used and I didn't help matters because I was still reeling with the loss of my football career, and I said some less than flattering things."

"Then how did you reconnect?"

"Do you remember when Porscha sang the national anthem at the Atlanta Cougars game last year?"

"Yeah, I do. You've been together since then?" Roman asked.

Xavier nodded and sipped his drink. "At first, she was really angry with me and let me have it. The chemistry between us was still there. And the rest, as they say, is history."

Roman shook his head in disbelief. "And you've managed to keep this to yourself without saying a word? That's impressive."

"Her rules. Not mine," Xavier said tightly.

"And now? I sense you would like to change them?"

"I'm not saying I'm ready to jump the broom like the rest of you," Xavier responded, "but it doesn't have to be about sex all the time, either. I think I proved that to Porscha this weekend when I cooked for her, and we talked. I wanted her to know we didn't have to hit it and quit it every time we're together."

"Sounds like you want more, Xavier, but you're afraid to admit it."

Was Roman right?

Xavier certainly remembered what it had been like between him and Porscha at the clinic. Losing football had been like losing the part of himself that made him him, and Porscha had been a safe harbor in the midst of the chaos of his life. "I don't know. Maybe, but don't go inferring I'm ready to settle down."

"You might want to figure out what it is that you want."

"Why is that?"

"There are rumors circulating she's dating that famous actor Ryan Mills," Roman stated.

Xavier shook his head. "Nah, you're wrong. He's just the costar in her first film."

"Are you sure about that?"

He thought he was, but then again, he and Porscha weren't exclusive. Xavier had no idea if she was dating other men. Were the rumors true? If so, he would find out, because he wasn't about to give up. At least not yet. He would see how this played out, because one thing was for certain: there was no way Ryan Mills and Porscha could possibly have the fire between them that Xavier and Porscha had.

Seven

Porscha watched her reflection in the mirror as she executed the dance moves with the choreographer and her backup dancers. The song was fast and there were lots of intricate arm, leg and head movements that had to be sharp and crisp. They would all have to be in unison, because when they performed onstage for the BET Awards, she wanted the world to be amazed by their hard work. But she was tired, and it was only the middle of the week.

When they finished the rehearsal, Erin rushed over with a towel and bottle of water.

"Thanks." Porscha guzzled the drink.

"We have some of the couture outfits and high-heeled boots you're going to be using for the show," Rachel said, coming toward her. "We'll need you to start practicing in them."

Porscha nodded. Sometimes her career was exhausting,

now especially. With the movie and soundtrack, Porscha was going to be everywhere, which left little time for herself. Now that the choreography session was over, it was off to the film set because she had to refilm a scene with Ryan that the director hadn't liked when they filmed the day prior.

Porscha was anxious. Both of their teams had gotten together and agreed they would have a date on Saturday night. They would hit one of the popular celebrity spots for dinner, followed by an appearance at a nightclub where the entire VIP area would be roped off for them. From a professional standpoint, the date was a no-brainer. The buzz from their date would keep everyone talking. But personally, Porscha was starting to wonder if she'd made the right decision in agreeing.

She and Xavier had had such a great weekend. He'd cooked for her and openly discussed his family life, and she'd seen another side to him. The softer side she'd discovered when they were in Denver. Perhaps they could be more to each other? Except she had a bad case of stage fright after her experience with Gil.

Am I projecting my fears and past hurt onto our relationship? She hadn't yet told Xavier about this date but maybe she should. No matter how much distance she wanted to keep to prevent herself from falling for Xavier, she didn't feel good about keeping the date with Ryan from him. She had to tell him.

Porscha left the dance studio and headed to the car waiting to take her to the film set. A crowd of fans along with the paparazzi were gathered outside. A few lobbed questions at her.

"Is it true about you and Ryan?"

"Are you secret lovers?"

Porscha chuckled to herself as she slid inside the vehicle. *If they only knew.* Erin and her mother soon followed, and Jose was the last to hop into the passenger seat next to the driver.

"You were right," Porscha said once the car was on the move. "The rumor mills are as active as ever."

"They are," her mother said from beside her. "I've already had requests from *People* and *In Touch* hoping to get an interview with you both about your love story."

"Ha!" Porscha snorted. "Like that's going to happen. I don't mind going along with the ruse of a public date to benefit both our careers, but I'm not going to outright lie." Although she and Xavier weren't monogamous, Porscha was already regretting her decision.

"All right, all right," her mother replied. "I was merely telling you your options. You don't have to bite my head off."

Was she? She and her mother hadn't always had a contentious relationship. Once upon a time, Porscha had wanted to be like Diane, but after her father left them, her mother had changed. She'd become hard and brittle. The hugs and soft words had gone away and she had transformed into a taskmaster constantly pushing Porscha to succeed. But she did love her. "I'm sorry, Mom."

Diane glared at her. "Are you, Porscha? You take for granted everything I do for you. I only want the best for you."

She hated when her mom acted put-upon, because Porscha's success gave her mother an extremely comfortable lifestyle.

"Dating a man I barely know hardly qualifies as wanting the best for me," Porscha replied and turned to stare out of the window at the Los Angeles skyline as they whizzed by on the freeway.

They spent the rest of the journey in silence and when

they arrived, Porscha hopped out as soon as Jose opened the door. She rushed to her trailer and once there, shut and locked the door. She needed some time to herself, which she rarely got. There were always people milling around and sometimes there was no space to breathe. She could feel herself becoming anxious.

Porscha tried the breathing technique the therapist at the clinic had taught her to use when she felt her world spinning out of control. It didn't work. Instead, she pulled out her phone and called Xavier.

She was afraid of needing anyone. Self-reliance and self-confidence had been a big part of her recovery and she was proud of herself, but there were times it would be nice to be held. And when she was in Xavier's arms, she felt safe and protected.

He answered after several rings. "Hey, what's up?"

His voice sounded weird, strained even. "Is everything okay?" She'd been calling him to boost her spirits, but something was off.

"I'm fine."

Her intuition told her something was up. Xavier was usually more talkative when she called. Had he heard about her and Ryan?

"Listen, Xavier, I need to tell you something."

"Let me guess—you're dating Ryan Mills?" Xavier offered.

Porscha nearly dropped her phone. "You know?"

"I'd have to be in a cave not to," Xavier said. "I have a phone."

She heard the sarcasm in his tone.

"The date means nothing." Porscha hated saying it because it was exactly the words Xavier had used to describe their relationship once upon a time. "It's just business."

"If it were nothing you would have told me," Xavier responded hotly.

A knocked sounded on her trailer door. "Porscha, we need you on set in ten minutes."

She glanced down at her Cartier. "I'm sorry, Xavier, I have to go. I need to shower and get on set. Can we talk later?"

"If you can find the time." His response was curt and then he ended their call.

Porscha stared down at her phone. Had he just hung up on her? He was pissed that she hadn't told him about Ryan and he had every right to be. She should have told him about the arrangement. Maybe she hadn't because she was afraid of getting too close to Xavier. But now, thanks to her keeping secrets, she'd gotten her wish and put distance between them.

Xavier was furious with Porscha. How long had she been planning to keep the date with Ryan from him? If he hadn't confronted her, how long would she have kept up the ruse? He would have to think about it later, though; he had his own issues to deal with. He was meeting his agent, Jevon Butler, for happy hour. Jevon had been insistent Xavier take the meeting because he had *big* news.

He was ambivalent about his on-air career. Being a sportscaster was the last thing on his mind when he'd been sitting in that Denver clinic, but then his father had called him during the end of his stay to tell him he'd gotten him a sweet deal with ASN, one of the big sports networks in Atlanta.

Xavier would have rather taken some time to get his head on straight. Instead, mere months after his knee injury, he'd been seated in front of a camera talking *about* football. He should have put his foot down, but who could say no to Josiah Lockett?

Jevon was waiting for him at a table outside, wearing a slim-fitting, ruthlessly tailored suit. His dark waves were combed back from his face and he had a hint of a tan. He rose when Xavier approached. "Good to see you, my friend. What can I get you to drink?" He motioned a waiter over.

"A Scotch, if you don't mind."

"I'll get it started for you," the waiter said and left them alone.

"So?" Xavier quirked a brow. "What's the big news?"

"Shelby Mitchell, the top sports anchor at ASN, is taking a leave of absence to deal with some personal matters, so the league is looking for someone to replace him."

"What does that have to do with me?"

"Duh," Jevon said. "They are looking at you, Xavier. In you, they see a good-looking former quarterback who knows his stuff. You've got loads of charisma on camera, and by having you in the seat they could reach millions in the younger demographic."

"I don't know, Jevon. I was going to tell you that I was considering stepping away from the camera and doing something more fulfilling with my life."

"C'mon, X. As one of the top anchors for ASN, you would have an even bigger platform to support the charities you love and bring in even more money."

"It's not just about the money," Xavier said. Since losing football, he'd been trying to find his purpose, and the charities brought him joy.

"You're honestly willing to turn down this gig and give it to someone else?"

"If they are more passionate about it than I am, yes," Xavier said. "I'm still quite wealthy because I was smart with my income early on in my career and with my endorsements." Even though those had soon dried up once the companies realized he no longer had a football in his hand.

Jevon sighed. "I didn't realize you'd gone soft on me, Xavier. I thought you would jump at the chance. It's a high-profile position. A lot of eyes would be on you and every lady would certainly want to know you."

High-profile.

Xavier's ears perked up at the term. He hadn't thought about it like that. If he were to consider taking on the role, he would be making his current seven-figure salary several times over. Maybe then Porscha would be willing to explore the possibility of dating him exclusively, and *publicly.*

"All right, I'll consider it."

A large smile spread across Jevon's angular face. "Oh, thank God. I was beginning to think you'd lost the fire in your belly to prove you were back on top."

"Oh, I'm back!" Xavier stated.

Now he had to show Porscha he was just as big a star as Ryan to be seen on her arm.

"Don't be nervous, darling," her mother stated from Porscha's bedroom at her Palisades home on Saturday evening. Rachel had made the final touches on her outfit for the evening, which was a low V-cut crop top with a large pendant necklace, accompanied by a slim-fitting miniskirt, a gold-chained belt and killer Manolo Blahnik heels.

"Your abs look amazing," Rachel said, adjusting the chain on the skirt, "but I do think the top needs a little something." She returned several minutes later and placed two silicon breast enhancer pads into her bra. "There, that's better. Now that gives you some cleavage and accents the pendant necklace."

Then there was Kristen, her personal double threat because she could do hair and makeup. She'd put Porscha's hair in a messy but glam updo and accentuated her eyes with smoky makeup, a bold swipe of red lipstick and a red manicure that showed off a chunky gold ring.

"Thank you, Kristen." Porscha stepped away from all the pampering to look at herself in the mirror. At least no one could fault her look. Her image was exactly what her label and her team wanted her to project.

Sex.

Sex sells, but it wasn't who Porscha was underneath. It was all a mirage. She would rather wear a pair of comfy sweats like she'd done nearly every day in Denver. Her life had been simpler then, but then she'd gone there to escape her grief and failing career.

Was she doing the right thing going out with Ryan?

"You ready?" her mother asked, coming up behind Porscha and looking at her through the mirror. "The car is ready."

Porscha spun around. "I don't know if I can do this. If I *should* do this."

"Clear the room," her mother ordered.

Everyone was used to Diane's brusque tone and quickly exited Porscha's bedroom. Once the door was closed, her mother grabbed her by the shoulders. "What are you doing, Porscha? Do you have any idea how serious this is?"

"Of course, I do, Mama," Porscha said, spinning away and out of her grasp. "Because you won't let me forget it."

"Then you *know* the ball is already in motion and we can't change the tide of events tonight. We worked this out with Ryan's team. He's expecting you. To not show up would *ruin* you. Do you hear me?"

"Yes," Porscha said through clenched teeth.

"Then go do your job."

"Fine, but know this." She pointed at her mother. "Just because you and Ryan's team have concocted this elaborate ruse for publicity doesn't mean I have to buy into it."

Porscha turned on her heel and left the room. Erin was waiting for her outside the door. "Are you okay?" she asked, searching Porscha's face. "Diane is in a real mood."

"I'm fine," Porscha responded. She'd gotten herself into this mess, so she would have to get herself out of it. Gingerly, she walked to the end of the hall, down the staircase and outside in the spiky heels Rachel had chosen. Jose was waiting for her and helped her into the car.

At least in the Bentley, on the way to meet Ryan, she was blessedly alone with her thoughts. She opened her crystal-studded Jimmy Choo satin purse and found her phone. She wanted to call Xavier back and explain, tell him the date was business. Surely once she clarified it was for publicity, he would understand. It wasn't as if she'd betrayed him. And there was no ring on her finger. No commitment between them that they couldn't see other people.

But she never had.

Until now.

And as far as she knew, neither had Xavier.

Since they'd been together, Xavier hadn't been photographed on social media with other women like he'd done after their breakup almost four years ago. Did that mean he was exclusively seeing her? Or should she say exclusively *sleeping* with her? They'd never set those parameters and she certainly hadn't mentioned it this weekend because she hadn't wanted to seem needy or desperate.

When the date was over, Porscha would call Xavier, clarify her arrangement with Ryan and make things right between them. It wasn't like their relationship was over. They'd just hit a minor bump, but they could fix it, right?

Eight

"Deal 'em." Xavier ordered. He, Julian, Roman, Wynn and Silas Tucker, Wynn's friend, were spending a rare Saturday night together at Roman's house because the wives had decided to go to some fashion show with Angelique Lockett, leaving the men to their own devices.

"Bossy much?" Julian asked with a smirk as he continued shuffling the cards. "Don't forget you're the baby in this family and we—" he glanced at Roman across the table "—are your big brothers. You need to show us some respect, otherwise we'll have to show you who's boss and take all your money."

"And you think that's you?" Xavier laughed and then tipped his beer back for a swig. "You do realize I have about twenty pounds and four inches on you."

Julian shrugged. "Size doesn't matter. Just because you knuckleheads got Dad's height means nothing. I got Mom's eyes." He pointed at his face. "Trust me when I say the ladies, including my wife, have no problem with this package."

Roman burst out laughing, spitting out some of his beer. "Julian, you're a ham. You know that?" He reached for a napkin and dabbed his face.

"We're playing poker. We're supposed to trash-talk," Julian retorted evenly. Then he dealt one card facedown to each of them and then went around the table again to deal another four cards until they all had five.

"So we're playing five-card draw?" Wynn asked.

"Yeah, anyone got a problem with that?" Julian snapped.

"Nah, just want to know. Because when I wipe the floor with you, you won't see it coming," Wynn countered.

"I love all the trash talk," remarked Silas, who was a celebrity chef with a slew of restaurants and television shows. His wife, Janelle, was the hottest supermodel around. They'd recently reunited after a long separation.

"You're all playing with the king of poker," Xavier announced, joining the fray. "Back in the day, when I was on the road with some of my teammates we would play until the break of dawn, or until the bets were so outrageous you finally gave up."

"You think you can best me?" Roman asked. "Good luck."

Their banter continued late into the evening. They laughed, talked, drank beer and ate pizza. Eventually the betting was in the thousands, and Xavier knew he had his brothers on the ropes. Both had to replace or discard dozens of cards, but Xavier had become quite adept at card counting. He was going in for the kill, but then his phone pinged.

Glancing down, he saw it was an alert about Porscha.

He'd put them on his phone months ago. Whenever she was mentioned in the press, Xavier wanted to know, in case she needed him or he could help with any fallout. She hadn't asked him to, but he remembered the anxiety and depression she'd experienced from the negative media attention.

However, he was angry when he opened his Instagram app.

America's Next Super Couple: Ryan and Porscha!

"Damn!" Xavier didn't realize he'd said it out loud until he felt Roman and Julian coming behind him to glance at his phone.

"Why do you care who Porscha Childs is dating?" Julian asked. He walked to the refrigerator, pulled out another beer, unscrewed the cap and began to drink.

"Since he's been tapping that for months," Roman replied.

Xavier glared at him. "Do you have to be so crass?"

"My apologies," Roman responded. "Our dear brother has been sleeping with the songstress since last year."

"Wow!" Wynn said, shocked. "Is that why she sang at our engagement party?"

Xavier shrugged. "She wanted to keep it a secret."

"And why am I the last to know?" Julian came toward Xavier and thumped him on the chest with his middle finger.

"Because it wasn't exactly open for discussion," Xavier replied. "I mentioned her completely by accident to Roman and had to spill the beans, but that's beside the point. Porscha is out on a date with Ryan Mills, Sexiest Man Alive. How can I compete with that?"

"You can't," Julian said.

"Julian, do you have to be so blunt?" Roman asked.

"Don't get in your head," Silas interjected. "It's tough

having a wife in the public eye. I know. Janelle and I were estranged for five years. I had no idea who she was messing with while she was living the supermodel lifestyle, but at the end of the day, we were able to come back from it. You can, too."

"That's all fine and good, Silas," Julian said. "But Xavier can only be who he is and if that's not good enough for her, then Porscha Childs is not the one for him."

Xavier shook his head. "You don't understand."

"Yes, I do," Julian stated hotly. "You have feelings for her and it's like a kick in the gut to imagine your lady with another man."

"Yeah, but she waited until the absolute last minute to try and tell me, and even then I had to help her out," Xavier replied. "And all she said was its business and she'll call me later."

"And what would you have done if she told you earlier?" Roman inquired. "Asked her not to go?"

"Of course."

"Then you're going to have come clean with Porscha and tell her what you want. Do you know that?" Roman asked.

Xavier shook his head. He wasn't sure what he wanted from Porscha. All he knew was that he didn't want their relationship to revolve purely around the bedroom. But what did he want it to be? Boyfriend-girlfriend? Their relationship had never been clarified because Porscha wasn't sure she could trust him. So instead, she'd gone out with another man. It burned Xavier.

"I suggest you figure it out before you talk to Porscha," Julian replied. "Because if you're asking her not to date other men, you better be offering her something else in return."

"I don't want marriage."

"Then what? Dating? Exclusivity?" Roman asked. "Figure it out, Xavier."

After he left Roman's, Xavier headed home to the guesthouse. To afford himself some privacy, he'd moved in, and he was glad he had. He wouldn't want to face his parents—his mother in particular, with all her questions. Because she would know instantly he was upset.

And he was.

To arrange a date of this magnitude took planning—Porscha had to have known about it for a while, but she'd kept it from him. He was mad and jealous. Jealous that another man was spending time with Porscha. Those moments were his and no one else's.

Damn her!

Julian was right.

He was starting to have feelings for Porscha, and he needed to figure out what to do next.

"You look fantastic," Ryan told Porscha at dinner that evening. She'd arrived at the restaurant with much fanfare to find the press in high occupancy. Crowds were screaming her name and holding up pictures of her and Ryan together, saying they'd make beautiful babies.

The whole situation was out of control.

But Porscha did her part and stopped for photos, waving at all the fans and press before heading inside. Ryan was already waiting for her at their table. He rose when she walked up and pulled out her chair. She wondered if he was always chivalrous or whether it was for show, because all eyes in the restaurant were on them.

"Thank you. You aren't too bad yourself," she offered. It was the best she could do. Ryan was handsome and slim, but he was several inches shorter than Xavier.

Xavier was tall with a broad chest and powerful shoulders, and had a commanding presence.

"I'm glad our people set this up," Ryan said, sitting back in his chair to regard her. "I've always been a huge fan of your work."

"Really?"

"Oh, yeah, your first album was amazing and this last one, *Metamorphosis*, was pure genius."

Porscha laughed. "Has anyone told you you're good at stroking egos?"

Ryan shrugged. "It's a gift."

"If we're passing around compliments, then I have to tell you your last film was epic. I really think you should have won the Oscar." Ryan had been nominated but hadn't won, even though he'd picked up statues at the Golden Globes and Screen Actors Guild Awards.

"I've come to accept Academy voters don't get me," Ryan replied, reaching for his wineglass and taking a sip. "But that's not going to stop me from trying."

"That's admirable. And I understand. When you fall, you still have to get back up," Porscha replied.

Ryan nodded. "I assume you're referring to your second album?"

"Yes." And that was all Porcha was going to say on the topic. She wasn't about to share confidences with Ryan, a man she hardly knew.

Ryan must've gotten the hint, because he moved on to a different topic. He opened a bottle of champagne and they toasted to the evening. Then he began discussing their movie. What he felt was going wrong and what could use improvement, but all Porscha could think about was Xavier. He was upset she hadn't confided in him, the one she normally shared her secrets with. Surely, she could smooth the waters with Xavier. She was dying to know. After dinner, while the waiter went to get their dessert, which she had no intention of eating, Porscha rushed to the ladies' room to powder her nose. The real reason was to check her phone. When she did, she went to a stall and closed the door. Unclasping her purse, she glanced down at her phone. There was a text from Xavier.

Hope you're enjoying your date with the Sexiest Man Alive.

He'd obviously meant it to be sarcastic, but it had the opposite effect, because Porscha went from feeling guilty to anger. How dare Xavier stand in judgment of her? It wasn't like they'd made promises. They never discussed next month, let alone next year. Up until this weekend, he was keen for sex and had agreed to the no-strings fling.

He had asked her to consider them becoming more than bedmates, but she hadn't agreed. She wanted to take baby steps because she was protecting her heart and shielding herself against getting hurt. And she'd done that, but had she also kept Xavier at arm's length?

The text told her he was bothered. She wanted to call him and tell him the date was a media ploy, but she couldn't. Not here in the bathroom of one of the most notorious celebrity restaurants. Her conversation could be overheard and spread on every press outlet before she made it back to her table. She would have to deal with Xavier in private.

Porscha returned to the table and Ryan rewarded her with the movie-star smile he was known for. "I hope you don't mind, but I took the liberty of telling the waiter dessert wasn't needed."

Porscha smiled. "Thank you. Carbs and sugar are a no-no for me."

"Completely understand. Are you ready to go? I believe our team arranged a nightclub appearance. My car is just outside."

Porscha nodded. Her mouth was as dry as the Sahara Desert. Once she walked out those doors with Ryan, they would be photographed together. Add that to the pictures people had snuck of them at the dinner table; she had caught a few fellow diners pulling out their phones when they thought she wasn't looking. Xavier would see it all.

"Yes, of course." She rose to her feet and Ryan, ever the gentleman, pulled out her chair. He placed his hand on the small of her back and led her out of the restaurant. Porscha hated that. She wanted Xavier's hands on her, not his, but she feigned happiness especially when they walked outside.

They were greeted by a large mob of reporters that had doubled in size from her earlier entrance. They all were yelling and throwing questions out at them. She and Ryan paused at the door of the dark Escalade idling at the curb and posed for pictures, which Porscha knew would run on every entertainment show, social media outlet and blog. She waved one final time before climbing inside and braced herself for what was to come.

Because there would be a price to pay for this escapade.

The end of her affair with Xavier.

Nine

Xavier didn't usually box. He much preferred the weight room at the family home gym, but today was another story. He was hitting the punching bag with all the force of a Mack Truck. He was so angry that he could spit nails. He'd called Roman and Julian to join him, but they were otherwise occupied, so his soon-to-be brother-in-law, Wynn, would do in a pinch.

The two men had come to an easy alliance after Giana had gotten engaged to Wynn. Xavier was often at their home for dinner or just to play pool, but today, Xavier needed to blow off some steam. He'd seethed when his phone kept beeping with photos of Porscha and Ryan on a night out on the town. Eventually, he'd turned off the damn notifications, but that had done nothing to calm him. He was still furious with the little minx for gallivanting around town with another man while he couldn't stop thinking about her.

"Easy, man," Wynn said, walking up to Xavier as he pummeled the punching bag. "That bag did nothing to you."

Xavier stopped to glare at Wynn. Wynn had an athletic and lean build from all the running he did. He had a tawny, light brown complexion and a perpetual five-o'clock shadow. "Ouch. Did I do something to offend you?" Wynn asked.

He shook his head. "It's not you, Wynn. It's me. I'm angry that I let someone get under my skin when I shouldn't have."

Wynn placed the gym bag he came with on the floor. "Care to talk about it?"

"Not now. Get changed and meet me in the boxing ring."

"All right. Give me a few," Wynn replied and rushed off to the locker room.

Xavier reminded himself Wynn wasn't the enemy. He was a sounding board. When he returned several minutes later, Xavier had gotten himself under control and was already in the ring wrapping his hands.

Wynn was dressed in a T-shirt and shorts and holding his gloves and mouth guard. He jumped up, lifted the ropes and entered the ring. "So, you ready to tell me what's got you hot and bothered?"

"Let's spar first," Xavier said, putting on his gloves and guard.

"All right, this is your funeral," Wynn replied with a smirk. "I'm pretty good at this."

Xavier didn't mind. He was more than up to the challenge.

They sparred for nearly an hour, with Xavier giving as good as he got. Wynn wasn't lying when he said he was excellent. Xavier managed a few jabs to catch him off guard while Wynn nearly knocked Xavier down a few times, but Xavier righted himself quickly.

He probably wasn't in the right head space to be here, but he needed something to burn off some tension, and boxing did that. Eventually, they called it quits and took off their gloves.

"Good match, Xavier," Wynn said, wiping his face with the towel he'd left on the ropes. "If I didn't know any better, I would think you sparred all the time."

"I don't do it often enough, but I know my way around," Xavier responded, wiping his face with the bottom of his tank top.

"I can see that. So, what did you want to talk about?" Wynn headed over to the water station and poured them both cups of water. He handed one to Xavier, which he quickly drank.

"Women."

Wynn laughed. "Why am I not surprised? It's true what they say that men are from Mars and women are from Venus, because we see things differently. Are you still upset about Porscha? If I recall from our convo last night, you guys never outlined exclusivity."

"Don't you think I know that?" Xavier responded hotly. "It's why I'm so upset." He stood up and began pacing the floor. "I guess I assumed that was a given." At Wynn's look of incredulity, he continued, "And yeah, I get that was a bonehead move. I just never thought she'd be looking somewhere else, especially not a famous movie star."

"You feel like you can't compete?"

"Of course, I can't," Xavier returned. "I can get any woman I want, but sometimes I doubt myself. I look in the mirror and see a washed-up former quarterback with a knee injury. I want the glory I had before."

"You might not be tossing a football around every Sunday, but you picked yourself up, dusted yourself off and found a new career. Second, what you've done with the Lockett Foundation is nothing short of kick-ass. I was just telling Giana that my company is going to donate."

"You don't have to say that, Wynn."

"I'm not saying it because I'm about to be your brother-in-law. I'm a businessman. Do you have any idea how many charities come to me for a donation? But I only choose those I have a real connection to and your work with underprivileged youth speaks to me. I don't know if you knew, but Silas and I grew up using the Boys & Girls Clubs services. So trust me when I say this, you're doing magnificent work."

Xavier had heard about Wynn and his celebrity chef friend's ties to the organization. "Thanks, bro. I appreciate it." Wynn's words meant a lot. Xavier couldn't let the past continue to rule him, but that was easier said than done.

"Ryan Mills is just a pretty face after all," Wynn responded.

Both men laughed.

"That may be so, but Porscha didn't tell me until the very last minute and didn't give me any details. That sticks in my craw."

"Then tell her. Keep it one hundred."

Wynn had a point. He was going to tell Porscha exactly how he felt about her rendezvous with America's favorite actor. And afterward, he would decide how to proceed with their current arrangement.

"You killed it last night, darling," her mother told Porscha the next morning while she lounged in her bed. "I've brought you some hot tea." She placed the teacup and saucer on the nightstand beside Porscha's bed.

"Thanks." Porscha pushed herself into the upright position and placed several pillows behind her so she could drink the tea. "What are they saying?"

"That you and Ryan are the next supercouple. The movie is going to be smashing. How great you look together. It's all positive," her mother replied, sitting on the edge of the bed.

Porscha sipped her tea. "Good."

"Good?" Her mother's expression showed her disappointment. "That's all you have to say?"

"What do you expect, Mama? An attagirl?" Porscha asked.

"I don't expect to be mocked, Porscha. I would think you would be happy to have all the positive press. We changed your narrative. People no longer remember the sullen, depressed and overweight Porscha. All they can see is a happy, fit and successful singer and actress."

Was that all she was? Porscha wondered. Like she wasn't a human being with feelings and emotions? Well, she had them. Just because she tried to fit the mold everyone expected of her, it didn't mean she was a robot.

"Can you please go? I'm tired."

"I thought perhaps we could do something fun together."

"Not today." It was one of her rare free days with nothing on the calendar and she wanted to lie in bed and mope. Mope because Xavier hadn't answered a single one of her calls or texts.

At first, she'd thought about ignoring his sarcastic congratulations. And she'd done a good job of it. Going with Ryan to the club had kept her mind off Xavier. But once there, she'd had a challenging time faking interest in Ryan when all she wanted to do was clear the air with Xavier. In the end, the date had limped along until eventually Ryan brought her home. When he'd gone in for a kiss, it landed on Porscha's cheek, and she bade him good-night, much to his consternation.

"If that's what you want…" Her mother's voice trailed off as if she was expecting a different answer, but Porscha didn't change her mind. She wanted to be alone.

Once the door closed, Porscha fell back against her pillows. She understood Xavier was upset. She hadn't told him in advance about the date and once she did, she had to rush off the phone. But they'd never set the parameters of their relationship. If he wanted more, if he wanted exclusivity, then he would have to tell her. She wasn't a mind reader.

The week whizzed by. Xavier met up with Curtis and discussed partnering with the Lockett Foundation on their inner-city youth programs. He also completed the interview with De'Sean Jones that Vincent had requested. Vincent was right: with his background and player insight, the interview went great. The network was happy and, consequently, the job as top anchor of ASN was within his grasp. Jevon was still negotiating the particulars of the agreement, but soon Xavier would be in the driver's seat. And this time, he'd done it on his own, with no help from his father. In no time, he would be a household name among sports enthusiasts and Porscha would be proud to have him on her arm.

Xavier tried not to let it bother him that the media were saying Porscha and Ryan were an item. Their date was splashed all over the internet, social media, everywhere he turned. He couldn't escape them. And nothing he seemed to do took his mind off the fact that the woman he'd been having an affair with was creeping out with another man. It was made harder by her repeated calls and texts, which had stopped a few days ago after he refused to answer them.

The shoe really was on the other foot. He wasn't used to being in the *wronged* position. Usually, he was the playboy wronging unsuspecting females, but in this case, Porscha was the player. It wasn't enough that he was in her bed. She craved the fortune and fame that came from being with someone as wildly popular as Ryan Mills.

As a quarterback, Xavier had had his share of dates, but there was something about movie stars, like the Idris Elbas, Michael Ealys and Morris Chestnuts of the world, that women seemed to love. A sportscaster wasn't sexy to all the ladies, but his name in Atlanta went far.

Maybe that was what he needed. To get back on the horse and get his groove back. Women did it all the time. He was Xavier Lockett after all. He wasn't going to sit and whine about Porscha keeping her options open; he would do the same.

He called up his former teammate, Allen Lewis, a known womanizer, and arranged to meet him on Saturday night. Why not? He was single and ready to mingle.

Saturday came quick and Xavier needed the distraction. He donned black slacks and his favorite purple silk shirt and met up with Allen at a new restaurant that was all the rage. He knew it was juvenile of him to go tit for tat with Porscha, but he wasn't about to sit home and worry about what she was up to.

"Xavier, my man." Allen gave him a quick hug when Xavier found him and several of his compadres in the VIP area of the restaurant. "Can't believe we managed to get you out on a Saturday night. We all figured you were booed up and some woman had her legs wrapped tight around you."

A few of the other men laughed, but Xavier frowned. He didn't appreciate being the butt of anyone's jokes. "No one rules me," Xavier said curtly.

"Glad to hear it," Allen said. "Should we get you a bourbon or a Scotch? I can't remember your poison."

"A Scotch will be fine," Xavier said through tight lips. He'd forgotten how annoying Allen could be.

After Allen signaled the waiter and ordered his drink, he returned to the group. He bumped shoulders with Xavier. "Did you catch those gorgeous ladies that just walked in?"

It was hard not to, Xavier thought, glancing at the trio of beauties sauntering past them. One was a platinum blonde wearing the tiniest dress he'd ever seen; it might as well be a shirt. There was a leggy brunette in a fire-engine red catsuit with the zipper low enough to see her bountiful breasts. Rounding out the trio was a stunning Latina with a high ponytail, in a skintight, hot-pink dress that didn't leave much to the imagination.

They were there to be noticed, and every man in the room did, including Xavier. He was tired of chasing women, but he didn't have to wait long. Once the women set eyes on their group and recognized some of the Atlanta Cougars players, they quickly made their way over, introducing themselves as Dawn, Skylar and Marissa.

The Latina named Marissa came over to Xavier. "I don't think I know you."

"Do you want to?" Xavier inquired.

Marissa smiled. "A tall drink of water like you, heck yeah."

And that was how Xavier's night went, from hanging with the boys to having a bevy of beauties at their side.

Conversation was banal at best, but Xavier refused to leave early. If nothing else, he had something to prove to himself—that he was still *the man* and no female, Porscha included, could break him.

Marissa was extremely willing to laugh at his jokes, and that worked for Xavier. He needed a boost of confidence.

Eventually, the night moved from the restaurant to a men's club in town. The drinks flowed among the group until everyone began coupling up, by the end of the evening. Marissa stayed by Xavier's side, and he hadn't minded it, but when it was time to go, Xavier knew he was going home *alone*. As much as he'd enjoyed the night out with the fellas, he did miss being with one woman.

And she wasn't just any woman.

She was Porscha Childs.

Gorgeous. Sexy. Talented.

"Who is she?" Marissa asked, sitting across the couch and staring at him.

"Who is who?"

Marissa laughed wryly. "The woman you're thinking about right now, because it's certainly not me."

Xavier started to deny it, but she cut him off.

"C'mon, I'm in this dress." She motioned downward to the hot pink number. "Most men would be trying to take me home and get it off, but not you. You're looking off into the distance as if you can't wait to get out of here."

Xavier chuckled. "Really?"

"Oh, yes, baby," she purred. "You've got it bad."

"Nah, we're just kicking it," Xavier replied. And apparently Porscha had gotten bored with him, because she was looking to replace him.

"If you say so, but I think you have unfinished business. So let me give you a piece of advice. Talk to her."

Xavier wasn't sure if he should or even if he wanted to. He was angry with Porscha for going behind his back and dating another man. Although they hadn't defined the rules of their arrangement other than the secrecy she demanded, at the very least, he thought they were honest with one another.

"Thanks for the advice," Xavier said. "Can I give you a ride home?"

Marissa glanced around and noticed her two girl-friends had gone, most likely home with Allen or one of his friends, and it was just the two of them. "Yes, I would like that. Otherwise, I'd have to call an Uber."

"No worries," Xavier said. "I've got you covered."

The crowd was winding down, so they easily made it outside with minimal disruption. Xavier's driver was waiting outside. He opened the car door and Xavier and Marissa slid inside the limo.

Nobody noticed the photographer across the street snapping pictures.

Ten

Xavier Lockett leaving men's club with unidentified female. Who is the mystery woman?

Porscha scanned the online post Erin showed her early the next morning as they sat in her bedroom going over next week's agenda. She tried to temper her response and not show how upset she was. "Thanks for showing me this, Erin."

"I wasn't sure if I should," her assistant replied. "But I knew you would want to know."

Was this his retaliation to her date with Ryan?

Xavier had ignored her texts and calls all week. And now this? He was clearly telling her he didn't give a damn who she was with because he was having fun himself. But could she blame him? She'd set all of this in motion but her date with the famous actor was just a media ploy. Xavier going home from a nightclub with a beautiful woman was a direct hit to her solar plexus. If he wanted to strike back at her, he'd achieved his goal.

She was angry.

She was jealous.

Porscha wanted to tell him where he could go. That she didn't want or need him. But for now, she'd bide her time.

She had a workout with her trainer lined up and then the rest of the day was free before she had to be back on set tomorrow afternoon. Filming was winding down and Porscha couldn't be happier.

The last week had been wild. The media furor over her date with Ryan hadn't died down. In fact, it had only grown stronger as the week progressed. There were rumors she and Ryan were lovers, that they were getting married. It was all hogwash, but both their teams played coy with the press, releasing statements that they'd enjoyed the evening. When asked about future dates, Porscha told her mom to evade the question.

Ryan was a nice person, but he wasn't Xavier. She wanted to tell Xavier she'd made a mistake, but he'd ignored her attempts to rectify the situation. Instead, he'd gone out, found a hot chick and bedded her.

"You ready for your workout?" her trainer asked, coming into the room and clapping her hands. "We have to keep you fit for your tour coming up this summer."

"I'm ready." Porscha rose to her feet. She would use her frustration about Xavier's silence to fuel her workout.

And it worked.

Until the hour was over.

But then her anger at the situation came roaring back and her mind wouldn't settle. Glancing at her watch, she saw it was still only 9:00 a.m. If she hurried and had the private jet fueled, they could take off in a couple of hours.

She would make it to Atlanta by evening and she and Xavier could have it out.

It was the only way she would get peace of mind. She refused to mope on her day off. She knew it was crazy to fly across the country when she had to be on the set to-morrow afternoon, but it was time she and Xavier cleared the air about where their relationship stood.

Xavier slept in on Sunday because he was recovering from a major hangover. He wasn't used to staying out late anymore, hanging with the fellas and drinking. Those days were long behind him. He stayed home all day, relaxing and watching television. He had no plans and was looking at a solitary evening. His siblings were all coupled up and his parents were going out to dinner with another family.

Xavier was left alone with his thoughts and his phone. Call him a masochist, but he scoured the internet and so-cial media looking for more images of Porscha and Ryan. He knew it was stupid, but he couldn't stop himself. From what he could tell, the gossip sites were still rehashing Porscha's date with Ryan.

And why did it bother him so much who she was dating anyway? Women should be allowed to date more than one man. He'd certainly dated more than one woman. Women came to him at the snap of his fingers, and over time he'd become jaded by too much choice and opportunity. He'd enjoyed sex with them like any other red-blooded male, but it equaled lust and satisfaction, nothing more.

He'd become good at cordoning off his feelings, but Porscha was different. She could have any man she wanted, but she wanted him. Perhaps that was the turn-on. Now that she'd signaled that she didn't need him, it made him want her more. And though he wasn't looking to get mar-ried or have children, Xavier did want exclusivity. He wanted to be the *only* man Porscha was sleeping with. And the fact she didn't see it the same way had his pulse racing.

He was about to get off the couch and scrounge up some dinner when he heard gravel crunch in the driveway. He wasn't expecting anyone and went over to peer out the window. A stretch limousine had just pulled up to his door.

Who in the hell?

Xavier didn't have to wait long to find out who his mystery visitor was, because the driver came around to open the passenger door. To his shock, Porscha emerged, wearing an edgy black leather jacket over a utilitarian yet chic white jumpsuit and carrying a Louis Vuitton duffel bag. Xavier pushed the curtains back. He hadn't expected her visit, but he was glad she'd come. There was a lot that needed to be said and there was no time like the present.

Xavier didn't wait for her to knock. Instead he went to the door and opened it wide. Porscha stepped into the entry, and they stared at each other for several long moments. Xavier broke first.

"I'm surprised you could find the time to visit with your busy dating life. Did you come to slum it?" he inquired. "Or are you here for a quickie before you have to get back to Ryan Mills?"

He knew the words were cruel, so he wasn't surprised when Porscha came toward him and pushed him back, with her palms on his chest. He stumbled inside the house and she followed behind him, slamming the door.

"You don't get to do that." She pointed her finger at him. "You don't get to be mad at me, Xavier. Not after the stunt you pulled last night." She took out her phone and brought up an image of him and the beautiful woman he'd left the nightclub with.

"Like hell I don't," he said, righting himself to face her. Although he had no idea who took the photo, he had nothing to be ashamed of. "You're the one who started us down this path, Porscha. So you sure as hell don't get to come to *my* home and tell me what to think or how to feel."

"And how do you feel, Xavier?" Porscha asked, removing her leather jacket and flinging it over the back of his sofa. "Please tell me, because you didn't answer any of my calls or texts."

"Why would I? You were with another man!"

"Damn it, Xavier. Answer me! I just flew thousands of miles to come here tonight. The least I deserve is the truth."

"The truth?" Xavier asked, nearly shouting at her. "I don't think you know it, Porscha, because if you did, you would have told me about your date with Ryan much sooner, but you didn't."

"Did I have to? Since when? I don't owe you anything. And you didn't seem to care last night when you were all over another woman."

"I'm only following your lead."

"I didn't sleep with Ryan!" she yelled at him. "The only reason I went out with him was for publicity."

"And I didn't sleep with the woman last night, either," he responded hotly. "I needed to blow off some steam with my friends, but therein lies the problem. You may not *owe* me anything, Porscha, but you don't share anything with me, either. You could have told me about the media stunt, but you didn't. You set all the rules and I'm supposed to go along with them like a good little puppy dog? Well, guess what? That doesn't work for me."

"I'm sorry. I should have told you."

"Finally, we're getting somewhere, so let me be clear on another topic. I don't want you to date other men."

"Why not?" She continued pressing him.

"Because I'm jealous!" Xavier roared. "It kills me to

see you with another man. Knowing he's touching you, possibly kissing you. Those lips—" he looked at her pink-tinted lips "—belong to me."

A slow smile spread across her face at his words, and he could see her pulse point beating frantically at the base of her throat. He had the inexplicable urge to cover it with his lips. With his tongue. "My lips are my own."

"You think so?" Xavier said, storming toward her. They stared at each other; both were breathing hard with the exertion of keeping their distance. "Would you like me to prove you belong to me?"

Her pupils dilated and her eyes darkened with desire. "Yes, if you dare."

Xavier hauled Porscha toward him and nudged her thighs wider with his knee so she could feel what she did to him. Her eyes flew to his. Then he lowered his head and touched his lips to hers in a searing kiss that told Porscha she was his in every way. She let him take control, so his tongue speared boldly into her mouth. She softened against him, allowing him to taste her essence, and her hands flattened over the hard muscles of his chest to slide upward and snake around his neck. Then she began moving her lips beneath his in an age-old request for more. Xavier gave it to her.

Nothing else mattered in that moment. Not his anger. Not Ryan Mills. It was just the two of them. And they came together like magic. Like it always was between them. When he lifted his head a fraction and they broke apart for air, he peered into her eyes. "Now, tell me again, you're not mine?"

How was it possible to feel so much for one person? To want so much.

Porscha knew it was emotional suicide to let her heart

rule her actions, but her entire body had caught fire with Xavier's kiss. She wanted him even though she'd been furious when she arrived. She wanted everything Xavier could give her. Wasn't that why she'd come? Flown halfway across the country—*for this*?

She gripped the back of his head and tugged him back down. His mouth captured hers in a sweet, lingering kiss that caused her to moan for the aching pleasure only he could give her.

"Xavier."

He swept her into his arms and strode toward the bedroom. "I'm going to make to love you, Porscha, and remind you how good it is between us. Until you won't so much as think about another man." His voice was raw and hoarse with need and Porscha believed him.

He lowered her to the bed, but Porscha rushed to get up on her knees, hastily pushing the hem of his T-shirt over his head and tossing it away while Xavier unzipped her jumpsuit. He clawed at the sleeves until he could slide them down her arms, then she was leaning back against the duvet so he could drag the entire garment along with her thong down her legs. Then he was unbuckling his pants and they followed the same path as his shirt. When he was naked as she, he smoothed on a condom and joined her on the bed.

"You drive me crazy," Xavier said, and then he was cupping her.

Porscha nearly dissolved when he parted her slick flesh and delved between her legs to glide his thumb and fingers over her in all the right places.

"Xavier, please—" she moaned.

He lowered his body on top of hers and his smooth thick hardness opened her up, penetrating deep inside. For a minute, they were both completely still as if suspended between two worlds. Xavier's eyes looked dazed as they met hers. There was nowhere for her to hide. His eyes glittered with hunger and Porscha knew that when he took her this time, it wouldn't be slow and gentle. It was going to be fierce and urgent because he was going to claim her and make her his.

He did just that.

Xavier crashed his mouth down onto hers and his tongue thrust deep as he plunged deep inside her. He was up on his forearms, his body sliding over hers, each stroke more intimate than the next, winding her tighter and tighter. And when he opened his mouth wide to bear down on one of her nipples, she nearly screamed at the sensation of having his greedy mouth on her once again.

Porscha wrapped her legs around his hips, a torrent of need flooding her. Xavier drove into her harder and deeper and she simply clung on as he took her to new heights. He grunted in pleasure. "Tell me if I'm too rough."

She shook her head. "No. Give me more. I want more."

"Ah, hell, Porscha." He began moving faster. He was tipping her toward the edge of an exquisite release, the kind she had only ever experienced in his arms, making her his with each thrust. She almost didn't want to let go, but then she opened her eyes at that exact moment and found Xavier watching her. The connection was so elemental it hurtled them both over the cliff into a mindblowing orgasm that had Xavier roaring out his pleasure and Porscha screaming.

Afterward, Xavier bent down and kissed her sweetly on the mouth. His big body swamped and cocooned her in a delicious warmth that made Porscha in her weakened state blissfully happy.

He'd proved his point.

She, or at least her body, belonged to him.

Eleven

Xavier wanted to feel relieved. He'd shown Porscha how good they were together. But he wasn't sure he could trust her. She hadn't been honest with him about the media stunt. Yes, she'd come to him tonight. For what? They hadn't yet settled anything between them or agreed to be exclusive. Instead, they'd done what they always did and torn each other's clothes off.

Porscha provoked a physical response in him he couldn't seem to understand. She simply took his breath away and he found himself consumed with her. He tried to analyze her appeal and what it was that kept him coming back for more. She was beautiful. Yes, she had a great body, and whenever they were together, desire, hot and hard, flared inside him, obliterating everything else in its path.

He felt murderous seeing her with Ryan. It was why he'd gone out with his boys and flirted with that woman, all in the hope he could beat whatever this was out of him. But he couldn't. Porscha was the sexiest woman he'd ever met. He didn't know why; he just knew it felt good and he wanted the feeling to last.

And so he made love to her again. This time it was different than the first. It was slow. He put his mouth on every inch of her body where he could find purchase, licking her one inch at a time. And when he settled between her legs, he drank deep of her core until she was sobbing out his name like an incantation.

Then he set her on her knees and with his hands on her hips, he took her from behind in a slow, steady rhythm that was so intense...it was too much...but not quite enough. Her cries of abandon filled the room, especially when he reached around her to push two fingers inside her. His thumb traced, found and circled the swollen bud and she gasped aloud, but he wasn't letting her go. His arm was clamped around her waist so he could pleasure her while simultaneously pressing farther inside her.

And when she was nearly pleading with him to end it and give her release, he flipped them so she was astride him and could take him deeper. He looked up at her and her head was thrown back as she rocked her hips wickedly against him.

"Look at me," he ordered.

Her eyes fluttered open, and she didn't look away as he began thrusting upward to meet her. She was right there with him and when the tempo began building, his thrusts became swift, sending excitement racing up his back. Porscha leaned forward, her breasts coming into direct contact with his face. He reached upward and laved one nipple lightly with his tongue. That was all it took for her to fly apart. Her detonation was something otherworldly and caused a deeply animalistic growl to escape his lips as Xavier met her in a state of utter ecstasy.

Porscha awakened in the middle of the night slightly disoriented. She felt different. Her entire world had been upended. Somehow Xavier had managed to strip away all her bravado as well as her willpower and made her a mass of sexual need. If he was in her presence, she wanted him to touch her. If he touched her, she wanted him to make love to her. Her desire for him was all-consuming, so much so she'd flown here to Atlanta when she was due back at Los Angeles to be on the set by early afternoon tomorrow.

But they did need to talk. She couldn't, wouldn't leave until they did. Until she understood what he wanted, what they both wanted to make sure this arrangement worked for both of them. Because she'd heard resentment in Xavier's tone when he mentioned doing things her way. And she'd insisted on conducting the affair on her terms to protect herself from him. She'd never once considered how he might feel.

She was going to do that now.

"Xavier." She shook his shoulder.

"Hmm…," he said sleepily.

"We need to talk."

He turned around, glanced at the clock and tried to pull her back down onto the pillows. "We can talk tomorrow."

"No." Porscha reached for the lamp sitting on the nightstand and turned it on, flooding the room with light. "It has to be now."

Xavier sighed and rubbed the sleep from his eyes as he sat upright. As much as she loved his muscled chest and firm abs, she needed to stay focused. She couldn't leave until they had a discussion like two normal adults. She would go first.

"I'm sorry," she said. "I'm sorry I didn't tell you about Ryan sooner. I should have, but honestly, I was afraid. Afraid of how you might react if I mentioned dating another man."

"Damn right! I don't like it."

"Fair enough. I only agreed to the date with Ryan because my mother suggested it would be good for my career and boost sales for the album."

"And that's your excuse?"

She lowered her head in embarrassment. "Yes. And it's the truth."

"Porscha, I've known you to go against your mother if you felt strongly enough. You didn't in this instance. It tells me a lot." He threw back the covers and started toward the bathroom.

"Xavier...wait!" Porscha followed him, uncaring of her nakedness. "Why are you mad? You proved your point when you went out with your friends and flirted with that beautiful woman."

She watched as he turned on the taps to the shower. "I'm not mad. You've told me the truth, so now I know."

Her brows furrowed. "So why do I feel as if nothing has changed between us?"

"What's changed is that I want exclusivity, Porscha," Xavier said. "I didn't think I had to spell it out since we're sleeping together, but I'm saying it again." He stepped into the shower and Porscha didn't hesitate to join him.

"I want that, too." She smiled, circling her arms around his naked waist and looking up at him. She didn't care if she got her hair wet. "You're the only man I want to be with." She stroked his cheek with her palm. "In fact, I haven't been with another man since we've been together all these months."

He raised a brow.

"It's true. I know you may find that hard to believe, but it is. And as far as the date is concerned, nothing happened with me and him other than a boring dinner and a choreographed outing to a nightclub."

"Will you see him again?" Xavier asked.

"Probably not."

Xavier pushed her away. "If you don't mind, I think I can shower alone."

"Don't push me away, Xavier," Porscha said, moving toward him again. "I don't want Ryan. I want you." She went to take his hardness in her hands, but he gripped her arms to stop her, even as he hauled her toward him.

"We can't. I need a condom."

"Where?"

"Bottom drawer in the cabinet by the sink."

Porscha stepped out of the shower long enough to grab a foil packet, and when she returned, they picked up where they left off. They reached for each other at the same time, kissing and touching. The passion between them was a strong as ever despite the fact there were still unresolved issues between them.

But it all went away the moment their bodies connected. Porscha felt an emotional bond to Xavier as deep as the physical one they shared. Their foreheads touched and they began moving together as one. She could hold nothing back and soon her world splintered into a trillion pieces.

Xavier swore as he continued driving into her. With her back against the shower wall, Porscha wound her legs around his waist as yet another orgasm began to roll through her. Unable to contain his own climax, Xavier threw back his head and shouted out his release. In that moment, Porscha realized it wasn't just about phenomenal sex anymore. She was developing feelings for Xavier. Feelings she wondered if she'd had all along, ever since they first met.

"Do you have to go?" Xavier asked when instead of coming back to his bed after their shower interlude, she dressed. His clock read 7:00 a.m.

"Thank God, you're a couple of hours ahead, but yes. I must get back. We're wrapping up filming soon," she replied.

He nodded. "Okay, let me get dressed. I'll walk you out."

She shook her head. "No, let me remember you like this." She glanced at his bare chest and continued moving her hands lower until she could open the towel around his waist. "All sexy and very—" she paused for a beat when she laid eyes on his length "—very aroused."

"You sure you don't want to help me take care of that," he said with an unabashed grin.

"Afraid not. I have to get a move on it, if I want to make it back to the West Coast." She was silent for several moments and then asked, "Are we good?"

"Sure." But even as he said the word, Xavier wasn't sure. She had never definitively answered his question about whether she would stop seeing Ryan for publicity. Instead, she'd sexed him up in the shower until he could no longer remember his own name.

Porscha sighed. "I'm not convinced. Listen, Xavier. I promise I will keep you in the loop going forward."

"And Ryan?"

"The media attention will fade once I make it clear it was a one-time thing. You'll see." She glanced down at her watch. "I have to go." She brushed her soft lips over his, but he didn't let her leave so fast. His hands tangled in her hair and he brought her mouth toward his in a demanding kiss. She groaned with pleasure, but gently removed herself from his embrace.

"You don't play fair. I'll call you from the plane." And with that, she left the house.

Xavier heard the click of the front door as she closed it. He folded his arms behind his head and thought about last night. Porscha's visit had been a surprise. After seeing her with Ryan, he'd assumed their affair was over. He'd anticipated receiving the brush-off. Instead, Porscha had come to him and admitted she'd made a mistake. She'd agreed to his request for exclusivity and claimed he was the only man she'd been with. He wanted to believe her, but he wasn't sure.

He remembered Tyra Daniels, a woman he'd casually dated, and the lie she'd told. She'd claimed he was the father of her baby, which could have destroyed his career. Luckily, the truth had come out because his father had put Nico Shapiro, the Lockett organization's investigator, on the case. Nico's sleuthing had revealed that Tyra had been sleeping with several members of the team, not just him. She'd known Xavier wasn't the father based on the timeline of when the child was conceived, but she lied deliberately because she wanted the fame and money that came with the Lockett name. Xavier could have been caught up in quite the scandal. He supposed it was why he had such a hard time trusting women and believing Porscha when she said it was over with her and Ryan.

He hoped that she was being truthful, but was he fooling himself because he didn't want to give her up?

Twelve

Porscha arrived back in Los Angeles just in the nick of time. It was just past 10:00 a.m. on the West Coast, and she had just enough time to get home and changed to be on set by noon. She'd only had a few hours of sleep on the plane, but she wouldn't have traded her night jaunt to Atlanta for anything. She'd been angry, jealous and confused when she'd flown there, with no idea how she would be received.

Xavier had been angry because she hadn't told him about her date with Ryan beforehand. But he'd also admitted he hadn't deliberately set out to hurt her by being photographed with another woman. He'd gone out with his boys to get her out of his system, but he couldn't. She couldn't let him go, either; he had entered her bloodstream like a powerful drug.

As she took in the scenic view on the way to the Pacific Palisades, all Porscha thought about was Xavier.

About the way he made her gasp out his name orgasm after orgasm. How he stroked her skin and whispered to her about how her body was everything a woman's body should be. Her senses were reeling, and she could still taste him on her lips.

God, she was in serious trouble of falling for him as she had in Denver. Was she a fool for believing in the same man twice? Xavier had the power to break her heart all over again and Porscha was scared senseless. Her mind told her to retreat. Take this time away from him to be sure Xavier was what she really wanted, but her body…her body craved his and she wondered how she would ever live without his kind of pleasure.

The limo slowed and soon they were easing into the driveway of her home. Her mother was standing outside the doorway dressed in jeans and a light sweater, but the look on her face wasn't casual. It was angry.

Porscha sucked in a breath. After her magical night with Xavier, she was in no mood for her mother's histrionics. She was no errant schoolgirl coming home after a night out.

When Jose came and opened her door, Porscha slid out. "Hello." She greeted her mother with a kiss on the cheek and was about to walk inside the foyer, but Diane was on her heels.

"Well? Are you not going to talk about the elephant in the room?"

Porscha spun around. "Which is what exactly, Mom?"

"That you left Los Angeles without a word to me," her mother replied swiftly.

"I didn't realize I had to answer to you about my whereabouts every single second of every single day. I'm a grown woman." She turned and began stalking up the staircase. She needed to shower and head to the set, but her mother wasn't letting this go. Diane followed her to her bedroom.

"For Christ's sake, Mom. Back off!" Porscha yelled.

"I won't! Not when I see you making a horrible mistake."

"According to you," Porscha said and started stripping off her leather jacket. "The great all-seeing Diane Childs who knows everything and thinks she knows best. You don't."

When she was down to her undies, Porscha walked to her master bath and to the sink to brush her teeth. Yet again, her mother was in the doorway.

"He's going to hurt you, Porscha. *Again.*"

Porscha slammed down her toothbrush and faced her. "You don't know that."

"I know how devastated you were when you got back from the clinic. You were there to heal from losing your father and your career tanking and you came back with another heartbreak."

"I misunderstood the situation," Porscha replied. "Plus, this isn't the same thing. *I hurt him* this time. *I* went on a date with Ryan."

"And what did he do? Did he call you up to find out what happened?" her mother asked. "No, he went right into the arms of another woman. Erin showed me the post."

"What did you do, Mom, browbeat my assistant until she gave up my location?" Only Erin had known she was with Xavier.

Her mother lowered her head and didn't answer. Instead, she said, "I only want what's best for you. Why is that so hard to believe?"

"I don't have time for this. I have to shower. Can I get some privacy?"

Her mother stared at her for what seemed like an eternity before she pushed off the doorway and slammed the door shut behind her. Porscha was thankful to be alone. She wanted her mother to be wrong in her prediction that she and Xavier would end up like they had nearly four years ago. This time *could* and *would* be different.

"You have three and a half minutes left," the producer told Xavier in his ear as he finished wrapping up his *Q and A on Atlanta Sports Night* segment later that morning.

Xavier continued asking the questions on the script on the screen in front of him, but if he had his way, he would be on a football field instead of just talking to a player. He ended the interview shortly afterward and allowed one of the production crew to take off his mic.

"Thanks, Dan." He was walking off the set but stopped when he saw a familiar face standing off to the side. She was dressed in a red suit dress and four-inch heels and looked every bit the CEO that she was.

"Giana, what you are you doing here?" Xavier asked, pulling her into his arms for a hug and a kiss.

"I was hoping I could take my little brother to lunch," Giana replied once they parted. "If you didn't have any plans."

"None at all."

"Excellent." She looped her arm in his and together they walked toward the bank of elevators down the hall. "So, what's new with you? I feel like you've been quiet of late."

"I've been busy."

"With a certain female?" Giana asked.

"Are you fishing for details, big sis?" Xavier asked, peering down at her.

"Absolutely. And you can tell me over lunch."

Once outside, they walked a short distance to a nearby restaurant the ASN staff liked to frequent. The food was good and the service top-notch. The ambience was grand with dark oak paneling and white tablecloths. After they were seated and the waiter had taken their orders, an ahi tuna bowl for Giana and a salmon salad for him, his sister wasted no time going in for the details.

"What's this I hear about Porscha Childs dating Ryan Mills?" Giana asked, filling her glass from a bottle of Perrier on the table.

"The date was purely for show."

"That's not what I heard. There's rumors they've been seeing each other the entire time they've been filming."

"All of which are unsubstantiated and false," Xavier responded. "C'mon, Giana. Do I look like the type of man that likes to share?"

Giana shrugged. "Hey, you're my baby brother. I have no idea what you like to do in the bedroom, and I don't want to know."

Xavier laughed heartily. "You, my dear, have an overactive imagination like everyone else in America. Just because the press says it's true doesn't make it so. You recall that's how rumors got started about me fathering Tyra's baby when I was in college."

A serious expression returned to Giana's face. "Yes, I do. How could I forget? Daddy was furious about how the negative press might sideline your career. And he wasn't having it."

"It's one of the few times I appreciated his heavy-handedness. If he hadn't hired Nico, Tyra would have ruined me."

"Fortunately, that didn't happen, and you still went on to win the Heisman," Giana responded.

Xavier nodded and his mind drifted to accepting the award onstage. How happy he'd been and how everything had seemed possible back then. He came back to earth when he felt his sister's hands covering his and giving them a gentle squeeze.

"I'm sorry. I shouldn't have brought it up."

He shook his head. "You can't walk on eggshells around me forever, Gigi. I've learned to deal with the hand I've been dealt, but on occasion, the memories pop up. I'm starting to think of them more fondly now."

"That's good to hear," Giana replied with a half smile.

Their lunch entrées arrived shortly afterward, and they tucked into their meals with gusto. That was when Giana returned to the original topic of conversation. "I'm curious, Xavier. If the date with Ryan Mills was just for the media, what does that mean for you and Porscha?"

"We're not looking to get serious, if that's what you're after."

"No?" Giana quirked a brow. "Wynn told me you were quite upset at the gym when you heard about it."

"I was jealous, but Porscha explained the situation."

"When?"

Xavier smiled as he thought about Porscha astride him during the wee hours of the morning, taking him to heaven. "Last night. She flew in to see me."

"And you didn't take the day off to be with her today?" Giana inquired. "Xavier…" She shook her head in dismay.

He laughed. "I'm not completely dense, Gigi. Porscha left this morning. She had to get back to the film set. I'm sure I'll see her again."

"You're telling me she literally flew overnight to be with you?" Giana inquired. "Hmm…"

"What does that 'hmm' mean?"

"It means that you claim the two of you aren't a couple or getting serious, but you were quick to anger when you thought she was with another man. And a woman doesn't just fly cross-country overnight and back again for someone she doesn't care about."

"You're wrong. Porscha has always been clear about what she wants from me. And now, that's dating and sex *exclusively*."

Giana brows furrowed. "If you say so. Listen, will I see you at Julian and Elyse's baby shower on Saturday?"

"I guess. I was invited."

"You'll have fun. Just wait and see."

But her words gave Xavier pause. Was there more to his and Porscha's relationship than he was willing to admit? He had come to care for her, and she wasn't just a bedmate anymore, if she'd ever been. In the past, he had never wanted love in his life. There hadn't been any room for it because he had to keep his mind clear and sharp for football. But it wasn't clear or sharp right now. Whenever he and Porscha were apart, it left an ache.

This morning when they'd been in the shower with their foreheads against each other and their bodies fused together as if they were designed to fit, like two pieces cut from the same mold, Xavier had wondered if there was more yet to be discovered between them. And if so, was he finally ready to make room in his life and his heart for love?

Thirteen

"The press isn't happy that we aren't fueling the fire," Ryan said after he and Porscha finished filming later that day and he walked her back to her trailer. "I think everyone was expecting the next Brad and Angelina."

Porscha chuckled. "I'm sorry to disappoint them, but…" She was trying to figure out a way to say she wasn't interested, without hurting Ryan's feelings. He was a big star, and she knew he'd lobbied for her to get the role after she screen-tested with him, but she couldn't ignore her feelings after last night.

She and Xavier had agreed to be exclusive.

And after what happened in Denver, it was a big deal. The trust issue between them wasn't completely resolved. She'd sensed that in Xavier's response to her this morning in the shower and when she'd left. If she went back on her word and continued to date Ryan, it would make any sort of relationship between them untenable.

"But…?" Ryan prompted her to continue.

"There's someone else," Porscha answered honestly.

"And they don't understand what this means?" Ryan asked, cocking his head to one side and peering at her. "It's just publicity to help our careers. They should understand. You can still see them in private."

"Why should we have to?" Porsha whispered. "It was all a media stunt anyway."

"Sounds like he means something to you."

Porscha nodded because Ryan was right.

She had developed feelings for Xavier, but it was so complicated because it was mixed in with past hurt. It wasn't easy letting go and making herself vulnerable again.

"All right, I won't push," Ryan responded. "But I do think it's a wasted opportunity." He left her alone in the trailer, but not for long. Her mother was climbing the stairs to be with her shortly afterward.

"I just spoke to Ryan. He told me you're done with dating him."

"That's right."

"I think it's a mistake, Porscha."

"Well, I didn't ask for your opinion," Porscha replied sharply. "This is my life. *I* get to decide."

Her mother frowned at her. "You really think you're in love with a former quarterback with a bum knee you met while you were in a mental health clinic? You were out of your mind with grief, and he wasn't in his right state, either."

Porscha's eyes grew wide. She couldn't believe her mother could be so cruel and unfeeling. Or that she thought so little of Porscha's judgment. "Out!" She pointed to the door.

"Porscha, I'm sorry." Diane started toward her, but Porscha backed away.

"I said I want you out now!"

Diane held up her hands. "All right, I'll leave, but I'll be close by." She started down the stairs and stopped. "I'll be right outside if you need me." She glanced at Erin, who was behind her on the trailer steps. "Take care of her."

"Ohmigod!" Porscha scrubbed her hands across her face and plopped down onto the small sofa couch.

"Are you okay?" Erin asked, coming to sit beside her. "Should I leave you alone, too?"

"No, no." Porscha shook her head as tears slid down her cheeks. "You've been wonderful, Erin. Thank you so much. What would I ever do without you? I'm so sorry my mother harassed you while I was in Atlanta. She had no right to. You work for me."

"It's okay."

"No, it's not," Porscha replied. "She crossed the line."

"Don't worry about it. I'm okay. It's nothing I'm not used to," Erin responded.

Erin had been a godsend and a wonderful edition to her team the last few years. She was smart and savvy and Porscha knew she wouldn't be able to hold on to her long, but she was happy to have a confidante. Someone she could trust.

Right now, that person wasn't her mother. She knew Diane could be cold and heartless, but usually it was never directed at Porscha. She'd always thought it was for other people, never her, but the line between mother and manager had been blurred for far too long.

Porscha was going to have to make some changes.

"I can't believe men are required to come to baby showers now," Xavier said as he, Julian, Roman, Wynn and Silas stood outside on the terrace of the Lockett mansion in Tuxedo Park while the women in their family oohed and aahed over baby clothes, bassinets and the like.

The rest of the week had gone fast. Although he and Porscha were apart, they texted and spoke on the phone as often as her schedule permitted. And certainly, more than they'd done in the past. It seemed that by his telling Porscha he wanted exclusivity, somehow they'd walked themselves into a relationship. And Xavier didn't mind so long as she didn't hear wedding bells.

"I don't know when it happened, either," Roman said with a chuckle, "but men are no longer on the sidelines handing out cigars in the waiting room when the baby is born. Oh, no, we are in the thick of it, from the birthing classes to the delivery, to taking off for paternity leave to help with the baby."

"We haven't told anyone, but Janelle and I are expecting as well, so I'll be looking to you guys for advice when the time comes," Silas said from the sidelines.

"Congratulations." Wynn stepped in and gave his best friend a one-armed hug while everyone else shook his hand. "I'm happy for you. I know you both have wanted a family for a long time."

"We have. Janelle is excited and we've been reading *What To Expect When You're Expecting*."

"Pregnancy has been eye-opening," Julian said, taking a swig of his beer. "We started Lamaze classes about a month ago."

"Lord! Am I honestly standing here talking about birthing classes with my brothers?" Xavier asked in a huff.

"Hey, don't knock it, Xavier," Roman said, laughing. "The same thing could happen to you one day."

Xavier shook his head. "Me? A father. I don't think

so." He honestly never thought about being a parent. It wasn't like he believed he would be a bad one, but it had never crossed his mind. It always seemed like far-off in the future. Maybe because he'd never met someone he wanted to marry.

But if anyone could make him *want* to consider marriage, it would be Porscha.

Julian snorted. "I think I said that, too. And look at me now. Mr. Playboy himself about to be a father, but I have to tell you, X—" he glanced at the doorway to the house "—I'm the happiest I've ever been. Elyse completes me in every way."

"Oh, now you're sounding like a sap." Roman laughed.

"Make fun all you want," Julian returned, pointing a finger at him. "You were head over heels for *my friend* and I recall how extremely territorial you were when it came to Shantel."

"Don't you start with that 'my friend' stuff," Roman growled.

"See?" Julian turned to Xavier, laughing.

"He's right, Roman," Xavier responded. "You are acting possessive. Admit it."

"That I adore my wife?" Roman asked. "Absolutely." He turned to Julian. "You not showing up at that bachelor auction was the best thing that ever happened to me."

Julian was supposed to attend the auction with Shantel but had been a no-show, leaving Shantel alone to bid on Roman instead. One thing had led to another and soon Shantel was not only wearing Roman's ring, but carrying his baby.

"See? I'm indirectly responsible for the two of you getting together," Julian shrugged. "You should be thanking me."

"Julian!" Elyse's voice rang out from inside the manor.

"You're being summoned," Roman teased.

Julian rolled his eyes at their older brother before heading inside.

"I'm glad you both are happy," Xavier said, "but don't wish your domesticity upon me."

"Maybe not domesticity, but certainly love and affection," Roman replied. "With someone who is worthy of you."

Xavier rolled his eyes upward. "Not you, too. Don't judge Porscha harshly. I already told Giana that Porscha dating Ryan was a media stunt. Get to know her before you say she isn't good enough for me."

"Oh, I know," Roman responded. "Giana told me. I just worry about you, Xavier. You've always been rather guarded when it came to the opposite sex, especially after that incident with Tyra."

"Wouldn't you? She tried to ruin my reputation," Xavier pointed out. "It's why I talked to Curtis and Wayne and told them my cautionary tale. I wouldn't want them or any of our players in a similar circumstance. It's extremely easy to get caught up these days."

"You're being careful. And I get that," Roman said, "but Porscha means something to you, or you would have let her go months ago. And on that note, we're being called in."

"For what?"

"You'll see."

Several minutes later, Xavier found himself along with Roman, Julian, Wynn and Silas in a baby-bottle chugging contest to see which of them could finish sucking all the apple juice out of the tiny hole in the bottle first. Xavier won that round, but the games continued with a good, old-fashioned change-the-diaper-blindfolded game.

Roman took that win thanks to lots of practice changing Ethan while being half asleep.

Then there was the great stroller race. Everyone went onto the terrace to watch the men race across an obstacle course in the backyard without crashing their strollers with baby dolls inside. Julian was much faster on his feet and won the race hands down.

Afterward, they retired back to the main living room where their mother, Angelique, had laid out an amazing spread for the guests. After Elyse and Julian made their plates and the ladies dug in, Xavier filled his plate with veggies from the crudités platter, along with quiche, tea sandwiches, Swedish meatballs, chicken satay, mini mac-and-cheese bites and bacon-wrapped scallops.

"This is delicious, Mom," Elyse said from the sofa. "You really outdid yourself." Xavier's sister-in-law had taken to calling their mother Mom because her own mother had died from cancer when she was young.

"You're absolutely welcome, my darling," his mother said from the chair opposite her. She was looking like a refined hostess in a yellow one-shoulder batwing cape dress that reached her knees. "Has everyone had enough to eat?" She glanced at Xavier's full plate, then up at him, and winked.

Xavier went to the dining room to escape from the couples and babies some of Elyse's friends had brought with them. He was settling down to his meal when his father walked in and sat across from him.

"I see I'm not the only one escaping all the brouhaha."

"Yeah, there are too many women and babies in there," Xavier said. "Don't want it to rub off."

His father eyed him. "Of all my sons, I thought you'd embrace fatherhood."

"Why is that?"

"Because you probably had more of my time and attention than even Roman."

That wasn't always a good thing, Xavier thought, but he continued eating and chose not to comment. His father wanted something. He was a calculating man and wouldn't have followed Xavier in here otherwise.

"I'm really proud of everything you've done with the foundation, and I hear the mentorship with the players is going well."

"And?"

"I'm wondering if you're finally ready to come back to the fold?" Josiah asked.

And there it was. The real reason his father came to talk to him.

"Coaching."

His father nodded. "Being a sportscaster isn't your thing and you and I both know it. It was only a stopgap measure to keep your head in the game and not fall into a deep depression after you couldn't play football anymore."

"And you think you know me so well?"

"I know the son I raised sacrificed everything for the love of the game."

"Those days are over."

"Playing, yes, but you are talented, Xavier. You always have been. I saw it in you when you were just a young boy. It's still there, if you can only believe in yourself like I do."

"You don't think I'm a failure?" Xavier asked.

"Have I ever said that?"

"No, but it was implied in the disappointment in your eyes."

"Yes, I was disappointed *for* you, but not *in* you. Never in you," his father responded. "And I'm sorry you felt that way. I wish you had told me, because I would have corrected you. Told you how immensely proud I am to have you as my boy."

"How can you be?" Xavier wondered aloud. "I didn't live up to my full potential."

"Life handed you a raw deal," his father said. "And you wallowed in it for a couple of months. But when the going got tough, you dug your heels in and brought yourself back to the other side. Reinvented yourself. How could I not be proud?"

Xavier was about to say more, but then his cell phone rang.

The display read Porscha. "Excuse me for a minute, Dad." Xavier left the dining room to walk into the corridor and take the call.

"Xavier, it's me," Porscha said from the other end of the line.

"Why are you whispering?" he inquired.

"I'm outside."

"Outside where?"

"Your parents' gate," Porscha said. "I called but your butler refused to buzz me in so the security guard won't open the gate. He didn't believe me when I told him I was Porscha Childs. He said the family wasn't expecting any guests."

"You're here!" It was impossible. Xavier raced down the hall, grabbed a key fob for the gate from the entryway and was out the front door as if he was the quarterback he used to be. It was harder for him to run because of his injury, and he quickly found himself stopping abruptly halfway down the driveway.

He was close enough to the see the front gate, and sure enough, Porscha was standing there. He pushed the button on the fob and soon the gates were cranking open, and to his delight Porscha ran toward him, wearing a baseball cap, jeans and a bomber jacket.

He hugged her and she held on to him tightly as if she never wanted to let him go. When they finally parted, he could see something was horribly wrong. Her tawny-brown cheeks were stained with tears and her eyes were red and puffy.

"Dear God, Porscha." Xavier tilted her chin upward to face him. "What happened?"

"It's awful." Porscha leaned her head against his chest and began sobbing.

"It's okay," Xavier said, lifting her into his arms. "I've got you." He carried her away from the main house and toward the guesthouse. No one would bother them there.

When they arrived, Xavier walked over to the couch with Porscha still in his arms and sat down. He rubbed her back as she cried until eventually her tears subsided and she grew quiet. He had no idea what could have upset her and why she was in Atlanta alone without her bodyguard Jose or any support. He wasn't going to pry, though; she would tell him when she was ready. They were silent until she finally spoke.

"Filming stopped because the director asked for some scene rewrites, so I headed home. As soon as I left the set, I was accosted by the press. My assistant, Erin, the woman I've trusted with my entire life the last three years, sold me out," Porscha said.

"Really? Erin's always been so great and supportive. What did she do?" Xavier inquired.

"She told the press I was hospitalized for a mental breakdown. She told them about Denver."

"Oh, no! Sweetheart, I'm so sorry," Xavier said and clutched her to his chest a bit tighter. How had he not heard about this? Then it dawned on him: he'd turned off the notifications about Porscha on his phone after her date with Ryan and he'd never turned them back on.

"I can't believe I trusted her," Porscha sniffed. "Erin has been my go-to person since I got out of the clinic. The person I relied on, other than my mother, and she *betrayed* me."

"That's horrible. I'm so sorry, babe." Xavier squeezed her tight against his chest.

"I've always treated her with nothing but respect. I paid her two times the normal salary because, silly me, I thought I was buying loyalty and trust, but at the first sign of a big payout, she stabbed me in the back."

"It's going to be all right."

"How?" she cried, glancing up at him. "How can it be? America thinks I'm disingenuous because I lied. I told everyone I was exhausted after my father died. No one knew I'd gone to the clinic for my mental health."

"You can't blame yourself for what happened. Erin betrayed your trust. That's not your fault."

"Yes, it is, Xavier. It makes me feel like I can't trust my own judgment. First Gil and now Erin." Her head fell back against his chest. "Am I fooling myself about you, too?"

He grabbed her chin and forced her to look at him. He didn't know who Gil was, but Porscha would tell him about it when she was ready. "If you thought that, you wouldn't be here, Porscha. You know you can trust me. I'm here for you, babe."

She nodded. "Thank you. I just need a place to lie low for a while and get my head on straight."

"Then you found it," Xavier said. "I will protect you."

Fourteen

Porscha awoke the next morning and at first, she didn't know where she was. All she could see was turquoise waters from a bedroom door that opened out to the ocean. The furniture in the room was white and lacquered, and a white shag rug lay on the floor. Across the hall, she caught a glimpse of a modern bathroom.

She most certainly wasn't in her Palisades home where a crowd of paparazzi were probably staked out in front. Then it came back to her. Erin's betrayal. Porscha had never wanted anyone to know about her mental breakdown. It was her truth, no one else's, and now the entire world knew her secret.

Looking around, she knew she wasn't in Xavier's guesthouse, either, where Xavier had taken her yesterday when she'd been in a state of sheer panic. She'd felt as if the walls were closing in on her and there was nowhere and no one to turn to.

Only one person had come to her mind in her distress. Xavier.

She hadn't known why. She just wanted someone else to take the wheel because she clearly wasn't good at it. And right now, she felt as if Xavier had lived up to his promise.

She felt protected.

Cared for.

Loved?

No, she mustn't think the word because love was not part of the equation when it came to them. Yet in her darkest hour, the person she thought of first had been Xavier. It hadn't been her mother, who had wasted no time reminding Porscha she was a loser for having put her faith and trust in another human.

Porscha hadn't wanted to hear that. She just wanted to be comforted. Held. But Diane didn't know how to do that.

But Xavier did. After crying on his expensive shirt yesterday afternoon, he'd chartered his father's jet and flown them to Turks and Caicos last night.

Xavier made her feel as if she could take on the world as long as she had him by her side. Throwing back the covers, Porscha found herself not nude as she would have imagined after a night spent with Xavier, but rather wearing an Atlanta Cougars T-shirt. It had to be Xavier's, but it fit her like a dress.

She heard music playing from somewhere in the house and followed the sound, padding barefoot down the hall. She quickly noted the color palette in the home ranged from white to splashes of turquoise. The decor was beachy, with an island feel and rattan furniture. She found Xavier in the small kitchen, which was modern, with white cabinets and stainless steel appliances.

He was bare-chested, and she took in the line of hair that arrowed down his stomach past the waistband of the shorts he wore. Porscha's throat felt as dry as the desert and she couldn't breathe, let alone speak. Xavier was so brutally sexy. She longed to touch his chest and tease his nipples with her tongue. She sucked in a quick breath. She very much needed the physical connection they shared with each other.

He was at the kitchen island with three wicker stools tucked neatly underneath. He was dicing vegetables and singing the Wayne Wonder song, "No Letting Go."

"Good morning."

He jumped when he noticed her.

"I'm sorry. Didn't mean to scare you." She blushed.

"It's all right." Xavier put the knife down on the counter. "You didn't scare me."

"Good." She moved toward him. She rarely instigated lovemaking unless they were in bed, but today she was leaving her inhibitions at the door. She pressed herself against him suggestively. She caressed his chest, abdomen, lowered her head to flick her tongue across his nipples, and tasted him like she wanted.

Xavier took the hint. His hot palms cupped both sides of her face and drew her upward, and before she knew it, he was lifting the hem of the T-shirt over her head and she was standing naked in front of him. But this wasn't about her. It was about him. She dropped to her knees and shoved his swim shorts down his legs so she could take his length in her hands. She worshipped him with her mouth and tongue, rhythmically using heat and suction so she could take him all the way over the edge. She felt his surrender when his hands tangled in her hair, and he cried out her name.

Afterward, she glanced up at him and licked her lips.

"Damn, Porscha!" He helped her up, then gripped her by the waist and lifted her up onto the countertop. "Now it's my turn."

His hands moved downward to the place where she was already wet and damp, to give all the pleasure she could bear. Porscha lost herself to the delight of Xavier thrusting his fingers inside her. And when he opened his mouth over her neck and sucked, she gasped, clenching around his fingers. While she was still quivering, he put on protection from his shorts' pocket and drove deep inside in her slick heat.

Porscha twined her arms around his shoulders and when she glanced at him, she found they were eye to eye. Man and woman. Hard and soft.

"Hold on to me," Xavier rasped, and she closed her legs around his waist.

Then he began moving, withdrawing and returning. He would thrust in deep and hold her there, suspended for a moment, before dragging out slowly. He aroused her with each thrust until the tempo began to build. Porscha couldn't turn away from his watchful gaze. Soon she was flying apart, and he was right there, too. Her heart raced along with his, and time and space swirled in an epic moment that left them both shattered and shouting each other's names.

Xavier stared out at the ocean from the open door of the living room terrace while Porscha slept in the other room. He liked coming here to Turks and Caicos. He'd found this place soothing when he'd been looking for a retreat after his injury. It gave him a calm he desperately needed at the time. He hoped bringing Porscha here would do the same for her.

Instead, once again he felt out of control and was looking for something to hold on to. He wasn't a weak or needy man when it came to women, but Porscha was a habit he'd become addicted to.

She was a sexy goddess, and he was unable to resist her. And it wasn't just physically. When she'd come to him in Atlanta crying for help, Xavier had nearly lost his mind. He'd been angry at those who betrayed her and fiercely protective, ready to fight anyone who might harm her. He didn't want to love her, wasn't even sure he understood what those feelings might look like, but he knew something had changed between them. Somehow, he'd left the vault door open and forgot to check the lock on his heart. And Porscha had become an expert safe-cracker who intuitively knew how to turn the padlock.

It was why he wasn't in bed with her now. The intense feelings he felt scared him. He and Porscha didn't have the best track record. Nearly four years ago, he'd screwed things up royally when he'd been afraid to acknowledge what was between them. Fast-forward, and Porscha was in the driver's seat, telling him she only wanted to scratch an itch and have a secret affair.

Now, here they were, months later, and the itch hadn't been scratched. It wasn't unusual for them to make love two or three times a day when they were together. Sometimes it was hot and fast, other times it was slow and sexy. Today was no exception, because after he'd made love to her on the kitchen counter, they'd gone back to the bedroom and immersed themselves in each other.

They had ignored their phones when they rang and beeped, and then turned them off. They ignored the growl of their stomachs and instead feasted on each other until they were a tangled, exhausted heap of limbs on the bed and all he could hear was the panting of their breaths and hearts beating in unison.

It was heady stuff, and Xavier took a shower and escaped from the bedroom because he realized he could be half in love with a woman he wasn't entirely sure of. Was he good enough for her? Although Porscha had explained she'd only dated Ryan for her career, he couldn't help but wonder if she wanted Xavier for himself? Or was he just a distraction? An escape from the drudgery of her famous lifestyle? Would accepting the top anchor position at ASN be enough to keep her?

He felt a presence behind him seconds before he felt the tips of Porscha's breasts against his back. She was naked.

Damn her.

"Xavier? Is everything okay?"

He nodded. "Yeah."

She slid around to face him and caressed both sides of his face. "Are you sure?" She searched his face, and he did his best to hide his inner turmoil.

Could she sense his unease at the feelings he just discovered? "Of course. But I am a bit hungry. You've exhausted me, woman."

She blushed and lowered her head. "So am I. I believe I thwarted your earlier attempts at making breakfast."

"I'm not complaining," Xavier said with a bemused smile, "but I do think we need to feed our bodies. You go shower and I'll have something rustled up by the time you're out."

She rose on her tippy-toes to brush a kiss across his lips.

"If I haven't told you already, you're amazing." Then she padded away, and Xavier couldn't help but watch her naked bottom as she departed.

Had she imagined the wary look in Xavier's eyes? Porscha wondered as she showered underneath the rain showerhead in the master bath several minutes later. There had been something in Xavier's stance as he stood staring out at the sea that made her nervous.

Was he regretting bringing her here?

He shared with her in bed how this was his happy place. The place he came to for peace, quiet and clarity. Did her coming with him change that? She knew she had a lot of baggage. And she was attracting a slew of unwanted attention. It was why when she'd first set out for Atlanta yesterday, she'd switched cars with Jose, dressed in some of Erin's old clothes, worn a wig and flown coach. She hadn't wanted anyone to recognize her.

It had worked. She'd arrived at the airport in Atlanta with the press being none the wiser, but for how long? Erin knew about her arrangement with Xavier. Would she tell the press about that, too?

And was *arrangement* the right word? In Porscha's mind it was a relationship. But did he feel the same way? Was that why he was uneasy—because he feared she would want more than he was able to give? They'd only discussed exclusivity in the terms of being bed partners, but never anything more.

Porscha didn't want to be with any other man, in or out of bed. Xavier was *her man*. Whenever she was around him, he overloaded her senses and made her knees weak. Over all these months, she'd sought refuge in her work hoping it would cure her of her infatuation with him, but it hadn't. The feelings had only grown stronger. It was why she'd told Ryan the truth—that she couldn't fake-date him.

But how did Xavier feel? She hoped this time together would not only bring her clarity about what to do next with her career, but clarity on what to do about Xavier the man she'd fallen in love with.

* * *

"Want some company?" Porscha asked Xavier when she found him outside laid out on the terrace watching the sunset later that evening. He had finished dinner and it was warming on the stove.

"Of course." He patted the lounger beside him. "Have a seat."

When she did, he caught a whiff of her floral scent. She'd changed into one of his T-shirts and shorts that he'd left out for her while she showered. When Porscha arrived at his parents' place in Atlanta, she'd come with nothing. He realized then how much she must have needed to escape, if she didn't even have time to pack a bag.

"It's nice here," Porscha said, leaning back to enjoy the view. "I can see why you come."

"It's my happy place, but it's even better now that you're here."

She turned sideways to face him. "Do you really mean that?"

"I do. Listen, Porscha," Xavier began. "I need to know what we're doing here."

"What are you asking me?"

Xavier chuckled. He'd heard these words before from women he'd been dating, but now the shoe was on the other foot. "You know what I mean. We've been skating around this topic, but if I need to be the one to put my cards on the table first, then fine, I'll do it. I know I said I wanted exclusivity before, and I think you interpreted that as us just sleeping together."

"I did."

"I don't want us to be just exclusive bed buddies," Xavier said, glancing into her light brown eyes. "I want more. I want to see where this—" he pointed back and forth between them "—goes outside the bedroom." He knew every man around the world licked his lips in lascivious heat over Porscha and the image she presented, but he wanted them to know she was his and his alone.

"Are you saying you want a relationship?" Porscha asked.

"That's exactly what I'm saying."

"Then the answer is yes," Porscha said, hopping up from the lounger and tackling him. Xavier captured her mouth in a firm, hungry kiss and Porscha returned his passion. He grunted and his hands went low to her back, pressing her bottom and pulling her tighter against him. She didn't protest. She merely shoved herself closer.

The kiss was explosive, with each of them flicking their tongue back and forth across the other. A wash of delirious pleasure overtook Xavier. He wanted to cover her, push inside her, and take them both to a place where nothing and no one could touch them. He lifted his head and cupped her face as he looked into her eyes.

"You know this changes everything," Xavier said when she moved backward and they were eye to eye. "I won't share you with other men."

"And I won't share you with other women," Porscha returned. "You're mine."

Xavier smiled. "I've only been in a meaningful relationship once before, and it was years ago."

"Will you tell me about it?" Porscha asked.

He nodded. Only his family knew what happened in college because he never shared it with anyone else, but he felt comfortable enough with Porscha now. "Her name was Tyra. We dated while I was in my senior year in college. She wanted to get serious, but I was up for a Heisman, so all of my energy went to football. Tyra was angry. To get back at me, she slept with other players and when she fell pregnant, she claimed I was the father."

"What happened?"

"Her lies threatened to derail my professional football chances and my dad wasn't having it. He had our private investigator look into it. He discovered the truth."

"So you know what it's like to be lied to, to be betrayed," Porscha said.

"I do. It's why my relationships became transient and I put my career before everything else. But I don't want to do that this time. I want to get to know you better. I want you to believe in me again. Like you did in Denver."

Her brows furrowed in consternation. "I do believe in you, Xavier. I wouldn't have come to you if I didn't. I want a relationship with you, too. I was afraid to ask for it because I thought you only wanted me physically."

"Although I enjoy making love with you, Porscha," Xavier said, "you're more than just your looks and your body."

"For so long, in my personal and professional life, it's always been about my appearances," Porscha responded, "so it's been hard to separate what's real and what isn't. But as time went on with you, I've come to realize you are the person I met in Denver on those longs walks on the mountain trails. I judged you too harshly back then because of my own insecurities. I want to wipe the slate clean. Can we have a fresh start?"

Xavier felt like he had waited forever for Porscha to say those words, but she finally had and he was thrilled. "Yes, we can."

Fifteen

After telling her mother she wouldn't be returning to Los Angeles until the movie restarted, Porscha spent an idyllic several days with Xavier on the island. She knew Diane wasn't happy with her, but she didn't care. She ignored her mother's repeated calls and texts. For the longest time, she'd listened to her advice, but it was time for Porscha to make her own decisions about what was right for her. Right now, she needed peace of mind and she got it in Turks and Caicos. There were long lazy days spent swimming in the ocean, sunbathing by the pool, writing lyrics for new songs or eating one of the Creole dishes Xavier liked to cook. Then there were the passion-filled nights spent wrapped up in each other's arms. But more than that, there was companionship, an ease they had found with each other.

They laughed and talked about their favorite films or music. In Xavier's case, Porscha discovered he loved classical, which she had never known. It was what they were listening to now as they sat on the beach on a blanket underneath the stars, sipping wine Xavier had gotten delivered earlier that day, along with a slew of groceries and other things. He'd had no idea she liked country music and that she would love to sing a duet with one of the popular stars in country music.

"Country?" Xavier quirked a brow. "I would never have guessed. Why haven't you tried to record a song?"

Porscha sighed. "Why do you think? Between my mother and my record label, they don't think it goes with my brand."

"That's bull. You should sing what feels right to you."

"That's easier said than done. You know my mother."

"I do, but you have to put your foot down, Porsch. You can't let her run your life. You're the one putting yourself out there day after day, night after night. I've seen your grueling work schedule. There's no time for you to rest."

"It's why the last few days have been so idyllic," Porscha said. "I know I have to go back to the real world and face whatever is being said about me, but I've enjoyed this respite to just breathe and be me. And that's because of you. You give me the space and freedom to be completely free."

"I feel the same way," Xavier said. "As much as I tried to act like your bed buddy, it was never just about sex for me."

"No? I rather thought you enjoyed that part." She gave him a saucy smirk.

A large grin spread across Xavier's features. "I did. And I do. Talking with you gave me the courage to mentor the Atlanta Cougars players."

"I only encouraged you to do what was in your heart."

"How would you feel if I went back to football?"

"How so?" She remembered from the clinic that his injury was too substantial for him to ever play again.

"My father keeps offering me an assistant coach position."

"I thought you decided to stay where you were."

Xavier shrugged. "I admit there's a certain freedom I have being on television, especially when the season is over."

"Is that when you do your work at the Lockett Foundation? How would that work if you coached?"

"It would be hard to juggle," Xavier answered honestly. "Even though there's an off-season, you don't get much time to yourself because you have to get the players ready for the next season. It's been four years since I had to live my life by that kind of rigorous schedule. I'm not sure I want to go back. And I don't want to put our relationship under any kind of pressure because of my schedule."

Porscha shook her head. "As much as I appreciate you putting us first, I want you to do something you *love*. That you're passionate about. Whatever *that* is, we'll make it work."

Xavier leaned over and brushed his lips tenderly across hers. "Thank you."

"For what?"

"For being you and not pressuring me either way. My father has been so insistent that getting back into football is the right thing, but I've hesitated."

"Because your heart isn't in it anymore?" Porscha offered.

He nodded. "I think I've found my purpose with the Lockett Foundation and mentoring others. And now ASN is offering me a top anchor position. It would not only be a high-profile position, but a platform to help raise awareness for my charities while still allowing me a glimpse of the sport I love."

"Then maybe that's your answer."

Xavier stared at her, but she knew he wasn't thinking of her in that moment. He was probably figuring out his next step. Porscha was simply happy that he wanted her opinion in his decision-making process. *This* was the relationship she always wanted, but never thought she'd have.

Xavier was amazed at how being with Porscha away from all the noise and the distractions brought him the clarity he'd been searching for. Was it because his walls had come down and they both admitted they wanted a relationship?

Knowing Porscha felt the same way had been a surprise to him. When he went backstage all those months ago after hearing her sing the national anthem, Porscha had been so angry with him. He never thought it was possible to get back what they had in Denver, but they'd come full circle, as if *this* was where they were always supposed to be.

He reached for a tendril of her hair that was flying in the breeze and tucked it behind her ear. "You're pretty amazing, do you know that?"

"Me?" She shrugged. "I'm nothing special. Don't believe the hype."

"Don't say that. Because you are. You're special to me," Xavier said, caressing her cheek. "You always put yourself down. Why do you do that?"

"I don't know."

But he knew she was lying. She was covering up her feelings because they were uncomfortable to talk about. But she'd just helped him make a breakthrough about a big decision. He wanted to help her. "You can tell me anything."

"Tell you what?" Porscha asked. "That every day when I'm out there singing, I'm waiting for the other shoe to drop? Waiting for everyone to realize I'm a fraud and don't deserve to be there? You mean that?"

"Why would you feel that way? You're super talented."

"Because there's always someone telling me I'm never quite good enough—that I have to work out a little bit harder. Practice dancing a little bit longer. Eat a little bit less. Get bigger boobs. Sometimes it's like I can't do anything right and I feel like I'm on a never-ending treadmill with no destination insight."

"Who makes you feel this way?"

"My mother. My record label. The public. My ex-boyfriend."

"Tell me about him," Xavier said.

She shook her head. "Why? He's long gone. He got what he wanted, and it was on to the next meal ticket."

"He's obviously not gone if you're still holding on to the hurt." He wanted to be there for Porscha like she was there for him when he told her about Tyra.

She regarded him and then looked back into the dark night. Xavier thought she wasn't going to share her feelings, but then she began speaking. "I met Gil when I was twenty and working on my first demo," Porscha said. "I had never been in love and Gil was older. He was good-looking and charming. Oh, so charming. And I fell for him *hard*."

"What happened?"

"I was discovered by my record label. Fame came instantly along with the accolades for my first album. I was giddy with excitement, but the more successful I became, the angrier Gil got. Even though during every interview, I said I owed my success to him for always being in my corner. That wasn't enough for Gil. He didn't like being the man on the side. He wanted to be front and center because he's a narcissist."

"Some men can't accept their woman being more successful than they are."

Porscha nodded. "He was definitely one of those. He sold my story to a tabloid that paid him thousands of dollars to talk about what a spoiled diva I was. He even threatened to publish pictures of me that were for his eyes only, if I didn't pay him off."

"What did you do?"

"I paid him." Xavier could see the pain Porscha felt as she relived the story. A single tear trickled down her cheek, which she quickly brushed away with the back of her hand. "He threatened my career and the clean-cut image my record label had established for me. I couldn't let him do that. I had to shut him down before he parlayed his five minutes of fame into fifteen."

"I'm sorry, baby." Xavier scooted closer to her. "That's terrible. You should never have had to endure something like that."

"I suppose that's why I flipped out in the clinic, when I thought you, too, were using me. It was a trigger and made me think that yet again I'd fallen for the wrong man."

"I was trying to protect your privacy and instead made the situation worse. I caused you to doubt *me*."

Porscha reached across the distance and stroked his cheek. "I don't doubt you, Xavier, not anymore." And to prove it, she moved forward and their mouths met in a searing kiss right before they fell back on the sand in a tangle of limbs. Xavier wanted Porscha like he'd never wanted any other woman. He didn't stop kissing her. He couldn't. She inhabited him completely, not just in body, but in mind and soul.

* * *

Xavier's hands were everywhere, clenching in her hair, stroking her back and molding her breasts, but his mouth never left hers and she wouldn't want it to. Every inch of Porscha's skin heated as it came into contact with his tall, powerful body. And the scent of him filled her head, electrifying her senses. By the time his fingers brushed against her taut nipple in the polka dot bikini she wore, her back arched, craving for a deeper touch.

She looked up at him and found herself staring into his dark brown eyes fringed with long lashes. He always managed to hold her in his thrall. She tore at his T-shirt, lifting it up and over his head so she could run her palms along his hair-roughened chest. She reveled in his hot skin and sculpted muscles.

Xavier's breath came out in a hiss. "I want to feel your skin on mine," he told her and then he was reaching behind her to untie her bikini top and bare her breasts to his incendiary gaze. Then he bent his head and his mouth touched her everywhere his hands had been. He left her senses spinning with every nibble and suckle of his lips.

Porscha clutched his head to her, sobbing in pleasure as he tasted her, but she needed more. Xavier intuitively understood, because his fingers were deftly finding and stroking her over her bikini bottoms.

"Please… Xavier."

He gave her what she needed by untying the damp fabric and plunging two fingers inside her. The pleasure was so acute that Porscha gasped. She reached for his shorts, fumbling to push them down.

"Porscha, I need…"

As hungry as she was, she appreciated Xavier being responsible and when he moved away for a few seconds and returned fully protected, she parted her legs. His invasion was swift, but so sweet. Tears stung Porscha's eyes because she wasn't just giving Xavier her body, she was giving him her love. Every time he caressed her, her carefully guarded heart became undone.

She wrapped her legs around him, taking him even deeper inside her. Xavier reached for her hands, placing them above her head and entwining them with his, then started to move faster. Porscha matched his rhythm and with each thrust, her body responded, opening up to him like a flower. Dizzying pleasure filled her, and she began climbing to a far-off summit.

Porscha thought she wouldn't reach it until Xavier brought his hand between their rocking bodies and intimately caressed her with his clever fingers and sent her into a free fall.

"Xavier!" She called out his name and he called out hers as his climax rushed over him and their bodies shuddered in tandem. In the aftermath, Porscha lay there, Xavier's body on top of hers, and she realized she could stay here in this moment with him forever.

Sixteen

Forever proved to be a fantasy because the next morning, reality came roaring back.

After making love on the beach the previous night, they'd come back to the house, showered and fallen asleep in each other's arms. It felt so good until the morning called and Porscha awoke.

The memory of how honest and truthful they had been was a turning point in their relationship. Porscha had shared things with Xavier no one else knew, not Erin and not even her mother. With Xavier, she felt safe enough to reveal her deepest thoughts and fears. He hadn't judged her or told her she was wrong. He listened and allowed Porscha to see that she needed to make some changes in her life.

It wasn't going to be easy.

Walking naked to the kitchen, Porscha began making coffee.

She'd been in a rut for far too long allowing everyone else to tell her how to live her life, but that was over. She needed to live her life *for her*. Doing what made Porscha happy. Because at the end of the day, *she* was worth it.

Once the coffee was brewed, she poured her and Xavier a cup and went to the bedroom with the steaming mugs. Xavier was still sleeping soundly, so she left his cup on the nightstand. She would have walked out naked on the terrace but saw Xavier's robe lying at the edge of the bed. She slid it on, not bothering to tie it. Instead, she left it open because theirs was a private beach. They'd had complete privacy all week.

She walked outside on the terrace and within seconds was greeted by camera flashes as paparazzi took pictures of her from every angle. The coffee cup she'd been holding flew out of her hands and crashed to the terrace floor.

"Porscha! Have long have you been hiding out with Xavier Lockett?"

"Is he the reason you dumped Ryan Mills?"

Porscha was frozen and unable to move as she stared at the crowd of reporters and camera crew on the sand.

Xavier must have heard the crash, because he was behind her within seconds, closing her robe and leading her back inside the bedroom. He slammed the door shut.

How much had they seen of her?

"It's okay, baby. I've got you."

"How did they find us?" Porscha asked, sitting down on the bed. They'd been so careful all week. They'd never gone out.

"I don't know." Xavier scrubbed his hand across his beard and began pacing the floor.

The only time they'd seen anyone was when the delivery driver dropped off the wine, food and the few items of clothing Xavier purchased for her during the trip. He had to have told the press.

"It was the delivery guy," Porscha said. "He must have recognized me. Oh, Lord!" She rolled her eyes upward. "How are we going to get out of this?"

"Get out of what?" Xavier said, turning to face Porscha. "There's nothing to get out of. Listen, baby—" he crouched down in front of her "—we haven't done anything wrong. There's nothing to be ashamed of."

"They caught me outside half-dressed," Porscha replied, her voice rising.

"Yes, you were a bit compromised, but it's not that bad, Porscha. You were clothed."

"But I looked thoroughly tumbled. As if I just rolled out of your bed after a night of hot sex."

Xavier smiled at the memory of Porscha on top of him as she'd ridden him hard and fast. "It *was* hot."

"Don't be cute," Porscha replied, rushing to her feet and pacing the floor. "The press will crucify me. If they haven't already." She left the room and Xavier followed behind her to see her grab her purse. She pulled out her cell phone, which she hadn't touched the entire time they'd been on the island, and turned it on.

He heard beeps as her messages and voice mails filtered in, followed by her audible gasps. "Is it bad?"

"The press thinks I've gone off the deep end, and add highly sexed-up, once those pictures of me in your robe surface," Porscha said bluntly.

Xavier reminded himself that he was new to her world and that Porscha needed his patience, not his ire.

"Whatever comes, we'll handle it together," he assured her, taking in her forlorn expression. "As long as we go out there together and publicly acknowledge we're a couple, it'll blow over. Maybe even spin this to our advantage. My sister-in-law Elyse is in publicity. Last year, when our most popular player, Curtis, got in a bit of trouble, she was there to bail him out. His reputation remains untarnished. I'm sure she can help us."

"That's easy for you to say, Xavier. You haven't been in my position. You don't know what kind of vultures they can be."

"Maybe not the same as you, but when I injured my knee, the press was terrible. There was no amount of optics to fix the fact I was never going to walk the same or be able to play football."

"I know and I'm sorry, honey." Porscha came rushing toward him and touched his arm. "I know you've had your share of tussles with the press. I just don't know if I can deal with any more drama. First the Gil incident, then when my second album bombed and the truth about my mental breakdown. Now this."

"What's so bad about being with me?" Xavier replied. He couldn't understand why she was making a mountain out of a molehill about the press discovering their relationship.

"Nothing. I… I just wasn't ready to put our relationship out there for public consumption. I wanted it to be between the two of us."

"So you want to keep us a secret?"

She shook her head. "No, it's not like that, Xavier. I just need to get back home and figure out my next move."

"What is it like, Porscha?" Xavier wondered aloud. "Here I am asking you to stay here with me so we can figure this out together, but you're ready to run back to Los Angeles with your tail between your legs. I don't get what's happening here."

"I need to call my mother." And without another word, she turned and rushed to the bathroom, closing the door.

"Do you have any idea what you've done?" her mother railed on the other end of the phone at Porscha as she wore a hole in the tile floor.

"I'm not a child, Mama, so don't talk down to me like I'm one. I took some much-needed time off after someone I trusted betrayed me," Porscha responded.

"So what if Erin said you'd been at a mental health facility? Celebrities have breakdowns all the time. We could have spun it, but this? Going off and gallivanting with that Lockett boy? The press is labeling you a cheat."

"A cheat?" Porscha asked, confused. "On who?"

"On Ryan!" her mother yelled. "We were setting it up to look like the two of you were headed for supercoupledom and you've gone and blown it up. You're trending, but not in a good way."

Porscha sighed. "I should never have agreed to go along with that charade in the first place."

"Are you blaming me for this mess? I'm not the one that was just caught half-naked coming from some strange man's bed."

"Mama! That's enough," Porscha hissed. "I will not have you talk about Xavier like he's some random hookup, because he's not."

"Fine. What do you want to do?"

"Oh, I get to choose?" Porscha asked tightly. Usually, her mother—and everyone else for that matter—was telling her what to do, how to look, what to eat, every single minute of every single day. The last week had been a breath of fresh air.

"Don't be smart, Porscha."

"Well, I choose to stay here with Xavier. We'll walk

out together and when we're ready we'll issue a joint statement."

"Do you really think that's wise?" her mother asked. "You haven't even been seen with Xavier. The press think you and Ryan were an item. Now all of sudden you're leaving hand in hand as lovers? The media already has doubts about your mental health, and now they'll call you a cheat. Don't stoke the flames. Come home alone."

"I don't know." Porscha didn't want to leave Xavier. Not like this. Their relationship was still so new, so fresh. It needed to be nurtured.

"Trust me, Porscha. Have I ever steered you wrong?"

"Other than with Ryan, no, you haven't," Porscha admitted, but that didn't mean this wasn't the exception.

"I've already called a private plane service. A driver and bodyguard will be there to pick you up within a half hour to bring you back to the States. They need you back on the film anyway."

"Fine."

"And, Porscha? Please do something with yourself," her mother said. "From the candid, I saw your hair is a mess, and you didn't have on a lick of makeup."

Porscha ended the call. She hadn't needed makeup because Xavier liked her just the way she was. She glanced at the door. She wasn't looking forward to what she had to do next, but there was no way around it. She had to tell Xavier she was leaving *without him*.

Xavier could hear Porscha in the bathroom talking to Diane, but he couldn't make out what they were saying. Eventually, the call must have ended because he heard the shower. What was going on? Why hadn't she come out to talk to him, to tell him where her head was? He thought they were in this together. They'd agreed to work on their relationship, but at the first test, Porscha seemed to be getting cold feet.

When she finally returned to the living room fifteen minutes later, she was wearing one of the summer dresses he'd purchased on the island for her. Her long hair had been swept up into a simple knot and her normally bare face held lipstick and, if he wasn't mistaken, some mascara. He liked Porscha's bare face. She was not only beautiful without all the adornments, but it showed she trusted him enough to be real with him, flaws and all. Not that she had any.

"Porscha?"

She looked down at the floor and when she gazed back up at him there were tears in her eyes. "I have to go."

"Have to?" Xavier asked, raising a brow. "I don't think so."

"Xavier, please understand that I need to go home. Everything's a mess and I have to strategize on what to do next and how not to make a mockery of my budding acting career, not to mention the singing career I've worked so hard to build."

"I get that, Porscha," Xavier said, coming toward her and taking both her hands in his. "I do. But why can't we do that together? I thought we agreed to have a relationship, and if we're doing that, you have to make space for me. I'm asking you to publicly acknowledge what's between us so we can walk out of this house united."

He wanted her to show him how she felt about him. Show him he was worth it, worth fighting for.

"And I will," Porscha said. "But not now. I don't want to add fuel to the fire. The press is all over me right now about Ryan and the mental breakdown. Let me just get back home and once this dies down, we can come out as a couple."

"So you're refusing to tell everyone we're together?" Xavier pressed. "Are you embarrassed to be seen with me?" He knew he wasn't Ryan Mills, but he also thought they'd made progress in their relationship.

"Of course not."

"Then why won't you publicly commit to me?" Xavier asked. "Why won't you tell the media out there—" he pointed toward the door "—that I'm your man. That you're here with me because you want to be."

"I can't comment about us right now. It's bad timing. I was just now dating Ryan. How would it look if I said I was with you instead? The public already think I'm flighty and a complete mess. Please let me do this *alone*."

"Fine," Xavier said. "Go out there alone as if the last week, hell, all these months with me meant nothing. I'm just the man you've been sleeping with, after all, and in the eyes of the public and apparently you, I'm not good enough to be seen with."

"You're deliberately misunderstanding me and making this all about you."

"When has it ever been about me?" Xavier shouted. "The one time I ask you to do something *for me*. To show me *you care*. God." He turned away because he couldn't face her. "I don't know why I'm fighting so hard for a relationship that's obviously not important to you."

"If it wasn't important to me, I wouldn't have flown to Atlanta after my date with Ryan to make things right between us. I wouldn't have stayed here with you this past week." The doorbell rang and Porscha glanced at the front door. "I have to go."

"Of course, you do," Xavier said. "But just know, I won't be waiting for you anymore."

"What's that's supposed to mean?"

The doorbell rang again. This time a little bit more insistently.

"It means it's over between us, Porscha. I'm tired of fighting for us. I'm tired of being the one constantly giving and getting nothing in return." When she began to speak, he interrupted her. "And I'm not talking about sex. We've always had a problem with communication and apparently that hasn't changed."

The bell rang a third time and this time Porscha began walking toward the door. "I'm sorry you feel that way, Xavier. I've given you all that I'm able to right now. I'm sorry if it's not enough for you."

Seconds later, she closed the door, leaving him alone.

Xavier was angry. Angry that Porscha had left him again. Why was she the one always doing the leaving? It was just like Denver. She hadn't stayed to hear what he had to say back then, either. Except this time, there was a difference. This time he was in love, and the woman he adored had walked out on him and hadn't looked back.

Seventeen

"Can I get you anything, Ms. Childs?" the stewardess asked Porscha on the flight back to Los Angeles.

Porscha shook her head. "No, not right now." As much as she wanted a stiff drink, nothing would ease the pain she felt right now.

Xavier had ended their relationship.

She was sitting on the plush reclining chair in utter disbelief. She didn't care that her mother had sent a luxurious private jet to retrieve her, or that it had every amenity Porscha could need—from a stewardess serving drinks and light snacks, to a private bedroom in the rear with its own master bath.

None of it mattered because she wasn't here with the man she loved. It was true: she loved Xavier. The minute she pulled away from their beautiful island retreat, she'd known she wasn't just falling in love, she was *in love* with Xavier. With his smile. With his warmth. With the way he made her feel. The way he made her feel beautiful, safe and protected.

But had it been real?

Or had she created a world in her mind because she desperately needed something to believe in after the betrayals she'd endured. All she asked for, all she needed from him, was a little patience, so she could figure out her next move. The entertainment world was so fickle. She couldn't react and think about the consequences later. She'd done that when she fled to Atlanta and to Turks and Caicos.

And Xavier had taken her in. Comforted her. Assured her it was going to be all right. And maybe it would be, but she had to start doing things on her own. Porscha knew it was selfish of her to not include Xavier in this journey, but she had rediscovered herself on that island. Learned she was strong and resilient and would make it through this snafu like she'd done all the rest.

The only difference was she would be doing it on *her* terms. She'd made some decisions while she'd sat on the beach day after day with Xavier. And as soon as she returned to Los Angeles, she intended to implement them, but first she had to get all her ducks in a row. Once they were, somehow, someway, she would get her man back.

"Appreciate the ride, big sis," Xavier said when Giana picked him up from the airport later that evening. Once Porscha had left, Xavier couldn't stay in the house anymore. Because memories of her and the two of them together haunted him and it was no longer his happy place. It was a place where relationships came to die, and he would never go there again.

Leaving had been problematic. Hordes of press had been waiting for him to leave the villa, snapping pictures and throwing out questions and comments about him and Porscha. He refused to answer them and instead slid into the town car and headed to the airport. Though there was a handful of reporters there, he'd evaded them, making it off the island without further incident.

"Of course," Giana replied. "When you told me what happened, I was angry. Angry that you were by yourself, and I wasn't able to be there for you. But I am now."

"I'm a big boy, Gigi. I can take care of myself."

"Yes, you can," Giana stated evenly, returning her eyes to the road. "But you will always be my little brother. And if I want to be angry with the woman who hurt you, then let me."

"It was my own fault," Xavier responded. "I think I was starting to believe all the hype. Probably came from hanging around you and my brothers lately. Must be something in the air."

Giana chuckled. "I don't think you *catch* love."

"Who said anything about love?" Xavier countered. He didn't even want to think about the word ever again, because if this was what it felt like, his siblings could have it. He wanted no part of this heartache.

"You didn't have to," Giana said. "I have two eyes." She glanced over in his direction. "And they see a man hurting because the woman he loves walked out on him."

"You don't know what you're talking about."

"Like hell I don't," she responded fiercely. "I know because I've been where you are, Xavier. Don't you remember me crying on your shoulder when Wynn thought I'd betrayed him—with Blaine Smith, of all people. I can't stand that guy."

Xavier nodded. "Yeah, I recall."

"So, then you also can't forget who was there to comfort me," she returned.

He smiled and looked warmly at her. "No. I haven't." He, Roman and Julian had been ready to string Wynn up by his shoelaces and beat him to a bloody pulp. It was only because they promised Giana they'd leave him alone that his future brother-in-law still had his teeth.

"Good, because I'm returning the favor," Giana replied. "I'm not taking you back to the guesthouse, where you will be alone to brood like Lockett men do. I'm taking you back to my place."

"Giana…"

"Don't whine, Xavier, because it may have worked with me when you were eight years old, but it's not going to work on me now."

Xavier laughed. When he was younger, he'd always made big puppy dog eyes at her and she would give him whatever he wanted. "I don't want to cramp your and Wynn's style. You're nearly newlyweds."

"Not until this summer," Giana said with a grin. "Because Mama has to have her big wedding. And as for cramping our style, you will have an entire wing of the house to yourself."

"All right." Xavier didn't have it in him to fight. He went along with Giana's request and let his big sister flutter around him, from getting him settled in the guest wing, to making one of her vegetarian concoctions. He was happy when the day ended, and he could shuffle off to bed and sulk.

Giana was right.

He was angry.

Angry at Porscha.

Angry at himself.

He should never have allowed himself to fall in love. He'd seen the train wreck coming, especially when he found himself wanting to cook for Porscha and show her they were more than just sex. But had he heeded the warning? No. Instead, he'd walked headfirst into disaster, and he only had himself to blame, because he had allowed his feelings of tenderness for Porscha to grow from lust. He hadn't kept this heart locked. He'd left the door open and Porscha had entered. Or perhaps love had always been there from years ago?

Xavier didn't know. All he was left with was the memories and they came by the truckload. Flooding his body and his mind with all the places he'd touched her, kissed her, made love to her. And there had been some interesting places. Her dressing room the night she sang the national anthem. A broom closet during one of her shows. She'd flown him up for the show, but she'd been so tense he'd known of only one way to ease it.

Afterward, she'd been relaxed, and the concert had been killer. Then there was the time they became part of the mile-high club. Porscha had sat on his lap and given Xavier the best ride of his life. Then there was the villa in Turks and Caicos where they'd made love all day and all night until their empty stomachs growled in protest.

Xavier could feel himself getting hard as images of Porscha's face, her smile, her incredible body and her amazing voice flashed through his head. It seemed like they were on an interminable loop that he couldn't stop. Slamming the pillow over his head, he prayed for sleep because the morning couldn't come soon enough.

"Well, if it isn't the diva herself," Ryan said when Porscha joined him on set the following day.

"Did you enjoy your jaunt down to the Caribbean?"

"First of all, don't be a brat, Ryan," Porscha responded. At his frown, she amended her words. "Don't be so sensitive, it was a joke. Seriously though, I had a great time in Turks and Caicos, thank you very much. Perhaps you should try it. Maybe you'd be more relaxed."

Ryan stared at her for several beats and then burst out laughing. "I like you, Porscha. You give as good as you get. And you're going to need that in show business."

"This isn't my first rodeo."

"No, but Hollywood is. It helps to have a friend. And I can be a friend or a foe."

Porscha was going to take his advice. "Well, then, Ryan." She leaned toward him. "How about you give me some advice about changing managers."

His brow rose. "You would fire your mom?"

"Quite frankly, it's long overdue," Porscha responded. "It's time I start doing things *my way*."

Ryan reached into the pocket of his button-down shirt and pulled out a business card. "Call my manager. He only reps the best and if I vouch for you, you're in."

Porscha smiled. "Thank you."

"I think you've got talent, Porscha, and not just to be a singer. You can be a breakout star, the next Jennifer Hudson, but don't tell anyone I told you so."

Porscha laughed and pinched her index finger and thumb together and ran them across her mouth. "My lips are sealed."

Later that day, after Ryan arranged for Porscha to meet with his manager and after they came to a handshake agreement, she returned home and went to her safe to retrieve the contract she had with her mother. She took it to her room and settled in on the bed to read it.

There was a provision for a thirty-day termination without cause, but her mother would receive a payout for any deals Porscha had in progress that were signed during her mother's tenure.

For some time, Porscha had known it was necessary to end their business relationship. It was the only way they would ever get back to being mother and daughter. Because right now, Porscha had it up to here with her mother as her manager.

It wasn't long before her mother came knocking on her door. Diane wasted no time giving her another lecture for leaving without notifying her.

"You're not my keeper," Porscha responded.

"No. I'm your manager and when you disappear without a word, I have to deal with it. You had several appointments that needed to be rescheduled."

"I'm sorry, it couldn't be avoided."

"Because you were with that Lockett boy?" her mother asked.

"He's not a boy. He's a man."

"Yes, I know," her mother responded tightly. "I just don't think he's the right man for you. With your looks and your talent, you can have any man in the world, but you choose a former quarterback with no future."

"That's not true. There's so much more to Xavier than how famous he is. And I know because I've gotten to know him."

Her mother sighed. "You've always been tender-hearted, Porscha. Even when you were a little girl, you wanted to take in every stray cat and dog, but I didn't let you. Otherwise, our house would be riddled with fleas." She grabbed both of Porscha's shoulders. "Listen to me, you need to be with someone like Ryan. He's a star." Her eyes grew wide with excitement. "I'm sure if I called Ryan's people, we could smooth things over. Make it appear as if you had a lovers' tiff and are reuniting. Think of the optics."

"Stop it!" Porscha yelled, pushing away from her mother.

"What's wrong? I'm just trying to help."

"I don't need your help. I haven't needed it in a long time. I'm capable of standing on my own two feet and looking after myself, and I'm going to do that. Starting now."

"What do you mean?"

"You're fired!"

"Excuse me?" Her mother stared at her in confusion.

"You heard me. You're fired." Porscha said it louder and with more conviction. Not just for her mother, but for herself. She was putting her foot down and taking back her power.

"You can't fire me. I'm your mother."

"Oh, now you want to be my mother? When it's convenient for you?" Porscha asked, shaking her head in disbelief. "You don't get to pick and choose which role you want. You're either my mom or my manager, but you can't have both. Pick one."

"Porscha!"

"All my life I have done everything by your rules, but no more. You told me how to look, how to dress, what to eat, what to sing, how to dance. I've been your bloody puppet. Well, I won't be that person anymore."

"Where is this coming from? Xavier? Did he put you up to this?" her mother asked, staring back at her with quiet anger.

"No. He didn't. He didn't have to because I've felt this way for a long time. Because you're always pushing me. Do you know how to be a mother anymore or is it all about business with you?"

"How dare you speak to me this way after everything I've done!" Diane pointed her finger in Porscha's face.

"After everything I've sacrificed to get you to this position. You wouldn't be here without me. I made you a star."

"Sacrificed?" Porscha laughed bitterly. "Well, that's a joke. I was the one in dance and singing lessons in middle school and high school. I missed out on school games, homecoming and prom because *you* told me I was destined for greatness and none of that meant anything. My entire childhood was stolen from me because I was trying to fit in the box you and my label and the whole damn world put in me. It all ends tonight!"

"Porscha, I had no idea you felt this way." Suddenly tears were slipping down her mother's cheeks. "You never said anything to me before—that you didn't want this life. All I have ever done is work hard to help you achieve your dream."

"Was it my dream, Mom?" Porscha asked, narrowing her eyes. "Or was it yours?" When her mother started to speak, she interrupted. "No, don't answer that. The choice is simple. You can bow out gracefully and pray we can have some sort of relationship in the future. Or you can keep fighting me on this, but you won't like the outcome."

"Is that a threat?"

"No, Mom. It's the facts," Porscha replied. "I don't want to lose you, but I can't keep going like this. When I went to that clinic, it was a cry for help because I was drowning. And yes, I picked myself up, but I did it because I had Xavier by my side. He helped me see the good in me and that I was special and perfect just as I am. Can you say the same?"

Her mother stared back at her in disbelief. "You're my baby girl, Porscha. I have loved you from the moment I laid eyes on you. And when your father left us, I guess I didn't know how to show you that love anymore. Instead, I put all my hopes and dreams on you. I'm sorry if you were smothered by my expectations, but I love you, Porscha. And if it's a choice being your manager and being your mother, there is no choice but one."

"I'm glad to hear you say that." Porscha hadn't been sure what her mother would choose, but it wasn't going to be easy rebuilding their relationship after years of neglect.

Diane nodded. "Thank you for giving me the chance to make things right with you."

Porscha thought about cutting all ties with her mother and making a clean break, but she did love her. She just refused to be ruled by her a second longer. "You're welcome."

"So, what do we do now?" her mother asked.

"How about we try being friends?"

"I would like that," her mother responded.

Finding her voice had helped Porscha and her mom turn a corner. And maybe someday they would have the mother-daughter relationship she'd always wanted.

Eighteen

"I'm proud of you, son," his father said after Xavier came to the Atlanta Cougars corporate headquarters and informed him he would *not* be coaching for the team.

He had a done a lot of soul-searching after Porscha left him in Turks and Caicos. She'd gutted him when she walked away, but she hadn't broken him. Xavier had given her everything he had and showed her the life they could have together. If she wasn't willing to take a risk on him, he wasn't going to wallow in it like he did when he lost football after his injury.

Xavier had already come to the realization he couldn't go back and recapture a past life. Instead, he had to embrace the man he'd become. Surprisingly, it had been Porscha who made him see that. Being a sportscaster still gave him the taste of football he loved but being a philanthropist and helping others in the

Lockett Foundation and as an Atlanta Cougars mentor was his true life's work.

"You are?" Xavier said. "I thought you wanted me to coach."

"I do," his father responded, "but you have to do what's in your heart. I've tried for so long to rule your brothers and sister and get them to do things my way. But I only hurt them in the process. I don't want to do that with you. I want you to be happy, and if working at the foundation is what you love, then so be it."

"Thanks, Dad. I appreciate your support," Xavier replied. "When I came here, I was certain you were going to try and change my mind."

His father shook his head. "I won't try to sway you, but I would like to offer a piece of advice."

"About?"

"Porscha Childs."

"How much do you know?" Xavier inquired staring into his father's dark brown eyes that mirrored his own.

His father laughed. "C'mon, Xavier. There were pictures of you and the girl all over the news and social media."

"Yeah, I wasn't happy about that, either. I can't believe the press followed us all the way to the island."

"And that surprises you? Porscha Childs is big news and you're a former quarterback turned sportscaster. You're both high-profile. Nico has been keeping an eye on the situation to ensure there's no blowback on the family or the team."

Of course, his father would think of business first. "And? I assume you have something to say about my relationship?"

"Why haven't you brought the girl around to meet the family?"

Xavier laughed. "Are you kidding me? After the reception Shantel received and your machinations with Elyse and Wynn, my siblings' significant others, that's a hell no."

"Because you don't think you have something real with her?"

"That's the thing, Dad. I do," Xavier responded. "Or at least I thought I did, but I was wrong. Porscha wants to keep our relationship hidden and out of the public eye. I think she's ashamed to be seen with me. Her mother certainly thinks so and has been pushing Ryan Mills on her."

"That actor has nothing on my son," Josiah roared. "When are you going to get it through that thick skull of yours that you haven't lost anything because you're not playing football. You're a strong, proud and caring Black man and I couldn't be prouder to have raised a son like you."

Xavier felt a broad smile spreading across his face. "Wow! I don't think I've ever heard you speak so passionately before except maybe the other day when you asked me to consider coaching again."

In his mind, Xavier had always thought he'd let his father down, but that was his own insecurity talking and not how Josiah felt. He'd said it before at the baby shower, but it hadn't really sunk in until now.

"Believe it, Xavier. You can compete with the likes of some Hollywood actor, and if Porscha Childs doesn't know that, I'm sorry for her because she's missing out on the best thing that ever happened to her."

"I didn't know I was coming for a pep talk," Xavier responded with a smile. "But I'll take it all the same."

"You're welcome. Now come here and give your father a hug."

And Xavier did just that. His father had come a long way from his boorish ways with Xavier's siblings, and he was glad to be the recipient on the other end.

"What are you still doing here?" Porscha's mother asked when filming ended a couple of weeks later and Porscha was packing up her movie trailer.

She hadn't found another personal assistant yet. It was going to take a minute for her to be able to trust someone after Erin's betrayal. She still had a tough time believing she'd gotten it so terribly wrong. So her mom was helping her out until she could find someone new.

"What did you say?" Porscha asked distractedly.

"I asked why you were still here in Los Angeles."

Porscha frowned as she glanced at her mother. "What do you mean?"

"Why aren't you in Atlanta trying to get your man back?" Over the past few weeks, on the road to getting back to a mother-daughter relationship, they had talked a great deal. One night over a cup of tea, Porscha had shared with Diane how important Xavier had been when they first met at the facility and afterward during their affair. She confided that she'd fallen in love with him.

"Why didn't you tell me how deep your feelings were for Xavier?" her mother had asked.

"If I admitted them out loud, that meant they were real, and I was so afraid of getting hurt again. This time, however, Xavier was different. He accepted the little I was willing to give him until I opened my heart to more between us. He was patient, kind and everything I've ever wanted."

"I'm sorry I misjudged him."

"You did. And I was so determined to show I could take care of myself that I turned my back on Xavier."

Now Porscha released an audible sigh. Her mom was right. As soon as the film wrapped, she should have been rushing to Atlanta, but she was afraid. Afraid of Xavier's reaction. What if he didn't forgive her for walking out of the house in Turks and Caicos without him and not telling the world they were committed to each other?

She wanted to go desperately, but she'd listened to everyone else's voice in her head for so long. It was hard to break old habits. Instead of standing by Xavier's side, she'd bolted because she'd been afraid to face her own inner demons and to let the public see the real her. She'd wanted to keep her and Xavier in a bubble where nothing and no one could hurt them, but life wasn't like that. There were going to be bumps on the road and they needed to face them together.

Yet she still hadn't called or texted him. *What could she say?*

That if she had to do it all over again, she would shout from the rooftops to anyone who would listen that she loved Xavier and couldn't live her life without him? The last couple of weeks had been misery. She'd gone to the set and back home, but she'd been unable to sing, which usually helped soothe her. And even if she could, she would sing love songs about Xavier, but she'd hurt him. She knew that. She needed to apologize and beg him to take her back.

But would he listen? Or she had she lost him forever?

There was only one way to find out. She had to go to Atlanta and try to win him back. She would have to pull out every trick in her short playbook and fight for Xavier. Make him see they had the real thing.

"You're right!" Porscha threw down the box she'd been tossing random items in and said, "I'm going to Atlanta to get my man back."

* * *

"Mama, you've outdone yourself yet again," Xavier said, rubbing his full stomach. "The meal was divine."

"I wholeheartedly concur, Angie," his father added from the head of the table, where the entire Lockett family was gathered for Sunday dinner. His mother was at the opposite end while his siblings, Roman, Julian and Giana, and their respective partners, Shantel, Elyse and Wynn, sat in the middle, along with Xavier.

His mother had cooked one of her famous Creole dishes of shrimp, chicken and andouille gumbo, and they'd all cleaned their plates and had seconds.

"You mean you don't have enough room for dessert?" his mother inquired. "I made my famous whiskey bread pudding."

"Listen, Ma," Julian said from across the table. "You know I love your food, but only one of us—" he glanced beside him to stare adoringly at his wife "—is eating for two."

Everyone laughed at the joke.

"That might be true," Elyse said, "but, Mom, even your granddaughter and I are stuffed." She patted her protruding belly. Xavier's sister-in-law was due to give birth any minute.

"Ditto on that," Giana said. "My wedding is around the corner and I have to keep this body tight."

"You have no problem in that department," Wynn said from across the table.

"Oh, Lord." Xavier rolled his eyes upward and prayed for inner strength. He couldn't bear to watch all his siblings in love with their partners while he was alone. Because the woman he loved didn't want him.

"How about we adjourn to the living room?" his

mother asked. Just then the doorbell rang. "Who on earth could that be? All of you are already here."

A few seconds later, Xavier heard the click of heels on the marble floor and to his utter astonishment, Porscha stood in the doorway of the dining room. Was he imagining she was here in his family's home in Tuxedo Park?

"I was hoping there was room for one more," Porscha said, slowly walking toward him.

"And who are you, my dear?" his mother said, but his father shook his head, and she became silent as did everyone else in the room.

All eyes were on him, but Xavier couldn't move. He didn't dare, because he couldn't believe Porscha was standing in front of him. These weeks had been miserable without her. She'd become part of his DNA. He'd tried to move on as best he could, but seeing her now told him he'd failed miserably.

She looked absolutely stunning in a burgundy dress with cap sleeves. Her hair was a simple, high ponytail, and her makeup was minimal and artless.

"I'm sorry to disturb your family dinner, Mr. and Mrs. Lockett," Porscha started. "My name is Porscha Childs, and I have been seeing your son Xavier for nearly a year, though we did know each other several years ago."

"I had no idea," his mother said softly from the other end of the table and turned to look at Xavier questioningly.

Xavier finally found his voice. "Porscha..." He didn't know what she was doing, but whatever it was, it was too late. He'd made his peace that it was over between them. He'd had to, when each day passed with no word from Porscha. And he certainly wasn't about to pick up the phone especially when he felt she'd made the wrong decision to leave him that day.

She ignored the caution in his tone. "I did Xavier a disservice and I've come here to correct that mistake."

"Yes, you did," Giana stated fiercely from across the table. "How do we know this isn't a publicity stunt?"

"Because it's not," Porscha defended herself, turning to Xavier's sister.

Xavier could tell Giana wanted to say more, but when he rose to his feet and turned to glare at her, she clammed up.

"I made him feel like he wasn't worthy of being with me, that I was ashamed of him, when that was far from the truth." Then Porscha turned her beautiful light brown eyes on him and what Xavier saw there nearly razed him to the ground. "You *are* good enough for me and I'm sorry if I made you feel otherwise. I love you, Xavier. And I would give up the fame and the glory because all of it means nothing if I don't have you by my side. Please give me another chance to be your lady."

His father coughed loudly and just like that, everyone in the room slipped away until it was just him and Porscha standing alone in the dining room.

Xavier was afraid to move, because he was afraid to believe the words coming out of Porscha's lips. It was everything he wanted to hear but hadn't thought he ever would.

"Please tell me it's not too late," Porscha whispered. "That I haven't lost you for good."

As much as Xavier might want to deny her, he couldn't. His heart wouldn't let him. "You could never lose me, Porscha," Xavier replied. "Because I love you, too."

"You do?" Wonder was in her voice as if she hadn't been sure of his response.

"Can't you tell?" Xavier asked. "It's why I was so jealous when I found out you were dating Ryan. It's why

I wanted to walk out of the house with you on my arm in Turks and Caicos. I wanted to tell the world just how much you mean to me."

"Oh, Xavier!" Porscha rushed toward him and jumped in his arms. He caught her and closed his mouth over hers. He deepened the kiss and their tongues dueled until they were both breathless and in need of oxygen.

Eventually, he slid Porscha back to her feet.

"I love you in ways I hadn't thought possible," Porscha said, holding both sides of his face as she looked up at him. "I love you with my heart, my body and my soul, Xavier. I thought I knew love before, but I was wrong. And I nearly ruined everything because I didn't cherish what we found. We have something special. Something one in a million."

"Yes. We do," Xavier said. "I think I knew it when we were at the clinic in Denver. I didn't want to admit my feelings for you then. You were still grappling with the media and I didn't want to hurt you, yet somehow I did."

"I had a trust issue after Gil," Porscha replied. "He made me doubt myself and my instincts. So I latched on to the first sign of trouble in our relationship because I was afraid. I had all these people from my mother to my record label whispering in my ear for so long. I couldn't hear my own voice, but I can now. I fired my mother."

"You did?"

Porscha nodded. "It had to be done. And guess what? It's been a turning point for us. I said things to her I should have said a long time ago, but once again I was too afraid to. But I don't want to live my life in fear. Not anymore. The sad, insecure woman you met in Denver is gone and in her place is a strong, powerful woman who is taking back her joy. I won't be afraid to feel. It's the best part of being alive."

Xavier leaned his forehead against hers. "Porscha, I'm so happy to see the change in you. The last couple of weeks have been hell without you. I wondered if I pushed you too hard to choose me. I would never want you to think you had to choose me over your career. I support you wholeheartedly. I just want to be by your side, loving you and being loved by you."

"Good, because I want to spend a lifetime with you, Xavier," Porscha said, threading her arms around his waist. "I don't want to waste another second being apart."

"What are you saying?"

"Will you marry me, Xavier Lockett?" Porscha asked.

Xavier traced his fingertips down the side of her face and then cupped her chin. "Yes, I'll marry you." And with that, he scooped her legs right out from under her and began walking down the hall to the delight of the entire Lockett family standing there eavesdropping.

And once in the guesthouse, Xavier made sweet love to Porscha as she softly sang to him. That was when he told her, "You're my forever love."

Epilogue

The applause never ended.

"Can you hear that?" the TV announcer was saying into the camera. "That's Porscha Childs and her husband, Xavier Lockett, coming down the red carpet and they look amazing. Porscha is ravishing in an Oscar de la Renta Zac Posen gown while her husband is looking quite dapper in a Brioni Vanquish suit. Let's hope we can get them over."

A famous entertainment host motioned her and Xavier over to the dais and she gingerly made her way up the steps thanks to the help of her gracious husband. She was three months pregnant, so walking the red carpet in four-inch heels wasn't easy, but she was proud to attend the Oscars to celebrate her nomination for best original song, "Forever Love."

"Porscha, congratulations on the nomination," the host said. "Your first film and you win a Grammy and an Oscar nomination. That's no small feat."

"Thank you so much." Porscha beamed. "I'm so excited to be here. The film was a labor of love. I can't thank my costar Ryan Mills enough for helping this newbie find her voice."

"But that isn't your only news, is it?" the host inquired.

Porscha shook her head and turned to Xavier, who was grinning with pride at her side. "No, me and my husband are expecting our first child later this year." She patted her still flat stomach.

"Congratulations on both fronts," the host said with a thousand-watt smile.

Porscha waved at her fans and together she and Xavier left the dais to head inside the auditorium.

Hours later, she and Xavier were in a limousine heading to the Governors Ball.

"I can't believe it," Porscha said, looking down at the golden statute in her hands.

She'd just won her first Oscar for her original song on the film's soundtrack. She was on a high, but nothing could compete with having Xavier's love. They'd made it through life's ups and downs and come out stronger on the other side. Their wedding a few months ago had been small and quaint, much to Xavier's mother's chagrin, but Porscha figured Angelique had gotten the big wedding of her dreams with Giana and Wynn's five-hundred-guest blowout affair in Atlanta over the summer. And at the end of the day, Porscha had walked away with the best prize.

Xavier.

She glanced up into his dark gaze and found he was staring right back.

"What are you thinking about?" he asked, caressing her cheek.

"I'm thinking about how happy I am," Porscha said, "and how I can't wait to be a mother to our baby." She rolled her hand over the swell of her small stomach.

He sealed his lips over hers.

"What was that for?" she asked, looking up at him.

"For changing my world for the better."

* * * * *

COMING SOON!

We really hope you enjoyed reading this book. If you're looking for more romance, be sure to head to the shops when new books are available on

Thursday 9th June

To see which titles are coming soon, please visit **millsandboon.co.uk/nextmonth**

MILLS & BOON

THE HEART OF ROMANCE

A ROMANCE FOR EVERY READER

MODERN

Prepare to be swept off your feet by sophisticated, sexy and seductive heroes, in some of the world's most glamourous and romantic locations, where power and passion collide.

HISTORICAL

Escape with historical heroes from time gone by. Whether your passion is for wicked Regency Rakes, muscled Vikings or rugged Highlanders, awaken the romance of the past.

MEDICAL

Set your pulse racing with dedicated, delectable doctors in the high-pressure world of medicine, where emotions run high and passion, comfort and love are the best medicine.

True Love

Celebrate true love with tender stories of heartfelt romance, from the rush of falling in love to the joy a new baby can bring, and a focus on the emotional heart of a relationship.

Desire

Indulge in secrets and scandal, intense drama and plenty of sizzling hot action with powerful and passionate heroes who have it all: wealth, status, good looks…everything but the right woman.

HEROES

Experience all the excitement of a gripping thriller, with an intense romance at its heart. Resourceful, true-to-life women and strong, fearless men face danger and desire - a killer combination!

To see which titles are coming soon, please visit

millsandboon.co.uk/nextmonth